BENEATH THE GRID

B. IVER BERTELSEN

ISBN: 978-1-4834-0471-4 (sc)
ISBN: 978-1-4834-0473-8 (hc)
ISBN: 978-1-4834-0472-1 (e)

Library of Congress Control Number: 2013919815

Lulu Publishing Services rev. date: 7/3/2014

PART I

CHAPTER 1

She lay gently against his chest, cradled in his arms—so young, so beautiful, her auburn hair matted but lovely still. Her breathing was deep, and her eyes were gently closed, as if she was at peace. But O'Brian knew better—utter exhaustion.

He'd propped himself up against the rusted, damp wall of the landlocked and abandoned cargo ship's hull to better see if or when they might come. He tenderly squeezed her shoulder, exposed by the rip in her bloody shirt. Her blood? His? Probably both. The surrounding stench was overwhelming—mold, garbage, and rotting animal carcasses. No doubt the rats that lived here also died here.

His entire body was wracked with pain, except those parts that had long since gone numb. The place was dark, except for the streams of light that exploded through the few cracks in the hull walls as dawn emerged.

How did they wind up here? Bad luck? Bad choices? It didn't matter now. *Damn, we were so close to making it,* he thought.

A noise? It's nothing. No … Shit! They're here! O'Brian shoved the young woman aside, grabbed his gun, and started to get up. The half-hinged, sagging hull door in front of him suddenly burst open. A shot rang out; the first intruder moaned and then dropped like a dead weight. The second entered. O'Brian fired again, but nothing—the gun had jammed. Now there were three … no, four.

What do I do? Think!

He turned to look at her. She had awakened, the fear in her eyes pleading for him to do something. He, for just that instant, hesitated—a fatal error that sealed their fate. Shots were fired, and she slumped dead with her eyes now vacant but still pleading.

O'Brian reached toward her as the next volley of shots rang out. Gripped in paralyzing fear, he thought, *I'm a dead man.*

*   *   *

Christopher O'Brian jumped up and shuddered as he woke up with a frightening start. Completely covered in sweat, he cursed. "Damn, not again. Another fucking dream."

His mind raced in agony. When did it start? One, two years ago? He no longer could remember. No order, no sense, just a series of disconnected vignettes always ending badly. Why? What did it all mean? When would it end?

O'Brian dragged himself from his rumpled Murphy bed and gazed around his condo—a third-floor efficiency located in the heart of the nation's capital. It was a temple of perfect order with everything meticulously clean and in its place: books neatly stacked on the shelves, framed photos from a past he would like to forget but couldn't, a spotless kitchen, and a closet that could have been a display at a Brooks Brothers store. He laughed to himself, as his orderly appearance was the perfect disguise for the mental chaos that raged within him.

O'Brian pulled the sweat-soaked sheets off the bed and dropped them in the nearby hamper. Although it was only 3:30 a.m., he knew that sleep was over for the night.

Stumbling to the kitchen and dressed only in his navy-blue boxer shorts, he grabbed the half-empty bottle of Cooper's Mark bourbon from the counter and an oversized goblet from the cabinet. After filling the goblet with the golden elixir, he took a healthy belt.

He wandered back into the living room, dropped into his black Barcalounger, snatched the remote, and flicked on the TV. His only joy in life: a new fifty-inch Sony plasma TV. *If you're going to escape from reality, do it in style,* he thought.

O'Brian took another healthy gulp from the goblet and then placed it gently on his sweaty stomach. At 215 pounds, the six-foot-one O'Brian was at least twenty pounds overweight. But otherwise, at forty-two, he had retained his rugged good looks and his wavy, jet-black hair.

Surfing the TV channels at nearly the speed of light, he settled on the Turner Classic Movie channel, which happened to be showing his favorite movie: *Casablanca*. He grabbed his pack of unfiltered Chesterfield Kings and lit a cigarette—the first of five he would smoke that night—and sat back to enjoy his little piece of heaven. He wanted to forget both the dream and the almost unbearable life he led.

In twenty minutes, he had emptied the bottle and reached a near-catatonic state—not exactly sleep but at least not dreaming. Morning would come soon enough.

CHAPTER 2

April 8
Montgomery County, Maryland

Today's the day, Ronnie Chapman thought as he turned on the water for his morning shower. Fifteen minutes later, Chapman was dressed and ready to go. He gently kissed his wife, who was lying half asleep in their bed.

"Don't forget the kids," she said with a smile.

Chapman hit himself with a mock blow to his forehead, conceding he had forgotten. He rushed quietly into the kids' bedroom and kissed Cody, four, and Danny, two. As he left the kids' bedroom, he glanced at a hall mirror and saw a fit, good-looking, brown-haired, thirty-five-year-old. "Is that a gray hair?" he said after spotting an errant strand. With a surgical pluck of his fingers, he removed the evidence of advancing age.

Chapman loved his simple life. He was happy to be one of those anonymous civil servants who toiled within Washington's massive federal bureaucracy. The work as a chemist was interesting, and his hours were regular, leaving him time to enjoy his family and his mountain biking. Also, the pay was enough to support his rather modest lifestyle. However, that was all about to change. He had asked for a private meeting with his boss to discuss something that had been troubling Chapman for some time.

But now I have proof to substantiate my theory, he thought as his heart raced. *Today I'm going to fire the shot heard around the world and go from nameless bureaucrat to* Washington Herald *headliner.*

During his drive to the Shady Grove Metro, Chapman couldn't get his female coworker, Ann Hastings, out of his mind. He had made a big mistake getting involved with her.

"What was I thinking?" he said quietly.

But she was young and beautiful, and Chapman simply couldn't resist.

Chapman always left home early to avoid the peak rush hour. He was a creature of habit, which didn't go unnoticed by others. At precisely 7:30 a.m., he entered an empty Red Line subway car and sat in his usual seat at the back.

Chapman barely noticed the fiftyish, pale-white, overweight man dressed in a gray suit who entered the same subway car and sat at the opposite end.

The ride to Metro Center was a quick twenty-seven minutes. During the ride, he resolved once again to end things with his coworker. *I was stupid getting involved with Ann, and now I have too much to lose. God, I hope she'll understand,* he thought, shaking his head while knowing full well that breaking it off would be messy.

At the Metro Center station, Chapman quickly exited the train. He walked along the platform and down the escalators to the lower platform, where he would catch another train to the Federal Triangle station. The platform was pretty empty, so he was surprised when someone bumped into him.

"Sorry," Chapman heard as he looked around. He saw the same middle-aged gentleman who had boarded his train earlier. "Should have watched where I was going," the man said.

"No problem," Chapman replied, somewhat suspiciously. Chapman instinctively felt his back pants pocket and, with some relief, felt his bulging wallet still where it belonged.

A subway train was entering the station as Chapman checked his front pants pocket. His keys were there, but so was something else: a piece of paper. He started to remove it but suddenly found himself falling forward into the path of the arriving train. His arms flailing with nothing to grab onto, the young chemist hit the tracks and screamed, "*Nooo!*"

CHAPTER 3

April 8
Washington, DC

As morning broke, O'Brian painfully slipped into full consciousness, his head throbbing from the previous night's massive alcohol overload. He grabbed a cigarette, lit it, and took a deep draw. He was running about twenty minutes late, so he showered and shaved quickly, selected one of his well-starched and box-folded pinstripe shirts, and tied his tie in a double Windsor knot. He capped off his "uniform" by putting on his nicely tailored, dark blue suit. The pants were too tight, even though he had his tailor expand the waistline on three occasions over the past two years.

Despite the lax business-casual dress code at the US Environmental Protection Agency, O'Brian took perverse pleasure in dressing up, and the outwardly professional appearance was the perfect disguise for the ever-increasing malaise and despair that was eating away within him. Besides, it seemed the single thing that O'Brian's boss, Office of General Counsel Deputy Director Conrad Martin, found acceptable about O'Brian was the way the staff attorney dressed. A few quick swipes with a brush through his black hair, and he was out the door of his condo building and heading down Connecticut Avenue, NW, toward the Van Ness Metro stop on the Red Line six blocks away.

The temperature was already pushing into the sixties on this early April day, and the azaleas and dogwoods were just bursting into bloom. The air was crisp and fresh. *God, Washington is truly beautiful in the spring,* O'Brian thought.

But more than the flowering buds and refreshing breeze, this was the time of year in Washington that unveiled the parade of beautiful young professional women who had recently shed their winter uniforms of black or dark gray for an explosion of colorful spring clothes with dropping necklines and shorter skirts. It was one of the few times O'Brian allowed himself to imagine being with a woman again, as unlikely a possibility as that was. O'Brian was pretty much a hopeless failure around the opposite sex. They found him boring.

Normally, the walk to work was one of his three favorite parts of the day—number two was leaving the EPA hell hole precisely at 5:00 p.m., and, of course, number one was having a smoke and getting stone-cold drunk when he returned to his condo in the evening. But today was different, and his bright mood changed abruptly as he began to contemplate the impending doom that awaited him: a 9:00 a.m. meeting with the "Dragon Lady"—EPA General Counsel Jackie Goldberg. It wasn't going to be pleasant. O'Brian's train wreck of a legal career would most definitely meet its ignominious end today. Goldberg was a tough ass and didn't put up with any crap, including O'Brian's sometimes less-than-stellar performance and his penchant for making trouble as an EPA staff attorney.

As he walked, O'Brian's mind drifted to his past. His career started off well enough—graduating near the top of his class at the Georgetown University Law Center. He worked as a summer associate for a prestigious law firm and was hired on as an associate after graduation. He picked the firm because of its reputation for being one of the few big liberal firms in DC. He soon discovered two painful truths: liberal, conservative, whatever—it was first all about the money, and second, as a lowly associate, he was a cash cow for the firm. He'd researched lots of documents and performed similar tasks that any paralegal could do, but at a higher hourly fee that brought more revenues into the firm. After less than a year, O'Brian jumped at the chance to join the EPA's legal team, ready to save the world. What he loved about EPA was that the agency threw its new lawyers right into the mix—sink or swim. He was a quick learner and had the raw talent. During the next seven years, he earned the reputation as an effective litigator, scoring some major victories in court against

9

industrial polluters, including some of the largest US oil and utility companies.

When he first came to EPA, it was definitely an "us versus them" spirit, and all the young staff attorneys in EPA's Office of General Counsel loved the "fight to save the planet." But like all regulatory agencies, as EPA matured over time, the relationship between the regulator and the regulated industry became cozier. Compromise and political reality became the standard, and many attorneys left.

O'Brian decided to stay and fight. He couldn't keep his mouth shut—he was always trying to push the envelope in terms of EPA enforcement actions against polluting industries. He was outspoken, controversial, and a general pain in the ass.

And so began the staff attorney's long, slow decline to oblivion. Finally, O'Brian was reassigned to the lowly position of reviewing EPA technical reports on automobile, truck, bus, and other mobile source pollution and the strategies to reduce that pollution in support of EPA's regulatory rulemakings. The stuff made interesting reading for O'Brian's somewhat nerdish brain, but the legal issues that arose were few and far between. In fact, it was pretty much a waste of time. But EPA policy required that all regulatory documents be reviewed and approved by the Office of General Counsel, and he was their man.

O'Brian often asked himself, "Why the hell do I stay here?" He never could come up with a good reason. His marriage to Sarah had fallen apart eight years before. He was never sure whether the marriage's demise was another casualty of his pathetic legal career or his personal disaster of a life in general—maybe a little of both.

Well, at least I'll get some closure today in my pathetic life, O'Brian mused.

As he neared the Van Ness Metro station, O'Brian was greeted by Chester Jones with a mighty "Good mornin', Captain" that snapped O'Brian back to the present. He reached for the copy the *Washington Herald* and handed the newspaper vendor two dollars—double the price of the paper.

"Good day, my friend," O'Brian replied. "Anything interesting in today's news?"

"All mysteries will be revealed, but you'll have to find the real meaning," Jones whispered.

O'Brian chuckled awkwardly and nodded as he headed down the long escalator that would take him down to the subway platform. To him, Chet Jones, a black man who wore his hard life on his face and looked at least sixty years old, was a mystery himself. The newspaper vendor had greeted O'Brian virtually every weekday for the past eight years, wearing the same tattered Redskins cap and faded burgundy and gold jacket. He thought of Jones as a friend, but he knew absolutely nothing about the man, including why the old paper vendor called him "Captain." At the bottom of the escalator, O'Brian raced to the subway train platform just as a Metro train arrived. As he entered, he looked at the high-arched station ceiling and the clean subway car. *Metro is one of the few things in the nation's capital that actually works reasonably well.* No sooner had that thought passed from his mind than the train operator blurted in a barely audible voice over the PA system, "We'll be holding at this station due to an incident at the Metro Center station."

"Perfect," O'Brian blurted out as he took a seat. "Now I'll be late—late to my own execution."

Normally, O'Brian had little time to read the paper before he got off the train. But today was different, so he decided to accept his fate and actually read the paper.

His eyes were immediately drawn to the lead article on the *Herald*'s left column: "Senate Environment Committee Chairman Blasts EPA for Failure to Act on Greenhouse Gas Reduction Technology Approval."

"Hey, that's my project," he wanted to tell his fellow passengers. Well not exactly his project, but he was conducting a legal review of the extensive documentation that the EPA staff had collected in considering EMCO Consolidated Corporation's application to commercially introduce a chemical gasoline additive called EZ-15. The product was regarded by many as the major scientific breakthrough that could reduce Carbon Dioxide (CO_2) emissions—the major global warming gas—from cars and other gasoline fuel engines like small pickup trucks and lawnmowers. The article hammered EPA for delaying approval of EZ-15 and had lots of juicy quotes from Michigan's senior senator and the committee chairman, Maxwell Goodman. "The damn application is going to be approved, and Goodman knows it. Just looking to grab some favorable press as the 'champion of the environment.' What a joke; he's in the pocket of industry," O'Brian grumbled.

He moved on to the main article—something about President Richard Keller and his recent drop in the public opinion polls.

"Ah the Great Communicator, who has absolutely nothing to communicate," O'Brian mumbled, shaking his head. "The guy has zero vision other than trying to make everyone like him. Good luck with that."

After about ninety minutes, the subway train doors closed, and they were on their way. As always, no explanation for the delay was provided over the intercom. O'Brian finally arrived at the Federal Triangle station and left the station platform to face his doom. Glancing at his watch, O'Brian realized he was nearly two hours late for his meeting with Goldberg.

"Damn," he mumbled as he reluctantly pushed the brass-framed doors opening into the EPA building lobby. As he entered the building, O'Brian sensed that something was wrong—terribly wrong.

CHAPTER 4

April 8
Washington, DC

The guards at the EPA building security checkpoint, usually half-asleep on a Friday morning, seemed uncharacteristically energized. When O'Brian reached the fourth floor and the Office of Air Quality, it was like entering a wake—no sounds, no eye contact.

Does everyone know I'm about to get canned? O'Brian thought. *No, nobody here would give a damn. It's way more than that.*

Then he saw her. Sonja Voinovich, the twenty-six year-old resident office weirdo—but damn good research analyst—wandering aimlessly around the office entrance with tears streaming from her reddened and swollen eyes.

My getting fired definitely would never elicit that kind of reaction from her.

In fact, O'Brian was pretty sure Voinovich hated him or at the very least had no regard for him. Not that it bothered him, given the awful dark makeup she wore, the grotesque ear piercings, the long, straight, unkempt, black hair, and a wardrobe that had one color—black.

Many people would say that the US government serves no purpose, but where else besides the government could someone like Sonja Voinovich get a job? O'Brian thought. *She does have a quick wit and hides her considerable intelligence well, but what a total freak.*

Voinovich's shoulders, as usual, were slumped down and inward, making her tall frame appear much shorter. O'Brian had always assumed her poor posture came from a lack of confidence. But today there was something different in her body language. Was she trembling?

Voinovich looked directly at O'Brian and said with a slight eastern European accent, "He's dead. Ronnie's dead."

O'Brian felt weak and sick to his stomach. "What? What did you say?"

But then her words sank in, and he said, "My God. Sonja, what happened?"

"He fell … on the tracks at Metro Center and … was crushed by the train."

"Are you sure?"

"The police found Ronnie's wallet with his EPA ID lying on the Metro tracks and called here almost immediately. He was your friend, wasn't he?"

"Yes," was all O'Brian was able to offer in reply.

Her bright reddish-purple lips quivered, but she could speak no more. In what was totally out of character for him and without a doubt the most bizarre gesture O'Brian had ever made at EPA, or perhaps anywhere, he gently took hold of Voinovich and wrapped his arms tightly around her to comfort her. Tense at first, she completely collapsed into his arms.

"I know he was your friend, too."

"He was my only real friend," she cried.

After more than a brief moment, they pulled slowly apart, still holding each other tentatively and staring into each other's eyes. Once separated, they drifted off in opposite directions. The tender moment had passed, and from that point on, O'Brian began his crash into hell.

O'Brian slowly made his way to his office, an eight-by-eight-foot cubical near the center of a patchwork maze composed of other cubicles and narrow passageways. This was "The Pit," as he and others called the large, square room that housed seventy-five EPA employees.

O'Brian's work space was neat but without personality. Two four-by-six-inch photos in a brass frame of a young boy were the only adornments in his office, the only thing linking O'Brian to his cubical. One photo showed a happy four-year-old at a birthday party, and the other photo—the same boy, but taken many years later—captured a rather good-looking teenager with sheer joy on his face as he kicked a soccer ball.

O'Brian, as he did every day, picked up the picture frame and, after making sure no one was looking, gently kissed each photo that served as his only link to his son—now a sophomore and soccer star at the University of Maryland.

O'Brian returned the photos to his desk, and his mind drifted. Depression, yes, but also a sense of dread that seemed to be intensifying—Ronnie's death, his own once-promising legal career and marriage wasted, his impending doom, combined with the sadness that he was no longer allowed to visit his only son. *Maybe all of it*, he thought.

No sound emanated from within The Pit. The news of Ronnie's horrific death had spread quickly and left O'Brian's fellow EPA workmates stunned into silence. No sound, save the distinctive footsteps of Conrad Martin as he marched on the vinyl floor ominously toward O'Brian's cubical.

Martin, looking every bit the Ivy League jock that he was, made his grand entrance. His six-foot-four, athletic frame seemed to fill the remaining open space of O'Brian's cubical. While O'Brian was only three inches shorter and hardly skinny, he always felt a little intimidated by Martin's physical presence.

"Nice tie, O'Brian. Sad about Chapman. Doubt he fell—suicide seems more likely."

How appropriate—the first thing he mentions is fashion and then disparages, without any evidence, the good name of a fellow colleague, O'Brian thought.

"It's horribly tragic about Ronnie. Poor Laura and the kids— God, what will they do?" O'Brian finally replied.

Then O'Brian added with an edge in his voice, "Frankly, I doubt it was suicide. Ronnie seemed pretty excited about some research he was doing—in fact, he wanted to talk to me about it, and he was also planning on meeting with Bennett today."

As soon as the words passed his lips, he regretted disclosing this information to Martin.

"Interesting … well, I guess we'll find out soon enough," Martin said. Then just as quickly, his tone changed as his eyes focused on Chris. He raised his finger and, pointing somewhat menacingly, said, "Your appointment with Goldberg has been postponed until Monday, so I guess you get a reprieve. It doesn't change anything. I've made my recommendation to Jackie, and she's in agreement. Don't expect to talk her out of it—come Monday, you're history."

Martin had joined EPA in the late eighties and had risen in the ranks to become EPA's second-ranking attorney. He was bright, a good writer, but not much of a lawyer, in O'Brian's mind. O'Brian believed Martin's greatest talent, and the reason he rose in the ranks, was an uncanny ability to work the system, including being a "yes man" to the right people at the right time. Martin and O'Brian never got along. Over the past several years, Martin had been building his case against O'Brian. Little things like tardiness—sometimes it was hard to get to work on time when O'Brian had nailed a bottle of bourbon the night before. Even O'Brian would admit that his work at times was spotty. He did a great job on things he felt had some environmental significance, but much of what O'Brian did he felt was meaningless, and he just wasn't interested.

But the incident that finally sealed O'Brian's fate was a casual, off-the-record conversation with Robert Levy, a reporter at the *Washington Herald*. O'Brian expressed his belief that EPA was giving a less-than-thorough review of the EMCO application that would enable the corporation to sell its carbon-dioxide-reducing chemical fuel additive EZ-15.

Levy wrote an article accusing EPA of caving to political pressure from the White House and Congress. The story was buried in the Saturday federal page of the *Herald* and generated little interest. Little interest, except that both the White House and EPA's Office of Public Affairs were most displeased, and both launched investigations. Unfortunately, Levy, usually very careful to protect his sources, included some information that only O'Brian could have known.

O'Brian was "dead meat" and he knew it. He wanted to rail at Martin about what a complete pompous ass Martin was, but he knew there was no point in doing so. He just wanted to end the conversation.

"Have a nice weekend," he said sarcastically to Martin and then turned to his desk and opened a file like he was going back to work.

Martin stood awkwardly for a moment and then, as always wanting the last word, said, "Don't take any of your files out of here—it's all government property."

O'Brian ignored Martin, who then turned and exited with an audible grunt.

CHAPTER 5

April 8
Washington, DC—Evening

As Martin stomped away, O'Brian began to spiral even further downward, filled with a sense of depression that he had rarely experienced. He felt weak, tired, and numb. He did little and said nothing to anyone. Finally, at 5:00 p.m., he meandered out of the office, eyes down, acknowledging no one except Voinovich. They made eye contact, and he gave her a quick nod good-bye, which she returned. It didn't register with him that Voinovich was doing what she could to console her fellow worker, Ann Hastings, who seemed considerably more distraught than anyone else at Chapman's tragic death.

O'Brian left the EPA building with his mind in a fog. He didn't gain full consciousness until he reached his condo forty minutes later. Collapsing in his chair, he pondered the day, his miserable life, and what was in store for him on Monday and beyond. It wasn't a pretty picture. O'Brian well understood that he had lived his life without passion or purpose for nearly a decade. Now, as a result of an unending series of bad decisions, he had become totally irrelevant to anything or anyone.

O'Brian lowered his head in his hands and held that pose for several minutes. Then raising his head, he began to devise the first inkling of a plan of action. He was both energized and unsettled as he accepted what he must do. A simple act that in an instant would solve all his problems: end his misery and, most importantly, secure the financial future of his ex-wife and son. The thought had entered

17

his mind before, but he was too much of a coward to carry it out—but not this time.

Rising purposefully, O'Brian crossed the room to a small mahogany secretary and opened a drawer. Simultaneously, he pushed the two barely visible brackets and flipped the back of the drawer forward, exposing a small compartment. The contents contained a faded manila accordion file that bore the wear and tear of being opened and closed numerous times, a small brown, velvet ring box, and a black leather pouch.

O'Brian opened the pouch and carefully pulled out a steel-black .45-caliber handgun and a clip filled with shells. While in college, in a moment of patriotic fervor during the Persian Gulf War, he had joined the ROTC. He actually enjoyed the six-week summer camps provided by the US Army, learning to shoot a handgun, M-16 semiautomatic rifle, and the M-60 machine gun, to say nothing about the chance to learn a little hand-to-hand combat at which he prided himself as being pretty adept. He was never called to active duty, but he did serve six years in the army reserves.

During the early years of his marriage, Sarah and he lived in a residential fringe area on Capitol Hill—not the safest place to live in those days. O'Brian loved living there, but Sarah grew increasingly fearful and finally insisted he get a gun for protection. O'Brian had made friends with a Hispanic family that lived in the house next door. The father gave him a tip where to buy an unlicensed gun. O'Brian kept the pistol for reasons he was never sure of even after he and Sarah moved to the suburbs and subsequently divorced. "But tonight I'll finally put it to good use," he said sadly.

Snapping the loaded clip into the weapon, he placed it on the desk with his now-sweaty hands and removed both the ring box and folder, placing them next to the handgun.

The folder contained a healthy stack of stock certificates, a handwritten will, and an "in the event of my death" note to Sarah. He never paid much attention to the stocks that he had inherited when his father and mother died suddenly in a horrific auto accident years before. His father was a hard-drinking, mean-spirited Irish textile worker in Boston. It was his somewhat airy and spiritual mother who had had an uncanny knack for picking stocks and selling or buying them at just the right time.

The note and will were prepared several years earlier when O'Brian was in one of his "let's get organized" phases and had no immediate thoughts of dying. The document left everything he had to Sarah. He opened the folder and read the note one more time. It meticulously detailed all the steps required to handle the estate. What the note provided in useful guidance, it lacked in compassion— it simply closed with "Sorry for everything. Love, Chris." He pulled the stock certificates and set them down neatly on the desktop next to his will.

Hesitating at first, he finally picked up the ring box and opened it slowly. Inside were two handmade wedding rings, one much larger than the other, but in all other ways matched in their intricate design—a material symbol of commitment gone bad and a sad reminder of love lost. He removed the larger ring and forcibly twisted it on—it was considerably tighter around his ring finger than when he last wore it eight years ago. The snugness of the ring felt strangely good as if Sarah was squeezing his finger one last time. He took the smaller ring out of the box and gently placed it on top of the note and then placed his wallet on the desk.

A sense of profound sadness overwhelmed him again, but he had no doubts about his course of action. He went to the kitchen area, poured himself a generous slug of bourbon, and savored what he knew would be his last taste of liquor. Surveying his abode, he was satisfied that everything was in its place.

Well, whoever gets stuck handling my affairs should have an easy task. Sarah should get the money quickly and painlessly. It's the least I can do after ruining much of her life.

O'Brian grabbed his parka and baseball cap, placed the gun in his pocket, and put his driver's license in his pants pocket. *Need to allow for easy identification*, he thought as he headed out the door of his condo.

A cold gust of frigid, damp air blasted O'Brian's face as he opened the outer lobby door and left the building. *So much for spring*, he couldn't help thinking as he recalled how beautiful the morning had been.

O'Brian had already decided on the exact spot to end his life. He took the shortest route to a small park only minutes away. He was always amazed that in just five blocks off Connecticut Avenue, the neighborhood went from luxury condo buildings to modest-sized single homes built in the 1930s and 1940s. The neighborhood was mixed both racially and economically—black, middle-class families that had lived there for several generations and a few young, white couples seeking an urban lifestyle at a price they could afford.

During the day, the neighborhood was as safe as anywhere in the nation's capital. But at night, things changed—the local residents stayed away from the park while thugs frequented the area to traffic in drugs.

By the time he found a park bench and sat down, O'Brian was shaking uncontrollably. Reaching into his left parka pocket, he removed the gun. He paused for a moment and thought, *Just do it—end it now.*

He snapped the gun up, placed it on his temple, and pulled the trigger.

Click. The shell in the clip hadn't properly seated in the chamber and failed to discharge. He pulled the gun down and bent forward, his whole body shaking. After a moment, he regained his composure and re-chambered the clip. Steadying the gun with both hands, he raised it toward his temple again.

But before he could complete his exit plan, a piercing scream not fifty feet from where he was sitting rang out. Without thinking, he raced toward the sound with the loaded pistol still in his hand.

"No, please, no!" a slight, young black woman no more than twenty pleaded hysterically to the four young thugs pounding on a young black man.

"We've got his wallet. Let's get the hell out of here," one of the assailants yelled.

"Not till we finish him off and fuck that bitch," yelled the biggest and meanest-looking one in the bunch.

But before another punch could be thrown, a piercing shot rang out, and a large branch shattered with a resounding crack just inches above the tough guy's head. Everyone froze and then turned to look at O'Brian, now poised and aiming directly at the obvious leader of the bunch.

"That shot was a warning. You've got exactly two seconds to get the hell out of here or the next shot will split your head wide open," O'Brian yelled.

O'Brian surprised even himself at how deadly serious he sounded. The four punks looked briefly at each other in desperation and then ran off into the darkness.

The young lad tried raising himself as the girl and O'Brian raced toward him.

"Thanks," was all he could muster before his legs gave out, and he grimaced in pain.

"We've got to get him some help. Do you have a cell phone?" O'Brian asked the young woman. But she didn't hear him as she hugged her boyfriend.

"Listen," O'Brian started impatiently.

But the young man interrupted, "No 911, no cops … I live near here. Can you help me get home?"

Without speaking further, O'Brian reached over to help him up. The young man's shirt had been shredded in the fight, and his face looked like he had run into a cement wall at full stride. He had several cuts on his arms, no doubt the result of fending off the knife attack.

"Which way?"

"He lives on Oak in the two-hundred block," the girl replied as she hugged her boyfriend again.

At first O'Brian thought it was odd that no one came out at the sound of gunfire. But then he thought, *Guess it's not all that unusual in this neighborhood at night.*

They got to the house in just a few minutes, and by then the young man was walking pretty much under his own power. The front porch light glistened in the mist as they reached the front door. The young woman pounded on the locked front door as the young man cried out, "Dad, it's me."

A voice from inside called out, "Leon?" Then the door swung wide open, revealing the presence of a neatly dressed, older black man.

"What happened?" the man said.

"Mugged," the couple replied in unison.

"This kind man saved us," the young woman added.

O'Brian's eyes met those of the large black man.

"Captain?" the boy's father said in disbelief.

"Chet?" O'Brian replied.

*   *   *

"Thanks Captain for coming to Leon and Tanya's rescue," Chet said as he grabbed Chris's hand and lead him into the modest but well-maintained home. "But what the hell were you doing out in this neighborhood at this time of night—trying to get yourself killed?"

When he looked at Chris, Chet saw no smile on his unexpected guest's face. Chris started to mumble a reply when Chet was suddenly distracted by Tanya's cries.

"Leon's collapsed!"

They carried Leon to a room in the back of the house and laid him on the bed. The next thirty minutes were a blur to Chris, who was escorted into the living room. If there was a Mrs. Jones, she was nowhere to be seen. Chet and Tanya were shouting into cell phones, and moments later a parade of people rushed in the front door to help or to check up on how Leon was doing.

Chris, a forty-two-year-old white guy sitting in Chet Jones's living room, drew more than one stare of curiosity as friends and relatives arrived. But otherwise, he was largely ignored. He could see not only the deep concern of those who arrived, but the incredible affection and caring they all shared with one another, a stark contrast to the solitude in which he had lived the past several years.

To pass the time, Chris surveyed the cozy living room. Faded family pictures adorned the walls. A framed citation honoring Police Sergeant Chester Jones, a US military Bronze Star medal in a glass case, and other memorabilia displayed on the fireplace mantel, spoke of a man who had obviously led a very full life. Chris thought little about his brush with self-annihilation. It all seemed, at least for the moment, strangely distant.

After a period of intense activity, a growing quiet emerged. People hugged and started to leave.

"Is Leon okay?" Chris asked Chet.

"He's doing just fine. The cuts were largely superficial, and no broken bones. He's going to be pretty sore for a couple of days. Hopefully, the two of them will show better judgment in the future about where and when they decide to take a romantic stroll."

Then Chet grabbed his Redskins jacket and motioned to Chris. "Let's get you home."

"I can walk home."

"Like hell you will. Let's go."

They both got into a tan 1998 Toyota Tercel that obviously had seen plenty of use. As if he had read Chris's mind, Chet said, "No sense having a decent car sitting on the street in this neighborhood. Where to, my friend?"

"The Palmer House on Connecticut," Chris replied with a sense of embarrassment.

"Nice digs."

"It's only a small studio," Chris replied, somewhat defensively.

As the car pulled away from the curve, Chet, looking at Chris's bulging jacket pocket with the pistol partially visible, cleared his throat and said with considerable conviction, "I don't know what possessed you to be out in that park tonight, and it's none of my business. But because you were, a terrible tragedy was averted. Whatever you might have been thinking or planning to do tonight doesn't change the fact that a lot of good was the result."

Rather than try to reply to Chet's mini-sermon, which was hitting pretty close to home, Chris opted to change the subject.

"Police commendations, a Bronze Star—looks like someone who had a pretty good career in the military and with the DC police. Probably has a pretty good pension, too. So why get up at 5:00 a.m. to sell newspapers?"

"Don't need to, but I'm an early riser. I like people, and I do a little citizen surveillance. I've helped my old buddies on the police force nab a few molesters and one or two pickpockets. What about you?"

"EPA attorney, but I'm about to make a life change," Chris replied with a touch of irony.

The car pulled up in front of Chris's condo, so the conversation ended abruptly. Chris rushed to get out, but Chet firmly grabbed his hand. "Thanks. Leon is my life. If you ever need help ... I'm your man."

Chris looked at his hand and saw a small piece of paper with what looked like a telephone number written on it. So as not to appear ungrateful, Chris stuffed it in his pocket. He really had no use for it and figured he would throw it away later.

"Thanks." And then without looking back, Chris entered the front door and headed to his condo. Exhausted, he collapsed in the nearest chair. He thought about grabbing the whiskey bottle but he was completely spent. Too exhausted to even begin to contemplate the meaning of the evening's bizarre events, Chris closed his eyes.

CHAPTER 6

April 8
Ballston, Virginia—Evening

At about the time O'Brian ventured out in the drizzle to kill himself, Ann Hastings, a natural-blonde, twenty-four-year-old EPA statistician, sat sobbing uncontrollably in her modest one-bedroom, sixth-floor apartment located just south of DC in Ballston, Virginia. Like most young professionals, Hastings was not a Washington, DC, area native, but like others had come to the capital from a small town to find fame and fortune—and a high-quality spouse. In all three categories, she had failed miserably.

Her eyes were almost swollen shut from crying, and her whole body was limp and chilled as she thought about the horrible death of the man she loved deeply, Ronnie Chapman.

He was going to leave his wife—I'm sure of it.

She hadn't wanted to be alone that night, but she knew there was no she could talk to about her brief yet passionate affair with her now deceased EPA colleague. *No one at EPA besides Sonja knew about our relationship, and I'm not going to ruin Ronnie's memory by disclosing to anyone now about our affair,* she thought as tears dripped down her cheeks.

Lost in thoughts, Hastings was suddenly jarred back to reality by a loud knock on the door.

Who could that be at this hour?

A little unsteady from three glasses of the inexpensive Chardonnay she had consumed to help numb the horrific shock of Chapman's death, Hastings made her way to the door. "What do you want?"

Hastings asked tentatively as she peered through the peephole, wishing she had been able to pay the extra rent for an apartment with a concierge and a better security system.

"Sorry to disturb you, Miss Hastings. I'm with the FBI," a voice on the other side of the door answered quickly. "We would like to talk to you concerning a Mr. Ronald Chapman," the man replied as he flashed what looked like an FBI badge.

Somewhat confused and apprehensive, she opened the door slightly. "Could you please come back tomorrow?"

Opening the door, even a little, was the biggest and last mistake of this beautiful girl's unfulfilled life. Without replying, the same middle-aged man who had dealt with Ronnie Chapman earlier that day stormed in with his younger, taller companion right behind.

The man grabbed the young girl forcefully and spun her around, her back pressed tightly against his chest as his left hand cupped over her open mouth. She tried desperately to scream and thrashed in vain to break his grip.

With a complete absence of emotion, the assailant quickly pulled a pearl-handled knife with a serrated five-inch blade from his back pocket and ripped it deeply across the young woman's exposed neck. Blood exploded forward as she gagged, choking on her own blood, and then went limp. The man shoved her forward to avoid being covered in blood, and she collapsed. By the time her face hit the floor with a sickening thud, she was dead—her face contorted. "Check the desk for the CD. I doubt if she tried to hide it," the man growled at his accomplice.

In a matter of seconds, the taller man reappeared from the bedroom. "Got it. Let's get out of here."

"Not so fast," the middle-aged man said to his young, less-experienced partner. "You're always too quick to leave the scene before the staging is complete. Smash the computer, and let's tear up the place to make it look like a break-in."

They grabbed the woman's purse from the couch near her lifeless body and took all of her jewelry from a jewelry case in her bedroom.

Completing their tasks with cold efficiency, the two men left the apartment and closed and locked the door. The older man jimmied the lock to create the appearance of a break-in with the perpetrators unexpectedly finding the resident at home. In less than ten minutes from the time they entered the apartment building, the assassins were gone.

By now the blood that had gushed from Hastings's neck had turned the small, white Berber rug in her apartment a ghastly dark red—the very rug on which the now-lifeless woman and Ronnie Chapman had enjoyed, on more than one occasion, some carefree sex.

* * *

They drove toward Washington, DC, for a few minutes and then pulled over. "I'll be in touch when I'm contacted again," the older man said as his partner got out, nodded, and headed off to his car that had been parked on a side street earlier that evening.

Leaving his colleague, the man drove across Key Bridge into Georgetown and made his way up the hill to a large, nicely appointed townhouse less than ten blocks from the White House. As he had done on other occasions, he walked carefully around the back of the building to a small but well-maintained carriage house in a back alley. He approached a door on the alley side of the carriage house, lifted the brass flap on the mail drop, and dropped the CD in. *This time a CD, last time a manila folder. Next time—who knows?*

Driving away, he wondered, *What the hell is this all about?*

CHAPTER 7

April 9
Washington, DC

The late-night streets of downtown DC were empty as Christopher O'Brian raced as fast as he could down a rain-soaked sidewalk in the shadow of the US Capitol building. His pursuers were rapidly closing the gap as fatigue overwhelmed him. *I can't outrun them; got to lose them,* he reasoned in desperation.

O'Brian cut sharply down a dark alley and then into a narrow side alley. Seeing no way out, he scrambled over an open, rusting dumpster filled with week-old, rotting garbage and closed the lid.

Damn it, he thought, gasping for air, his heart pounding audibly. *Once I could have outrun them, but all that stupid smoking and drinking—*

He never got the chance to finish his thought. His antagonists peered menacingly at him from the lip of the dumpster. Without speaking, they aimed and fired away.

*   *   *

"No," Chris wailed as he woke with a start. Completely disoriented, he struggled to gain complete consciousness. Covered in sweat, he panicked. "Where am I? What day is it?"

Slowly Chris drifted back to reality—safe in his condo, not dead in a dumpster. He twisted his neck and raised his arms over his head in an effort to relieve the aching, full-body stiffness that had set in as a result of falling asleep six hours earlier in an awkward position in his chair.

Chris tried to push himself up, but his efforts were in vain, and he sank back into the soft, overstuffed leather cushions. He sat motionless for more than a few minutes, pondering the significance, if any, of his recurring dreams, the events of the previous day and night, and what he would do with the remainder of his life, as short or as long as it might be.

Sometimes change simply never happens. Other times it evolves slowly and goes largely unnoticed. For Christopher O'Brian, it came as an explosion—blasting his senses.

"Why the hell not?" he finally said as he pounded his fists on the padded arms of his chair with a determined expression.

Was it the fear of facing death, the agony of hitting rock bottom, the rush of saving someone's life, Chet's odd words of encouragement, or the need to understand the meaning of those damn dreams, or all of it together? Chris pondered.

In rapid succession, he grabbed the open pack of cigarettes on the table beside his chair, the unopened carton of smokes in the kitchen cupboard, and finally a nearly full bottle of bourbon. Without hesitation, he tossed the cigarettes in a trash receptacle and poured the contents of the bottle down the drain. In a flurry of motion, he gathered up all the alcohol present in his domicile, including some rather expensive Cabernet, and they all met the same fate.

Next Chris stripped to his blue, striped boxers, put his hands firmly on his hips, and said, "So now what?"

With a jerk, he yanked open the top drawer of a teak bureau and searched frantically for his jock strap. Tucked in a back corner, he found it. Next he grabbed a pair of black shorts, white socks, and a ragged, gray T-shirt with red lettering proclaiming "Washington Nationals." He slipped on his running outfit—the pants and shirt fitting a little too tightly. Chris pulled out a shoe box containing a pair of unused running shoes he bought five years earlier when he had decided but failed to make a change in his life.

"This time I won't fail," Chris said with conviction as he headed out the door.

He hit the pavement on Connecticut Avenue at 6:30 a.m. on a cool Saturday morning. "From now on, life is going to be more exciting," Chris said with considerable resolve.

It's been awhile, Chris thought about his running as he headed down the steep grade on a side street to a bike and running path that ran down the middle of Rock Creek Park, one of the many beautiful urban parks in the capital city. Chris quickened his pace as he ran down the path toward the city center.

In his prime, he had trained hard and run the Marine Corps marathon in a respectable three hours and fifteen minutes. At first, despite the added pounds, lack of training, bad habits, and passing years, he felt great. Unfortunately, the bliss was short-lived, and by the time he had run a little over a mile, he was breathing heavily and felt lightheaded. Stopping abruptly, he put his hands on his hips and bent forward, struggling to catch his breath.

"Not goin' to quit," he muttered, "even if I have to slow to a crawl, rest often, or walk. I'll get on my hands and knees, if necessary, but today I'm going a full five miles."

The five-mile journey took over an hour. Chris was sweaty, exhausted, and ached all over. He ran again on Sunday, and his time was even worse—the stiffness and blisters on his feet brought on by Saturday's run made Sunday's outing even more agonizing. But Chris didn't care. Despite the pain, he felt great. He didn't even mind the numerous disdainful glances he got from the younger, fitter runners who raced by him as he struggled to maintain even a modest pace.

The rest of the weekend passed quickly as Chris pondered his future. He knew he was finished at EPA. "So what? I'll go to work for an environmental group. And I'm going to get fit again—eat right, no booze, and certainly no smokes."

Chris even contemplated attempting reconciliation with Sarah—quickly dismissing the idea as preposterous. He knew she hated him, and nothing he could say or do would change that. While Chris revisited several times and was still severely shaken by the memory of that fateful Friday night, his resolve to move on and face life anew only strengthened.

CHAPTER 8

April 11
Washington, DC

It's only 6:45 a.m., Chris thought, looking at his watch on Monday morning as he left his condo building. *I'll get to EPA well before 8:00 a.m. That'll be a record.*

Despite the early hour, Chris had already run five miles and, upon his return, discovered, to his delight, that he had already lost three pounds. But now his mind was focused on the confrontation awaiting him at EPA. *The quicker I get that meeting with the Dragon Lady over with, the quicker I can move on.*

As he approached the Metro station, and Chet Jones came into view, Chris's pace slowed. After that rather remarkable Friday night, Chris wasn't sure what to say or do. But Chet took care of that. "Great to see you today alive and kicking, Captain."

Chris understood the meaning behind Chet's carefully chosen words and laughed nervously. "It sure beats the alternative. I think things are definitely looking up."

Chris bought a *Herald* from Chet, but his mind was racing about his new life, and he never opened the paper. When he arrived at his cubicle, a note was ominously taped on his chair. Written in red magic marker, it simply read, "Goldberg wants you in her office as soon as you arrive!" and was signed "Conrad."

"What an ass," Chris mumbled as he headed up to the tenth floor, where Goldberg and the other senior EPA officials were located. When he arrived at the general counsel's office, Karen Black, Goldberg's administrative assistant and go-to person, greeted him with a friendly hello. And then with a touch of concern, she added, "She's waiting for you."

Chris smiled at the woman, who had always been friendly to him on those rare occasions when he had been summoned to the general counsel's office, and said, "Thanks," as he opened the door to Goldberg's office.

Jackie Goldberg's large office, with its high walls and large windows looking out on the courtyard, appeared more like a receiving hall than a government bureaucrat's office. On the left were four leather chairs and several small tables, with lamps creating a warm and friendly environment for discussions. However, they were only for show. The EPA general counsel preferred to sit behind her enormous black walnut desk and hold court for anyone who was visiting. In front of her desk were two small, hard, wooden chairs for visitors. The choice of seating was no accident. Goldberg liked to tower over her visitors—be they industry representatives, persons from other government agencies, or EPA staff—and to make them as uncomfortable as possible.

Chris hesitated as he entered the room. But Goldberg, with her head down, apparently reading some document, called out gruffly, "Come over and sit down."

The EPA general counsel didn't look at Chris as he walked slowly toward her. Plopping down in one of the chairs and sitting for what seemed like an eternity, he began to fidget with his tie.

While Chris had come to terms with being fired from EPA, he dreaded the prospect of the verbal dressing down he was about to receive. His growing anxiety came with good reason. The general counsel, while less than five feet tall, was perhaps the most revered, if not feared, person at EPA.

Her career had started modestly enough as a Department of Justice trial attorney in the Antitrust Division. But her legal skills, political savvy, and tenacity saw her quickly rise through the ranks. Then at the peak of her remarkable career, she quit to raise a family over the ensuing fifteen years. That all changed three years before when Bingeman Foster, a former colleague at the Justice Department, who had been named to President-elect Richard Keller's transition team, called Goldberg about becoming EPA's general counsel.

President Keller had run a modestly pro-environment platform, and it paid off on Election Day. Foster knew EPA needed a strong figure to handle the turf battles between EPA and the other departments and agencies whose officials had their own agendas. Goldberg, who had remained politically active, dabbled in environmental issues as a private citizen and worked part-time for a mainstream nonprofit group. She had lost none of her toughness over the years. For as long as anyone could remember, she had been called the Dragon Lady, because when she was angry, her eyes turned red as she figuratively spit fire with words so cutting they ripped deep into her victims' souls.

Goldberg was the perfect choice to be EPA general counsel. After initially resisting the offer, she heeded the call to serve the president. And while President Keller's commitment to the environment tended to ebb and flow depending on what was politically expedient at the time, Goldberg remained the good soldier, fighting it out in the trenches, doing what she could to protect the environment. The fifty-eight-year-old warrior even helped score some pretty impressive wins for EPA within the administration. But Goldberg also understood well that more often than not environmental concerns would have to take a backseat to more pressing considerations, like doing whatever it took to make sure that Keller wouldn't be a one-term president.

Goldberg finally looked up, a deep frown across her face as she shook her head. "Chris, you're a first-class fuck up. In all my years in government, I've never seen anyone with as much raw talent as you have just completely waste it."

While Chris, like everyone else, feared the Dragon Lady, he also really admired what she stood for and respected her, so her opening salvo cut pretty deep.

"Was it my work? I always thought it met the standards," he meekly replied.

"Chris, you damn well know your work was more than adequate, although, with your talents, you could have done so much better."

With her impatience growing, the general counsel continued, "If it were simply a matter of the quality of your work, you probably wouldn't be sitting here. But over the past several years, you've seemed to go out of your way to piss off your superiors and coworkers. I've beaten back Martin's attempts to get rid of you in the past, but that leak to the *Herald* about EPA being politically pressed to expedite approval of the EMCO's EZ-15 application leaves me no choice."

"Where's Martin's proof that it was me?"

"There you go again. Everyone knows it was you."

Breaking the ensuing silence, Chris gathered what dignity remained. "I can't argue with anything you've said, except I won't admit I was the leak. I won't try to justify my actions here at EPA. I agree that it's best for me to leave. You won't have any more trouble from me. In fact, I'll save you the trouble of firing me. I'll resign today," Chris said with little emotion as he lowered his head.

"No you won't," Goldberg shot back. "You're not going to quit. In fact, you're going to challenge the dismissal."

"What?" Chris said as he raised his head and stared blankly at Goldberg in disbelief.

Goldberg leaned toward Chris and in a totally changed tone said, "Chris, I need you to do something very important before you leave EPA. It will require about a week of your time—just about the time it will take the Office of Human Resources to process your dismissal."

"But—"

"Chris, for once, can you keep your mouth shut and just listen?"

When Chris offered no further interruptions, Goldberg continued in a more measured tone, "You were right that EPA is being pressured politically to rush the approval on EZ-15. It's coming from several sources. Obviously, the stakes are high. Depending on how EPA rules on EMCO's EZ-15 application, there will be major winners and losers. But not everyone at EPA is caving to the pressure. You were wrong on that score. Some of us think there are genuine problems with EZ-15, and we are working diligently to find out."

Then, much to Chris's amazement, Goldberg slowly stood up, came around her desk, and sat in the chair next to Chris. Leaning toward him, she looked at him with sad eyes and in an almost motherly fashion said softly, "Chris, something is wrong here, very wrong. I can't tell you everything now, but please believe me; this isn't your 'politics as usual' situation. The more you know, the more you're at risk."

She paused, letting her words sink in, and then moved even closer to him. "It's as if someone wants EPA to make a decision before something bad concerning this product is discovered."

"But as part of my job, I've read every document in the public docket on the EZ-15 application, and nothing exists to even suggest there may be a problem," Chris replied.

"I can believe that because I know how thorough you are and that you'd have enjoyed nothing more than finding a problem just for the fun of sticking it to someone," Goldberg said with a chuckle. Then she continued, "Ronnie Chapman told Ted Bennett that he had found something that could raise serious questions about EZ-15. Bennett and I were scheduled to meet with Ronnie on Friday, and he was going to explain to us what he had discovered. Now Chapman's dead ... and under what seems to be suspicious circumstances."

Chris looked at Goldberg in shock and then muttered as if speaking and thinking at the same time, "Ronnie told me last Thursday that he had done analysis on some of the emission testing performed at the EPA laboratory and had found some anomalies that he was going to discuss with his boss."

"Chris, did he say anything else to you?"

"Only that if he was correct, it might require an entirely new round of testing and analyses that could delay approval of the EZ-15 application for at least six months or more. Frankly, I thought Ronnie was being a little too dramatic, and I didn't give it much thought. Has anyone checked Ronnie's computer?"

"Bennett came in over the weekend and checked Ronnie's desktop computer. He said he went through Ronnie's paper files and checked his box of CDs in his office—nothing. If Ronnie had any data or analysis, he must have put it on a CD and hidden it somewhere else or given it to someone." Jackie then added, "But why would he download files and hide them?"

"Are there any leads as to where the analysis or other information might be?" Chris asked.

"No," Goldberg replied.

"What's being done?"

"Surprisingly, not much, and that's why you can't leave EPA just now. I need you to go to Europe to attend the Seventh Annual Climate Change Science and Policy Symposium in Brussels. There are people there you need to contact who may be able to shed some light on this matter. The background information you need is all here in this file," Goldberg said as she handed Chris a two-inch-thick accordion file.

"Your tickets, your itinerary, and information on how to contact the people you need to speak with, and some of my thoughts are in the file, as well as a hard copy of the EPA presentation you'll be making on Wednesday at the symposium."

Somewhat dazed, Chris looked through the file and then said, "I leave tonight?"

"You've plenty of time to make the flight, if you get going. Until your termination is finalized next week, you're being reassigned directly to my office. For the conference, you'll have the title of Director, General Counsel Office of International Affairs. We made you business cards and supplied everything you'll need. You do have a passport?"

"Yes," Chris replied dutifully and then added, "but how did you get this pulled together so quickly?"

"Karen and I came in on Sunday and I made a few phone calls. Being EPA general counsel does have some benefits."

Without speaking further, Goldberg rose abruptly, motioning Chris to do the same. As she ushered him toward the door, she whispered, "Download anything you need from your computer and get the hell out of this building as quickly and quietly as possible. Don't try to contact me while you are gone. When you return, call me, and we'll arrange to meet in person."

As he was about to open the door, she grabbed his arm firmly and cautioned, "Be very alert and be careful who you trust. I'm truly sorry about getting you involved in this, but I had no one else to turn to. Good luck, Chris."

As Chris exited Goldberg's office, he saw Conrad Martin waiting impatiently to speak with the general counsel. Chris started to whisper, "What about—"

Goldberg interrupted. "I'll handle Conrad. Karen has a few other items for you."

Conrad Martin beamed as he marched past Chris and into Goldberg's office, but before entering, he couldn't resist one last dig. "Well, at least we've eliminated a little government waste today. So long, Chris."

Goldberg's assistant handed Chris the papers he needed to sign in order to contest his dismissal. As Chris handed the signed documents back, Karen gave him some additional travel documents he would need. As he left, Karen's smile turned to an expression of concern. She grabbed his hand and said softly, "Be careful."

The last thing Chris heard as he walked out of the reception area was a loud voice shouting from within Goldberg's inner office, "What do you mean you're sending *him* to Brussels? That was my trip!"

* * *

Back in his cubicle, Chris grabbed a few essentials and the photos of his son. There was no need to download anything from his office computer. He routinely downloaded his key files onto a thumb drive, and he had done so on the previous Friday. He took one quick look around and then left.

Even though Chris had a few friendly relations with several others at EPA, there were no good-byes. His colleagues had every reason to believe that Chris had just gotten canned by the Dragon Lady, and they went out of their way to avoid eye contact. That was fine with Chris because he had lots to do before his United Airline flight to Brussels took off at 8:35 p.m. that evening.

Shoving The Pit doors open, he didn't look back. His days as a drone EPA staff attorney were now mercifully history. His current assignment, while only a week in duration, would be a nice way to salvage what he could from his last eight years at EPA. Chris was energized, and even Goldberg's unsettling words of caution couldn't dampen his sense of excitement.

Completing his farewell march down the long hall, Chris turned the corner to the bay of elevators. What he saw stopped him dead in his tracks. Staring back at him was an ashen face filled with horror and pain. Sonja Voinovich slumped against the wall, her eyes red from crying, and her arms hanging limp at the sides of her black slacks. In her quivering hands, she clutched what appeared to be shredded white tissues.

"She's dead," Sonja moaned.

"Who?" Chris shot back.

"Ann ... Ann Hastings. The police found her body in her apartment late last night ... something about a robbery ... I saw it on the *Herald* website ... Nobody here knows yet," she cried out but couldn't continue as she moved to Chris and collapsed in his arms.

He held her tightly for the second time in four days as she shook uncontrollably. Her body molded against him, and he felt her soft breasts press against his chest. While he felt awkward, he continued to hold her.

"That's horrible," Chris said.

But before he could say more, Sonja abruptly pulled away, regaining a measure of composure, and whispered, "There's more, much more, but we can't talk here. I've been waiting for you. I knew you'd come this way once the Dragon Lady cut you off at the knees. Here's a number where you can reach me. Call me tonight. It's a matter of life and death."

Chris took the folded note and stuck it in his shirt pocket. While he always felt Sonja had a penchant for the dramatic, something was clearly wrong. He started to speak, but she cut him off again. "Call me … please."

"I will," was all Chris could say before she put her hand gently on his lips to block further conversation. She looked around carefully and then started to turn away. "Everything is going to be okay," Chris said, trying to sound convincing.

Sonja's expression didn't change. She turned once more and walked unsteadily down the hall back toward the Office of Air Quality. Her footsteps faded into the distance as he boarded the first available elevator.

As Chris rode down the empty elevator, he wondered what Sonja had meant. *This is insane. What the hell is going down here, and what have I gotten myself into?*

CHAPTER 9

April 11
Washington, DC—Afternoon

On the subway back to his condo, Chris tried to clear his head and start making a list of things to do to get ready for the trip. *Now more than ever, I need to get focused.*

Exiting the subway station, Chris made a stop to pick up his laundry, which fortunately included a cleaned and pressed black pinstripe suit and four pressed and folded oxford shirts. A quick stop at a pharmacy to restock his Dopp kit and a quicker stop at an ATM to withdraw $500 in cash came next. Finally, Chris arrived at his condo to pack and to pick up his passport, which he fortunately had kept current even though he hadn't traveled internationally in over fifteen years.

He started to leave but stopped abruptly, spun, and opened his desk. He pulled open the panel to the secret compartment and grabbed the file with his stock certificates. *Just in case*, he thought.

Chris quickly walked the two blocks to his stockbroker's office in a renovated three-story brownstone building. Daniel Witt, Chris's broker, was an amiable fellow who represented a dying breed of financial advisers who operated essentially independently. He also was an old college friend, and Chris had wanted to throw some business Dan's way.

Chris's investment account was modest and consisted mainly of a money market fund where he had his paychecks automatically deposited and that he used to write personal checks and withdraw cash from ATMs. He also had some mutual funds and a few stocks he had bought on recommendations of others that had all performed horribly. Chris just wasn't all that interested in the financial markets, and he earned more than enough as an EPA attorney to pay for his modest and incredibly boring lifestyle.

"It's been awhile," Witt greeted Chris. "What can I do for you today—you've got another hot stock tip?" he said as he invited Chris back to his office.

"Dan, it's good to see you, but to be honest, I'm in a hurry," Chris replied as he placed on Witt's desk the file containing the stock certificates given to him as part of his inheritance years ago.

Pushing the file toward Witt, Chris said, "Deposit these certificates in my account, and I'd like Sarah made the beneficiary in the event of my death. Do you still have all the information on Sarah from our days of marital bliss?"

"Yes. Old habit, I never throw anything away."

Opening the file, Witt began furiously pulling out one stock certificate after another.

"Holy Christ—where the hell did you get these? They must be worth millions. And why didn't you put them in your account?"

Chris laughed as he watched Witt's expression. "All good questions, but I don't have time to explain. I can assure you, however, that they're mine, and it's totally legal. Please total the amount for me. I'll endorse the certificates and leave the rest to you."

Then Chris added almost as an afterthought and picking an amount that he simply guessed he might need, "And I need to take out $300,000 in cash. When can I pick it up?"

Witt didn't look up or answer as he totaled the number of shares of the various stocks and checked the current market values.

"It comes to about $3.5 million, and yes I can draw you $300,000 in cash. But it will take five business days ... that would be a week from today. Also, I can change your account today to make Sarah the beneficiary. Should I notify Sarah?"

"No, don't tell her. I'll be by next Monday to pick up the cash," Chris replied. Then completing the paperwork, he thanked his broker and left.

*　　*　　*

Looking at his watch, Chris could see that he was right on schedule as he flagged a taxi to take him to Dulles International Airport. But traffic was horrendous, and it took twice the normal time to reach the airport. When Chris finally arrived, he barely had enough time to catch his plane. By the time he arrived at his gate, the ground crew was announcing the final boarding of the flight to Brussels. While he was flying economy class, he had lucked out and gotten an aisle seat. He stowed his travel bag and slid his computer case under the seat in front of him.

Settling in for the flight, Chris remembered his promise to call Sonja Voinovich. Pulling out his cell phone, Chris quickly punched in the number she had given him. The phone rang, but Voinovich didn't answer, so he left a voice message.

"Sonja, sorry I missed you. I'm on my way to Europe—no time to explain. I'll call again, but if we don't connect, let's meet at Bus Boys and Poets on U Street next Monday night at 10:30 p.m." And then he whispered into his phone, "Sonja, be careful."

Chris spent the first two hours of the flight reviewing the material Goldberg had given him, including a hard copy of the presentation he would give at the conference. Since he had reviewed and edited the presentation two days earlier in his capacity of reviewing all presentations prepared by the Office of Air Quality for possible legal issues, he was familiar with the material and wasn't concerned about presenting it.

Chris declined, with great reluctance, the flight attendant's offer for free alcohol, one of the few remaining perks of international flying. No longer the international flight gourmet experience of the past, his meal was little better than a frozen dinner. Nevertheless, he hadn't had the chance to eat all day, so he cleaned his plate, except for the dessert.

The passenger next to Chris was a well-dressed woman with brown, shoulder-length hair, probably a few years older than Chris, who barely acknowledged his presence. Being ignored was fine with him. Unfortunately for her, the fifty-year-old, overweight traveler sitting in the window seat next to her had been taking full advantage of the free drinks and had plied himself with liquor. He repeatedly tried to engage the woman in conversation. At first she was polite, but she grew increasingly impatient and uncomfortable.

"I'm on my way to Brussels … big high-tech deal … lots of money," the man spit out as he leaned in her face.

Chris resisted the temptation to tell the man to shut up and instead tapped the woman on her shoulder and whispered, "Would you like to change seats?"

"That's okay. I'm fine," she replied, but her look of desperation belied her words.

"Really, I don't mind, and I can sleep through anything."

"Thanks," she finally whispered, and they changed seats.

As Chris sat down in the middle seat, the drunk, looking surprised, muttered in protest, "Hey, what's up?"

Chris leaned toward the jerk and whispered affectionately, "I hope you don't mind, but you looked like someone who may share a common interest with me. I'll be in Brussels, and maybe we could get together for a drink or … something?" Then Chris briefly brushed his fingers along the man's left leg. The fat guy got the message and immediately moved in his seat as far away from Chris as possible. No further conversation occurred between the passengers seated in Row 36. Within minutes, Chris fell asleep.

*   *   *

As Chris traveled over the Atlantic Ocean toward Europe, Sonja Voinovich wandered aimlessly around Columbia Heights. The area, not far from the Washington, DC, business district, was increasingly a haven for young, white professionals looking for affordable housing in the nation's capital. Certain side streets and alleys, however, were still fringe areas where walking alone at night wasn't a great idea.

But this night, Voinovich was oblivious to the risks of her surroundings as she thought about the horrible deaths of her work colleagues and pondered her own miserable life. She had no real friends, with the exception of Ronnie Chapman, and no one special in her life. Of course, there was the group of musicians with whom she regularly played "Europop" for tips at local dives. She played an electric keyboard/synthesizer and arranged and composed the band's music. But beyond the music and her work at EPA, the young woman's life was empty. She wasn't a loner by choice, but simply alone.

41

Around eleven o'clock, she decided to head to her apartment—an English basement with a combined living room/dining room and kitchen, and two very small bedrooms that she shared with two other women. Voinovich barely knew either of them, and they rarely spoke. She had answered a classified ad about a year before, seeking a woman to share space and costs with the two current tenants. It was an arrangement of convenience.

Nevertheless, things worked out pretty well for all three. Sonja typically arrived home late from practicing or performing with her fellow musicians, and she was the first to leave in the morning. Normally, she was happiest when one or both of them were away—her roommates spent most nights, including this one, hooking up and frequently sleeping overnight with various men in an unending search for the "right guy." But this night Voinovich longed for the company of someone—even her roommates.

As Voinovich approached her apartment and started down the stairs, she noticed a light on. *Maybe, I left it on,* she thought. But the light seemed to move.

"A flashlight," she gasped. "Someone's in the apartment."

She quickly spun around to climb back up the stairs but tripped and fell, hitting her shin on the sharp edge of a brick step. She let out a scream of pain that she tried to mute with her hand. Scrambling to her feet, she raced up the remaining steps and fled.

Her scream hadn't gone unnoticed, and within seconds her apartment door flew open, and two figures emerged, racing up the stairs chasing after her. She wanted to scream for help, but running as fast as she could, she only could gasp. It didn't matter—at that time of night, the sidewalks and streets were pretty much empty.

Horrified, Voinovich could hear the sounds of footsteps closing in on her. She glanced back and almost stumbled again. Abruptly, the young woman turned down a dark, dead-end alley. There was a back door to a club where her band often played near the end of that alley. She hoped it was open. The door was supposed to be locked, but it typically was left partially ajar by the wait staff so their friends could sneak in without paying the cover charge.

Once inside the club, I'll be safe, she thought. And when she reached the door, she gasped, "Made it."

As she struggled to gain her breath, she shoved the door inward. "Oh no! It's locked," she cried out as the two strangers reached out for her. With all the strength she could muster, Voinovich pushed the door again as she looked back in horror at a man with his arm above her head, holding a black steel billy club poised to hammer her with a blow to the head.

CHAPTER 10

April 12
Brussels, Belgium

Once the airplane landed at Brussels International Airport and the all clear to deplane announcement was issued, the fat businessman pushed his way past Chris and, without looking back, muttered, "Fuck you."

Tapping Chris on the shoulder, his female flight companion said, "Thanks for switching seats. What did you say to him to shut him up?"

"Just guy talk," Chris replied. Extending his hand, he added, "I'm Christopher O'Brian, an attorney at EPA here to attend a very boring environmental conference."

"I'm Nancy Carter, a news analyst at Cable News Programming, and I'm attending a very boring media business conference," she replied, with a laugh. "I owe you big time. Here's my card, if I can ever be of help."

"Thanks. My pleasure," Chris responded as they parted.

The EPA travel office had made a reservation at a Marriott that was a short walk to the Palais de Congress de Bruxelles, where the symposium would be held. His room was spacious and nicely appointed. It was more upscale than Chris expected for a government bureaucrat, but then he remembered that his room had originally been reserved for his boss.

Martin must have had a hand in making the travel arrangements, he thought.

"Your luggage, sir," a voice from the other side of the door called out. Chris opened the door, and the porter placed Chris's luggage on the baggage stand and turned toward the door.

"Thanks," Chris said as he handed the young man a generous tip. "Any recommendations on a good place to go for a run?"

The porter replied without hesitation, "The Parc de Bruxelles. Go out the front lobby door and turn left. It's only a few blocks, and you can't miss it. It's spectacular this time of year."

As the porter turned and left the room, Chris looked at his watch, which read 3:39 a.m. He did the calculation in his head and reset the time for 9:39 a.m., Brussels time. Even though those traveling east to Europe often suffered some jet lag the first day, Chris felt great and decided to spend a few hours poring over his computer files on the EMCO EZ-15 application and then to go for a run.

But first he needed to call Reginald Longshank, the first person named on Goldberg's contact list, to see if he could arrange a meeting. With a little help from the front desk in making the call, he was able to reach the office of the International Association of Emission Control Manufacturers, a worldwide association representing manufacturers of motor-vehicle pollution-reduction technology.

"Bonjour, IAECM," a female voice at the other end answered.

"Hello, this is Christopher O'Brian from the US EPA calling for Sir Reginald Longshank. I believe he is expecting my call," Chris said slowly, carefully enunciating each word to the woman speaking French.

The voice at the other end quickly shifted to perfect English. "Ah, greetings, Mr. O'Brian. This is Carin Holsten, Sir Reginald's administrative assistant. He is indeed expecting your call and is looking forward to meeting with you."

"Great. When would be a good time?"

"Sir Reginald is out for most of the day but was hoping you could come to our offices around six o'clock, and then perhaps you would be able to join him for dinner."

"That would be wonderful; I look forward to it," Chris lied. A meeting at 6:00 p.m. and then dinner; he wouldn't get to bed until nearly midnight.

"We're located at 121 Rue de la Champlain, a five-minute walk from your hotel. We'll see you then."

Chris spent the next three hours immersed in his computer files, searching in vain for something that might give him a clue to what Ronnie Chapman had discovered. Most of the reports, data, and testimony were fluff. No one had provided a full explanation of how EZ-15, a proprietary chemical formula added to gasoline fuel, worked other than that it resulted in a substantial reduction in carbon dioxide emissions that otherwise would be emitted from an internal-combustion gasoline engine.

Chris fully understood that with the ever-increasing, elevated levels of carbon dioxide (CO_2) being the most serious cause of global warming, or climate change as many called it, and with literally billions of tons of CO_2 being emitted from the hundreds of millions of internal-combustion, gasoline-powered engines worldwide—any product that could reduce those CO_2 emissions cost effectively would be in demand and probably worth billions of dollars. Tests in the data Chris reviewed demonstrated that the EZ-15's proprietary chemical formula, when added to gasoline fuel, reduced carbon dioxide by over 40 percent in the post-combustion exhaust of a gasoline-powered engine.

Disappointed that his review of the records revealed nothing new, Chris decided to head out for a run. Maybe it was the perfect sunny day or the incredible majesty of the huge five-hundred-year-old park, with its tree-lined paths, ancient statues, endless fountains, and gardens in full spring splendor. Whatever the reason, Chris glided with ease at a running pace he would have thought impossible just four days before. An hour later as he completed his run and entered the hotel lobby, covered in sweat but smiling, he proclaimed to no one in particular, "I'm back."

Chris had such a rush from his run that he decided to throw in a set of push-ups and sit-ups, which would become part of his daily workout routine. He then took a long, hot, steamy shower, dressed, and headed for Longshank's office

CHAPTER 11

April 12
Brussels, Belgium—Evening

The IAECM offices were located in a four-story, stone, Victorian-age building that no doubt once served as a residence for a very wealthy family. Chris found the IAECM's brass nameplate and rang the appropriate button. At the sound of the buzzer, he pulled the heavy, white-painted door open and entered. Longshank's office was on the second floor, and Chris walked up the somewhat worn, red-carpeted spiral staircase. If there was an elevator, he didn't see it.

When he arrived, an attractive, young, stylishly dressed woman greeted him. "Mr. O'Brian, I'm Carin Holsten. Welcome."

Chris was instantly impressed with the young woman's professional persona, as he was with the office's high ceilings and elegant decor. He stole a glance at Longshank's inner office, which was, in a word, grand. But for the computers and printers, the office looked like it was right out of the seventeenth century.

What a contrast to my workspace at EPA, Chris thought.

After an awkward moment of silence, Holsten finally said, "Sir Reginald should be arriving at any moment. May I get you a coffee?"

"No, thank you. I'm fine," Chris replied with a growing sense that he was way out of his league.

Around seven o'clock, Longshank finally arrived with a flurry of apologies. While Chris could have easily been annoyed at the late arrival, he took an immediate liking to the seventy-five-year-old, tall, and distinguished-looking British gentleman who would be his host for the evening. Longshank was at once proper and engaging.

"Jackie rang me up yesterday to tell me you were coming and asked me to share my 'wisdom' on the EZ-15 matter," Longshank said. "But I'm sure you must be weary from your travels, so let us skip the formalities and have a chat over dinner."

Chris nodded with approval, and they headed off to what Longshank had described as a modest bistro with decent food. Nothing could have been further from the truth. The restaurant was small but truly elegant in every respect. The food was magnificent. Longshank selected each course and an appropriate accompanying alcoholic beverage—an aperitif, a wonderful Chardonnay, a Bordeaux, and a healthy glass of the finest port Chris had ever sampled.

Chris drank only enough to be polite, but Longshank, who had no need for restraint, drank freely. Rather than dull his senses, the alcohol seemed to energize Longshank, and the tales he told kept Chris riveted.

Longshank talked of the "early days," when concern about pollution from automobiles began to grow in the post-World War II era of the 1950s and early 1960s. "Lots of studies on both sides of the Atlantic began to expose the growing problem. I'm sure you remember seeing old films of the incredible smog that blanketed Los Angeles and Tokyo in the 1950s and of people wearing surgical masks to reduce inhalation of harmful air pollutants. Research performed by Dr. Haagen-Smitt and his colleagues in Los Angeles found that this brown urban haze, or 'smog,' was caused by a chemical reaction of hydrocarbons and oxides of nitrogen in the presence of sunlight.

"As you know, Chris, both hydrocarbon and oxides of nitrogen are gases that are emitted by all internal-combustion engines, regardless of the fuel used, as well as, from some industrial and commercial facilities. Ozone was found to cause a number of respiratory and cardiovascular health problems, to say nothing of making life unbearable. Carbon monoxide, another engine pollutant, adversely affected people with heart decease and became a target for reduction as well."

Longshank paused, took another drink of his port, and with great enthusiasm, continued. "California was the first to regulate auto pollution in the late 1960s, and then a national grassroots environmental movement sprang up, culminating in Earth Day on April 16, 1970. In response to growing public pressure to protect the environment, President Nixon, of all people, called on Congress to pass legislation to reduce air pollution. Not to be outdone, Congress took Nixon's somewhat modest legislative suggestions and enacted comprehensive legislation, calling on the automakers to cut hydrocarbons, carbon monoxide, and oxides of nitrogen pollution by 90 percent in about five years as part of the now-famous Clean Air Act Amendments of 1970."

Chris, who while at EPA, had focused on the legal issues related to industrial and motor-vehicle pollution reduction was less familiar with the technical intricacies. So he asked, "How did the technical solutions evolve to meet the new automobile standards?"

Longshank smiled and went on. "Many thought the only way to achieve such reductions was to reinvent the internal-combustion engine—a task that was both formidable and seemingly impossible to achieve in the short time period before the standards were scheduled to go into effect. But chemists and engineers in the States and in Europe were all working on a radically new strategy—the catalytic converter—that could be used with a conventional internal-combustion engine to significantly reduce exhaust pollution. The auto industry at first resisted using the technology, but when no other feasible options presented themselves, they reluctantly embraced it.

"The catalytic converter is simple in its elegance. It has no moving parts and is placed in the exhaust system downstream of the engine. The technology consists of a stainless steel canister with a ceramic or metallic brick that looks like a bee's honeycomb. The thin walls of this brick, or 'substrate' as we in the industry like to call it, is coated with various precious metals like platinum, palladium, and rhodium. These precious metals act as a catalyst to facilitate the chemical conversion of the auto exhaust pollutants into harmless gases and water, without being consumed in the process.

"Catalytic converter technology was introduced commercially in automobile applications a mere four years after passage of the 1970 clean-air legislation. The first-generation catalytic converters were called oxidation catalysts because they oxidized harmful hydrocarbon and carbon monoxide emissions into water and carbon dioxide. Several years later, the technology was further refined to simultaneously convert oxides of nitrogen to nitrogen and oxygen, while lowering carbon monoxide and hydrocarbon pollution as well.

To make the three-way catalyst work most effectively, fuel injection and electronic controls were introduced—both of which added significantly to the vehicle's performance and fuel economy."

Longshank poured himself another glass of port and continued. "The original 1970 auto-emission standards themselves were modified several times, but eventually the 90 percent pollution reduction requirements were implemented, and the catalytic converter was the central element of the control strategy. Today, as you probably know, gasoline-powered autos and pickup trucks in the US are up to 99 percent less polluting than vehicles sold in the 1960s. Catalyst-based technology is also playing a key role in reducing diesel exhaust pollution from trucks, construction equipment, and, more recently, train locomotives and even marine vessels. I must say it's deeply satisfying to be a part of this history."

"You're being too modest, Sir Reginald," Chris said. "I believe you were knighted by the queen for your role in the development of the catalytic converter."

"Thank you, Chris," Longshank replied, beaming with pride. "But while Her Royal Majesty, the British government, and the London press tried to give me all the credit, I actually played a small role. The truth is that catalyst technology has evolved through a series of chemical and technological breakthroughs and enhancements. Many scientists and engineers from the emission control and motor-vehicle industries on both sides of the Atlantic Ocean and in Japan made significant contributions to developing catalytic-converter technology, including Sergio Sanchez, with whom Jackie mentioned you will also be speaking."

"But now at the forefront comes the issue of carbon dioxide, which is emitted from every internal-combustion engine with or without a catalytic converter, as a global warming gas. Does catalyst technology once again come to the rescue?" Chris asked.

Longshank paused for a moment and replied, "Virtually every chemical company involved in developing catalyst technology— be it catalyst coatings on catalyst substrates or catalyst chemical additives added to the fuel—has been working on this issue since the early 1990s. With EMCO and its additive EZ-15 being the possible exception, no other company has come close."

Chris, leaning forward, softly whispered, "You said that EMCO possibly found the solution. I take it you aren't convinced."

Longshank looked around the room and then whispered, "The EZ-15 chemical formula is proprietary, but there are only a limited number of precious and base metal species that can be used in a catalyst formula to attempt to reduce carbon dioxide. Scientists from every IAECM member company have tried them all and in every conceivable formula. They simply haven't been able to come close to duplicating the results claimed by EMCO for EZ-15."

Longshank stared at Chris and added, "It simply doesn't add up. Something very wrong is going on with that EZ-15 product. But we haven't been able to figure it out yet."

A long silence followed, and then Longshank finally said, "Maybe Sergio will have some ideas."

"What's IAECM's official position on EZ-15, and why isn't EMCO a member of your association?"

"EMCO Consolidated Company would qualify for membership, but the company has always been a bit of a loner when it comes to joining industry associations. In answer to your other question, IAECM doesn't have an official position. Our association exists to promote its members' products and not to attack others. But as I said, there's definitely something that doesn't add up with the claims EMCO is making about the product."

The dinner conversation then drifted back to small talk, and they departed the restaurant shortly thereafter. As the two men went their separate ways, Chris glanced at his watch, which read 11:15 p.m. As he walked down the now-empty boulevard back toward his hotel, Chris heard distant footsteps on the sidewalk and had a distinct feeling he was being followed. He shrugged it off as growing paranoia and arrived safely in his room ten minutes later. He tried to call Sonja Voinovich, but again she didn't answer.

CHAPTER 12

April 13
Brussels, Belgium—Morning

As Chris started to leave his hotel room, he hesitated. He suddenly thought, *What if I was being followed last night?* Recalling Goldberg's admonishment to be careful, Chris decided that taking some precautions wouldn't hurt. First, he removed any documents in his suitcase or lying around the room that could provide any clues regarding his true mission to Europe or that revealed anything about EPA's review of the EZ-15 application for certification. He then stuffed those materials in his computer case.

Then Chris sat down and pulled out the conference program. He looked for and quickly found the list of attendees. Running his finger down the list, he randomly stopped at Charles Gibbons, a professor at George Washington University in Washington, DC. Chris grabbed a hotel notepad and wrote down Gibbons's information, which included his phone number and e-mail address, and added a note: "Call Gibbons re: EZ-15."

Chris placed the handwritten note on one of the hotel's tourist guide magazines, carefully observing exactly where on the magazine cover the top of the note rested. He then strategically placed the magazine on his desk where he felt the hotel cleaning people would likely leave it undisturbed. Chris had no idea who Charles Gibbons was, but he figured any intruder would be interested and might tip their hand by contacting Gibbons.

I'll have to give Gibbons a call when I get back to the States to see if he received any strange calls inquiring about me or EZ-15. Pleased with his scheme that was inspired by one of the many action adventure movies he loved, Chris headed out the door to the conference and checked his computer case with the hotel's bellman.

During the short walk to the symposium venue, Chris became increasingly uncomfortable with every step. First, despite the late night, rich food, and libations the previous evening, he had forced himself to run five miles and perform his morning exercises. That left him with a lingering full-body ache. Second, Chris knew that as the EPA representative, he would be the prime target for verbal abuse at the symposium since EPA was the lone roadblock to allowing EMCO to make its "wonder product" commercially available.

The Palais de Congress was elegant, with high ceilings and marble columns in the entrance lobby. A large banner hung high in the air announcing the Seventh Annual Climate Change Science and Policy Symposium. The banner also listed the symposium sponsors—some corporations and associations Chris recognized and some he did not. But one sponsor stood out: EMCO Consolidated Company.

"Great," Chris mumbled. "They've bought themselves a showcase to hawk EZ-15."

The three hundred or so symposium attendees milled about the lobby, engaging in conversations in small groups. To the right was the symposium meeting room with theater-style seating and the walls covered with elaborate tapestries depicting great moments in science and medicine.

In the front of this grand room were a long table, at which the symposium panelists would sit, and the speakers' podium. An enormous, two-story-high projection screen hung behind the stage. Chris noticed a roped-off area to one side with lots of mikes and cameras. *No doubt the press box,* he thought, his anxiety growing. He turned and walked slowly to the end of the main lobby and registered.

The morning sessions were about to begin, and Chris found an inconspicuous seat near the back of the meeting room. He hadn't recognized anyone and was happy to avoid notice as long as he could. He expected that once he made his presentation, everyone would be trying to track him down to elicit more insight on EPA's position.

After a lengthy introduction by the symposium moderator, which was filled with flowery praise for the organizers, sponsors, symposium staff, and the coming speakers, the first panel discussion finally began. The panelists spoke of the key contributions that private sector industry had made recently to reduce global warming gas emissions. Chris noticed that each of the speakers represented one of the companies sponsoring the symposium.

I see a definite pattern emerging for this symposium, Chris thought.

Despite his best efforts, Chris dozed off several times. At the midday break, he skipped the elegant lunch for the symposium attendees because he wasn't hungry and wanted to avoid getting into any conversations. He went for a walk in the old town section of Brussels, returning just in time for his 2:00 p.m. panel discussion on EZ-15.

The walk had helped clear Chris's head, and now approaching the stage, he felt as ready as he could be.

Chris introduced himself to the session chairman, who, in turn, introduced Chris to his fellow panelists: Pamela Russell, a PR person from EMCO; Joanne McKay, legislative assistant to Senator Goodman; and Barbara Simon from the environmental group, Protect the Environment Consortium. The greetings were formal but at least cordial, and the panelists took their seats at the speakers' table.

The session began with glowing introductions of the panelists, including Chris. *Only Goldberg could have written my bio—if anyone else at EPA even saw it, they would have died laughing,* Chris thought. The bio was obviously designed to make it sound like Chris was intimately involved in all the details of the EPA review of EZ-15 in order to add credence to his presentation.

Pamela Russell was a strikingly beautiful woman in her late twenties, with long, blonde hair loosely pulled back by a black, satin band. She wore a silk, cream-colored, button-down blouse with a deep V-neck that showed off her rather stunning cleavage. Her black skirt captured the lovely contours of her waist and hips, and her black, very high heels encased her tiny feet and pulled taut the firm muscles of her long, thin legs. Chris had trouble not staring at her, and he was sure the other males in the audience were doing the same.

Russell's presentation was a stock EMCO PR piece, with creative, colorful slides that included animation and other audio/visual effects that entertained the audience while presenting very little in the way of real information or data on how EZ-15 actually reduced carbon dioxide emissions. But Chris had to concede the message was clear and convincing that EZ-15 had been developed by a century-old chemical company with a proven track record, that millions had been spent on EZ-15's development, and that the product could prove to be the most significant weapon against the growing threat of global warming and climate change. As a speaker, Russell proved to be a master in grabbing the audience. She was at times funny, passionate, and deadly serious. When she finished, Russell received warm applause. As she returned to her seat, she glanced, with a smirk of satisfaction, at Chris. He looked down at his shoes.

Next up was Barbara Simon, a rather bookish-looking forty-year-old. Simon covered the question of "promise" in the session's title. She spoke with considerable conviction, describing the growing global warming/climate change problem and the potential beneficial role EZ-15 could play. She cited data from air-quality monitors in Tokyo and Osaka where, as a pilot program, EZ-15 had been added to the fuel used by tens of thousands of municipal and other gasoline-powered fleet vehicles over the past six months. That data showed a measurable reduction in carbon dioxide emissions.

Simon next presented data that extrapolated the carbon dioxide reductions that could be achieved over a five-year period in the several key cities around the world if all gasoline-powered motor vehicles used fuel containing EZ-15. The estimated carbon dioxide emissions were shown to be in the millions of tons. There was an audible gasp from the audience as the attendees contemplated the significant reductions that could be achieved. She closed her presentation by showing a list of twenty environmental groups that had recommended EPA approval of EZ-15 for commercial use.

Joanne McKay, a rather attractive, young but stern-looking blonde, followed Simon. As Chris had expected, the legislative staffer first traced her boss's long support of environmental issues, and then the legislation he had sponsored and helped get enacted into law.

"Without question, Senator Goodman has been the leading champion of environmental programs in the US Congress for the past quarter century," she said.

A bit of a gross overstatement, Chris thought.

Next, McKay turned her comments to Senator Goodman's responsibility as chairman of the Senate Environment Committee to provide oversight of EPA, including the agency's action on EMCO's EZ-15 application.

McKay listed all of the actions the senator had taken and added, with considerable conviction, "Senator Goodman isn't trying to substitute Congress's judgment for EPA's, but he does feel the review process has been bogged down far too long, and it's way past the time for EPA to reach a decision. No credible evidence exists in the record to this rulemaking that in any way suggests EZ-15 doesn't reduce CO_2 as demonstrated by EMCO. Nor has any information been presented by EPA or any other source that suggests there are any adverse impacts from using EZ-15."

McKay then pointedly turned to Chris and frowned. "The enormous potential of EZ-15 to help address the most far-reaching environmental challenge facing the world today calls for immediate action, not more bureaucratic delays." As the audience applauded with enthusiasm, Chris's Irish temper began to rise, and his face became flushed.

Finally, it was Chris's turn. He rose slowly. He had sat through most of the panel discussions worrying about his rather dry presentation that contained little of the pizzazz of the previous speakers' presentations. But by the time he got to the podium, he was seething and decided to shake things up a bit.

Chris went through the formal presentation that outlined the EPA review process and all of the data that had been collected. When he came to the last slide that indicated EPA was very close to completing the technical review and a decision could be expected very soon, Chris looked at the audience and saw some nods of approval. If he had stopped at that point, everything would have been fine, but Chris couldn't resist.

"EPA has not been - and never will be - pressured by the regulated industry, special interests, or their allies in Congress to rush to judgment at the risk of putting the public health in jeopardy. A favorable decision on the EZ-15 application will only occur if EPA is completely satisfied that the product performs as claimed and that there are no adverse side effects from use of the product. Thank you."

The audience was stunned, and an eerie silence hung over the room. After more than a couple of uncomfortable moments, the moderator got up and said somewhat nervously, "Well, what an informed and spirited discussion we have had."

The now totally flustered moderator took a few questions. Only one question was directed at Chris, and it concerned the expected timing of the EPA decision. Chris was vague but hinted it could be a while. Then he added a reminder that under the US Administrative Procedures Act, even if EPA approved the EZ-15 application, a thirty-day waiting period would follow before the decision would be final and the product could be introduced for commercial sale in the United States. Chris also noted that anyone could challenge the EPA decision during the thirty-day period based on new evidence not contained in the EPA public record when the initial decision was made. This statement brought yet another chorus of moans from the audience.

As Chris prepared to leave, he was surrounded by the media, all pushing and shoving, hoping to get one more juicy quote. He disappointed the crowd by calmly stating that he could issue no further comments on behalf of EPA.

As he made his way down the stage stairs, he caught a glimpse of Barbara Simmon, who was visibly annoyed, and Pam Russell, who looked a little stunned. As he stepped off the last stair, still glancing at his two fellow panelists, he bumped into Joanne McKay.

"You must have a death wish giving that performance. I hope you hadn't planned a long career at EPA, because, believe me, you have been on Senator Goodman's shit list since that leak you made to the *Herald*. Your showboating today will most definitely result in some rather nasty phone calls from Senator Goodman to your superiors. You're toast, asshole," the young woman said with a smug smile and then walked away.

Notwithstanding the audience's reaction or McKay's ominous threats, Chris was quite satisfied with himself at having stirred the pot. *Jackie would be pleased,* he thought.

As he passed through the meeting room exit with his head down, he heard a voice with a heavy Spanish accent say, "Very interesting presentation."

Chris turned and saw a jolly-looking gentleman with a round, bald head, bushy sideburns, and thick, black eyebrows, smiling at him.

"May I introduce myself? I'm Sergio Sanchez," the short, rotund man said as he handed Chris a business card.

"I'm glad you enjoyed it. I suspect you're my one and only fan," Chris said. "I'm very pleased to meet you, and I look forward to discussing a subject of mutual interest."

The smile on Sanchez's face abruptly changed, and he leaned toward Chris and whispered, "Not here—the date, time, and location for our meeting are written on the back of my card. It's better that we converse no more."

The Spaniard then turned and walked away. Chris resisted the temptation to look at the back of Sanchez's business card. *I'll check it out later when I'm alone.*

Chris contemplated leaving but decided to check out the reception. Besides, he didn't want his adversaries to think he was afraid of being confronted by them. The extravagant reception buffet and the marble-topped bar, with an unending selection of libations, like everything else at the symposium, were completely over the top.

To his surprise, no one approached him. In fact, it was almost like he had the plague. After a few awkward moments, he decided to leave and started to walk out of the room.

"Leaving the scene of the crime so soon?" a sexy female voice called out.

Startled, Chris turned and, to his surprise, there stood Pamela Russell, looking every bit as drop-dead gorgeous as before.

"Let me buy you a drink. Just because we're on opposite sides doesn't mean we can't be civil," she said warmly.

"Normally, the EPA code of ethics would require me to decline your kind offer, but since the drinks are free, why not?" Chris said, smiling.

She grabbed his arm and led him to the bar. Russell selected a glass of the most expensive cabernet, and Chris ordered a Heineken light. "Light beer? Very cosmopolitan," Russell said mockingly as she raised her glass to a toast. "Here's to burying the hatchet—well, at least for this evening."

They moved to a quiet corner of the reception area. The sight of an EPA official casually chatting with an EMCO representative caught the eye of several symposium attendees, and soon a small crowd gathered around. The tone of the conversation was light as Chris and Russell exchanged friendly barbs.

After a few minutes, Pam touched Chris's elbow gently and said quietly, "Let's get out of here. Interested in getting a bite to eat?"

The effect on Chris of an extremely attractive women touching him somewhat affectionately and proposing dinner was immediate. He blushed and felt his heart race. "Sure, how about one of those small cafés just off the Grand Place? I've been told mussels in Brussels are incredible."

As they exited the symposium reception hall, Chris said he wanted to make a quick stop to wash his hands. He entered the men's room, which was empty, and quickly took Sanchez's business card out of his coat pocket, flipped it over to the back side, and read the instructions.

Chris read the note again, making sure he had memorized the information. Then he tore the card into pieces, tossed them in a toilet, and flushed them away.

Russell was waiting outside as a broad smile came to her face. Again she grabbed his arm and said, "I know just the place to dine."

CHAPTER 13

April 13
Brussels, Belgium—Evening

About a ten-minute walk from the symposium venue, Russell and Chris arrived at the Grand Place, a medieval cobblestone courtyard surrounded by fifteenth-century buildings beautifully restored and now crowded with tourists, business people, and students.

"Magnificent, isn't it?" Russell said as she grabbed his hand. "I love this place. I love Brussels. I guess I just love to travel internationally. It's one of the big perks of working for Miller and Braxton."

"But your business card says Vice President, Public Relations, EMCO," Chris responded.

"Oh, I work for M&B, but you could say I'm on assignment to EMCO."

"I guess that's pretty common in your line of work."

As they cut diagonally across the ancient court, Chris marveled at how Pam negotiated in a very elegant manner the journey over the bumpy cobblestones in her ridiculously high heels. Exiting the Grand Place, they strolled down a narrow street lined with beautiful two- and three-story buildings. On each side of the street was a mix of small cafés and shops, many beautifully displaying an array of fresh seafood in ice-filled, colorful, wooden, stainless steel-lined bins. "That's the spot," Russell said with girlish excitement as she pointed to a small, quaint café to their left. "Shall we sit outside? I love to watch the people," she added.

Chris suspected that the "spontaneous" suggestion to go to dinner was a setup and part of Russell's plan to ply what information she could from him. He guessed she was pretty good at it. Yet he was struck by the fact that sometimes she seemed so youthful, innocent, and naïve.

Is it all an act or is there more than one facet to this incredibly gorgeous woman staring playfully at me? Chris pondered.

They were shown to a table that gave them a great view of the street while also providing a measure of privacy. No sooner had they sat down than Russell said, with a seductive smile, "I need to freshen up. Why don't you order us a couple of Cosmos—they're fantastic here."

Chris held her chair as she rose, brushed against his leg, and headed into the dimly lit, indoor portion of the restaurant. Just before she disappeared into the darkness of the inner confines, he saw Russell pull her cell phone from her purse.

Checking in with home base, no doubt, Chris thought.

A young, neatly dressed waiter asked politely, "May I bring you and your lady an aperitif or cocktail perhaps?"

"Two Cosmos." Then Chris added, "Could you go very light on the vodka in mine? I have an important business meeting later this evening. But the lady prefers her Cosmo strong."

The waiter smiled and said, "Ah, yes, a business meeting. One needs to keep himself sharp."

Chris guessed the waiter assumed Chris wanted to keep the upper edge on his beautiful dinner partner, and he was right, but not for the reason the waiter probably suspected. Chris knew he needed to keep sharp for his coming duel with Pamela Russell as each tried to extract information from the other.

As Russell returned to the table, Chris thought, *Pamela Russell, the beautiful, ruthless hunter from M&B—you are about to become the hunted.*

"We came here Sunday night. The mussels are the best in Brussels."

Chris pondered, *Who was the 'we'?* But he didn't ask. He'd wait until Russell had a few Cosmos, and then the probing would begin. The drinks arrived, and the two adversaries raised their classes for a toast.

"To the speedy approval of a product that will help address the global warming/climate change nightmare we face," Russell said with a huge, infectious smile.

And Chris quickly added as their glasses touched, "But not before a thorough analysis of this wonder product is completed." They both laughed as they took a swallow of their drinks.

"Do you mind if I smoke?" Russell asked as she reached for the pack of cigarettes in her purse.

"Not at all," Chris replied—realizing he still had a strong craving for a smoke.

Russell offered Chris a cigarette, but with a surge of willpower, he declined. The young lobbyist looked incredibly sexy as she lit her Fatima Turkish cigarette with her slender fingers, drew in a long breath, and then playfully exhaled a cloud of smoke in Chris's direction. Chris could feel his heart rate jump. He had a sudden craving not only for a cigarette, but also for the seductive woman sitting so intimately close to him.

As they consumed first one and then another Cosmo, the conversation drifted amicably through a series of safe topics: where they were from originally—she from Wisconsin, and Chris from Boston; where they went to school—she the University of Wisconsin, and Chris Colgate; families—she one of six kids, and Chris the only child; marital status—she single, and he divorced; and how they got to where they were professionally. On the last topic, Chris was less than candid, and he suspected Russell had left out a few details as well. Since she had been to the café before, Chris encouraged Russell to do the ordering, and as he would discover, she would do a masterful job of selecting each course.

As she had promised, the mussels, served in a big, steaming, ceramic pot, were unbelievable. Chris couldn't help staring at his stunning dinner companion. She even looked incredibly sexy as she delicately removed each mussel from its shell, raised it slowly to her open mouth, and savored the taste.

As the waiter cleared the table, Russell suggested, "Shall we have one more Cosmo for the road?"

"Let's," Chris quickly replied as he tried to remember whether that would be the third or fourth of the evening. "Those drinks do pack a bit of a punch. I have to admit I feel it," Chris lied.

Russell playfully laughed and said, "I feel a little buzz myself, but this has really been fun." Then, still smiling, she added, "How about we end this wonderful dinner with some honest conversation—and we agree that anything we say won't be shared?"

"Sounds good to me," Chris replied, thinking, *Does she really think I'm that stupid?*

Russell then moved closer to him, crossed her legs, and put her hand near his. At the same moment, the toe of her left high heel brushed against his ankle and rubbed gently up and down in a circular motion. Chris's whole body tingled in response as he put his hand on hers. He leaned toward her and whispered, "Okay, you first. Tell me something about EZ-15 or EMCO that I don't already know."

The young woman smiled and said, "A large percentage of EMCO's stock is owned by Crown Prince Abdul Syed. His extended family is one of the five wealthiest families in the world."

"I could have found that out by checking EMCO's annual 10K report," Chris replied.

"But, did you know that the crown prince has loaned EMCO hundreds of millions to finance the development, production, and marketing of EZ-15? The simple reason EPA is getting so much political pressure to approve EZ-15 quickly isn't because anyone doubts the effectiveness of EZ-15 or is trying to get EPA approval before anything negative is discovered. The pressure is coming because people genuinely and correctly believe EZ-15 will make a difference in addressing global warming. But, thanks to your agency's unjustified bureaucratic delays, EMCO is running out of time to repay its loans to Crown Prince Syed and the royal family. If there are further delays, EMCO could be in serious financial difficulty. EMCO has a lot of friends in Washington who don't want to see the company placed at financial risk when there is no good reason to further delay approval. It's not about some great international environmental conspiracy, but about keeping a corporation, which employs nearly forty thousand workers worldwide and over ten thousand in the United States, financially strong."

"Sounds plausible," Chris replied even though he doubted that the intense political pressure on EPA was entirely the result of concern for EZ-15's environmental benefits or because EMCO needed the revenues from EZ-15 to repay its debt to some Arab sheik.

"If that's true, it's ironic, because the main reason some folks at EPA are so concerned about rushing approval of EZ-15 is that they fear the overwhelming political pressure to approve the product quickly might be because there's something wrong with the product itself."

"EZ-15 has no skeletons hiding in the closet. I can assure you of that," Russell responded with conviction.

Russell tossed her long, flowing blonde hair back and said, "Now it's your turn."

Chris deliberately paused a moment to heighten the drama and then whispered, "As the EPA attorney overseeing the EPA technical review of EZ-15, I have been charged with reviewing every bit of data, analysis, and testimony related to EZ-15. Between you and me, I haven't seen anything that would remotely call into question the benefits of EZ-15 or that suggests there are any potential adverse issues with the product itself."

Everything he said was true but incomplete, because he also knew that Ronnie's analysis, which he hadn't yet read, could raise critical issues that would prevent EZ-15 from being approved by EPA.

Russell's expression remained unchanged at hearing Chris's words. *She's good at what she does*, he thought.

"Enough talk about business. What are your plans for after the symposium?" Russell asked.

"My flight back to the States is on Monday. EPA got a great fare, but I'm stuck here for a couple of days. Thought I might head to Paris and spend the weekend," Chris lied convincingly. "How about you?"

"Unfortunately, I head back to DC on an early flight tomorrow. In fact, I should be heading back to the hotel. Will you walk me back?"

"Certainly, but maybe we should pay the bill first?" Chris said.

"I already took care of it—gave the waiter my credit card when you weren't looking. My treat."

Chris protested, citing EPA's conflict of interest rules that didn't allow EPA employees to accept gifts or meals from the regulated industry.

"You're such a bureaucrat. We're in Brussels, and I don't think there's another EPA official within hundred miles of here, so you're safe," she said as she affectionately squeezed his hand.

"Okay, as long as you don't assume you're buying any special treatment," Chris said with a smile.

As they walked arm-in-arm back to her hotel, which was across the street from his hotel, Chris said, "Seriously, thank you very much. It was a delightful dinner, and I very much enjoyed the company. Was I as much fun as your guests the other night at the café?"

Russell responded with a hug on his arm and a kiss on his cheek. "You're much better company. Monday night was all business. I met with EMCO's CEO, a Swede named Jorgen Johansson, who loved to hear himself talk, and Hassid Kabar, an adviser to the crown prince whose family lent EMCO the money. The Arab guy said virtually nothing and stared lustfully at me, trying all night to look down my blouse. The other guy was someone EMCO hired for security. His name was Dietrich, I think."

"Sounds like a grim evening," Chris replied as they reached Russell's hotel. He couldn't believe she had divulged so much information. *Was it the booze or is she simply just that clever and is throwing me a curve?* Chris pondered.

"Come up for a night cap?" she asked seductively as she gently rubbed his shoulder.

Chris nodded, without speaking, and they took the opulent elevator up to the top floor. As they reached her room at the end of the hall, she handed Chris the key in a somewhat obvious gesture that signaled she was "letting him in." After fumbling for a moment with the brass key—no plastic electronic cards at this luxurious, five-star hotel—he opened the door into a huge, beautifully decorated suite. When he closed the door behind them and turned, she kissed him playfully and pressed her knee where she knew it would elicit the right reaction.

She pulled away abruptly and playfully whispered before Chris had time to fully react, "There's some wonderful champagne on ice. Would you open it and pour us a glass while I get out of my Bonnie business costume and into something a little more comfortable?"

When Russell returned, she was dressed in a black, sheer teddy and panties that left little to the imagination. Her body was a thing of beauty. As Russell slowly approached Chris, he couldn't help staring at her and tried to speak, but nothing came out. Finally, he handed her a glass and toasted, "To finding a new friend in a faraway place."

"I'll drink to that," Russell responded warmly as she put down her glass and kissed him deeply, removed his tie, unbuttoned his shirt, and loosened his belt buckle. They pressed close together as she pulled him onto her bed. The mild scent of the expensive body powder she was wearing was intoxicating.

It had been a long time since Chris had been with a woman, but Russell was an expert and took the lead. When their lovemaking reached a climax some twenty minutes later, they both were soaked in sweat. They kissed tenderly and both put their heads on the pillows, surveying the carnage that was once a neatly made bed—the comforter and sheets wrinkled and tossed about, and pieces of clothing scattered from one end of the room to the other.

"That was pretty good stuff for a bureaucrat."

"Gee, thanks for the high praise," Chris replied somewhat breathlessly as he pushed back his black, sweat-soaked hair.

"Seriously, you're a damn good lover—sometimes tentative, but always tender and concerned about pleasing your partner," she said, sounding sincere.

"You're pretty damn amazing yourself," Chris replied.

"Maybe, we can get together in DC once this EZ-15 issue is put to rest," Russell said as she turned and hugged him.

"That would be great," he replied, knowing that the odds of that happening were less than zero.

"Let's seal the pact by each of us telling the other one more secret, and this time you go first," Russell said affectionately as she kissed him once more tenderly on his lips and pressed her naked breasts into his chest.

Without hesitating, Chris said, "My educated guess is that EPA will announce approval of the EMCO application within ten days." Chris had no idea when the decision would be made, but he hoped his prediction would cause EMCO and its allies to back off for at least a short period and give EPA more time to evaluate EZ-15.

"Okay, my turn. When EMCO gets EPA approval for EZ-15, and I do mean when, not if, the corporation has another product, EZ-20, that will reduce carbon dioxide emissions from diesel engines and be even more beneficial in reducing greenhouse gases that cause global warming and climate change."

They lay together a few minutes longer, and then Chris lifted himself up and said he should be heading back to his to his hotel.

"Besides, you need to get some sleep. You have an early flight tomorrow."

Looking at her watch, which said 10:05 p.m., she pleaded, "Can't you stay a little longer? Maybe we could go another round."

Chris laughed affectionately at the suggestion. "I gave you everything I had, and you wore me out. Seriously, I really need to get going."

Chris sensed Russell was annoyed, but she reluctantly acquiesced, and they both gathered up their clothes and dressed. As they reached the door, holding hands, Chris turned and kissed Russell one more time. She gazed affectionately at him as he turned to leave, squeezed his hand one more time, and closed the door.

*   *   *

As soon as Chris was gone, Russell's mood changed abruptly. She searched for and grabbed her cell phone and made a call. "Hans? Are you still in his room?"

"Yes."

"Get the hell out of there! He's on his way back."

"I told you to keep him busy until 10:30," a gruff voice responded.

"I did everything I could to keep him here; just get out!"

Russell then walked to her bed and, surveying the scene of her triumph, made another call, this time to the United States. The phone at the other end rang, and a voice said, "Braxton here."

Russell responded with considerable excitement, "I just spent the evening with the EPA's international liaison legal official, got him drunk, seduced him, and plied some very interesting information from him that I think will be very helpful to our client."

*   *   *

Chris returned to his hotel, which now seemed far less grand than when he first checked in the day before. Retrieving his computer case from the bellman, he took the elevator to the third floor and made his way down the hallway toward his room. About halfway there, Chris noticed a muscular man about five foot ten, with short, blond hair and a face that looked like it was chiseled from stone, walking toward him. The man was dressed casually all in black, and as he passed Chris, he looked down.

As he reached his room, Chris couldn't contain his satisfaction at scoring such a success with Russell. Not only did he pick up a few pieces of information that might be useful to Goldberg, but he also had led Russell down the wrong path regarding EPA's review of EZ-15. He was confident that Russell would pass the misinformation he provided on to her superiors. *And the sex was pretty damn special, too,* he thought.

Looking carefully around the room, everything appeared as he had left it in the morning. Chris walked over to the desk and looked at the magazine with the note he had placed on it. The note was still on the magazine cover, but it clearly had been moved from its original spot.

An icy chill raced through Chris's entire body. "Damn, someone *was* in here and looking for *something.*"

The hour was late, but Chris knew it would be six hours earlier in Washington, so he picked up the phone and asked for an international line. Pulling out the now-tattered sheet of paper with Voinovich's number, he punched in the numbers. The phone rang, but again she didn't answer.

"Damn. First, someone breaks into my room, and now Sonja's still missing."

Suddenly, the joy of outsmarting Russell vanished, and in its place, a sense of dread consumed him.

CHAPTER 14

April 14
Washington, DC—Morning

While Chris slept, a global financial firestorm erupted that was way beyond anything he could have imagined when he made his off-the-cuff comments at the symposium on possible delays and uncertainly regarding EPA's approval of EZ-15.

Godfrey Thomas, a financial reporter for the *London Times*, had all but fallen asleep during the session on EZ-15. But then Chris dropped the bombshell that the EPA wouldn't be pressured to rush to judgment on approving E-15, and the reporter snapped back into consciousness. After fumbling for his glasses, Thomas started furiously typing notes on his laptop computer. When Chris suggested that even if EZ-15 were approved by EPA, it would be a month before EZ-15 could be introduced into commerce, Thomas knew he had his story. By the time the session on EZ-15 ended, Thomas had already e-mailed his story, "Future of EMCO's EZ-15 in Doubt" to his editor in London.

The story on EZ-15 made Thursday's early edition of the *London Times*. Indeed, it made the front page of the newspaper's financial section. The article also was picked up by the wire services and reprinted in the Thursday morning issues of the left-leaning *Washington Herald* and the right-leaning *Washington Daily*. A lot of influential people in London, Washington, and elsewhere awakened to read Thomas's article. They weren't happy, and phones started to ring.

*   *   *

The consternation and angst about a possible delay in, or disapproval of, EMCO introducing EZ-15 commercially was particularly evident among the members of the Heritage Study Group meeting at the Capital Club in the heart of Washington's business district.

The study group was an informal gathering made up of white, middle-aged men who had been carefully selected from among individuals representing the nation's key political, social, and business communities—a real Who's Who list. No written agenda, no minutes, and no record of the study group were kept.

The very private meetings were hosted by retired Federal Court of Appeals Judge Thomas Worthington, the only actual member of the Capital Club. Worthington was a gruff, seventy-two-year-old former Marine general, who diligently maintained his healthy physique and kept his gray hair shortly cropped like it was when he served in Vietnam. Worthington, or the "judge," as everyone called him, provided special-delivery, encoded plastic pass keys that allowed his guests to enter the magnificent building by a private side entrance and pass unimpeded through the rather formidable security checkpoint at the main entrance. Once used, the pass cards were electronically disabled to prevent reentry at a later time.

The stated purpose of the Heritage Study Group was to bring together key leaders of industry and government to discuss and reflect on the major issues and challenges facing the nation. The real purpose was money.

Judge Worthington, who started the group and picked the members, knew from personal experience that Washington insiders were often privy to information not publicly available, such as pending regulatory or court decisions or the future of key legislation. The judge had the vision to bring a group of these insiders together to share key information that could greatly expand the opportunities for financial gain. While each member shared key information that might impact a particular corporate stock, the rule was that no member bought or sold stocks for which he had provided the information or for which he was connected, in anyway, with the corporation in question.

The study group had been in existence for nearly two years, and every member had benefitted. Their latest success was buying large blocks of stock in a communication conglomerate whose request to the Federal Communications Commission for a renewal of a television license was widely rumored to be in jeopardy. Alan Hastings, an FCC commissioner, knew the rumors were false and that approval was imminent. He urged his study group colleagues to buy the company's stock. Most group members did, and within a week the company's stock value, which had fallen precipitously on the negative rumors, began to rebound and increased by ten dollars a share.

Group members were very happy with how things had gone over the past two years. That was until today. Based on insider information that EMCO's EZ-15 approval by EPA was imminent, members, over the past thirty days, had been urged to buy EMCO stock. During that period, the stock had traded in the twenty-six to twenty-eight dollar a share range.

But today, the buzz around the table was growing as members pored over the *Washington Herald*'s reprint of Godfry Thomas's article suggesting that EMCO's "product of the future" was now in jeopardy. EMCO's stock had opened down 10 percent on the news.

Franklin Moss, chief of staff for Congressman Allen Beasley, chairman of the House Environmental Committee, and one of two top congressional aids in the study group, flipped his cell phone closed and proclaimed, "I just spoke to my broker, and EMCO's stock has dropped to less than sixteen dollars. It's in a damn free fall."

A collective moan could be heard around the table as everyone turned and glared at Stanley Braxton, senior partner and cofounder of Miller and Braxton, one of the top lobbying firms in the nation's capital.

"There is absolutely no reason to panic," Braxton said confidently. "The entire article was based on some showboating by a low-level EPA bureaucrat looking to stir the pot and grab the spotlight."

Then thinking about the critical intelligence Pamela Russell had extracted the day before from O'Brian, Braxton added confidently, "We have it on good authority—solid inside information—that the EPA approval of EZ-15 is imminent. Any issues that had been lurking have been or will be addressed. I can guarantee it."

Braxton's words deflated the collective anxiety around the table. Discussion turned to other opportunities to benefit financially from shared inside information.

The meeting, as always, ended precisely at noon, and the study group members filed out of the room. As Braxton was heading for the door, Judge Worthington grabbed his arm and said sternly, "You better be right about that EPA approval. I'm heavily leveraged in EMCO stock." Then the judge added, with a menacing glare, "If this investment goes badly, I'll personally track you down and rip your guts out."

"Don't worry. We've got all of the contingencies covered. In fact, I think the EMCO stock is a steal at its current price, and you would be wise to pick up more shares."

Worthington, seemingly placated at least for the moment, turned and left without saying another word. Braxton pulled a handkerchief from his pocket, wiped his sweating palms, and headed back to his office to check if there were any new developments regarding EMCO's application to sell EZ-15.

CHAPTER 15

April 14
Brussels, Belgium—Morning

Chris decided to skip the second day of the symposium, thinking he could make better use of his time. *I'll go through the EZ-15 documentation again. Maybe I missed something. And I'll try to reach Sonja at EPA. She should be there by 2:00 p.m. Brussels time.*

Six hours later, after reading all the documents again, Chris pushed his hotel room chair away from the desk and agonized, "What a complete waste of time." He then called EPA and was told by the receptionist that Voinovich hadn't been at EPA since Monday.

Frustrated and with a growing sense of anxiety about Voinovich's well-being, Chris changed into his running clothes, headed to the park, and took off running, hoping a good, hard run would help clear his head.

He had been running for nearly sixty minutes at what he felt was an excellent pace when an athletically-built woman passed him.

"You won't get any aerobic benefits running that slow," the young woman said with a laugh as she raced by Chris.

"Joanne McKay," Chris sneered as he quickened his pace, attempting to catch her. His lungs burned, and his knees ached, but Chris began to close the gap on the Senate staffer. As he passed McKay, he cried out to her, "That was my warm-up pace."

Chris could see the east end of the park, which was a logical place to end the run. As he extended his lead, he thought, with considerable satisfaction, *Less than a quarter of a mile to go, and victory will be mine.*

But then he heard the pounding footsteps from behind closing in on him. He tried to pick up his pace, but he had nothing left, and with about 150 yards to go, McKay caught and easily passed him. "Nice try, old man."

Upon finishing, Joanne turned to watch Chris finish about ten seconds behind her. He stumbled to a stop and bent over at his waist, legs spread and hands on his hips, gasping for air. He wasn't sure what hurt more, his totally racked body or McKay's cutting words as she had passed him.

Looking at his stopwatch, Chris felt better as he calculated that he had run the approximately eight miles at an average per-mile pace that was thirty seconds better than any previous run. *Not bad*, he thought while still trying to catch his breath.

When Chris looked up, McKay was smiling. "Nice run. I never would have guessed you had it in you." But before Chris could reply, she went on in a more serious tone, "You missed all of the excitement at the symposium. Of course, the fact you weren't there was probably no coincidence."

Still trying to catch his breath, Chris sputtered, "I have no idea what you're talking about."

The young congressional staffer explained the *London Times* article concerning Chris's comments at the symposium and the resulting precipitous drop in the value of EMCO stock.

"You're a real fuck up," Joanne said with a note of exasperation.

"That's the second time in four days I've received that compliment," Chris replied, recalling that Goldberg had used similar words when she greeted Chris in her office on Monday.

After a brief moment, Chris said, "Look, I'm not the bad guy. We're all just trying to do what we think is right."

Joanne looked unconvinced, so Chris added hopefully, "How about getting a bite to eat? At least give me a chance to tell my side of the story."

Joanne, looking somewhat guarded, replied, "Okay, but I get to pick the spot, and we split the bill."

"Sounds good to me," Chris replied, wiping away the considerable sweat that was dripping into his eyes.

Joanne gave Chris the directions, they agreed to meet at 7:00 p.m., and she jogged off. Chris, his legs aching, hobbled slowly back to his hotel.

The restaurant McKay picked was in an area not frequented by tourists. The café itself was actually part produce store and part health food pickup restaurant.

"Hey, this place looks interesting. How did you find it?" Chris asked, greeting McKay, who was sitting at a small table in the back.

She got up and gave him a quick hug. "Don't get any ideas. It's the custom in Europe to give your dinner partner a friendly hug, even if he or she is your worst enemy."

They both laughed as she added, "I found this place on the Internet, and I've tried to eat all my meals here."

Chris enjoyed the hug, even if it was only a custom. He thought how attractive the young woman looked in her white cashmere sweater and gray slacks that complemented her lightly tanned face and beautiful smile.

"What's good here?" Chris finally asked.

"If you're game, I'll do the ordering."

Chris nodded with approval, and they walked to the counter to order. As they carried their trays back to the table, Joanne described the ingredients of each of the small-portion dishes she ordered for them. Some he recognized, and others he did not, but everything served was vegetarian. Chris was skeptical at first, but everything tasted fantastic. "This stuff is really great."

As they ate, they covered the same small-talk subjects that he and Russell had talked about the night before. McKay turned out to be thirty-five, but she looked much younger. She played soccer and ran track at the University of Michigan, where she had received an undergraduate degree in political science and a master's degree in economics—both with honors. Her family knew then-Congressman Goodman, and when Goodman became a senator, McKay was hired as the staff "gopher." Over the next ten years, she was given ever-increasing responsibilities and had become the number-two staff person behind Goodman's lifetime friend and chief of staff, Damon Kowalski. She described the fifty-five-year-old Kowalski as a "take no prisoners" guy who could get things done for the senator.

McKay talked about the long hours and the thrill of working on Goodman's staff. She didn't say much about her private life, and Chris guessed the dedicated staffer pretty much devoted her life to her job.

"Sounds like you keep pretty busy, but you've certainly stayed in great shape."

"I try to eat right, take martial arts courses, and I run virtually every evening—usually up Rock Creek Park from M Street to about a mile or two past the National Cathedral and back again. It really helps me unwind and get to sleep. It's a great way to end my day."

Chris was enjoying the conversation and time together, but then there was an awkward moment of silence. Looking at Chris somewhat pensively, McKay said softly, "I wish I could convince you that Senator Goodman is one of the good guys. I've spent more time with the senator than anyone else over the past ten years, with the obvious exception of Kowalski, and even in private conversation, the senator is principled, caring, and totally committed to what he believes is right. The man's actions come from his heart." She then added with a slight edge in her voice, "That's why he was so upset when you and your friend, Levy, portrayed him as a political hack trying to pressure EPA into a quick decision for political gain."

Chris knew when he was being taken to the woodshed, but he didn't get angry. Rather, he cautiously replied, "I wish you could believe that what I say and do is because I believe I'm right. EPA is being pushed to rush its decision, and I'm not alone in that opinion."

"I almost believe you, but after what you said yesterday about political interference and the delays in the EPA approval of EZ-15, and now the resulting reactions by the financial markets, I wouldn't be surprised if EPA pulls you off the EMCO review or even fires you. I know Senator Goodman will call Jackie Goldberg, who's a longtime friend of his, about what you said."

Chris laughed in response. "I've already been fired—last Monday, in fact."

"Then why are you here?"

He replied, still smiling, "Because I appealed the dismissal."

"But why did they send you?" McKay sputtered.

Chris paused and then decided to open up to the young woman, "Because Jackie Goldberg believes EPA is being pushed to rush a decision before all the facts come out. For some reason, she felt I was the right person to send to Europe."

McKay looked shocked at what she was hearing. Rather than try to pursue the matter further, she abruptly said, "It's getting late and time for me to head back to my hotel. I have an early-morning flight back to DC."

As they left the café, Chris offered to walk her back to her hotel, but she declined. "I'm a big girl and can find my way back, but thanks."

Chris, sorry the evening had to end on such a negative note, said with considerable conviction, "It was a fun evening, and I enjoyed the food, the company, and the conversation. I know you may have trouble believing me, but maybe we really aren't on opposite sides of the issue."

McKay raised her head and, looking into his eyes, said, "I don't know … maybe, but … I just don't know." With that, she gave him a hug that was a little less formal than their initial greeting and headed off down the street.

Chris turned in the opposite direction. He genuinely liked McKay and began to doubt his negative opinion of Senator Goodman. He also hoped that mentioning Goldberg's concerns wasn't a mistake. But he had a gut feeling he could trust McKay, and giving her the information about Goldberg had obviously gotten her thinking.

CHAPTER 16

April 15
Brussels, Belgium—Morning

Dressed in slightly worn jeans, a wool shirt, and a pullover parka and carrying only a small backpack he purchased the day before, Chris stepped out of the taxi in front of the Brussels train station just in time to catch the early-morning train to Bruges, as instructed by Sergio Sanchez. Chris had left his other luggage with the hotel bellman and would pick it up upon his return Sunday night.

Walking through the station toward the ticket window, Chris had a feeling that he was being watched. Glancing at the schedule of trains departing in the next hour, he said, "Perfect."

Chris had checked the train schedule the night before and had noted the train to Bruges left at 7:16 a.m. and a train to Paris departed on an adjacent track at 7:20 a.m. He could see now that both were scheduled to depart on time. Purchasing his ticket to Bruges, Chris headed toward the train to Paris.

At 7:10 a.m., Chris boarded the Paris train, grabbed a seat close to an exit, and peered out the window. "Damn, I was right," Chris whispered as he spotted the same muscular, blond-headed man who had passed him in the hallway of his hotel two nights before. The man rushed along the side of the train as Chris ducked so he couldn't be seen from the platform. He waited a moment and then looked out the window to see the man boarding the train three cars up.

Time to move, Chris thought, grabbing his backpack and walking briskly toward the back of the train. When he got to the last train car, he quickly exited and ran across the platform to board the train heading to Bruges. He hopped aboard, and within moments the train to Bruges started to pull out of the station. Finding a seat, he again ducked down in case he had been spotted leaving the train to Paris.

As the train to Bruges gained speed out of the station, Chris thought, *I'm getting pretty good at this industrial espionage stuff.*

Meanwhile, Hans Dietrich walked through the Paris train as it left the station and he discovered too late that his mark had given him the slip.

Chris settled in for the trip to Bruges, and his mind wandered. It had been just a week since he had tried and failed to kill himself. The very thought made him shake. But after a brief moment, he regained his composure.

Got to focus on what I need to accomplish today and not worry about the past, Chris thought as he reviewed in his mind Sanchez's instructions and the questions he wanted to ask the chemist.

In what seemed like no time, the train pulled into the station just outside the inner village of Bruges. As soon as Chris saw the village, he was struck with an overwhelming sense of melancholy, remembering the last time he was in Bruges twenty-two years before. "Sarah," was all he could mutter.

Entering the station, Chris put his backpack in a locker and headed for the bike rental stand. He saw that the rental bikes were all one speed, fat tired, and looked like they were at least ten years old.

Well, I guess I'll get my exercise for the day, he thought as he paid the fee and got directions. The Bruges-to-Damme Canal and Bikeway was only about a mile from the train station. Chris quickly found the packed-earth walking and biking trail. The tree-lined canal and bike path meandered through the rolling countryside. He passed several other bikers and walkers who were headed in the opposite direction, but otherwise he had the bike path pretty much to himself over the next two hours.

After riding about twenty miles, Chris rounded a bend in the canal and could see just off the bike path to the right a quaint, one-story thatched-roof building with white stucco walls and rough-cut wood window frames and trim. He looked up and down the bike path. Seeing no one, Chris pedaled off the path, parked his bike, and entered the inn.

The dining room at the inn was small and intimate, with a massive fireplace throwing off a warm glow that filled the room. Chris immediately spotted Sanchez sitting at a corner table near the fire. A half-empty bottle of red wine sat on the table. As Chris approached, the Spaniard rose to greet Chris as if he had been a friend for life. Chris noticed that no one else was in the restaurant and figured that was why Sanchez had selected such a secluded spot.

"Ah, my good man, you were able to follow my directions and arrive safely," Sanchez said as he motioned Chris to take a seat. They chatted cordially for a few minutes. Sanchez offered Chris a glass of wine, which he declined. Instead Chris ordered coffee from the young waitress. They then looked at the menus, Sanchez ordering the wild boar stew, and Chris a salad.

As the meals arrived, the conversation turned to more serious matters. "Jackie sends her best regards and told me you're the person to talk to about EMCO and EZ-15."

In response, Sanchez first described his forty years of experience as a chemist in the automotive catalyst field, and then turning to the subject at hand, the Spaniard began, "EMCO Consolidated Company is a highly respected chemical company. I actually worked for them in the late eighties and early nineties, before going out on my own as an independent consultant. Over the past few years, EMCO has been selling off many of its assets. I think it has done so, in part, to help fund the development, manufacture, and distribution of EZ-15. It's well known that EMCO has also borrowed large amounts to fund the project. But if EMCO gets approval to sell EZ-15, it stands to make billions of dollars annually."

"How can they make that much money?" Chris asked.

"EMCO expects to make about ten cents on every gallon of gasoline containing EZ-15. Worldwide, over 250 billion gallons of gasoline are sold annually. You do the math, Chris. The money to be made is staggering. What's more, oil companies likely will be happy to pay the price so they can take credit for making a substantial contribution to reducing global warming gases."

Chris thought back to Pam Russell's comments during their dinner together about EMCO needing to meet its debt obligations. "So, do you believe the main reason EMCO and its allies are pressuring EPA for a quick decision is all about the liquidity of the corporation and not about any environmental concerns with the product itself?"

"In part yes, but that's not the only reason for the onslaught of pressure being placed on EPA," Sanchez replied quietly. "Let me give you a little background about the product itself."

Sanchez took a healthy gulp of his third glass of red wine to wash down an overstuffed mouth full of stew and explained that the EZ-15 chemical formula was developed by a former colleague and highly respected chemist named Gunter Heinz.

"Heinz worked for EMCO and was a visionary who recognized that developing a catalyst formula that could chemically reduce carbon dioxide emissions would be worth billions of dollars. The key wasn't only finding the proper mix of base and precious metals, but the staging of the process during which the metal molecules where fused together in the proper balance to make the CO_2 reduction possible. Whatever Gunter did, only he was able to find a way to reduce CO_2 emissions."

"Boy, I'd love to talk to Dr. Heinz."

"So would I, but unfortunately eighteen months ago, right after the patent was issued for EZ-15, my good friend Gunter and his entire research team were killed in a crash of an EMCO corporate jet," Sanchez replied. "They said the pilot had a stroke, but it all seems a little suspicious. All of Heinz's preliminary research was also destroyed in the crash, and upon Gunter's death, the patent reverted to his employer—EMCO."

"But if the EZ-15 formulation really reduces carbon dioxide emissions, then what's the issue?"

Sanchez leaned toward Chris and simply said, "Unintended consequences."

"You lost me."

"Both Gerhard Mueller of the German Federal Environmental Agency, or the Umweltbundesamt or UBA, as the Germans call it, and I believe there is a toxic chemical by-product being emitted during the CO_2 reduction process," he whispered in a voice barely audible. He then added, "I understand you'll be meeting with Mueller tomorrow."

Chris looked at Sanchez in disbelief and said, "But I've looked at literally hundreds of pages of documents, and there has been absolutely no mention or evidence of any toxic byproducts. What's your proof?"

The Spaniard's expression telegraphed considerable offense at Chris's question, and he replied curtly, "I won't answer your question directly until Mueller has had the chance to run more tests in Berlin next week to confirm our theory. But I will say some proof already exists."

"What proof?"

"Let me just say asthma attacks are the canary in the mine as far as EZ-15 goes."

"What does that mean?"

"You're a smart fellow. Figure it out or, if you prefer, wait until Mueller has completed the tests in Germany," Sanchez said. "Actually, Gerhard and I previously shared our theory with your colleague at EPA, Mr. Ronnie Chapman. To confirm our suspicions, Mr. Chapman has been checking the most recent EPA test data to see if there is an anomaly in chemical balance equations of the test results on EZ-15. I spoke to Mr. Chapman last week, and he said he had found some very interesting issues with the test results. He promised to get back to me, but I haven't heard back from him. Based on Mr. Chapman's apparent discovery, the tests Gerhard plans to run in Germany next week are designed to generate a second set of data to confirm our suspicions."

"You haven't heard? He's dead. Ronnie Chapman was killed in an accident last Friday. He was crushed by a subway train."

Sanchez stared back at Chris, his mouth hanging open and his eyes locked in disbelief as his face lost all its color. "My God! The bastards may be on to us."

Feeling a sudden sense of panic, Chris exclaimed, "Who?"

"EMCO and its friends," Sanchez replied as he pulled his chair close to Chris and continued. "We need to be very careful. I'll try to reach Mueller today by phone and update him on the situation. If I fail, explain the situation when you see him tomorrow and watch your back," the chemist concluded, primal fear written all over his face.

Sanchez looked around the room that had started to fill with other patrons and said, "We both should leave this place now. I'll go first, and you leave in about ten minutes so we aren't seen together outside."

Sanchez paid the bill, handed Chris a thick file for Goldberg, got up, and said good-bye to Chris, who was still stunned by what had just transpired.

*   *   *

Quickly exiting the inn, Sanchez scurried to his 2009 BMW jet-black coup sitting in the parking lot. He climbed in, started the engine, and spun out of the gravel parking lot on his way back to Barcelona.

In his haste, Sanchez failed to notice the footprints in the soft damp dirt around his car or the person hiding behind the bushes bordering the far side of the inn's parking area. Unlike Chris, Sanchez hadn't been sufficiently careful to hide his visit to the inn.

As soon as the Spanish scientist departed, the thin young man crouching in the bushes made a call. "Hans, it's me. I followed the squirrel, and as we suspected, he met up with the rabbit. I've taken care of the squirrel, and I'll pick up the rabbit's trail when he gets back to the train station. I'll keep you informed."

"Excellent!" Dietrich replied.

CHAPTER 17

April 15
Bruges, Belgium—Afternoon

Chris waited ten minutes and headed back to Bruges. The weather had turned colder, and a chilling wind was blowing in his face. Rain began to pelt him as he rode along the bike path, which was rapidly becoming muddy, making pedaling more of a task. But neither the weather nor the conditions of the bike trail were on Chris's mind. He kept replaying the conversation with Sanchez, and his sense of despair grew with each turn of the bike's pedals. Several times he stopped and waited to see if anyone was following him. He saw no one.

Arriving back at the train station well over two hours later, completely soaked, Chris retrieved his backpack, found a men's room, and quickly changed into dry clothes. He went to the ticket window and asked, "When does the overnight train to Berlin depart?"

The kindly-looking woman behind the window said, in barely understandable English, that the train was scheduled to leave in four hours.

I've got some time to kill, he thought. After considering his options and debating with himself, he came to a decision. *What the hell. I'm stuck here for a while. I might as well take a walk down memory lane.*

Chris strolled across a stone bridge and into the ancient village of Bruges. The city was a maze of narrow cobblestone streets with quaint three- to four-story buildings with colorful tiled roofs. It took Chris a moment to get his bearings—after all, it had been over twenty years—but the strong memories returned, and he knew the way.

As he walked along the streets, Chris's mind raced back to that unforgettable day so long ago when Sarah and he shared the most wonderful hours of their lives together. They had met earlier at an international seminar—he in his junior year at Colgate, and she a Wellesley College sophomore. Their friendship blossomed at a time when both were in the midst of a life journey with no clue of what the future might bring, free from their pasts, and with no real plans for the future. They fell in love, and before heading home, the two lovers had spent the day in Bruges sightseeing, planning for their future, having a romantic dinner in a small French café, and sharing a night of intense passion in a small hotel. Remembering back on it all, Chris thought, *That night marked the beginning of the end of our magical relationship.*

After that night, they each headed in different directions, not only geographically, but intellectually and spiritually. Sarah went home; her brief summer of unbridled freedom from her controlling parents was over. Chris met up with a couple of buddies from the seminar, and they traveled another week through Germany.

When they returned to the United States, they continued to plan their future, but things had already changed. Somewhere along the way, the wonder of Europe, the passion of their love, and their collective naïve innocence gave way to the harsh realities of life.

Sarah's parents made no secret of their disdain for Chris, who they felt was unworthy of their daughter's affections. They regarded Chris's mother as a hippie freak and his father as a hopeless Irish drunk. Sarah sided more and more with her parents.

Their love child, Corbin, was probably conceived that night in Bruges and certainly accelerated plans for the wedding. Corbin's birth, at least for a while, brought them back close together. But then over the years, they slowly drifted apart.

Eventually, the memories became too painful, and Chris decided to head back to the station to wait for the train.

Several hours later as Chris settled into his seat on the train for the overnight trip, he pulled out and began to read the notes Sanchez had prepared for Jackie. He was disappointed to find that Sanchez's notes contained basically the same information the Spaniard covered during their lunch. There was one curious reference to "filter paper

X10B19-0.001 may be the key," but Chris had absolutely no idea what the notation meant.

Too tired to read anything more, Chris reclined his seat and had little trouble drifting off to sleep. He slept peacefully through the night, completely unaware that the same sinister figure lurking outside the country inn earlier that day had boarded the train and had Chris clearly in his sights.

CHAPTER 18

April 16
Berlin, Germany

Arriving at the Berlin Central train station around seven thirty in the morning, Chris caught a taxi to the hotel not far from the station. Once in his room, he took the opportunity to clean up and change his clothes.

Chris thought about Sanchez's statement that asthma was the canary in the mine for EZ-15. He knew about the old custom of taking a canary in a cage down into a working coal mine. If the canary suddenly died, it was a danger warning that the air in the mine contained dangerous gases, such as methane or excess carbon dioxide, and the miners should evacuate immediately before they died as well.

But what does that have to do with EZ-15? Chris thought and decided to search Google for information about asthma. But the sites were limitless, so he narrowed his search by typing in "asthma," "episodes," "attacks," and "increases." Again, he was faced with a long list of sources, but the fifth one down had a caption that grabbed his attention: "Asthma Attacks Spike in Tokyo."

The article, appearing in the March 28 edition of the *Tokyo Times*, reported that the rate of asthma attacks had significantly increased over a six-month period in small, isolated areas of the city. No explanation for the increase was proffered in the article other than a statement from the health authorities that the matter was under investigation.

Could there be a tie between EZ-15 and the increase in asthma attacks? Chris wondered.

Shortly before 1:00 p.m., Chris walked into the hotel lounge, but he saw no one who looked like a high-ranking official with the UBA.

Moments later, a tall, lanky, casually dressed German with a full, red, curly beard that matched his long, red hair, tied back with a black band, approached with a broad smile. "Welcome. You must be Christopher O'Brian."

Gerhard Mueller was a legend in the field of motor-vehicle emission regulations. While only in his midforties, he had risen high in the ranks of the German UBA as the result of his tenacity and sheer genius. He was principally responsible for developing the regulatory programs for reducing pollution from cars, trucks, locomotives, and off-road equipment, not only in Germany, but throughout the European Union.

The German and the American spent some time getting to know and trust each other over iced tea. They conversed about motor-vehicle emission control and global warming. Each took some time practicing a little one-upmanship on the other. Chris reminded Mueller that the United States led the way in reducing pollution from motor vehicles, and Mueller countered by pointing out that Germany had established stringent pollution control requirements for coal-fired power plants long before the United States got around to addressing those sources of pollution.

Despite Mueller's tendency to boast about his own accomplishments, Chris found himself liking and admiring the German scientist. Eventually, the conversation turned to EMCO's EZ-15, and the tone became more serious and subdued.

"Germany and the European Commission, the executive body of the European Union, are leaning against approval of EZ-15. But if the US EPA caves, and with Tokyo and Osaka already using the product and achieving measurable CO_2 reductions, Europe will have little choice but to approve the product as well," Mueller said, shaking his head in frustration.

"Jackie Goldberg hasn't given up yet. That's why she sent me to Europe. I gather you agree with Sanchez that the pressure on EPA to make a quick decision isn't just about the financial implications to EMCO."

Mueller nodded. "It's far more sinister."

Chris relayed his conversations with Sanchez, including the Spaniard's warning about asthma being the canary in the mine. "I checked the Web and found a report about incidents of asthma increasing in Tokyo. Is that what Sanchez was alluding to? Do you think there's a cause-and-effect link to EZ-15?"

Mueller took a deep breath and responded, "We believe there is a definite link between the two. If you had looked further, you would have found that asthma attacks are increasing in Osaka as well, where EZ-15 is also in limited use."

"But there could be lots of different causes for the asthma attacks. It may simply be a coincidence," Chris said.

"True, but what's telling is that the asthma attacks have occurred in places very near major highway intersections where tens of thousands of cars and trucks pass by every day. One of the triggers for asthma attacks is lung irritation from ultrafine particles that get deposited deep inside the lung. That's why I'm conducting new tests next week to see if there are any harmful byproducts emitted by the EZ-15 chemical process that have yet to be discovered in previous testing."

Without waiting for Chris to respond, Mueller continued, "We found an anomaly in our previous test results, and that's why we asked Ronnie Chapman to check the US EPA data. If the same anomalies exist in your agency's test results, then we have confirmation that we need to make several modifications to our testing protocols."

"Did Sanchez call you about Ronnie's death?" Chris asked with a sense of urgency.

"Yes, he called me immediately after your lunch yesterday," Mueller said, with a note of sadness in his voice. "It's tragic, but I don't share Sanchez's theory that Chapman's death is part of a conspiracy. It's too preposterous to believe. Nevertheless, we should be careful. We plan to run the new tests using newly available, more sophisticated, and finer filter media to see if we can detect any harmful byproducts missed by the previous tests. We should have the test completed by the end of next week and will have data soon after. Please tell Jackie to do everything she can to delay EPA's decision to approve the EZ-15 application until we have time to complete our work. If I'm right, we may be able to put an end to EZ-15."

"I'll do everything I can, but I can't promise anything. The pressure on EPA is intense."

"You have to succeed. Otherwise, we could be facing a horrific environmental disaster."

The conversation ended shortly thereafter, and Chris thanked Mueller for his efforts. Mueller handed Chris a folder of documents for Goldberg, and they agreed to keep in touch. Chris felt better about the prospects of blocking EZ-15 approval, and some of the paranoia he had felt after Sanchez's stern warning dissipated as well.

As Chris started up the hotel stairs, he was oblivious to the fact that he was being watched by the same man who had traveled on the train to Berlin.

CHAPTER 19

April 17
Brussels, Belgium

Chris's Sunday train ride back to Brussels was uneventful, and he returned to his hotel and retrieved the luggage he had stored. He wished he could have taken a direct flight from Berlin to Washington, but he understood that Goldberg wanted no evidence regarding his side trips to Bruges and Berlin on his official EPA itinerary.

Chris spent the rest of the afternoon looking through the material Mueller had given him for Jackie. One document caught his eye. It was entitled "Possible Shortcomings with Test Procedures," and it contained four bulleted items: "1) residence time?; 2) filter paper X10B19-0.001?; 3) measurement techniques?; and 4) technician errors?"

Sanchez's notes had the same reference to filter paper X10B19-0.001, but not the other three items.

Maybe one or all of these factors can provide the key to the harmful byproducts of EZ-15. I hope Jackie or Chapman's boss, Ted Bennett, can provide an answer, Chris thought.

When Chris finished reading both Mueller's and Sanchez's documents, he gathered all the papers and his computer and placed them in the hotel safe. Then, on the recommendations of the hotel concierge, he arrived at the unassuming café and ordered dinner.

"Excellent," Chris replied when asked by the waiter how he enjoyed his dinner. Keeping to his training diet, Chris skipped the wine and dessert. As he exited the restaurant, the street was empty— empty save for a person Chris noticed leaning against a building wall about two blocks away.

Just in case I'm being followed, maybe I should take a more circuitous route back to the hotel, Chris thought as he pulled out and studied his map of the city.

Having picked his route, Chris started off slowly. But as soon as he turned the corner, he broke into a run. He turned left at the first corner, then right at the next, and then left again. Confident that if he were being followed, his pursuer had surely lost his trail, he looked at his map and found a nearby, narrow, two-block alley that looked like a shortcut back to his hotel.

When he reached the entrance to the alley, which was dark and barely wide enough for one medium-sized vehicle, he stopped in his tracks. "I've been here before. I recognize that archway above the alley entrance," Chris said. "But when? I haven't been near here this trip, and this is the only time I've been in Brussels."

Chris didn't want to turn back, so he cautiously entered and started walking down the alley, which seemed familiar. Looking at a spot about ten feet in front of him, he said, "Right up there on the left is where it should be."

And when he arrived at the spot, he said "Yep, there it is. This is getting a little weird."

Chris started jogging toward the other end of the alley but stopped abruptly as another recollection entered his mind. "If I'm right, it should happen right about now."

At that precise moment, a red SUV turned into the alley at the opposite end from where Chris had entered and began racing toward him, its bright lights flashing. Grazing against one alley wall and then the other, the vehicle rapidly approached.

I was right, Chris thought, and without hesitating, he spun around and began running back down the alley toward where he had entered. Despite Chris's improved fitness, there was no way he could reach the far end of the alley before being crushed by the pursuing vehicle. Still, Chris kept running, his face down in determination, his arms pumping furiously, and his legs pounding like fast-moving pistons on the uneven pavement.

"Don't quit, you can make it," he urged himself on as the vehicle drew closer. *Thirty yards away, twenty, ten …* Chris looked back and saw the mangled front bumper of the SUV nearly upon him as he leaped to his right in desperation, plastering himself in the small, recessed space with the red door that he had spotted earlier.

"Are you all right?" a woman called out from a window above the alley after the car had passed through.

"I'm okay," Chris replied. "They must have been drunk ... nearly hit me, but I'm fine."

Chris was still trying to recover as he finally reached the hotel. Arriving at his room, he did a quick once over to determine whether anything had been disturbed in his absence, but everything looked to be in its proper place.

He flopped on his bed, pounding his wrists on his forehead, as he racked his brain, trying to figure out how he recognized the alley, knew precisely where the recessed doorway in the alley was located, and correctly anticipated the SUV entering the alley from the other end.

Then Chris sat up. "Damn, the dream. I remember that dream. I remember the alley, the arch at the entrance, the recessed doorway, and the vehicle racing toward me." He shuddered as he thought about his near miss with certain death. *Only, in the dream, I didn't make it to the recessed doorway.*

Lying in a pool of sweat, Chris couldn't fall asleep.

CHAPTER 20

April 18
Washington, DC—Morning

Pamela Russell, perplexed and devastated, squirmed in her chair while getting chewed out by Stanley Braxton and Peter McDonald, Russell's immediate supervisor.

The reception she had received moments before when she entered Braxton's posh office in the K Street offices of Miller and Braxton was totally unexpected. When she had called Braxton the previous Wednesday evening after her encounter with O'Brian, she had received high praise for feeding O'Brian misinformation regarding why EMCO was anxious for quick EPA approval of EZ-15. Even more important was the intelligence she had collected from him that EPA approval of EZ-15 was imminent—information that Braxton had shared with EMCO and many others, including the Heritage Study Group members, the previous Thursday.

"Great job, Pam," Braxton had said on the phone. "Take a couple of extra days on the continent, and we'll see you first thing Monday morning."

But now here in Braxton's office on Monday morning, he was shouting at her, the veins in his neck bulging. "O'Brian was on to you. Somehow you blew it. The information he fed you was crap, including the fact that he planned to go to Paris. He didn't go to Paris. He went to Bruges and then Berlin to meet with people trying to block EZ-15."

With a threatening look, Braxton added, "You're blundering has cost us valuable time."

Russell was in tears as she pleaded in her defense. "I did everything you told me to do, including fucking him. Nothing I said could have given him a clue I was—"

But before Russell could finish, Braxton's secretary rushed in. "Sorry to disturb you, Mr. Braxton, but Senator Goodman's office is on the phone. They say it's urgent."

Braxton got up immediately, shaking his head in frustration. "What now?"

He immediately turned and entered his inner office, but in his haste, he neglected to close the door behind him. As he grabbed the phone, he said, "Braxton here. What's up?"

After listening for a few moments, all the while becoming increasingly agitated, Braxton blurted out, "I thought you had that EPA issue taken care of."

Again, Braxton listened to the voice at the other end and then barked, "Goldberg! When will that bitch go away?" Finally, Braxton concluded, "Keep on it. I'll do what I can at this end to slow her down."

Slamming down the phone, Braxton returned to the outer office as Russell cowered in her seat. Looking at the helpless young woman, he simply said, "Get out of my sight."

Russell left without speaking, her head down. After she had exited, Braxton turned to his colleague and said dismissively, "Peter, send that bitch to Des Moines to work on that landfill approval issue."

"But, Mr. Braxton, Russell doesn't have any technological knowledge or skills to convince the Solid Waste Disposal Board to approve our client's landfill application," McDonald replied with a look of confusion.

"Ms. Russell has other, more subtle skills that she can use to help gain the support of at least one or two of the middle-aged, horny bastards who sit on that board," Braxton replied. They both laughed, and Braxton added, "And tell her if she fails to deliver, she's finished at M&B."

Braxton then picked up his cell phone and dialed a number he knew well. "Plans have changed. We need to take care of the fox immediately. We can't afford anymore screw-ups."

The voice at the other end said, without emotion, "Consider it done," and then added, somewhat cautiously, "Our associates in

Europe blew it and let the rabbit escape, but we'll handle him at our end as well."

"Good," Braxton replied as he hung up the phone and thought, *At least that's one person I can count on.*

Braxton then made his next call, one he dreaded because he knew the person at the other end would be furious at the way things were going and certainly would blame Braxton for everything. When the call was answered, his worst fears were confirmed. Braxton explained the current situation, and the person at the other end of the call went into an extended tirade. After several moments, Braxton finally said, "I'm on top of it, and we'll get back on track—immediately."

The person at the other end said, in a chilling voice, "You better," and ended the call.

"Damn it," Braxton muttered as the sweat streamed down his face. His secretary rushed in. "Is everything all right, Mr. Braxton?"

"Everything is fine," Braxton replied, knowing full well that things were far from fine and that his head was on the chopping block.

CHAPTER 21

April 18
Washington, DC—Afternoon

Chris cleared US passport control after his flight landed and found a quiet spot in a remote corner of the baggage claim area. Then he called Jackie Goldberg on her cell phone.

"Hello?" Goldberg answered in a voice that sounded both cautious and anxious.

"It's me. I just landed at Dulles. Should I come to your office?"

"No. It's not safe to meet here. Call me again at eight o'clock tonight at this number, and I'll name a place where we can talk in private."

"Ms. Goldberg, what's going on?" Chris asked with growing alarm.

"The forces behind EZ-15 have upped the stakes, and it's clear they'll stop at nothing to gain approval for their product here in the United States and elsewhere."

The general counsel then paused for a moment and whispered with considerable alarm in her voice, "They ... they killed Sergio Sanchez last Friday. I fear they've targeted others as well."

"Sanchez is dead?" was all Chris could utter as he quickly surveyed the area to make sure no one was nearby.

"The wire services said it was an accident—that his brakes failed and he was killed instantly when his car spun out of control and struck a highway concrete barrier on a sharp curve in the road on his way back to Barcelona. But I'm not buying that explanation," Goldberg said. Then she added quickly, "Chris, I can't talk now, but

I'll fill you in on more details when we meet. I need an update on what you uncovered in Europe, but we have to end this call now."

Chris wanted to talk more but accepted her instructions, "Okay, Ms. Goldberg, I'll call you at eight."

"Chris, please be careful ... be *very* careful ... and for god's sake, just call me Jackie. I think given the current situation, we can drop the Ms. Goldberg, at least for now," she said and hung up.

Chris retrieved his luggage and, on his way to the taxi stand, called Sonja Voinovich at the EPA's Office of Air Quality general number. He was told that she hadn't been seen or heard from in over a week.

Chris knew it was unlikely that Voinovich would miss an entire week of work because of illness. As far as he could recall, she hadn't missed a day of work during the time she had been at EPA.

Something terrible must have happened to her.

She had never called to confirm their meeting at Busboys and Poets, and he feared the worst. But he was determined to get to the meeting place by ten pm. Chris used the time in the taxi to start organizing and writing up the key information he had gleaned from his discussions with Russell, McKay, Sanchez, and Mueller, as well as his review of the documents Mueller and Sanchez had given him.

Jackie should find this information very interesting, Chris thought as he paid the cabbie and entered his condo building. A familiar and friendly voice call out, "Welcome back, stranger. Hope you had a good trip."

"Hi, Ruth. The trip was great, but I ate too much."

"I don't know about the eating too much part. You're starting to look a little skinny to me," the condo concierge, mail clerk, and welcome wagon replied.

The black, older woman was always friendly and efficient and went out of her way to help the residents. Ruth and Chris got along great. He was one of the few residents in the building who took an interest in her, and she always treated him like family. They often did small favors for each other.

Ruth grabbed Chris's mail from the slot behind her and leaned toward him over the counter as she handed him the stack of mostly junk mail. "You had a couple of visitors earlier today—two fellows flashing FBI badges. I told them I didn't expect you back until tomorrow or Wednesday. They said they would be back," she whispered.

"Did they say why they were here or who they were?" Chris asked as he glanced out toward the street.

"Only that they were with the FBI. Their badges looked like the real deal. They said you were a person of interest in an ongoing FBI investigation. One of them said his name was Michael something. I was so scared. I missed the last name, but I think it began with a C or K. Chris, are you in trouble?"

"I don't have time to explain. I promise you I've done nothing wrong. I need to get some stuff from my condo and get out of here without being seen leaving the building. Any ideas?"

The receptionist thought for a moment and then whispered, "The underground passage between this building and the building next door. The maintenance folks use it as a shortcut, but it's always locked. I have a key for emergencies, and I think this situation certainly counts."

Reaching under the counter, she pulled out a large ring with keys and removed one. "Here, return it when you can. The door is at the back northwest corner of the subbasement. Go through the passage to the building next door and then exit through the rear door. You can't miss it, and you should get away without being seen."

Chris wanted to give Ruth a big hug, but he settled for tightly squeezing her two hands.

"Thanks."

Rushing to his condo, he dumped everything out of his suitcase and took out what he needed to bring with him. Next, he rummaged through his bureau drawers and closet, taking clothes and tossing them on the pile he had started. Finally, he opened the secret compartment in his secretary, removed the remaining contents, and stuffed everything into a duffle bag with a carry strap.

"Got to travel light from now on," he said as he headed toward the door but leaving the light on so if anyone was watching they would assume he was still there.

*   *   *

While Chris was scrambling to pack, Michael Cavanaugh raced into the condo building's lobby. He flashed his badge at Ruth and raced over to the elevators. He knew O'Brian's unit number and pushed the button to O'Brian's floor. When the doors opened, Cavanaugh raced toward Chris's unit. The FBI agent drew his weapon, knocked once, and without waiting, kicked the door open. But when he stormed in, the condo was empty. All Cavanaugh found were dirty clothes scattered around the room and the secret compartment of a secretary open and empty. Cavanaugh returned to the lobby and, gasping for breath, asked Ruth if O'Brian had exited through the lobby.

"No one has passed by here since you arrived a few minutes ago."

"Is there any other way out of the building?"

"Not that I'm aware of," Ruth lied.

Cavanaugh pounded his fist on the counter and then stormed out of the building to see if his partner had seen O'Brian come out.

"Rich, he might still be in the building. Stay here and watch for a while, and then let's meet up at the usual place at 7:00 p.m. We've another matter to attend to tonight."

*   *   *

Chris ran down a back alley, carrying his computer case and bulging duffle bag while constantly looking over his shoulder to see if anyone was following him. In less than five minutes, he reached his stockbroker's office. Dan Witt happened to be standing in the front lobby when Chris stumbled in, his arms flailing and a look of panic spread across his face.

"Chris, are you okay?"

"No time to explain." Chris gasped for breath and then added, "Is everything ready?"

Witt motioned Chris into his office and quickly closed the door. Without saying a word, Witt went to a metal file cabinet and pulled out a canvas bag. He put the bag on his desk and said in a soft voice, "Here it is: $300,000 in Ben Franklins—thirty packs each, with a hundred bills."

Chris grabbed one pack worth a total of $10,000, put it in a large envelope, crammed it in his pocket, and pushed the bag back to Witt. "Is everything else taken care of regarding my accounts?"

"Everything is all set. What do you want me to do with this?" Dan asked, pointing at the canvas bag.

"Can you keep the bag, my computer, and this duffle bag at your place? You still live in Rockville, don't you?"

"Yes, still there, and no, I don't mind keeping this stuff for you," he replied cautiously. "Are you in trouble?"

"Dan, you know I wouldn't ask you to do anything that was illegal," Chris replied defensively.

"Come on, Chris, I know you wouldn't, but that's not my question. Are you in trouble?"

"There's some really bad stuff going down. I'm right in the middle of it. I can't tell you anything more right now. But either I, or someone I send, will pick up my stuff at your home. I'll call you on your cell phone."

Then Chris reached for and opened his computer case. "Forgot to grab these," Chris muttered as he stuffed a small notebook in his pants pocket. The little green book contained all the notes, observations, questions, and future "to dos" he had written up during his trip to Europe and upon his return home.

Dan started to speak, but Chris interrupted, "I've got to go."

Flagging a taxi, Chris headed downtown. Fifteen minutes later, he exited the taxi in the heart of the city's central business district and home of the famous K Street lobbyist corridor. The office buildings housed the lobbying firms, law firms, and associations that represented virtually every special-interest group known to man. Most of these firms, like Miller and Braxton, typically employed several former congressional staff members, and often a former congressman or senator as well.

The Founding Fathers never could have conceived of, or condoned, the manner in which the democratic system they created has become so corrupted by these incredibly powerful and politically influential groups. These industry and other special interest groups have ready, easy access to members of Congress and the Keller administration and have incredible and disturbing influence on every aspect of public policy. So much for the concept of "one man, one vote," Chris thought.

Glancing at his watch, which now read 6:30 p.m., he decided to grab a bite to eat at one of the numerous takeout/eat-in sandwich/salad bar shops in the area.

Continuing to refine his notes, Chris lost track of the time and was surprised when he looked at his watch, which read 8:05 p.m.

He cursed aloud and then dialed quickly. The person at the other end answered before the ring tone finished.

"You're late," Goldberg said in a stern voice.

Chris started to apologize, but she interrupted. "Eight thirty at the Parisian Cafe on Pennsylvania Avenue." Then she hung up.

The meeting place was a popular and expensive wine bar on Pennsylvania Avenue, the broad boulevard leading from the Capitol building to the White House. The wine bar was located at about the halfway point between those two Washington landmarks. Arriving fifteen minutes later, Chris grabbed a table outside so he could clearly see Goldberg coming, and she wouldn't need to search for him.

This part of town bustled during the day as lobbyists dined with members of Congress or congressional staffers, but by 8:30 p.m. it was pretty deserted. Chris felt a mix of excitement and anxiety. He knew he had some important information to pass along, but he also expected that she would chew him out for one reason or another.

He looked up and saw Goldberg on the other side of Pennsylvania Avenue, ready to cross the street. To his surprise, she waved and actually smiled at him. His sense of dread diminished considerably. The light turned green, and Goldberg stepped off the curb and into the street, still smiling at Chris.

Then Chris saw a black, late-model, full-sized car come out of nowhere, tires squealing, as it raced toward Goldberg, who was now about halfway across the broad boulevard.

"Look out!" Chris screamed.

The EPA General Counsel turned and froze as the vehicle raced directly at her. A millisecond later, the vehicle hit her with a sickening crunch, and Goldberg flew, arms and legs spread wide, over the top of the speeding vehicle and then landed with a horrific thump on the pavement. Goldberg rolled over several times before she came to rest on her back. As Chris raced to her, the car sped off down Pennsylvania Avenue and out of sight.

As he bent down to try to help Goldberg, he choked at what he saw. Her legs had been snapped at the knees by the car's bumper and were twisted back—her feet pointed toward her head. Her face was barely recognizable, having skidded on the rough street surface, and both arms were mangled.

"You'll be all right," Chris lied.

Goldberg, staring at him, struggled to speak. "Chris … no time for your bullshit … listen." Then she uttered, "EZ-15 thing … far more sinister than we imagined. They know everything we're doing."

She stopped for a moment, coughed up blood, and then said in a barely audible voice, "Trust no one." She pointed with her broken, bloody hand at a thin gold chain around her neck and whispered, "It … may … help."

Chris pulled the chain as gently as he could until it finally snapped. As he put it in his pocket, he noticed that a key was hanging from it. Other bystanders were starting to gather.

Grabbing his hand as best she could, Goldberg struggled to utter each word. "You're the … only hope … to stop them. Leave now; they're probably watching," were her final words as she squeezed his hand. Then she sighed and was gone.

Chris jumped up, turned to the crowd, and said, "I'll run for help." He, indeed, did plan to run, but he knew there was nothing more he could do for Goldberg. He needed to get away.

Chris started to run and soon realized he wasn't alone. As raindrops began to pelt his face, he raced down Pennsylvania Avenue toward the Capitol building. After running for several blocks and failing to put any meaningful distance between him and his pursuers, Chris cut into the first alley he found and raced down it.

"Damn, here we go again." He was in the exact alley that he had dreamed about the night after his attempted suicide. Chris remembered the dumpster and a voice saying, "There's always another way out." As he neared the end of the alley, Chris saw the battered green dumpster, but rather than jumping into it as he had done in his dream, he lifted the metal lid and slammed it down loudly as he raced farther down the alley. As he reached the end of the alley, he could hear his pursuers lifting the top of the dumpster and then the thumping sounds of automatic weapon rounds being fired through a silencer and crashing into the trash-filled interior of the dumpster.

Frantic, Chris looked around and finally saw that there was a narrow passage out of the alley to the left. He wasted no time in leaving and continued to run for several blocks before stopping.

Having successfully ditched his pursuers, he stopped in a futile effort to catch his breath.

Looking around, Chris knew he was somewhere near Union Station. He headed for the train station and tried to blend in with the crowd of folks waiting to catch the late train to New York City. Glancing at his watch, he figured he had about an hour before he would hopefully meet up with Sonja Voinovich.

Chris sat fidgeting on an unoccupied bench inside the station and tried to gather his wits. But a barrage of images—Goldberg lying dead in the middle of Pennsylvania Avenue, his two narrow escapes in the past twenty-four hours from unknown pursuers, his trip to Europe, and even his own suicide attempt filled his thoughts. Finally, he bowed his weary head and let his mind go blank.

*   *   *

At 9:45 p.m., Chris stepped out of the train station, went to the taxi stand, and entered the next available cab in the line. "Fourteenth and U Street, Northwest."

The cabbie, who had waited in line for nearly twenty minutes to pick up a fare, was less than happy with getting a passenger who would make a short trip that would yield only the minimum four-dollar fare. Seeing the angst in the driver's eyes, Chris reached into his pocket and pulled out the packet of cash Dan Witt had given him.

Chris handed the cabbie a hundred-dollar bill and said, "Make sure we're not followed and forget you ever saw me." Nodding, the cab driver drove off without uttering another word.

In the cab, Chris tried and failed once more to reach Voinovich on her cell phone. His anxiety over whether she was okay or if she would indeed show up consumed him. By the time he reached Busboys and Poets, he was convinced she wouldn't be there.

Chris entered the dimly lit restaurant/coffee shop, which was located in the U Street corridor about a block from the center of the race riots in the 1960s. Forty years later, the area was a multiracial and cultural hot spot with a growing influx of young professionals. New condo buildings, renovated townhouses, and great dining and drinking establishments dominated this once-blighted community.

There was a decent crowd in the place for that time of night. Chris scanned the room and saw several women, including a woman sitting alone with her back to him and dressed impeccably in a gray skirt and matching jacket. She had radiant auburn hair. But there was no sign of Sonja Voinovich.

"I'll wait at least an hour in case she's running late," Chris muttered as he grabbed an empty table. Suddenly, he felt weak, helpless, and totally alone, as if he was being pulled by a riptide out into a treacherous, dark sea of the unknown.

Maybe it would have been better if that damn gun hadn't jammed that night.

Chris started to take a swallow of the coffee he had ordered when he sensed a presence near him. He placed his coffee down and turned to his left. To his amazement, there stood the young woman he had spotted earlier. She stared at him with her beautiful, deep blue eyes. Her soft, pale complexion only added to the luster of her full, red lips.

Chris felt icy chills spike deep through his entire body as he realized that standing in front of him was *the* woman—the very woman who had haunted him on numerous occasions in his nightmares. He stared at her and said nothing for a long moment. Then he realized something else about this beautiful, young woman.

Finally he spoke, but only one word passed his lips. "Sonja?"

PART II

CHAPTER 22

"Sonja, is it really you?" Stunned, Chris got up, and they embraced. Tears started to well up in the young woman's eyes as they tightly hugged each other. Sonja alternately wept and laughed nervously.

"Why didn't you return my calls? What happened to you? What's with the disguise?" Chris fired question after question without giving her a chance to reply.

Finally, they slowly moved apart. "Thank God you're safe." Chris said nothing about Sonja being a dead ringer for the mystery woman in his dreams, nor did he plan to ever speak of it to her.

They sat down, and Chris ordered Sonja a cup of coffee black. He knew from their days at EPA that she drank black coffee pretty much nonstop all day long. They stared silently at each other, and Chris finally said, "So?"

Sonja took a deep breath and then recounted how a week before, she had returned to her apartment late at night only to spot someone inside. How she ran, was chased down an alley, and entered the back door of a night club.

"The door was jammed, but it finally opened just as my attackers were about to catch me. I got a pretty good look at one of the guys, even though they didn't try to enter the club. Once I got inside, my friends hid me and helped me escape later. Earlier in the evening, I got your voice message about meeting up when you returned from Europe, but at some point, I lost my cell phone. After that night, I dropped out of sight. I was taking care of one of my band member's cat at his place while he was away, and I decided to stay there. After a couple of days, I changed my look," Sonja said as she put her hands around the cup of coffee as if trying to warm herself.

"You sure did an amazing job changing your appearance," Chris said. Realizing his statement implied he didn't think much of how Sonja looked before, he added, "Not that your old look wasn't fine."

"Right, I'm sure you loved my old look," Sonja said with a laugh. "Actually, I had my dye job removed professionally. My natural hair color is auburn. My natural eye color is blue. I wore contacts that made them look greenish brown. All of the ear piercings were fake, so no leftover holes."

"Why did you change your appearance in the first place?"

Somewhat defensively, Sonja replied, "I'd rather not go into that right now."

Chris then recounted everything that had happened to him in Europe and upon his return to the United States. Becoming aware of the effect his saga was having on her, he stopped abruptly.

Taking her hands in his, he leaned forward, trying to reassure her. "I won't let anything bad happen to you. But we've got to get out of here. I think I know a safe place we can go."

The tenseness in Sonja's hands relaxed slightly at his words. But then she said, "My god, I almost forgot the most important thing. The day before he died, Ronnie Chapman gave me a copy of his report and the EPA data on a CD. I don't know why he gave it to me because he also gave one to Ann Hastings." She reached in her pocketbook and flashed a silver CD in a blank, white envelope. Chris gently pried the CD from her trembling hand and placed it in his pocket.

Reaching for his cell phone, Chris thought better of it. "Someone knew exactly where and when Goldberg and I would meet. Maybe someone intercepted my cell phone call to her."

Then he remembered noticing a bank of pay phones when he first entered the restaurant. He'd noticed them because they'd become almost an extinct species in big cities. Getting up, Chris asked the waiter if the phones worked or were only hanging on the wall to add to the place's 1930s atmosphere.

"The phones are in service. Some of our less-advantaged customers can't afford cell phones, so when the place was renovated, we kept the pay phones."

Chris reached in his wallet, pulled out the piece of paper with Chet Jones's telephone number on it, and dialed the number. After the fourth ring, a person at the other end answered in a sleepy voice, "Hello?"

"Chet, it's me, Chris O'Brian. Sorry to bother—"

Before Chris could finish the sentence, Chet barked back with concern and in no way resembling the sleepy, soft voice that had just answered the call, "Chris, where are you? Do you need help? What can I do?"

Chris said he needed a safe place for himself and a friend to hide. After a long pause, Chet explained with military preciseness exactly what Chris and his friend should do next. When Chet finished, all Chris could think to say was, "Thanks."

With a broad smile on his otherwise tired and weary face, Chris returned and said, "Here's what we're going to do." As Sonja and Chris got up, he squeezed her hand briefly, and the young woman headed out the door without looking back. As instructed, Sonja flagged a cab and told the driver to go to the Mayflower Hotel and drop her at the main hotel entrance downtown on Connecticut Avenue. When she arrived, she paid the fare without waiting for her change and entered the main doors.

As soon as she was inside the posh hotel, she raced straight ahead down the wide cathedral-ceiling central hallway that ran the full, block-long length of the hotel to a much smaller entrance on the L Street side of the hotel. If anyone had been following her, they likely would have lost her in this maneuver. Once outside of the hotel, she looked for an aging, tan, parked vehicle.

"There it is!" she exclaimed and ran to the waiting vehicle. A large, elderly black man spotted her and waved to her to get in. She hesitated for a moment and then entered. Before she could speak, the driver grabbed her head with his huge right hand and shoved her head down. For a moment, horrified, Sonja thought she was about to die.

But then Chet Jones spoke in a soft voice that belied his huge, gruff appearance. "Sorry about pushing your head down. Just a precaution; don't want the bad guys to spot you if they followed you through the hotel. I'll let you know when it's safe to sit back up." Then Chet gently removed his hand from Sonja's head.

As they drove up Seventeenth Street away from the hotel, Chet said, "It's okay to sit up now. We can't waste any time. Tell me what you can about what's going down."

Sonja then told Chet everything she knew. Chet reached for his cell phone and started making calls. Sonja had trouble following the conversations—something about "Code Red" and "meeting at my place, now." Twenty minutes after getting into Chet's car, she arrived at his house safely and was welcomed inside.

Chris left the restaurant ten minutes after Sonja, took three different cabs that crisscrossed the city, and was dropped off by the third cab six blocks from Chet's house. By the time he reached Chet's house, it was 11:30 p.m. As he entered, a small group of people were talking in the back corner of the living room, and Chet seemed to be barking out orders, laying out a plan of action for the next day. Chris recognized Leon and Tanya and the two black men he had met briefly at Chet's house the night Leon and Tanya had been attacked. Chris had never seen Chet so energized. Before, he had always seemed calm, easy-going, and soft-spoken, even the night Chris brought Leon home.

When Chet became aware that Chris had arrived, he stopped talking and approached his young friend. Giving Chris an enormous bear hug, he said, "Good to see you here, Captain."

Chet then walked to the center of the room and made introductions. "Chris, of course you know Leon and Tanya, and you met Casey Randolph and Otto Simpson that night." Both men were over six feet tall, and each probably weighed well over 250 pounds. He then introduced a middle-aged Hispanic man named Freddie Hernandez and a pale-looking, skinny white guy named Billy McGinnis.

"This is what I call the Crew. Casey and Otto handle logistics, Freddie takes care of security, and Billy is in charge of counterintelligence and communications. Everyone, meet Christopher O'Brian and Miss Sonja Voinovich."

Greetings were exchanged, and then Chet said, "It's late, and these two folks have been through a lot. Let's call it an evening and meet tomorrow at 11:00 a.m. at the safe house."

Within minutes all the guests had left.

"Miss Voinovich, Tanya will help you get settled in the back, and, Chris, if you don't mind sleeping here in the living room tonight, we'll give you both a chance to get some rest. Tomorrow is going to be a very busy day."

Sonja and Chris took the opportunity to clean up, but neither had a clean change of clothes. Chris grabbed the blankets and pillow Chet had provided him, sat back on the couch, and turned off the lamp. In the darkness, he sat, staring forward. His mind raced, and sleep seemed like a distant possibility. After a few minutes, he sensed a presence in the dark room. "Sonja?" he whispered.

Dressed only in her rayon blouse and half-slip, Sonja walked barefoot toward him. "I can't sleep. Can I join you?" Without waiting for a reply, Sonja sat down, tucked her knees up on the couch, and gently leaned in his direction.

"What's going to happen to us? I never thought I would be this frightened again. I'm not sure I have the strength to go on," she whispered.

Chris didn't understand the exact meaning of her words "frightened again," but he could feel her body trembling, like she was freezing, even though the house was quite warm. Putting his arm around Sonja's shoulders, he gently pulled her close to him. No longer did he feel awkward in holding the young woman.

"Sonja, we're safe now, and I know things will be okay," he whispered, trying to sound confident, but feeling the same fear. Sonja finally began to relax, and within minutes, she was deep in sleep.

After about an hour, Chris looked at his watch, which read 2:30 a.m. Sonja's peaceful presence next to him had helped him unwind somewhat. "I've got to get some sleep," Chris said quietly in a tired voice.

CHAPTER 23

April 19
Dessau, Germany

About the time Chris finally fell asleep in Chet's living room, Gerhard Mueller was striding purposefully through the glass-enclosed lab of the German FEA motor-vehicle emission-testing facility. The local time was 8:30 a.m. as Mueller greeted the group of nine lab technicians. As he and the staff inspected the testing equipment and all of the electronic data collection equipment, Mueller thought, with considerable satisfaction, *Today we generate the proof that will crush EMCO and bury EZ-15 once and for all.*

Mueller barked at his staff to start the test engine, which was fueled with gasoline containing the fuel additive EZ-15. The engine would produce the exhaust emissions that would be tested. The test gases, heated by propane flames, had reached the proper temperatures, and the actual emission testing began. Within minutes, test data began printing out on large sheets of paper. All was going well.

But then several of the test team members picked up the scent of gas in the room, and someone shouted, "Shut down the burners!"

Mueller cried out, "No time. Everybody out!" As they all raced to the exit door, Mueller reached out, grabbed the hand of a young female technician, who was frozen in fear, and pushed her toward the exit door.

* * *

Chet Jones climbed out of bed at precisely 5:45 a.m., just as he had done every day for the past ten years. But today he wouldn't be heading to the Metro station to sell newspapers. He walked quietly out of his bedroom and spied Chris and Sonja sleeping quietly together. *Mother wouldn't have been happy to see two unmarried, young people lying half-naked together under a blanket on her favorite couch*, he thought with a smile and headed into the kitchen.

Chet went to work making breakfast for everyone. But when he decided it was time for his guests on the couch to wake, he clanked a spoon on the side of a pot just loud enough to have the desired effect without embarrassing them.

Sonja woke first and gently moved away from Chris. When she moved, Chris awoke. She looked at him with thankful eyes. Without speaking, the somewhat embarrassed young woman quietly got up and headed to Tanya's room to get dressed. Ten minutes later, Chris, Sonja, Leon, Tanya, and Chet were sitting at the oversized breakfast table in the kitchen, enjoying a hearty breakfast. Chris tried to keep his portions small, but not so small that Chet might be insulted. Other than a few "good mornings" and "how'd you sleep?" comments, the conversation was pretty much nonexistent.

Finally, Chet announced, "I've thought it over, and we need to alter our plan of operations that we discussed last night." Then turning to Sonja, he said, "Young lady, you're going to stay here with Tanya until all of this madness comes to an end."

"No," both Sonja and Chris protested in unison.

"I'm part of this now, my only real friend was murdered, and I know I can help," Sonja pleaded.

"Sonja's a wiz with computers, and she understands the EPA testing protocols. She knows many of the players involved, and she's extremely clever and bright." Sonja's checks turned crimson at Chris's praise of her talents and the fact that he knew that much about her. She had believed that Chris, like most everyone else at EPA, barely knew she was alive.

"Chet, I'd feel a whole lot better if I knew Sonja was safe with us."

Chet rose from the table and seemed agitated, but to everyone's surprise, he said, "Chris, I don't like the idea one bit of having a woman placed in danger by coming with us. But you've got the lead on the operation, so it's your call." Then Chet added, almost as an afterthought, "If you come with us, Miss Voinovich, you must significantly alter your physical appearance."

Smiling, Sonja reached into her wallet and pulled out her EPA identification badge. "I think I've already taken care of that, and please call me Sonja."

Chet took the ID and stared at the young EPA analyst's picture. With a look of disbelief, he exclaimed, "My God. That's you?" He then handed the ID off to Tanya and Leon, who had similar reactions.

They all laughed, and Chet said, "Well, with that settled, let's talk about next steps."

"You're not leaving me behind all alone. I won't feel safe," Tanya said.

Looking at Chris and Leon, who were both nodding with approval, Chet simply exclaimed with considerable exasperation, "Fine."

They agreed that Tanya and Sonja would go shopping for supplies and pick up some clothes and anything else Sonja might need.

"Tanya, use your credit card. Sonja, give me any credit cards and any IDs you have. They have to be destroyed. We'll provide you with a new ID," Chet ordered.

Chris reached into his pants pocket, retrieved the wad of cash Witt had given him, and pulled out ten crisp hundred-dollar bills. Turning to Tanya, he said, "Use this to buy anything you need. There's plenty more where that came from."

To Chet, he said, "I need to pick up some stuff at a friend's house. He's expecting me. Also, I have this key that Jackie Goldberg gave me just before she died." Setting the key down on the table, he added, "It looks like a locker key—maybe from National or Dulles Airport?"

"I don't think so," Leon said as he picked up and examined the key. "It's from the bus station near the Convention Center. I've used those lockers before."

Standing up, Chet said with a sense of urgency, "Okay, Leon, take your car and check out the locker and then pick up Chris's stuff and meet us at the safe house. Get a move on it and be careful."

Leon got the address and telephone number for Dan Witt from Chris, grabbed his jacket and cap, and was on his way.

Looking at his watch, Chet said to Chris, "We need to get going."

Five minutes later, Chet and Chris were in the Toyota and on their way. "So, where and what is the safe house?" Chris asked.

"It's in upper Prince Georges County about fifty minutes from here. It's an old farmhouse that has been in Casey Randolph's family since the 1880s. We've used it in the past as a staging area when we've gotten involved in an operation."

As they headed out, Chet, most likely sensing that Chris was about to unload a barrage of questions, seized the initiative and began to describe the origins of the Crew. Chet explained that he, Casey Randolph, Freddie Hernandez, and Otto Simpson met in the early 1970s at Fort Bragg, where they were undergoing training to become MPs.

"Military policemen?" Chris asked.

"Yes. The four of us became close friends there. As luck would have it—or as I like to think, the Lord's will—at the completion of our training, we all were assigned to Fort Dix in New Jersey, and two years later, we all received orders to report to Saigon for active duty.

"I was promoted to sergeant, and upon arriving in Vietnam, my superior appointed me as a squad leader in command of my three army buddies—Casey, Otto, and Freddie—as well as two young black lads from Mississippi and two white guys: Billy McGinnis and another named Dyson Parker, who was a complete wacko. I always felt that putting all the black guys and a Hispanic together was hardly an accident and that Billy and Dyson had been put in my squad because they didn't fit in anywhere else.

"The war was coming to an end, and even before the final collapse of Saigon and subsequent takeover of South Vietnam by the Communists, life in the city had become increasingly chaotic and dangerous. My squad was assigned the task of trying to help maintain a semblance of order in one of the most notoriously dangerous sectors of Saigon.

"When the shit finally hit the fan in April 1975, all semblance of order disappeared in an instant. We found ourselves isolated from our military brethren. We did what we needed to do to survive." Chet paused. "Not everybody made it. The two boys from Mississippi were killed, and Billy and Dyson Parker were wounded. Billy was in really bad shape, and Dyson eventually lost his leg below the knee."

"Was that how the Bronze Star wound up on your mantel?" Chris asked.

"Yes. Not sure why I got it and why the other squad members didn't. I was no hero; I was acting on pure survival instinct.

"Anyway," he continued, "we all got back and received early discharges from the army. All of us settled in the Washington, DC, area and remained close friends. Otto, Casey, and I became cops in DC. Freddie joined the police force in Alexandria, Virginia, and Billy got a desk job with the Montgomery County, Maryland, Sheriff's Department. Dyson Parker spent five years in Walter Reed military hospital but never fully recovered. When Dyson was finally discharged, he moved to Los Angeles, but he still keeps in touch with Crew from time to time.

"Everyone except Billy put in their twenty years of service and retired in the late 1990s with decent pensions. Billy quit the sheriff's office after about five years and went to work for a security-consulting defense contractor. He's always been one of those technology nerds and fit in perfectly.

"At first, we all were content to enjoy our retirement in leisure, going to Redskins games when we could get tickets. But one night that all changed. We were sitting on Otto's front porch in the shadow of the old RFK stadium in a section of town that in the 1990s was changing but was still frequented by muggers and drug dealers. We heard a woman scream and jumped up and raced toward the scene. When we arrived, four young punks were shredding an elderly woman's clothes and hitting her mercilessly. We easily overwhelmed them, beating the muggers with our fists and a baseball bat Otto grabbed of the front porch. As they ran off, we warned them to stay away from the neighborhood.

"That night, the Crew was born. At first, we focused on organizing neighborhood watch programs around the city that proved to be pretty successful. Before long, the DC Police Department became aware of our activities and began to ask us to perform some unofficial tasks—mostly surveillance and an occasional undercover operation. The DC police could use our services because they were hopelessly understaffed, and we had the experience.

"One day, much to our surprise, the DC police chief asked if the Crew members would be willing to hide folks in the witness protection program who were waiting to testify in felony trials. The location of several witnesses had inexplicably been discovered, and they had been brutally murdered by unknown assailants.

"That's when Casey had the idea of using his family's farmhouse as a safe house. It had been recently left vacant when his last remaining relative died."

"What an incredible story," Chris said. Then noticing a somewhat crumpled, faded photograph on the driver's side sun visor of the same woman whose picture was in a gold frame on the fireplace mantel in Chet's house, Chris asked, "Is that Mrs. Jones?"

"My wife died ten years ago—cancer," Chet replied with what sounded like a mix of sadness, longing, and anger.

"I'm so sorry," Chris mumbled awkwardly.

He started to ask another question, but Chet turned toward him with an expression clearly indicating there would be no further discussion on the subject of Chet's wife. Wishing he had never mentioned Chet's wife, Chris glanced out the car window and saw that the urban landscape of the nation's capital city had changed to a more rural area, with small farms and an occasional housing development.

They eventually turned onto a two-lane country road and took it for about ten miles before turning down an even narrower road. After about another five miles and with no other houses or farms in sight, they turned on a loose-gravel driveway, with a sturdy, red, metal gate blocking their way.

Chet got out of the car, went up to the gate, and punched a combination into a huge lock on a chain securing the gate. After removing the chain and pulling the gate open, he drove the car though the passageway and then secured the lock and chain. They drove for what Chris guessed was a about a half-mile through a wooded area before turning and starting to gradually climb a small hill. As they reached the top, Chris could suddenly see a large and well-maintained farmhouse in front of them.

"Welcome to the safe house," Chet proclaimed.

CHAPTER 24

April 19
Prince Georges County, Maryland—Morning

The white, slightly weathered farmhouse with a large front porch was situated on the slope of a knoll overlooking a large pond. Surrounding it were acres of uncultivated fields and groves of trees that were just beginning to show their buds. The serenity and beauty in the early-morning light reminded Chris of an Andrew Wyeth painting.

The front door opened into a large living room/dining room area with a stone fireplace to one side. In the back was an enormous kitchen.

As if reading Chris's mind, Chet said, "There're four bedrooms upstairs and several bathrooms. Downstairs there're three bedrooms off the kitchen in the back. One of them is mine."

The furnishings were functional. Four small card tables with folding chairs were in the corners of the living room. Hanging on one wall in the living room, in lieu of the family photos, was a large blackboard. Next to it was an even larger cork board with lots of stick pins. In the dining area was a large, rough-surfaced oak table with eight wooden chairs. Chris guessed that the room had served the dual purpose of additional work space and the gathering place for meals. Looking out a back window, he saw what looked like a cell phone tower.

As the men stood in the center of the living room, Chet asked, "Would you like a cup of java? I'm going to make some for myself."

"What I would really like to do is take a shower and get cleaned up."

"No problem. Go upstairs and take the last bedroom on your left. It has a private bath and all the stuff you'll need. It's a little drafty in here. I'll start a fire to warm things up."

Chris climbed the steep, creaking stairs and made his way down the narrow hallway to his assigned bedroom. The shower felt great, but as he toweled himself off, he remembered he had no clean clothes and would have to put on the same clothes he had worn the past two days.

Looking at his watch, Chris was surprised it was just a few minutes past 8:00 a.m. He flopped back onto the somewhat lumpy but comfortable bed, put his arms over his head, and without planning to do so, immediately fell into a deep sleep.

After what seemed like only a minute, Chris was jarred awake. "Captain, get your sleepy ass out of bed and get down here. It's after eleven, and the Crew has arrived."

Coming down the stairs, Chris witnessed a flurry of chaotic but purposeful activity. Casey, Otto, Billy, and Freddie were busy bringing in load after load of boxes. Chris offered to help but was completely ignored until all of their appointed tasks were complete.

As things started to settle down, Chet barked, "Everyone, grab a sandwich and let's get started. We've no time to waste."

Chris, feeling a little like an outsider, walked cautiously into the kitchen, where the center of the mayhem had moved. Chet, Casey, Freddie, Billy, and Otto were playfully pushing and shoving each other as they grabbed their choice of premade sandwiches and bottled beverages—water, soda, or energy drinks. When everyone had their food, the group moved back into the living room, and things began to settle down.

Finally, Chet spoke. "Everyone, let's get started. Chris, why don't you bring everyone up to speed on what we're dealing with here."

Chris stood up, faced the Crew, and began to describe in detail all that had happened. He felt the need to inform the team on every aspect of the EZ-15 matter, including a tutorial on global warming and climate change, the alleged benefits of EZ-15, a history of the regulatory process, and the more recent, disturbing developments. After about fifteen minutes, Chris noticed the placid facial expressions of his audience. Casey and Otto, the twin black behemoths who Chris decided to affectionately call the Bubba Twins, looked like they were about to nod off to sleep.

Exasperated, Chris said, "Am I boring you guys?"

Before anyone could answer, Chet slowly stood up and smiled at Chris. "I'm sure all the information you're providing would be fascinating if we were scientists or politicians. But to be honest with you, these guys don't give a damn about whether the earth's average temperature is going to be five degrees warmer in fifty years. They all have loved ones just trying to survive on a daily basis. Their biggest concern is to protect their families and friends. Of course, they also want to help keep The Man from screwing with folks who can't defend themselves. Let me try," Chet said in a fatherly tone.

Then turning to face the Crew and clapping his hands together, he barked, "Listen up! Here's the deal—we've got a corrupt, multinational corporation, one of them Arab sheiks, and apparently some other bad guys yet to be identified who are pushing a product that's putting some crap into the air that could kill millions of kids and old folks not only here in the US of A but all around the world. We've got a government bureaucracy that is either incompetent, in on the fix, or both. Innocent people have died, and I don't think we have many allies out there. I can't stress enough the dangers we'll face, but it's up to us. Are you guys in?"

Almost in unison, the four Crew members jumped up, pumping their fists as Otto shouted, "Now that's what I'm talking about!"

"Let's get the bastards," Freddie chimed in, which led to a chorus of "Right on."

Chet turned to Chris and said, grinning, "It's all in the delivery."

Just as things started to settle down, and the attention was refocusing on Chris, Leon raced in the front door with a sense of urgency and proclaimed, "Got it."

He moved directly to Chris, placing at Chris's feet the large duffle bag, the computer case, and the large canvas bag retrieved from Dan Witt. He also handed Chris a letter-size, sealed manila envelope.

Chris picked up the canvas bag that contained the $290,000 in hundred-dollar bills. Turning to Chet, Chris handed him the bag. "Why don't you hang onto this?"

Chet opened the bag and looked inside. "Holy Mother of Christ. Where in God's name did you get this?"

"It's a long story."

Chet got up and took the bag to his bedroom, shaking his head in disbelief the entire time.

Next, ripping open the envelope, Chris pulled out a single sheet of paper and skimmed it. With considerable disappointment in his voice, Chris looked at Leon and said, "Is this all there was in the locker?"

When Leon replied, "Yes," Chris bowed his head. He had hoped that what Goldberg had stowed away would provide some answers. Instead, it simply raised more questions.

Chris reread the handwritten note and started pondering the next steps they needed to take. Jackie's sadly prophetic note began, "Chris, if you are reading this, then my worst fears have been realized. EMCO and its allies will stop at nothing, including my death, to get EZ-15 into commerce."

The chilling first two sentences were followed by six numbered items on the sheet of paper:

1. *Someone at EPA is leaking information to EMCO and its allies.*
2. *The White House has expressed more than the usual interest in the EZ-15 matter. There may be an inappropriate connection between someone high up in the White House and EMCO and/or its allies.*
3. *Ronnie Chapman almost certainly stumbled onto something important in the EPA tests results. Access Ronnie's data, and you might find the answers with the help of Gerhard Mueller. Try 547571 and then "dragon lady."*
4. *This telephone number might come in handy—011.866.545.2781 and a code (998345#).*

The fifth item contained a list of names, some familiar to Chris, and following each name was a notation either "Good Guy," "Bad Guy" or "?". In some cases, there were additional comments as well. The sixth item simply read: "Heritage Study Group?"

About the time Chris finished rereading the note, there was a commotion on the front porch as Tanya and Sonja barged into the living room, their arms filled with packages and boxes. They were both talking loudly. The commotion came to an abrupt end when Chet shouted, "Please. If you want to help, put those bags away, grab some lunch, and get your behinds back in here."

As things settled down, and Sonja and Tanya returned, Chris passed around copies of Goldberg's note that he had made on the old copier sitting on one of the card tables. He asked, "Any thoughts?"

After a brief moment, Sonja said in a barely audible voice, "Can I say something?"

"Of course," both Chris and Chet responded.

Hesitant at first, but with increasing confidence, Sonja began, "First, the code in the third bullet might be the General Counsel's Office and Goldberg's personal password to enter the EPA's computer network. If I'm right, with that code and password, we can access any computer in the EPA system. Goldberg must have been one of only three or four persons in the entire agency that had that kind of access. Second, I would guess the number in bullet four is EPA's toll-free telephone access for making international calls—the digits 011 are a dead giveaway. Third, Chris, you told me last night about that Spanish guy who was killed last Friday. Since Goldberg had given you his name, surely he should have been on the Good Guy list. The fact that he isn't suggests she wrote this note and placed it in the bus locker *after* she learned of Sanchez's death. Finally, I know several people on that list, but then so do you, Chris, and I assume we'll be discussing them one by one."

Chris, leaning toward Chet, who was sitting next him, whispered, "I told you she was good." Then he turned and nodded affirmatively to Sonja, who obviously was pretty pleased with herself.

Turning to Chris, Chet said, "What now, Captain?"

With all eyes on him, Chris hesitated and then mumbled, "Chet, maybe you should take charge from here on."

Chet said to Chris, "Let's you and I take a little walk outside."

As Chris rose hesitantly, Chet put his arm firmly around Chris's shoulder and guided him outside where they could converse in private.

"Look. You've got a great team in there, but we need a strong leader," Chet began.

"Why not you? You led these guys before."

"I'm the sergeant—I can come up with the tactics and implement the orders, but we need someone to oversee the operation, and that's you."

"But—"

"But nothing. You have the brains and the talent. It's pretty obvious to me that for some time you've been wallowing in your own self-pity and really haven't cared about anything or anyone. Hey, I got to know pretty well that meek, pathetic bureaucrat who bought a newspaper from me every weekday over the past eight years. I don't know how or why, nor do I care, but that all started to change the night you saved Leon and Tanya. It's pretty clear to me you're not the same person anymore. It's time you realized it.

"Also, Jackie Goldberg thought enough of you to trust you with that mission in Europe, and from what you've told me, it sounds like you did a first-class job. Look, the people in that farmhouse and those kids in Asia need you to step up now."

After long moment, Chris reached out and shook Chet's hand. "Looks like I don't have a choice."

"Excellent," Chet said as he slapped Chris on the back, and they reentered the farmhouse.

Chris, surprising even himself, took charge. "Here's what I suggest: first, let's write down what we know and need to find out on notecards and post them on the cork board; second, we'll make a list of action items; third, let's go over logistics; and fourth, let's assign tasks."

When Chris finished, he looked at Chet, who nodded with approval. Without speaking, Tanya jumped up and grabbed a handful of notecards. "I'm ready—fire away."

Chris did most of the talking, but Sonja chimed in several times with helpful comments. Over the next ninety minutes, the cork board was filled with three major columns of notecards. The first column was titled "What We Know." The second was "The Players" and was divided into three subcategories: "Good Guys," "Bad Guys," and "To Be Determined." The third column was titled "What we need to find out." When they finished, Chris stared at the board and said, "Well, at least it's a start."

Chet stood up and started to speak when a cell phone rang. Chris, realizing it was his and without thinking, pulled it out of his pocket, ready to answer.

"No!" Chet and Billy McGinnis cried out in unison as Otto and Casey sprang at Chris. The sight of the huge Bubba Twins lunging at him caused Chris to drop his phone.

When calm had been restored, Billy McGinnis rose and said, "Sounds like now would be a good time to talk about communications. First, everyone, give me your cell phone. If you need it to check for someone's telephone number or to check recent calls received, come to me, and I'll do it for you. I'm not kidding. Give them to me *now*."

The collective stares of disbelief and resistance suggested no one wanted to give up their cell phones.

"Okay, let me put it to you this way. We don't know who all the bad guys are, but we can be pretty damn sure they know what they're doing. If the government is involved in any way, they have the most sophisticated communications surveillance and tracking technology available. If you use your iPhone, smartphone, or any cell phone made in the past five years or so, you might as well be wearing a bright neon sign on your head saying, 'Here I am.' The same thing is true if you're using a computer that was made less than a decade ago. Even large corporations, and certainly defense contractors, have the tracking technology. If you're on the communications grid, they can find you. One screw up by any one of us, and we'll all go down."

"But if we go off the grid, how can we function?" Leon asked.

"We don't go off the grid. We can't operate without some type of electronic communications, but we can go beneath the grid."

Billy looked around the room at the blank expressions. "Look, we'll be like a submarine—just barely below the surface, and once in a while we'll surface, if absolutely necessary. But only when it's safe and only for a very short time."

"Okay. I got it, and we're the Crew that's being assigned to U-Boat EZ-15," Freddie said with a laugh.

"But how do we do what you suggest?" Chris asked.

"First, everyone please bring me your cell phones and put them in this box."

This time, everyone complied—looking every bit like they were saying good-bye to their very best friend.

"Second, everyone grab five of those little babies in the box. Use 'em for no more than a day. Then crush them and give what remains back to me."

Everyone peered curiously into the box and saw hundreds of old cell phones in every shape and color. Chris hesitated and asked, "Is it safe to use one of those?"

"Well, if you're talking about radiation levels, I can't say," Billy replied curtly. "But they're not stolen, and they're not easily traceable back to the original owners. As long as you use them only for a short time, I don't think even the National Security Agency or the Department of Homeland Security could track you down. Does that answer your question?"

Everyone came up and, in turn, reluctantly grabbed cell phones. Chris selected his five quickly. He wasn't picky, but he did avoid the pink phones. Then Billy opened the second box, which was loaded with old, clunky desktop computers and accessories.

"If you have your own computers, don't use them. In fact, give them to me. We'll set up three computers with Internet connections and a fourth that will house our database. Sonja, I understand you're pretty good with computers. Would you be willing to set up and manage the database on the main computer?"

"I'd be happy to. It's what I used to do for a living … in another life."

"Thanks," Billy replied. And then pointing at the database computer, he said, "No one, and I mean no one, gets on this computer without Sonja's or my permission and not without at least one of us present whenever the computer is in use. If you want to use any of the other three computers, ask Sonja or me first. We'll be switching all these computers out every few days, so if you want to save anything, download it on a CD."

Chet then asked, "Freddie, anything else on the security front?"

"Yes, at eight o'clock tonight, the security net will be turned on, so don't wander too far from the house after that. Also, the security cameras are all active, so just remember that anywhere near this building and at the front gate, as well as at some well-hidden locations, you'll be on *Candid Camera*."

Next the Crew discussed the action items for the ensuing twenty-four hours, including obtaining armaments, a task assigned to Casey and Otto. Each member of the group was given a room assignment, and they divided up various tasks, including cooking, cleaning up, and food shopping for the coming week.

Around four o'clock, Chet said, "Captain, if it's okay with you, let's call it a day. I, for one, like the idea of U-boat EZ-15, and if everyone agrees, I'd like to welcome Chris, Sonja, Leon, and Tanya as the newest members of the Crew." Everyone nodded enthusiastically.

But then Chet added, "We're done—except for you, Chris. You've got an appointment for a little makeover. Tanya, could you give Chris a ride?"

"Makeover? What the hell are you talking about?" Chris said with alarm.

"You'll see soon enough, my friend," Chet replied.

With that, everyone headed off in different directions, leaving poor Chris standing alone, completely befuddled.

CHAPTER 25

"Let's go," Tanya called to Chris as she grabbed his hand and pulled him toward the front door.

As Chris got into Chet's car, he asked Tanya, "Where're we going?"

"Jasmine's Beauty Salon and Tanning Parlor. When she finishes with you, even your best friend won't recognize you."

Chris was suddenly filled with a sense of dread. They rode in silence for about five minutes before Tanya finally spoke. "Leon and I never really had the chance to thank you for what you did that night to save us. I want you to know, speaking for both of us, we'll do anything we can to help you."

"I'm not totally comfortable putting all of you in danger. We're dealing with some really bad people, and right now I don't know what to expect from them next. But thanks. We can use all of the help we can get."

With the awkwardness broken between them, they engaged in small talk. In the course of the conversation, Chris said, "I understand from Chet that his wife died about ten years ago, but he didn't seem to want to talk about it."

"Chet has trouble talking about her. Martha died of lymphoma cancer after a long and painful struggle. The truly sad part was that she could have survived. Chet had health insurance as part of his pension plan, but the plan switched insurance companies just after the cancer had been diagnosed. The new insurance carrier refused to pay for treatment because they said she had a preexisting condition.

Chet fought the insurance company but lost. He spent everything they had saved and mortgaged the house to pay for her treatments, and the cancer went into remission. But when the money ran out, and she could no longer receive the meds, the cancer returned, and four months later she died."

"What a nightmare," Chris muttered.

"It wasn't the first or the last time Chet has been screwed by somebody," Tanya said bitterly.

Before Chris could ask what she meant, Tanya said, "Here we are."

She pulled into a small strip mall located in what looked like the middle of nowhere. They parked in front of a small storefront with an enormous, overhead pink sign that read "Jasmine's Salon and Tanning Parlor."

"No way. I'm not going in there," Chris protested.

Ninety minutes later, Chris emerged from the salon and got into the car. He looked in the mirror and barely recognized the face staring back at him. Gone was the wavy, black hair. Looking back at him was a man who looked at least six years younger with considerably shorter, sandy brown, curly hair. His thick, black eyebrows had been trimmed and plucked—their color matched his hair. Also gone was the pasty white complexion of a man who, until recently, had spent little time outdoors in the sun. In its place was a well-tanned face.

The conversation on the twenty-minute ride back to the farmhouse was all but nonexistent. When they finally arrived back, Chris really didn't want anyone to see him in his transformed state, but that wasn't possible. As he entered the house, everyone was sitting at the dining room table, and they turned to stare at him. After a brief moment of silence, save a few snickers of laughter, Chris threw up his arms, fully exasperated, and declared, "Enough. I'm going for a run."

Five minutes later, Chris was on his way out the door and took off running. The evening was cool and dry, and he had a lot of pent-up energy, so his pace was quick. As he ran along, his mind raced over the events of the last several days, and then his thoughts became fixed on the dreams he had had and what they all meant. He recalled the conversations he had with his grandmother when he was very young about his mother's gift to see into the future. But what he had previously forgotten until this very moment was that in the same conversation, the elderly woman had whispered to him, "You may have the gift as well."

Chris stopped and put his hands on his hips. *Can my dreams really reveal the future?* he thought, recalling the two recent events when he had been able to correctly anticipate what actions were needed in order to save his life.

He started running again, and his thoughts turned to the last time he had seen his mother alive. It was about twenty years ago. His mother had seemed uncharacteristically disturbed. She was arguing with his father about whether they should go to the grocery store or stay home. Chris's father insisted, grabbing and shaking her. Finally, his mother acquiesced.

Chris also remembered that at the last minute she announced that Chris and Sarah would remain behind. Then she gave Chris a deep, tight hug before getting in the car. Fifteen minutes later, his parents lay dead in their mangled car—the victims of a drunk driver who had crossed the double yellow line and crashed head-on into their car.

Did she have a premonition about the accident? If so, why did she agree to go? Chris thought sadly.

As Chris completed his run, the setting sun was hanging on the distant horizon. Chris calculated that he had run about six miles at a pace around seven minutes a mile.

He looked down toward the pond and saw Sonja sitting alone, deep in thought. A small breeze caused her auburn hair to flow gently over her back, and it glistened in the waning sunlight.

God, Chris thought as he walked to her, *she's beautiful.*

As Chris approached, Sonja turned. "I was worried about you," she said.

"No one could possibly know where we are, and besides, I'm a big boy."

"I wasn't worried about your safety. I was afraid you might sweat off that great spray-on tan."

Feigning annoyance, Chris sat down next to Sonja, and then as his expression changed, he asked, "How are you doing?"

"Okay. I'm struggling to hang in there. So much has happened so fast, but don't worry, I'll be okay," she replied, showing appreciation for his concern.

"Hey, I'm scared too, but I'm feeling better. At least we're starting to take some countermeasures," Chris said, looking into Sonja's blue eyes.

Changing the subject and hoping to lighten things up, he said, "Mind if I ask you a question?"

With a slight note of concern in her voice, Sonja said, "You can ask me anything you want, but you may not get an answer."

"Why did you change your appearance?"

"I told you before. It's none of your business," Sonja said firmly as she turned to leave. Clearly upset, she walked briskly to the farmhouse without looking back at Chris or saying another word.

Walking to the farmhouse as well but about twenty paces behind her, Chris realized that what he had thought was an innocent question apparently was not. He knew better than to try to reenter her space and pursue the matter further. It was likely the last he would see of Sonja that evening.

His mind turned to the task at hand as he entered the farmhouse. He used one of the cheap phones to check his voicemails on his old phone. He had one message, and he didn't immediately recognize the number. But then it came back to him—Pam Russell.

At first, he considered calling Russell right away, but then he thought better of the idea. *How to handle Russell should be a group decision. I'll bring the matter up at tomorrow's Crew meeting.*

Everyone had been assigned a room for sleeping, and most everyone had retired for the evening even though it was pretty early. Chris learned that Sonja and Tanya were sharing a bedroom on the far side of the kitchen, next to Chet's bedroom. Leon was upstairs in the bedroom next to Chris.

Chet's making sure there's no extracurricular activities between Leon and Tanya and, apparently, between me and Sonja as well. There's absolutely no physical attraction between us. That's for sure, Chris thought.

With no one to talk to and feeling ready for a good night's sleep, Chris grabbed the copy of the *Washington Herald* that Leon had brought and headed to his room. After a quick shower, he stepped on a scale and was pleased with the results. *Ten pounds in nine days.*

Chris flopped on his bed and spotted a story about Goldberg's death. The article described the death as an accident, resulting from a hit and run. The story went on to report that the car suspected of being involved had been reported stolen and was found abandoned with lots of drug paraphernalia. There was no mention of foul play. The article did indicate that there was an eyewitness to the accident who was being sought by the police. Chris knew that the witness in question was probably him. "So much for staying under the radar," he mumbled.

CHAPTER 26

April 20
Montgomery County, Maryland—Early Morning

Just after 3:00 a.m., the cell phone on his bedstand rang. The FBI agent jumped and then fumbled to find the phone in the dark. Cavanaugh didn't need to check the display to see who was calling. Only one person would have the gall to disturb him at this hour.

As Cavanaugh got up from his bed and headed out of the bedroom, speaking quietly into the phone, a voice from the bed called out with alarm, "Darling, is anything wrong?"

Without looking back at his wife, Cavanaugh simply said, "It's work, dear. Try to go back to sleep."

Their two children, a boy and a girl, were home from college, but Cavanaugh doubted he would wake them as he made his way past their bedrooms and went down the stairs and into the spacious chestnut-paneled study. He knew his spoiled and worthless children had been partying with friends earlier and were probably dead drunk.

"Any new developments?" the voice at the other end said with a mixture of impatience and displeasure.

"Parnak, they've both disappeared. If we continue to snoop around, people might start to get suspicious. Besides, from all we can gather about that woman, she's a loner and a total freak. And that dumb-ass lawyer is probably hiding in some closet after what he saw Monday night."

"I totally disagree with you. That freak, as you call her, and that attorney were both smart enough to evade you. What's more, she may have a duplicate copy of Chapman's CD. The fact you didn't find it in her apartment means absolutely nothing. As for Mr. O'Brian, Goldberg almost certainly shared at least some information with him before her, shall we say, accident. Also, we know O'Brian spoke with both Sanchez and Mueller when he was in Europe, and he was damn effective in making our counterparts in Europe look pretty incompetent. Damn it, Mike, for the first time that I can remember, I am disappointed in you—very disappointed."

Cavanaugh cringed and felt his palms getting sweaty. He knew it wasn't a good idea to be on the wrong side of Parnak Petrovic, a powerful and well-connected independent consultant working for the Department of Homeland Security. "We'll get them, Parnak. We won't let you down."

Then in a desperate attempt to regain a measure of credibility, he suggested, "How about going official. If we do, Rich and I can be much more open in our investigation."

"Way ahead of you. Yesterday, I called your boss and requested that the FBI expand its ongoing investigation into possible illegal activities of several EPA employees relating to the EZ-15 matter, including Voinovich and O'Brian, who were also persons of interest to DHS. I also asked that you and Adams be assigned to take the lead on the investigation. Wiseman had no problem with my request since you've worked with Homeland Security before. We've already agreed to meet at FBI headquarters. I'm sure he'll give you a call in the morning."

"Great. We have all of the pieces in place to implicate Chapman, and we can easily tie in the other two by association. Are you going to push for a simultaneous DHS investigation?"

"Not yet. I still need to build the link to an international terrorist group before I can get DHS to become involved. I'm working on it. Right now this is a matter for the FBI, and I'd prefer to keep me and the DHS as far away from the investigation as possible."

The conversation then ended abruptly, and Cavanaugh returned to his bedroom. He looked at the gray-haired woman who had shared his bed for the past twenty-five years. She was at least thirty pounds heavier than the day they married and hadn't aged well. Cavanaugh had seriously considered asking for a divorce on several occasions, but decided that his marriage, one with a dutiful wife and two children, was the perfect cover for his extracurricular activities. Besides, he knew he had other options when he wanted a little action of a sexual nature.

As he climbed into bed, his wife asked, "Everything okay?"

"Yes, dear," he replied and then forced himself to give her a kiss on her cheek.

CHAPTER 27

After a quick breakfast, the Crew reconnoitered in the living room, now looking more like a command center. All of the computers were operational. The large cork board was filled with neatly organized notecards containing various pieces of information and the names of individuals from Goldberg's list, and others like the two unnamed FBI agents. On the adjacent blackboard, Chris had chalked in the list of the day's action items.

"I guess someone needs to take the lead, and Chet seems to think it should be me. But the truth is each of you has something special to bring to this effort. If you disagree with anything I say, have an idea, or have something to add, just speak up at any time."

He handed Sonja the CD containing Ronnie Chapman's files on EZ-15 that she had entrusted to him. "Use the central computer and go through Ronnie's file. You're pretty familiar with what Ronnie was working on, so if you can get through it today, maybe we can go over what you found this evening—okay?"

Sonja, grabbing the CD without looking at Chris, said with just a hint of annoyance, "I'll have what you need by midafternoon, Captain Crunch."

Chris then turned to Tanya. "Could you do a computer search of the persons on the good guys, bad guys, and to be determined lists on the cork board and see what you can come up with? Also check out the Heritage Study Group that was on Goldberg's list."

Next he turned to Leon. "Please look for any recent news items on the Web regarding EZ-15, EMCO, or asthma, as well as the German Federal Environmental Agency and the Umweltbundesamt, as it's called in Germany."

"Consider it done," Leon replied as he got up and sat down at the computer next to where Tanya was already hard at work.

Looking at Billy, Chris said, "I'd like to call Reginald Longshank in Brussels and Gerhard Mueller in Berlin, two of the definite good guys to tell them about Jackie and warn them to be careful. I also want to return Pam Russell's call even though I put her on the bad guys list. I'll need my phone back to get the numbers."

"Okay, use the EPA access code and number that Goldberg provided to make the international calls. I'm not exactly happy with you contacting that lobbyist, but that's your decision to make. But one thing—copy down all your contact numbers quickly and don't use your cell phone again."

Billy then added, "Listen up, everyone. If anyone wants to check for messages, use one of the phones I gave you yesterday and just key in your message access number like Chris is doing. I've given the phone situation more thought, and I think we should only use a phone once. We don't want to create any patterns that can be linked … and that goes for Sonja too."

Without looking up, Sonja raised her arm to signal that she got the message, even though she wasn't part of the conversation.

Damn, she's sitting there working away on the computer, deep in thought, and at the same time she's listening to other people's conversations, Chris thought and decided he would be very careful anytime he spoke about Sonja with others. Then he said to Billy, "That's going to mean a lot of cell phones."

"Don't worry, there are plenty more of these if we need them."

"Billy, I have an idea I'd like to run by you. Those two so-called FBI guys who visited my condo building on Monday were probably caught on the building's security camera. Is there any way you guys could sneak in and check the video feed?"

"Don't need to sneak in," Freddie chimed in. "I can check to see who provides the security service for the building. The feed box is usually in a utility room that typically is on the first floor just off the lobby. Billy can gin up the needed identification cards, and Casey and

I can pay a visit to the condo for, shall we say, a routine maintenance check. When did those guys visit your building?"

"Probably sometime between 3:00 p.m. and 4:30 p.m. on Monday based on what Ruth, the concierge, told me," Chris replied. He then added, "Hey, is there any chance Ruth could get in trouble? If there is, I can't go along with the idea. She's been a real friend to me."

"No risk of that. We go in, find the utility room, download a copy of the video feed, and we're out of there in fifteen minutes. No one will be the wiser. It's going to take a little time to set up, but we should be ready to go by midday tomorrow."

With the day's assignments made and most Crew members already working on their respective tasks, Chet suggested to Otto that they head out to restock the supplies.

"Looks like we're going to be here for a while. Anyone need anything as long as we're heading out?" In response, Chet received a barrage of requests.

Chris picked up his phone and jotted down the telephone numbers for all of his key contacts. Next, he grabbed one of his cell phones, keyed in the EPA international telephone calling code, and called first Longshank and then Mueller. Neither answered. *I'll have to try again; I can't leave a callback number,* he thought.

He tossed the cell phone in a big box marked "Used Cell Phones Here," grabbed another cell phone, and called Pam Russell.

A voice answered at the other end, "Hello, who's calling?"

"Pam, it's Chris O'Brian."

"You bastard! You screwed me royally," Russell shouted.

"Hey, I thought the sex was consensual and pretty good at that," Chris replied as if he had no clue what she was really referring to.

"Really funny, asshole. You know damn well what I mean. You used me. You fed me a line of bull about EPA being close to approving EMCO's EZ-15 application when you knew all the time there were people at EPA who still had concerns."

Chris thought, *Oh gee, I guess you weren't trying to use me that night either,* but said instead, "Pam, I honestly don't know what you're talking about. What I told you was what I truly believed was the case."

"Cut the crap. I'm on to you."

"You're wrong. What's your source of misinformation?"

"First, I know you talked privately with both Sergio Sanchez and Gerhard Mueller after our night together in Brussels."

"The visits were simply courtesy calls," Chris replied.

"Bullshit! Second, you told me you were going to Paris after the conference, and you never did. Third, while I was sitting in Stanley Braxton's office on Monday getting chewed out for believing the line of crap you fed me, Braxton got a call from Senator Goodman's office telling him that Goldberg was still actively trying to stop EPA's approval of EZ-15."

Chris was speechless—his mind raced trying to process what he just heard.

"Because of you, my career at Miller and Braxton is probably ruined. Hell, they're sending me off to Iowa to work on some landfill construction project. I am sitting in the airport waiting for a flight to Des Moines of all places," she said, almost in tears.

After an uncomfortable moment of silence, Chris said, "Pam, I'm not the bad guy here. Goldberg and Sanchez are dead. There may be other victims as well, and something very bad is going down. You're right in the middle of it, and I think you're in grave danger. For God's sake, don't go to Iowa. Drop out of sight for a while. You have my number; call it if you need any help. I'm temporarily using a new cell phone, but if you need to reach me, use my old cell phone number, not this one."

"Screw you," the voice at the other end replied, and the conversation abruptly ended.

Chris sat silently for a long moment. He then got up, walked over to the cork board, and removed Maxwell Goodman, chairman of the Senate Environment Committee, from the good guys list and stuck the senator's name under the bad guys list. Next, he picked up a blank notecard, wrote a name on it, and stuck it under Goodman's name. The name written in red and doubled underlined read "Joanne McKay, legislative assistant to Senator Goodman."

Chris pounded his fist on the wall as he cursed himself for making the remark to McKay about Goldberg's lingering concerns regarding EZ-15. *I thought I could trust her. It's my fault Jackie's dead.*

Hearing his fist slam, everyone in the room—with the exception of Sonja—looked up and stared at him.

"I need a smoke," Chris mumbled. "Otto, mind if I bum a cigarette off of you?"

"Help yourself," Otto replied as Chris grabbed a cigarette from a pack sitting on an end table and headed out the front door.

"You'll regret starting up again," Sonja warned in a mocking tone.

Chris flipped her the bird, and Sonja, again without taking her eyes off the computer screen, raised her hand up toward him with her middle finger extended and said, "Same to you, Captain Crunch."

Does she have peripheral vision, too? Chris wondered as he rethought his decision to smoke, clasping the cigarette tightly in his fist.

Once outside, Chris stared blankly off in the distance. *Can things get any worse?*

CHAPTER 28

April 20
Prince George's County, Maryland—Afternoon

"Oh my God. Chris, come quick!" Leon shouted from inside the farmhouse. Chris threw down his still-unlit cigarette and raced inside. Leon was standing at his computer, staring at the screen as several others converged, gasping in shock at what they saw.

"Deadly Explosion at Germany's Umweltbundesamt Lab Kills Ten," the article, displayed on the *Der Spiegel* website, reported that a massive explosion had occurred during routine testing on Tuesday morning at the agency's vehicle-exhaust emission-testing laboratory. Among those feared dead was the agency's revered scientist and director, Gerhard Mueller. No cause for the explosion was offered.

"Now you can see what we're up against," Chris said quietly. "Almost everyone that I've come in contact with, who was identified by Jackie Goldberg as a good guy, is now dead. I can't ask any of you to risk your lives by staying here or being involved in any way."

After a long moment, Chet broke the silence. "I think I speak for everyone when I say that we're all in this now, and we don't plan to quit until we get the bastards."

Everyone else in the room joined with a chorus of "I'm in" or "Me too."

"Thanks, everybody," Chris said quietly. Then raising his voice, he added, "Okay, let's get back to work and figure out what's going on, who is involved, and how we can shut them down."

Walking slowly to the cork board, Chris removed the card with Gerhard Mueller's name and tore it into pieces. Everyone slowly returned to their stations, except Tanya, who came over to Chris.

"Sorry, but I found nothing on the Web about the Heritage Study Group. I ran several variations of the words, but none of the hits traced down to anything that looked relevant."

Chris thanked Tanya and encouraged her to get back to checking the other names on her list. Then an idea came to him regarding who might have some information about the mysterious Heritage Study Group.

I'll contact Levy. If anyone in Washington knows about the Heritage Study Group, it's Rob Levy. The guy's obsessed with knowing about everyone and everything related to the Washington power inner circle, Chris thought as he grabbed yet another cell phone and punched in Levy's number.

"Hello, Levy here."

"Rob, it's me, Chris."

"Hey, Chris, what's up? Hope you're not still pissed at me for running that story."

"No problem, Rob. Your damn article got me fired, but hey, the job sucked anyway, and I always wanted to travel," Chris replied, feigning annoyance.

"Chris, I'm truly sorry to hear you got canned, but I had, and still have, a really bad feeling about EMCO and EZ-15. The public has a right to know what's going down with EPA's review of the EZ-15 application."

"Rob, seriously, you don't owe me an apology. You did the right thing. I was just the collateral damage. In fact, I'm now convinced that there's a hell of a lot more to this EZ-15 story than either of us could have imagined."

"Where are you? Do you have information you can share with me?"

"We don't have time to chat about me or EZ-15. I promise you if and when I have solid information, you'll be the first to know. I'll give you the exclusive. But for now, I strongly suggest for your own safety that you don't pry too deeply into EMCO or EZ-15."

"What are you saying?"

"I've said more than enough. In the meantime, I need a favor. Have you ever heard of a club or organization called the Heritage Study Group?"

Levy thought for a moment and said, "It's funny you should ask. I was talking with my friend, Frankie Moss, you know, Congressman Beasley's chief of staff on the House Environment Committee. We were both at some reception a week or so ago, and I asked him if he would be interested in playing at Congressional Golf Course the following Thursday. I did someone a favor, and in return, I scored a tee time for a foursome, which is almost impossible for nonmembers to get.

"Anyway, Moss said that Thursday mornings were bad for him because that was when the Heritage Study Group met at the Capital Club. I asked him if he could get out of the meeting, but he said 'no way.' I'd never heard of the organization and asked him about it. It was clear from his response that he regretted even mentioning the group by name. He then tried to blow it off by saying it was just a bunch of old friends who got together to shoot the breeze."

"If it was just a weekly, informal gathering of friends, then why was it such a big deal if he missed one meeting?" Chris asked.

"Exactly. In fact, I thought about checking into the group, but I never found the time. You know, there are so many nutty groups in this city trying to push one agenda or another. I'm glad you brought it up. I think I will do a little snooping around."

"Don't," Chris said firmly. "Let me look into it. I'm flying pretty far below the radar right now, so it might be better for me to check it out."

"Do you think there's some connection between the Heritage Study Group and the EZ-15 application?"

"I don't know for sure, but I'll let you know, I promise."

The rest of the day passed by without incident, and at four o'clock, Chris called out, "Everyone, let's gather and see what we've uncovered."

Crew members finished what they had been working on and meandered into the living room—everyone except Sonja, who continued to work at her computer.

"Hey, Sonja. Come on, we're ready to meet," Chris said.

"Start without me. I'm not finished here," Sonja replied without looking up.

"Thought you said you would be finished by now."

"There's a lot more here than I thought, Captain Crunch. And this ancient, piece-of-crap computer is incredibly slow. I'll be there when I'm ready, not before," Sonja shot back, glaring at Chris.

If those eyes had been daggers, I'd be a dead man, Chris thought and decided to leave Sonja alone.

The Crew members took turns reporting in. Tanya reviewed the list of names she had been asked to check. Most of the information was biographical about each of the persons listed, such as Senator Maxwell Goodman and Congressman Alan Beasley, who were the chairmen of the two congressional committees with oversight of EPA, including EPA's consideration of EMCO's EZ-15 application.

"Nothing I could find in any way links them directly or indirectly with EMCO," Tanya reported. "Similarly, nothing unusual about Ted Bennett, who's the EPA assistant administrator for air quality, or the other folks listed by Chris, except the last three: the firm of Miller and Braxton, Stanley Braxton, and Sheik Abdul Syed.

"Miller and Braxton is a lobbying firm established in the late eighties by the two namesakes. Miller died six years ago as a result of an apparent firearm accident, and Ted Braxton took over as the managing partner. Over the years, the firm has had a number of clients in the energy sector—mostly oil, but some coal. M&B also has several defense industry clients that focus on national security issues and products.

"Since Miller's death, the firm has steadily lost clients. I guess Miller was the brains of the operation. But two years ago, M&B picked up EMCO as a client, and their billable revenues jumped even as they continued to lose other clients. The firm has been the spokesperson for EMCO on all regulatory matters and has really led the charge for EMCO's EZ-15 application. I'm just guessing, but it sounds like M&B's future hinges on EMCO getting EPA approval for EZ-15.

"Ted Braxton sounds like your typical industry lobbyist—focused and ruthless. Seven years ago, he was cited in a House Ethics Committee investigation for alleged improper lobbying activities on behalf of a coal mining company. The investigation went absolutely nowhere, but guess who was mentioned in the investigation?" Tanya asked, but didn't wait for an answer, "None other than a member of Congressman Beasley's staff.

"Second surprise is Sheik Abdul Syed, who is also his country's crown prince. Apart from his family's equity interest in EMCO, the Syed's family is also a direct client of M&B. The crown prince's family gets money from the US government because of its strategic geographic location in the Middle East. Apparently, Sheik Syed comes to Washington quite often. When he does, Braxton serves as his host. The sheik has a reputation as being a bit of a playboy.

"Finally, there's Karl Thurgensen, who was on Goldberg's list of good guys. I found several articles that listed his accomplishments in the evolution of that motor-vehicle pollution-reduction technology— the catalytic converter. The guy was a chemist from the early 1960s until the late 1990s for a US-based chemical company, NJC Chemicals, Ltd. After 2000, I couldn't find a single reference to him. That's all I have so far," Tanya concluded.

"Great, Tanya. I'll go next. Tanya was unable to find anything on the Heritage Study Group, but I called a source, and he gave me some information. We don't know who's involved or what the purpose of the organization or club is, but we now know that they meet every Thursday morning at the Capital Club in downtown Washington. Chet and I have discussed this, and he has an idea. Chet, I'll turn this over to you."

"Leon did some Internet searching and found a floor plan of the Capital Club building. There are two entrances: the main entrance is on Seventeenth Street and a private or service door on H Street. Leon and I will go into town after dinner to scope out the place. The current plan for tomorrow is for Leon to position himself where he can take pictures of those entering through the main entrance, and Tanya will do the same at the side entrance. Billy will equip Leon and Tanya with lapel cameras with a remote clicker. I'll go with Leon and Tanya tomorrow to provide backup in case it's needed."

"Too bad we can't get someone inside after the study group meets to check out whether they've left any useful stuff behind," Sonja said.

Chris couldn't resist the opportunity to jump on her suggestion. "Brilliant, Ms. Voinovich. Why didn't I think of that? Hell, after Leon and Tanya take the pictures tomorrow, let's have them march into the Capital Club and ask if they can check out the meeting room."

"Not so fast, Chris," McGinnis chimed in. "Sonja has a good idea. You're right, of course; we can't just walk in. But that building has a cleaning service, and if we can check out which company does the cleaning, we may be able to work something out. It wouldn't be the first time someone, including a couple of law-enforcement agencies I can think of, have used cleaning crews to gather evidence."

"I'll make some calls right now," Casey Randolph volunteered.

Chris couldn't help himself from stealing a glance at Sonja. The young woman, still sitting at her computer, was looking at him with an enormous "I told you so" smile on her face. Turning away quickly, Chris said, "Billy, you're up."

"Tomorrow, Freddie and I are going to visit Chris's condo building and check out the security video feed to see if we can capture a picture of the two so-called FBI agents who were looking for Chris."

Leon was next. "Nothing new searching under 'EMCO,' 'EZ-15,' or 'asthma.' But I found two articles on the other topics you gave me. The first, of course, was that horrific explosion at the German FEA building. The second was a story about Jackie Goldberg. Most of it was biographical. She really was an amazing woman. The rest of the story focused on the police's continued belief that drug dealers were driving the car that hit her."

Chris then looked over to Sonja and said, "Are you ready or do you want us to have dinner first and come back later?"

Sonja got up, walked over to the blackboard, and said to no one in particular, "Do we have some colored chalk?"

Otto handed her a box of chalk, and she took off her black sweater, revealing her very attractive figure, and rolled up the sleeves on her shirt.

"I'll keep this quick and simple. Bottom line: Ronnie Chapman discovered that the EPA test data indicated that the process by which EZ-15 reduced carbon dioxide emissions may also be creating undetectable harmful byproducts that could be putting lives at risk. Let me try to explain what the test data shows," Sonja began, but was interrupted by Chris.

"Sonja, I tried to explain the issue already, but I lost everyone."

"Chris, you're a damn lawyer; no one can understand what the hell you're talking about."

The EPA analyst then started by saying that chemistry isn't all that complicated as she drew a car on the blackboard. She pointed out that any engine needs fuel and air to initiate the combustion of the gasoline fuel that provides the energy to drive the vehicle. She next drew a picture showing the chemical byproducts of combustion from a gasoline-fueled vehicle in the form of connected little circles representing carbon monoxide, CO, hydrocarbons, HC, and oxides of nitrogen, NOx.

Next, she drew a little box representing the exhaust pollution reduction device called a "catalytic converter." She explained that the emission-reduction device contained a series of cells not unlike a bee's honeycomb that are coated with precious metals, and the metals promote or serve as a catalyst to bring about a chemical change in the pollutants to water, $H2O$, nitrogen, $N2$, and carbon dioxide, $CO2$. Next she drew a series of connected circles representing the compounds coming out of the exhaust.

"The key is that the number of atoms for each element should be the same, or balanced, before and after passing through the emission control device." She pointed to the drawing showing the same number of oxygen, hydrocarbon, and carbon atoms both before and after entering the catalytic converter.

Sonja then explained that EZ-15 was a chemical compound that was added to the fuel before it was combusted and combined with the exhaust constituents to reduce carbon dioxide to carbon atoms and oxygen atoms. "Here's the problem. When EZ-15 is used, the latest EPA emission tests reveal that a substantial amount of the carbon atoms that should be present at the end of the test simply aren't there—they've disappeared."

Next, she drew with brown chalk a number of small circles with frowns. "These are the potential harmful chemicals that may be making kids and old people sick. But why weren't they detected in the test and what exactly is their chemical makeup? We simply don't know. But good science tells us that these questions must be answered before EZ-15 can even be considered to be allowed to be used."

Chris looked around the room, and everyone was nodding in the affirmative. Sonja had taken an incredibly complex issue and made it understandable. "Nice job, Sonja."

"Whatever," was all she offered in reply before continuing. "Ronnie Chapman explained what I have talked about in much greater technical detail in his report. His theory, as well as Gerhard Mueller's, was that the filter media used to capture the carbon-based materials during the emission testing was simply too porous to capture the subatomic carbon-based particles, and they simply passed through the filter undetected."

Staring at Chris, Sonja quickly added, "I double-checked *all* of Ronnie's data references against the actual test results from the EPA lab, which were also on Ronnie's CD. Ronnie's report is completely accurate. In case you're interested, that's why it took longer to finish than I originally estimated."

By the time Sonja finished her report, it was around five thirty, and Chet said, "Maybe we should call it a day. Give me fifteen minutes, and I'll get some chow on the table."

After dinner, Chris went for a run. When he returned, he saw Sonja, as she was the previous night, sitting alone by the pond. At first he thought about going into the house, but something drew him to the young woman sitting on the grass. As he walked down to the pond, Sonja turned and looked at him without expression.

"Great job on your analysis," Chris said. And then he added with a smile, "You did a pretty good job of making me look like a fool as well."

"I'm sorry," she replied.

"No, seriously, what you said was really funny, and frankly everyone needed a laugh."

"I'm not talking about what I said or did today. You deserved that. I'm talking about last night. I'm sorry I was so abrupt with you. It just that … well, there's just a lot that I simply can't talk about right now."

"Sonja, I can respect your wish for privacy. But if you ever want to talk about anything, I'm here for you," Chris said as he rose and touched her on her shoulder.

When she didn't respond, Chris started to walk back to the farmhouse, saying, "Okay, I know you want me to leave you alone."

CHAPTER 29

April 21
Washington, DC—Morning

During their reconnaissance mission the night before, Chet and Leon had agreed that Lafayette Park, across the street from the Capital Club, was the best spot for Chet to be posted. Now seated on a park bench, Chet could see both the Club's main entrance on Seventeenth Street and the side entrance on H Street. It was a perfect spot if something went wrong, and he needed to come to the aid of either Leon or Tanya. Chet tapped his pocket concealing the .38 pistol, as if seeking reassurance that everything was ready should he need to take decisive action. Dressed in ragged and dirty clothes, Chet looked like a down-on-his-luck black person. As he had hoped, virtually no one who passed by him made anything close to eye contact.

At 10:50 a.m., an intermittent stream of white, middle-aged, well-dressed men began to arrive at the side entrance of the Capital Club. Each swiped a card key, opened the door, and entered without looking around. None of them took any note of the young black woman dressed in a stylish skirt and matching jacket and wearing a trench coat. The woman, who appeared to be waiting impatiently for a companion to arrive, was actually snapping numerous pictures of them with a well-hidden camera as they entered. By 11:00 a.m., nine individuals had arrived. No one else entered the side door after that.

Inside the Capital Club, the nine members of the study group greeted each other briefly and took their respective seats. One chair on each side of the table was empty. Seating assignments were made based on a combination of stature and seniority. No one needed a place card to know where they should sit. The chair belonging to Judge Worthington at the head of the thick mahogany table also was empty. The stately wood-paneled walls complemented the table. Two windows at the far end of the room looked out at the park, but the lace curtains had been drawn.

After about five minutes of meaningless chatter, Judge Worthington made his grand entrance. The man's ego knew no bounds, and his temper was legend. Whether it was some poor junior officer or enlisted man or woman in the Marine Corps or a clueless lawyer arguing a case before the judge, once a mistake or misstatement was made, Worthington showed no mercy. No one could even hazard a guess as to the number of men or women who unfortunately crossed Worthington and had their careers, if not their lives, ruined because of it.

"Two members of our group are missing," he said. "I talked to both of them, and they have valid excuses. May I remind all of you that missing a meeting without an approved excuse is grounds for expulsion from the study group."

Worthington called the meeting to order and announced the discussion items for the day. EMCO's EZ-15 was the third item on his list. Even though everyone around the table was most interested in that item, no one dared suggest changes to the order of discussion announced by the judge. The first item was a recently announced FCC renewal of a local television license owned by Tilden Media.

"I hope everyone took advantage of Alan's advice at our last meeting to continue to buy Tilden Media," Worthington said smugly. "The stock jumped another ten dollars a share and hit an all-time high at the market close yesterday."

Members of the study group joined to clap for Alan Hastings, Federal Communications Commission Board member, who had alerted everyone to buy Tilden Media in advance of the FCC license renewal announcement. Collectively, study group members, their clients, and even friends netted over three million dollars in profits.

"Item two, Cloverleaf Security," the judge said, turning to a bald-headed, well-built man in his early sixties and longtime personal friend of the judge. "Any new developments?"

The gentleman, like Judge Worthington, was an ex-Marine officer, but he now served as a consultant to the US intelligence and national security community. He was a man of few words. "Cloverleaf is dead in the water. It can't be saved. They were unbelievably stupid in the way they booked their overcharges. In three weeks, the Department of Homeland Security and the Justice Department will announce a joint investigation, and the company will collapse almost immediately. If you own it, dump the stock, but spread out the sales over the next few weeks."

Lester Moody, an investment banker with Miles Hatfield Securities, one of the largest investment brokers in the country, said without thinking, "Are you sure? My clients hold a lot of Cloverleaf. They've made a lot of money on the stock, and they'll be reluctant to sell."

The ex-marine turned directly toward Moody and growled. "You and your clients made lots of money on Cloverleaf because of me. Don't ever—and I mean *ever*—question any information I provide the study group."

Moody replied meekly, "Sorry, I didn't mean to question your advice." Then Moody grabbed the pen and pad in front of him and wrote down a note about Cloverleaf.

Finally, Worthington spoke the words that everyone was waiting to hear. "Item three, EMCO Consolidated Company. Stan, the floor is yours."

Everyone turned to Stanley Braxton and leaned in his direction, not wanting to miss a word.

"On Monday afternoon ..." He paused for affect and then continued, "EPA will approve EMCO's application to sell EZ-15 in the United States."

Comments like "Finally" and "All right" filled the stately meeting room. The mood was broken temporarily by Franklin Moss, Congressman Alan Beasley's chief of staff, who said, "Our office hasn't heard anything about the EMCO application being approved, and Beasley's the chairman of the House Environment Committee, for Christ sakes."

Braxton replied, his annoyance with the congressional staffer apparent, "EPA will notify key members of Congress Friday afternoon and make the public announcement on Monday after the markets close at 4:00 p.m. There are only three people at EPA who are aware that the decision has been made. You can start buying EMCO stocks as soon as you leave, but spread your purchases over today, Friday, and Monday so the stock doesn't move up too dramatically in advance of the EZ-15 approval announcement by EPA."

Braxton turned to the only stockbroker in the group and asked, "Lester, do you have any predictions on how high EMCO stock can go?"

After the tongue-lashing he had taken earlier, Lester Moody welcomed the chance for redemption and said, "EMCO stock has drifted to a low of twelve dollars a share. Our estimate has been that if EPA approves the application, the stock will jump initially to at least thirty dollars and continue to climb upward. Once EPA issues final approval after the thirty-day waiting period, the stock price will jump again and probably hit forty-five dollars a share by August. After that, who knows, but our firm's estimate is that EMCO stock will continue to rise as the product comes online and sales soar. It could hit sixty dollars a share by the end of the year."

When he finished, Moody wrote on his pad some notes about EMCO and tore that and the sheet that had his note about Cloverleaf from the pad and quickly stuffed them in his pocket.

"I believe that concludes the business for today, gentleman," Judge Worthington stated as he stood up. Everyone began gathering their papers and started leaving when Worthington spoke again. "One thing more, gentlemen. Today was a very good day for the study group, but I am profoundly disappointed that not once, but twice, a member called into question information provided by another member. Such outbursts won't be tolerated. May I remind all of you that membership in the study group is by invitation and is conditioned on following the rules."

Lester Moody and Franklin Moss said almost in unison, "Sorry."

"Good. I consider the matter closed," the judge replied.

The meeting room emptied quickly, and all but Worthington left by the club's side entrance. The wind had come up, and several members pulled their coats up around their necks to block the cold air. Leon, who had switched places with Tanya and was positioned across the street from the side door, dutifully clicked multiple pictures as the members exited.

Meanwhile, Tanya who was now stationed in the park across the street from the Capital Club main entrance, waited to take pictures of people leaving by the main entrance. Between 11:55 and 12:30 p.m., only one person, an elderly but distinguished-looking gentleman in a well-fitting camel hair coat left the building by that exit. She got several good shots of him.

Once Braxton had distanced himself from the other study group members, he reached into his pocket and grabbed his iPhone. Immediately upon hearing late the previous evening from his EPA contact that approval of the EZ-15 application was imminent, he had placed a call to the Middle East to alert Hassid Kabar and to Europe to advise Jorgen Johansson of the impending good news.

When he got up this morning, Braxton had checked the international markets, and EMCO stock had a small bounce in price from the higher-than-usual volume of buy orders, but not enough to attract any real attention. Now he wanted to alert the two study group members who were absent from the meeting.

Worthington imposed a strict rule against providing any news emanating from a meeting of the Heritage Study Group to members who had missed the meeting. The rule was designed to encourage attendance, but Braxton had discovered that sharing the information with members who had missed a given meeting was an important way to build up chips that could be used later when he needed a favor.

CHAPTER 30

April 21
Prince George's County, Maryland

While Chet, Leon, and Tanya were doing their photo shoot at the Capital Club, and Billy and Freddie were checking out the security camera feed at Chris's condo building, Chris, Sonja, Casey, and Otto remained behind at the farmhouse.

Chris decided to take a quick run before breakfast. The drizzly, cool weather fit his mood. While they had made some progress the previous day, it seemed like more questions had been raised than answered. He was worried about how things would turn out and what he had gotten everyone involved in. And, then of course, there was Sonja.

She's a royal pain in the ass at times, but she's undeniably talented. She can appear vulnerable and caring at one moment and distant, if not hostile, at other times.

Chris decided the safest course for the day ahead was to leave Sonja alone as much as possible. At breakfast, Casey turned to Chris and said, "I made a few calls and was able to identify the cleaning company for the Capital Club. As luck would have it, I've worked with the fellow who heads up the crew that will be there tonight. In fact, he said I could join them this evening. That's the good news; the bad news is that the Capital Club is their last stop, so it's going to be a late night."

"That's great. Thanks, Casey."

After breakfast, Otto and Casey left to pick up more supplies. Sonja and Chris cleaned up the kitchen without speaking.

Finally, Chris turned to Sonja and said, "I need to make a couple of calls. Would you be willing to check the Internet for any breaking news related to the names on the good guy and bad guy lists and the topics Tanya checked out yesterday?"

"Consider it done, Captain Crunch."

"I really wish you wouldn't call me that," Chris pleaded.

"Sorry, but I like the sound of it, and besides … it fits you so perfectly," Sonja said with a smile.

"Fine. If it makes you happy, call me anything you want," Chris replied, knowing it would be impossible to change her mind.

Chris tried and failed again to reach Longshank. With a growing sense of concern that something had happened to him, Chris hung up.

"Sonja, can you Google Sir Reginald Longshank and the International Association of Emission Control Manufacturers to see if there's anything new on him?"

"Yes, sir," she replied mockingly.

Next, Chris called Charles Gibbons, the man whose name he had left on the pad in his hotel room in Brussels.

"Chuck Gibbons here, how may I be of assistance?"

"Mr. Gibbons, my name is Daniel Donovan. I'm an investigator with the FBI, and I would like to ask you a few questions about a man named Christopher O'Brian, a corporation named EMCO, and their new product, EZ-15. It shouldn't take long."

"What's wrong with you guys? I've already spoken in person with two of your associates last Thursday, and I told them I don't know this O'Brian person. Nor do I have any knowledge or dealings with ENCO or EMCO or whatever the hell the corporation's name is. I don't even know what EZ-15 stands for. I'm a marine biologist, and my only interest in that damn conference, which I was unable to attend, was a presentation on the impacts of increasing ocean temperatures on the leatherback sea turtle."

"I'm so sorry for the inconvenience. There has been an unfortunate mix-up at our end."

"I apologize as well. Sorry to overreact."

"Do you happen to recall the names of the agents? It would really help us make sure this type of unfortunate incident doesn't occur in the future."

"Their names were … let me think. Yes, Agents Cavanaugh and Adams, or it could have been Andrews, something like that."

"Thank you very much, Mr. Gibbons, and again, please accept my apology on behalf of the FBI," Chris said and hung up. He crushed the cell phone and tossed what remained in the designated box.

"Yes!" Chris exclaimed, pleased that his clever ploy worked and had generated an important lead. He wondered if the two so-called agents were really with the FBI and if they were the same two men who had visited his condo. "The person who broke into my hotel room in Brussels and who may have tried to kill me is working with someone in the United States. If Cavanaugh and that other guy are really FBI agents, then we have—"

"Chris, come here quick," Sonja called out.

Chris rushed to Sonja and began reading the screen. The headline read, "EPA Scientist's Suicide Linked to Bribery Scheme."

The online version of the *Washington Herald* reported that late on Wednesday the DC Police Department and the FBI jointly announced that the death of Ronald Chapman previously thought to be a tragic accident at the Metro Center station was, in fact, a suicide. A suicide note had been found on the victim's body. According to the news report, the note indicated that Chapman had accepted a substantial bribe to alter EPA files and test data related to an application from EMCO to obtain EPA approval to sell its new greenhouse gas emission-reduction product, EZ-15.

The suicide note, found in Chapman's pants pocket, indicated that he, feeling remorse for his actions, decided to take his own life. The article went on to explain that the FBI had discovered that $200,000 had recently been deposited in the joint savings account of Ronald and Laura Chapman. In the suicide note, Chapman implicated a competitor of EMCO, Medico Fuel, which was also developing a greenhouse emission-reduction product. The news article pointed out that Medico was now under investigation and that Laura Chapman wasn't currently a suspect in the bribery scheme.

Next, the news piece quoted EPA assistant administrator for air quality, Ted Bennett, who stated that an internal EPA investigation had indeed found substantial evidence of tampering with EPA test data and that the accompanying analysis of Mr. Chapman calling into question the effectiveness of EZ-15 was completely fabricated, and his conclusions had no basis in fact. Bennett went on to say that the ongoing FBI investigation would have no impact on the timing and direction of EPA's review of the EMCO application.

Then came the real shocker. The article quoted FBI Director Calvin Wiseman, who announced at the press event that two additional EPA employees were being named that day as "persons of interest" in the ongoing FBI investigation of the EPA data alteration and bribery attempt. The first was Christopher O'Brian, an attorney at EPA, who had been fired on the previous Monday, and the second, Sonja Voinovich, a systems analyst in the Air Quality Division, who worked very closely with Chapman. Both persons were believed to be friends of Chapman, and both had recently disappeared.

The article concluded with a glowing description of EMCO and EZ-15 and stated that EPA was under considerable pressure from Congress to move forward with making a final decision on EZ-15. Adjacent to the printed article were pictures of Chapman, Sonja, and Chris.

Both Sonja's and Chris's photos were taken from their EPA IDs and looked nothing even remotely like their current appearances. In addition to the spray tan and new hairdo, Chris had lost significant weight since his ID photo was taken, and he had traded in his heavy black-rimmed glasses for contacts several years before.

"This story is a total bunch of bullshit," Chris said, feeling more outrage than fear.

"I know, but let's break it down sentence by sentence. Whoever is behind this crap may have given us some clues," Sonja replied calmly.

"You're right. Getting mad isn't going to do any good. So let's get to work," Chris replied, recognizing that Sonja had had a much more intelligent and thoughtful reaction to the news article. *Maybe she should be the captain.*

"I'll start," Sonja said. "First, Ronnie didn't commit suicide. When I spoke to him the day before he was killed, he gave me the disk, and he was excited—not depressed. He really believed he had uncovered something monumental about EZ-15. Second, Ronnie didn't alter any test data. I watched him download the raw test data from his computer onto the disk he gave me. That was the disk I studied yesterday. The data on that disk came directly from the EPA test lab. There is no way he could have altered the actual data. If something else was found on Ronnie's computer, it was put there by someone else *after* Ronnie left EPA for home. There are only three people who would have had the access code to Ronnie's computer: Ted Bennett; Carmen Davis, head of internal document security for EPA; and the chief legal officer at EPA, Jackie Goldberg."

"My turn," Chris began. "Third, Medico Fuel is a mom and pop operation that has been trying for years to get a black box fuel economy-enhancing technology approved by EPA. During the past decade, no one at EPA has ever taken the technology seriously. It's absurd to suggest that Medico engaged in such an elaborate bribery or fraud scheme. Fourth, several people alleging to be FBI agents visited my condo on Monday, but the article stated that you and I became persons of interest to the FBI only yesterday—that's two days after those guys paid my condo a visit. Whoever they were, they must have been using fake FBI identification. Finally, and most important of all, Ted Bennett told Goldberg he checked Ronnie's computer right after Ronnie died and found nothing unusual. It's pretty damn clear that Bennett lied to Goldberg."

About the time Chris and Sonja finished carefully going through the article and making notes, McGinnis and Hernandez returned. With a broad smile, McGinnis declared, "Mission accomplished."

McGinnis walked over to one of the computers, began downloading data from a small handheld recording device, and reported, "Should have some pretty good pictures in just a minute or two."

Twenty minutes later, Chet, Leon, and Tanya entered the farmhouse living room. "I think we got some great shots of the Heritage Study Group gang of thieves," Tanya declared.

"It will take us a while to go through the photos, enhance the quality, and make enlargements. We should have something by late afternoon," Leon said as he downloaded the pictures from the two cameras into a Photoshop program on one of the available computers.

By 3:30 p.m. everyone, except Leon and Tanya, had completed their assigned tasks for the day, and Chris called out, "Let's gather up and start going over what we've come up with today."

After everyone had settled in, Chris began describing his conversation with Charles Gibson about the visit by two purported FBI agents and the possible link with the thugs who tried to kill Chris in Brussels. When he finished, he went to the cork board and posted the names of "Cavanaugh, FBI?" and "Adams/Andrew, FBI?" on the bad guys list.

Chris reported on the news article about Ronnie Chapman's death and the ongoing FBI investigation in which he and Sonja had been named persons of interest.

"Sounds like a bunch of crap to me," Chet said, and everyone voiced agreement.

"You're right, it's all bullshit," Chris responded. He and Sonja then proceeded to take turns pointing out the discrepancies in the story. When they finished their report, Chris posted the names of Ted Bennett and Carmon Davis as possible bad guys.

Billy passed around stills taken from the condo security video feed and asked if anyone recognized either person.

When the photos reached Sonja, she exclaimed while waving one of the photos, "This is the guy who was in my apartment and chased me down the alley. Just before I entered the club, I got a good look at the creep."

"Are you sure?" Chris asked.

"You don't forget something like that."

After a moment's silence, Tanya called out, "We're ready, well almost ready. We have pretty good photos, or at least one good photo of nine of the ten men who we're pretty sure attended the Heritage Study Group meeting today. Leon is still trying to enhance a photo of the tenth guy. How about I pass the photos around and see if anyone can identify the men?"

Tanya handed the photos of the first person to Chris and said, "This is the guy who entered and exited the Capital Club by the main entrance, so presumably he must be a club member."

"This one's easy—Thomas Worthington, retired Federal Circuit Court of Appeals judge," Chris said.

Chris was also able to identify two other individuals: Stanley Braxton and Franklin Moss.

Tanya recognized one person, the Pastor Jeremiah McCormick, founder, spiritual leader, and chief executive officer of the ultraconservative Holy Union Ministry church. "The guy's a complete fraud. I can't believe anyone watches his crappy cable TV show, to say nothing of sending the jerk money."

No one could identify the persons in the other photos. "I'll text these photos to Levy. He knows everyone," Chris said.

Tanya then wrote the names of the four persons identified on their pictures and posted them on the board under "Bad Guys."

Just about the time Tanya finished, Leon called out, "Got it. It's not a great picture, but I think it will do."

Leon handed the picture to Chris, who studied it, shook his head, and passed it along. The picture quickly traveled around the room, and no one could identify him.

Finally, the picture was handed to Sonja. At first she was ready to pass the picture back to Tanya. Then, as if something in her memory exploded, she pulled it back and stared at it intensely. Her eyes opened wide, her complexion turned ghostly white, and her hands began to shake. "No. No. It can't be. Please No."

Without looking at anyone, Sonja dropped the photo as if she wanted no part of it, jumped up, and raced out of the house, choking and gagging as she desperately tried to breathe.

Everyone sat stunned.

"Chris, for God's sake, go after her!" Chet shouted.

CHAPTER 31

April 21
Prince George's County, Maryland—Late Afternoon

By the time Chris reached the front door of the farmhouse, Sonja was past the parking area and racing down the gravel driveway. She was running full out like someone was chasing her and closing in. The young woman's running style was at best awkward—her arms were flailing, and her legs moved awkwardly. Chris decided to jog after her but kept a distance between them.

After about two hundred yards, her running stride improved, and she picked up the pace, which surprised Chris because he had assumed Sonja wasn't very athletic and that she didn't engage in physical exercise of any kind. Even more surprising, she maintained that pace until she reached the metal gate over a half a mile from the farmhouse.

When she finally stopped, Sonja was breathing hard and bent over, with her hands on her hips. Her hair and forehead were damp with perspiration, and her low-cut, tight-fitting T-shirt was sweaty and no longer neatly tucked into her denim shorts. Both her cheeks and long, slender neck had a healthy, rosy glow, and Chris couldn't help but think how naturally attractive the young woman was.

Sonja fumbled with the lock on the gate but couldn't get it to open. Quietly coming up behind her, Chris grabbed the lock, opened it, and swung the gate open. Without looking at him or saying a word, she ran off down the road at a more moderate but still respectable pace.

"Run as long as you want, but I'm not leaving you out here alone," Chris yelled, fully expecting Sonja to flip the bird back at him, but she didn't. She ran for about another half-mile and then slowed to a walk.

Chris, coming up alongside her, stayed on the opposite side of the gravel road. They walked side by side, but not together, neither speaking for at least another twenty minutes.

Finally, Chris broke the silence. "I'll stay out here as long as you want, but at some point you're going to have to tell me what the hell is going on. The time for secrets is over. We're all in this together, and the only way we can hope to survive is if we're honest with each other and we have each other's complete trust."

Chris waited for Sonja to fire back with an acerbic reply, but instead, she turned slowly toward him with tears in her eyes and said, "Everything is so fucked up: me, my life, everything ... and now Petrovic. I wouldn't even know where to start."

Chris crossed the road, put his two hands gently on Sonja's shoulders, and said, "How about starting at the beginning."

As they stood in silence, Chris touched her back softly, guiding her to turn back in the direction of the farmhouse.

She spoke softly and slowly, without a trace of emotion. "My parents, Harold and Gertrude Zimmer, were spies in East Germany in the late 1970s and 1980s for the NATO countries. My father was a brilliant scientist for the East German government, doing highly secret research on nuclear energy, and my mother worked for the government-run radio station. Although they both detested the repressive Communist regime, they never spoke openly about it to anyone other than their very closest friends. As it turned out, someone they thought was a close friend was a spy for the West. He eventually approached my father, who was lured into service with promises of money and, far more important, an escape to the West."

Sonja paused for a moment, brushed the sweat-soaked hair from her face, and continued, "In the late 1980s, the East German government stepped up its anti-espionage activities as it became clear that the entire Eastern Bloc was in danger of crumbling. Somehow, my father was identified as a likely spy, and my mother was accused as well—simply for being my father's spouse. They were both placed under house arrest.

"I was too young to understand what was happening, and my parents were always very loving to me. I enjoyed the life of a normal adolescent—as normal as life could be under the repressive East German regime. Then world events took over. The Soviet Union collapsed, and the Berlin wall came down. Lost in the headlines of these world-changing developments was that several scores of Communist spies in the West and a like number of Western spies in the Soviet Union and East Germany were quietly exchanged.

"My family was relocated to Newark, New Jersey. For me, the sudden move from the life I had known for my first seven years was traumatic. The fact I couldn't speak a word of English only made things more difficult. But worst of all, my parents began to argue incessantly. What I didn't fully understand at the time, but would learn later, was that the subject of the arguments was whether they should flee. Run away from the federal agents and the US government that were supposedly there to protect us but who were becoming increasingly menacing."

Sonja stopped walking, her head bowed and her arms dangling limply at her side.

"Do you want to stop for a moment?"

"No, now that I've started, I want to finally get everything out. The end result of all the disruption and growing anxiety took its toll. While I'm sure my parents loved me, they were always preoccupied, and the previously close, nurturing relationship, particularly between my mother and me, became almost nonexistent.

"Apparently, my father had made an important discovery while in East Germany that could significantly enhance the effectiveness of small-scale nuclear weaponry. He had kept secret his discovery from both the East German government and then the Western allies. But somehow the CIA became aware of his work. CIA agents frequently visited our home, and those agents became increasingly hostile. Even though I was sent to my room, I could hear the arguing and screaming conversations.

"I remember one man vividly—a bald-headed man with bushy eyebrows and piercing, steel-gray eyes. I thought he was old, but he was probably no more than forty. The guy was truly creepy. He'd pat me on the head and stare at me with those frightful eyes. I've never forgotten his face," Sonja said as she shuddered.

Chris could see the fear etched upon her face and asked, "Petrovic?"

"Yes, Parnak Petrovic," Sonja replied, her voice shaking with a mixture of fear and hate. The young woman explained that, despite the growing pressure to reveal his secret, her father refused to disclose any information about his discovery. Eventually, fearing for his family's safety, he sent Sonja to live with distant relatives who at the time resided in one of the poorer slums in New York City, having escaped from the former Yugoslavia in the early 1980s. The plan was for Sonja's mother to join her and for her father to completely disappear for a couple of years. Her father had hoped that eventually they all could be reunited.

"Two days after my relatives, Nikola and Jasna Voinovich, came and secreted me away, a horrific explosion incinerated our house, instantly killing my mother and father. I've been convinced all my life that the man with the steel-eyed stare was the cause, directly or indirectly, of my parents' deaths. Some organization or someone must have decided that if my father wouldn't cooperate with the US government, there was a risk that he might give or sell his discovery to someone else."

Chris moved toward her to offer what comfort he could, but she raised her arm as if ready to push him away if he got any closer.

"I'm okay. Just let me finish this." Sonja explained that the case of the Zimmer family deaths was closed—either because the explosion was so devastating that she was assumed to have died in it or because whoever was responsible decided it was better to say she had died so the case could be closed.

"The Voinoviches had a daughter named Sonja who died two years before I went to live with them. After the explosion, and even though no one besides my parents knew that I was with them, Nikola became increasingly concerned for his wife and my safety and decided to move his family to upstate New York where no one knew them.

"Because Sonja had been only two years younger than I was, and I looked very young for my age, they decided to tell everyone they met in our new hometown, Buffalo, that I was their daughter, Sonja. From the day we stepped off the train in Buffalo, I became Sonja Voinovich, six-year-old daughter of Yugoslavian refugees Nikola and Jasna. They dyed my hair black, and I just kept it that way after I left home years later. The Voinoviches were very kind to me, but we all lived in fear.

"I always did well in school. Hey, I was two years older than everyone thought, and I picked up English very quickly. But because of what had happened to my parents and the fear of possibly being discovered by whoever killed my parents, I became increasingly introverted. Growing up, I never had any real friends."

As they approached and opened the entrance gate, Sonja continued, "Nikola had trouble finding work, but he eventually got a menial labor job with a chemical company cleaning the chemical by-product waste that was generated during the manufacturing process. In 2000, the company was cited for over 350 safety violations by the Occupational Health and Safety Administration. Little good that did my stepfather—he had earlier contracted lung cancer and died in 1998. By the time the lawyer representing my stepmother sued the company and won a $300,000 award in 2003, the company had declared bankruptcy, and she received absolutely nothing. What's more, Nikola's pension fund was bankrupt, and so Jasna received nothing.

"About two months later, she killed herself by taking an overdose of sleeping pills. I was never sure if she did so because of the injustice of it all or because life without Nikola was too much for her to bear. I loved Nikola and Jasna as if they were my own parents, and suddenly they, the only people I ever cared about besides my parents, were gone."

As Chris and Sonja approached the farmhouse, Sonja turned and walked toward the pond. Chris followed, understanding that Sonja hadn't finished her story and wished to continue.

"Because my grades throughout my school years were great, I received early admission on a full scholarship at the University of Maryland and enrolled in September 2001. I've always felt guilty about leaving Jasna, because she was alone. But she was the one who insisted I go to a new place and start a new life. When I started college, my majors were music appreciation and computer science, but between my junior and senior year, when Jasna died, I changed my second major from music to chemistry. It took me an extra year to graduate. I worked nights and weekends while in college to pay my expenses, so I made virtually no friends, and my social life was nonexistent. I loved music and got used to being alone. After a while, I realized that I greatly preferred the solitude, and because I still feared being discovered by the people who killed my parents, I kept my rather freaky disguise."

"So you switched majors and then went to work at EPA because of what happened to your stepparents?"

"Brilliant deduction, Captain Crunch," Sonja responded. Her follow-up laugh broke, at least for a moment, the mood that had been pretty somber up until that moment.

Without waiting for Chris to reply, the young woman continued, "I guess like a lot of people who go to work for EPA, I thought I could save the world. I found some of the people there a pain in the butt. Ted Bennett, my beloved boss, is a quintessential bureaucrat most concerned with covering his own ass. He never showed any initiative and had no leadership skills. Frankly, I'm amazed at the amount of really high-quality work that comes out the Office of Air Quality in spite of that asshole. Thanks to people like Ronnie who, despite his indiscretions with Ann Hastings, was a great scientist and a decent guy."

Chris was at a complete loss as to what he should say or do in response to Sonja's harrowing story. Finally, he broke the silence. "If Sonja isn't your real name, what is?"

Sonja looked up with her soft eyes staring at him and said, "The daughter of Harold and Gertrude Zimmer died that night with her parents. My name is Sonja Voinovich, and let's leave it at that, okay?"

Sonja leaned toward Chris and tapped him on his knee, "But thanks for asking."

Sitting together for a few more minutes, Sonja finally said, "Chris …"

Chris looked up and saw something in Sonja's face that he had never seen before—the look in her eyes was both clear and intense.

"I've been afraid my entire life, but I'm tired of running. I want to do what I can to help get the bastards who killed Ronnie, Ann, Goldberg, and your two friends in Europe, and most of all, I want to see Parnak Petrovic wiped off the face of this earth."

Without speaking, Chris reached out and grabbed Sonja's hand as they both stood up. They walked together into the farmhouse.

Everyone had just finished dinner, and they were doing their best to ignore Sonja so she wouldn't be uncomfortable.

"Hey, everybody. Sorry for the freak-out exhibition earlier tonight. But thanks to Captain Crunch here, I'm okay, and I promise you that it'll never happen again. Frankly, I'm exhausted. I need a good shower and some sleep. I'll let Captain Crunch tell you everything he thinks you need to know. See you all in the morning."

With that, she walked over to Chris and whispered in his ear, "Thanks for being such a good listener and friend." Squeezing his hand for just an instant, she left the room.

Chris proceeded to tell Sonja's life story, including identifying Parnak Petrovic as the person in the photo. "He used to work for the CIA, but I have no idea what he's up to these days. I'll ask Levy to check him out."

CHAPTER 32

April 22
Prince George's County, Maryland—Morning

As the Crew finished breakfast, everyone was present except Casey and Sonja. Casey had worked late with the office cleaning detail and was still sleeping. Sonja, despite her brave showing the previous evening, had spent the night alone crying and reliving sad memories she hadn't thought about for years.

Chris grabbed a cell phone from the box and tried once again to reach Reginald Longshank. He was about to hang up when Carin Holsten answered the phone.

"Carin, it's Christopher O'Brian. May I speak to Sir Reginald?"

"Certainly."

"Chris, great to hear your voice. I've been trying to reach you all week, but your phone at EPA has been disconnected. Are you all right?"

"I'm fine, but a lot has happened, and we need to talk. I've tried to reach you, but no one has been answering your office phone."

"Carin and I have been in Lisbon for our association's annual meeting. You could have left a message, and I would have gotten back to you."

Chris explained that he had been fired from EPA and then went on to describe generally all that had happened while he was in Europe and since he had returned to the United States.

"Sir Reginald, you're in grave danger. Everyone I have spoken to who had doubts about EZ-15—Sanchez, Mueller, and Goldberg—are dead. I'm convinced they were all murdered by the same group of conspirators. You could be next. You need to get out of Brussels now and go into hiding."

"I heard about Jackie, Sergio, and Gerhard. It's horrific. But I can't just up and leave," Longshank protested.

"You must. And either take everything you believe is relevant on EZ-15 with you or destroy it. Your life is at risk; please believe me. There have been two attempts on my life," Chris pleaded.

"Maybe you're right. I could shut the office down for at least a couple of weeks—springtime here is usually a very quiet time of the year."

"Do you have a safe place to hide?" Chris asked.

"My wife and I have a place where we can go. None of my business colleagues or contacts knows about it."

"Perfect. Of course you'll need to take Ms. Holsten with you."

"Are you daft? Carin has a four-month-old baby, and my wife would never put up with them joining us."

"I'm deadly serious. If Carin is left behind, she'll be in danger. These guys will stop at nothing if they think she knows anything that could jeopardize EZ-15 or knows where you're hiding. And the father needs to go with you as well."

"The infant's father was killed in an auto accident before the child was born. We'll take Carin and the child with us, but believe me, it won't be easy convincing my wife."

"Leave today and make sure you aren't followed."

"Okay," Longshank agreed. "Is there anything I can do to help you before we disappear?"

"There is indeed. Jackie Goldberg instructed me to track down Karl Thurgensen. Do you know if he's still alive and, if so, how I can reach him?"

"Karl, the crazy Dane, now there was an interesting person," Longshank said.

"I know a little about him, but I'd appreciate any information you can provide," Chris responded.

"Thurgensen was a genius and the best chemical engineer I ever met. He graduated from MIT in the late 1950s and went to work for NJC Chemicals—a large multinational conglomerate. Within two years, he became head of a research team working on the use of precious metals as catalysts to promote chemical reactions for a variety of applications. Thurgensen and his team made many breakthroughs in automotive catalyst technology from the late 1960s into the mid-1990s. Thurgensen himself was awarded over thirty patents."

"You said he continued to make discoveries until the mid-1990s. What happened after that?"

"It was tragic, simply tragic. His wife, Susan, died suddenly of a heart aneurism. Thurgensen was devastated. He had difficulty coping with the loss of his wife, who was his inspiration, soul mate, and best friend. Thurgensen's work began to suffer. He was always temperamental, but after her death, his erratic behavior reached a point beyond which his superiors and colleagues could tolerate.

"Since Thurgensen was nearing the company's mandatory retirement age anyway, the company, which had made millions of dollars in profits from his discoveries, decided to throw him a nice party and boot him out the door. Oh yes, and because the catalyst technology advances for which he had received all of those patents came from research while he was a NJC employee, the patent rights belonged to the company. In lieu of a pension, they gave Karl a one-time payment of $50,000."

"What happened to him?" Chris asked anxiously.

"Thurgensen just disappeared."

"I need to find him. Goldberg must have felt that Thurgensen could help unlock the truth about EZ-15."

For a long moment, there was no response, but then Longshank said, "Wait, I got a postcard from him in the early 2000s congratulating me on being knighted. I think I may still have it. Let me check. I'll be right back."

Chris waited impatiently, and finally Longshank returned.

"Found it. Karl didn't say much other than congratulating me. I can't make out the postmark, but the postcard is a photo of mountains, and the lettering reads, 'Come Escape to the Beauty of Mason County, Virginia.'"

Chris was ecstatic. *It was over ten years ago, and it's only a postcard, but it's something to go on.*

"Thanks, Sir Reginald," Chris said. "We should end this conversation. You need to get out of there."

Longshank gave Chris his cell phone number, and the conversation ended.

Turning to Leon, Chris asked, "Are they ready?"

"Yes," Leon replied, handing Chris a CD with photographs of the Heritage Study Group members and the names of those the Crew could identify. Chris picked up yet another cell phone and called Levy.

"Rob, it's Chris, and I have photographs of ten of the Heritage Study Group members. I need your help in identifying them. I can e-mail them to you. I was able to identify five of them, and I've noted those I've identified," Chris said, not wanting to reveal that he was working with others.

Levy gave Chris an e-mail address that belonged to his girlfriend. "Use her e-mail. No one at the *Herald* even knows we're dating. Once you send it, I can access her e-mail on my iPhone and get back to you."

"Don't try to call me. I'll give you a call later today," Chris cautioned Levy. "One of the study group members identified is a guy named Parnak Petrovic. At one time he worked for the CIA, but I'm interested in knowing where he is now. Be careful who you ask about this guy—he's a dangerous character. I'm sending your girlfriend the file now, and I'll call you around three o'clock."

*   *   *

About the time Chris ended his call with Levy, Sonja emerged. When Otto saw Sonja standing there somewhat unsure of herself, he walked over to her, extended his arms, and engulfed her in an enormous hug. When Otto finally released his hold on Sonja, she gave him a gentle kiss on the cheek and turned to everyone with an embarrassed smile. "Thanks, thanks all of you. Now let's get back to work."

As everyone settled back to their tasks, Leon said to his dad, "Isn't it time Casey got up, and we started looking through what he collected?"

"Someone go wake him and tell him to get his butt down here."

Five minutes later, a rather sleepy-looking Casey Randolph emerged with a plastic garbage bag over his shoulder and plopped it on the floor.

"Man, piece of cake. Everything went off without a hitch. But those guys sure generated a lot of trash for a one-hour meeting. All of the pads, pencils, and newspapers we found in the conference room are in the bag," Casey declared proudly.

Grabbing the bag and emptying it on the living room rug, Chris suggested, "Leon, Tanya, and Sonja, let's go through all of this and see what we have."

After about an hour, they had sifted through all of the trash. When they finished, Chris asked Leon to check the stock market online regarding several stocks, and in an effort to help Sonja get back into her grove, he asked her to report on what they had found.

Sonja explained that one of the notepads found in the room had pencil indentations on it.

"The top sheet of the pad, on which notes had been written, was ripped off, but by gently rubbing a pencil over the indentations, two bulleted items can clearly be read. The first bullet reads, 'Cloverleaf Security dead in the water—sell.' The second notes, 'EPA Monday. EMCO buy now!' Casey also retrieved copies of the *Wall Street Journal* left in the room. In the section listing individual stocks, two copies had underlined notations for the same two stocks: EMCO and Cloverleaf Security."

"That's all you got?" Casey said dejectedly.

"Not so fast, Casey, there's more, much more," Chris said and then asked Leon, "Find anything?"

"Give me a minute more—you aren't going to believe this."

Moments later, Leon got up and walked over to the group with an enormous grin on his face. "First, Cloverleaf Security. The company is a huge defense contractor, with a substantial business here in the United States, but also in Iraq and Afghanistan. On Thursday morning, the stock was trading near its five-year high of eighty-five dollars. Yesterday afternoon, the stock began drifting downward on more than average trading levels for that stock over the past few months. The stock value has dropped nearly 5 percent even though there's nothing in the news that can explain the decline. Second, EMCO's stock value yesterday at the market opening was trading at twelve dollars a share, down about fourteen points from ten days ago. But starting yesterday afternoon, EMCO stock began to climb, again on more than average daily volume for the stock. I just checked, and the stock has climbed to sixteen dollars a share—an increase of over 25 percent."

"So what does this all mean?" Casey asked.

"It means that we have figured out what the Heritage Study Group is. It's a damn investment club," Sonja replied.

"And not only that, it's an investment club whose members apparently have inside information on various companies. My guess is that EPA plans to announce approval of EZ-15 on Monday, at which point the value of EMCO's stock will soar. And you can be assured that if EPA does plan to announce approval on Monday, only a very small group of people will have had advance notice. With regard to Cloverleaf, my guess is that some major negative news about the company will be coming out real soon, and the value of the stock will plummet," Chris said confidently.

"Sounds like we made some good progress today," Chet said.

"Absolutely. And thanks, everyone," Chris said. "Why don't we knock off for the day and get an early start to the weekend. I'll check with Levy to see if he was able to identify any more of the Heritage Study Group members, and I'll post their names on the bulletin board."

Within a minute, Chris was left alone in the living room and decided to call the journalist. Levy answered before the second ring.

"I know three of the five you couldn't identify: Number one is Alan Hastings, an FCC commissioner and a real jerk. Number two I didn't recognize, but I'll keep checking. Number three is Roman Cherkoff, a naturalized citizen from Russia and one of the richest men in the United States. There has always been some question about exactly how he amassed his wealth when he was in Russia. Number four I don't know, but again I'll keep looking. And number five is Larry Wasserman, a high-priced lawyer who champions liberal causes."

"Thanks. Any luck with Parnak Petrovic?"

"Sorry, nothing yet, but I'll keep checking."

"Be careful with that one," Chris again admonished Levy.

"I hear ya, Chris. But when are you going to tell me what the hell is going on here?"

"Rob, I told you I'd give you the exclusive when the time is right, but for now, be patient. I need to go. Thanks."

Chris sat alone in the living room, pondering all that had happened the past week. He was exhausted but felt some progress was being made. He decided to relax until dinner and grabbed the copy of the *Herald* that one of the crew had picked up earlier in the week. Flipping to the sports section, he saw an article that caught his attention, and he didn't hesitate in deciding how he would spend the next day.

*   *   *

The mood at dinner was light and relaxed. After an incredibly intense week, everyone was ready for a couple of days off. Monday would come soon enough and with it EPA's expected approval of EMCO's request to market EZ-15.

Sonja sat quietly as if she was listening in on others' conversations, but her mind was somewhere else. She thought about how the Crew had greeted her so warmly earlier in the day and the kindness she had received since she first arrived at Chet's house. Then the realization came quietly to her that for the first time since her early childhood, she was surrounded by a group of individuals who, though she barely knew them, actually cared about her and, perhaps more remarkably, that she cared for them deeply as well. Christopher O'Brian was another matter—her feelings toward him only seemed to become more conflicted as time went on. She glanced at Chris, and he was staring at her almost as if he was reading her mind. She frowned, and he looked away.

After dinner, Leon, Tanya, and Chris decided to go down to the pond and headed out the door. Chet looked at Sonja and, reading the uncertainly on her face, said, "Why don't you join them and let us old farts sit in the living room and argue about whether the Washington Redskins or the Baltimore Ravens will be the better football team this fall?"

Reluctantly, Sonja walked out to join the others. She sat down next to Tanya rather than next to Chris—a move that didn't go unnoticed by Chris. Breaking the silence, Chris asked Leon and Tanya how they met, what they were studying in college, and if they had any plans for the future.

"We met at a frat party two years ago, and we've been together ever since," Tanya said as she squeezed Leon's hand.

Leon said, "I'm planning to go to Howard University Medical School next year. I'd prefer to go somewhere else. My grades and MCATs score are good enough to get into a better school, but the cost is too high."

Tanya chimed in, "I plan to get a master's in journalism after I graduate in two years. My parents barely had enough money to send me to college. Now my only hope is to marry some rich, fat-cat doctor." She laughed and smacked Leon hard on the arm, indicating that he would have to be the one to pay for her graduate school loans once he became a doctor.

"So, Tanya, how did you happen to be in DC this spring?" Sonja asked.

"Leon and I both did an independent study semester and we finished in March. I couldn't find a job in Miami, where my parents live, so Chet, after much lobbying from Leon, allowed me to stay at his house and look for a job. I don't think he's very happy about the prospect of the two of us living under the same roof, but he's so generous and caring—he just couldn't refuse. Both Leon and I found temp jobs until next fall, which, by the way, we happily quit when we all headed out here to the sticks."

Sonja asked Leon what happened to his mother, and Leon told her how his mother had died.

Tanya added, "It took Chet years to start to overcome his grief. Chris, if you hadn't stepped in that night and saved Leon and me, I don't think Chet could have survived the loss."

Sonja, who had been listening pensively, suddenly blurted, "What? What's this about Chris saving you and Leon?"

Chris quickly replied, "It was nothing—"

But Leon and Tanya cut Chris off and explained everything that had happened that night. Sonja looked at Chris, trying to comprehend what she had just heard and making it fit into what she knew or thought she knew about him.

Uncomfortable with where the conversation had drifted, Chris got up and said, "It's getting late, and I'm beat. I think I'll call it a day."

As they walked back to the farmhouse, Chris turned to Leon and said quietly, "I need to run an errand tomorrow. Can I borrow your car?"

"Sure, but check with my dad first. I know he doesn't want anyone leaving here without a good reason," Leon cautioned and handed Chris his car keys.

"Absolutely," Chris said.

Tanya and Leon entered the farmhouse, but Sonja lingered on the porch and said to Chris, "Come on, tell me more about you being a hero."

"Maybe some other time," was all Chris was prepared to say in response.

"You're so damned annoying," she replied with a frown.

CHAPTER 33

April 23
College Park, Maryland

Chris walked toward the University of Maryland's soccer field, where Maryland was about to play its archrival, the University of Virginia. If Maryland could win the match, they would qualify for a spot in the NCAA championship. He was excited to see Corbin play, but Chris knew he was violating the trust of Chet and the others.

When Corbin was young, soccer had been Chris's and his son's passion. They spent hours practicing, talking about, and watching soccer. Chris never missed one of Corbin's games—that was, until Sarah and Chris separated and eventually got a divorce.

Corbin never forgave his father for the divorce, even though it was Sarah who demanded they end the marriage. Over the next several years, Chris saw less and less of his son. Finally, on the occasion of Corbin's sixteenth birthday, when Chris showed up late and caused a scene that drove Sarah to tears, Corbin shouted in his father's face, "I never want to see you again!"

Chris painfully honored his son's wish until this day. He had no idea what the future would hold for him, but he wanted to see Corbin and Sarah for what could prove to be one last time.

When Chris arrived at the soccer field, he was so excited he could hardly contain himself as the Maryland team raced out and there was Corbin. He couldn't believe how much his son, now twenty and a sophomore, had grown.

Chris stood on the Virginia side of the field to avoid any chance of being recognized by Sarah or Corbin. To fit in with the Virginia fans, he wore a Virginia baseball cap, which he purchased earlier that day at a sporting goods store, where he also picked up clothes and supplies he needed.

Chris searched the other sideline to see if Sarah was there. It didn't take long to spot her. She looked as lovely as ever, and Chris sighed as he thought of all he had lost. Then he noticed a man, probably in his fifties, standing near Sarah. He had gray hair, was quite handsome, and was well dressed. The man moved closer to Sarah and put his arms around her neck. Her companion was no doubt everything Sarah had always wanted and what Chris never was or ever could be. When the man gently kissed Sarah on her cheek, and they hugged affectionately, Chris turned away.

Mercifully, the referee blew his whistle signaling the start of the game, and Chris turned to watch the game. The first half was hard fought and ended without either team scoring. Then, with less than a minute left in the second half, Corbin stole the ball from a Virginia player and raced down the field.

As Corbin neared the Virginia goal, two Virginia players closed in, and the goalie moved to defend against the impeding shot. But rather than take the shot, Corbin, using a trick play Chris had taught him years before, flipped the ball back to a teammate who was undefended. Corbin's teammate took the open shot and scored the winning goal. The Maryland supporters and the team went wild.

On the Virginia side of the field, Chris let out a great cheer and pumped his fists, much to the consternation of the Virginia fans who stared at him curiously.

"I always cheer a great play, no matter which team makes it," Chris offered up as an explanation to no one in particular.

Everyone had been following the ball as it went in the goal, and no one saw that just as Corbin passed the ball to his teammate, he was sandwiched by the two Virginia players and cut off at the knees. The celebration ended abruptly as teammates and fans saw Corbin lying motionless on the field. Both the Maryland and Virginia players circled the fallen player. The hit Corbin took wasn't intentional, but it appeared devastating nonetheless.

The coaches from both teams, Sarah, her companion, and the medical team carrying medical bags and a stretcher all raced to Chris's son. Chris felt sick to his stomach. He wanted to run onto the field as well but realized that he no longer had the right to be there at his son's side.

After what seemed like an eternity, Chris could see his son moving his head and arms. Corbin slowly got to his feet to the roar of the crowd. His teammates gathered around him, patting him on the back as he limped gingerly off the field. When Corbin saw Sarah, they embraced, and then Sarah's companion joined in the group hug. The scene was more than Chris could bear. He loved his son and realized that he still had feelings for Sarah, but he also knew painfully that they were lost to him now.

I should never have come today, he thought as he wiped away a tear from his eye and headed back to Leon's car.

*   *   *

"Finally," Joanne McKay said exhaling triumphantly as she jogged down the access path on M Street, NW, and onto the bike path that ran through Rock Creek Park. The park was a large, wooded, linear oasis that was nearly a mile wide in places and ran north through the middle of the nation's capital.

Things had been crazy the past week in Senator Goodman's office, and McKay had been unable to get out for a run since Monday. On top of everything else, EPA's pending decision on EMCO's application to market EZ-15 was generating all kinds of calls, e-mails, and visitors to the senator's office—mainly by those who favored EPA approval.

Normally, McKay would have been happy because now that EPA was close to approving the EMCO application, the pressure on Senator Goodman to get involved would diminish or even disappear. And as a result, it would make her life as a key staff person assigned to the EZ-15 application issue a little saner. But as she ran up the bike path and deeper into the park, she couldn't get rid of the nagging feeling that she hadn't seen the last of the whole matter.

McKay ran her normal route, which went out about four miles north and then back. As she neared her favorite stretch on the bike path, she glanced at her watch. It was already 8:00 p.m. "I'll pick up the pace and be home by 8:30," she declared.

Usually, even this late on a Saturday evening, she would pass at least a few fellow runners coming in the opposite direction, but it was a chilly and damp evening, and she saw no one. Deep in thought, she failed to notice some movement directly ahead in the bushes to the left of the path. Three strides later, she was hit waist-high with such a force that she flew into the air and crashed down hard on her back in a pile of brush four feet off the path.

Before she could regain her senses, her assailant, dressed in black and wearing a hooded ski mask, jumped on top of her and put a six-inch bladed knife to her exposed neck. With his other hand, he forcibly cupped her mouth. The back of McKay's head throbbed from the impact, and she felt for a moment she would lose consciousness. But she willed herself to stay focused.

The assailant pushed the knife deeper against her neck but pulled his hand off her mouth, motioning her with his finger to remain silent. He seemed to hesitate, and she spoke, "If you think you're going to rape me, you'll have to kill me first, and believe me, that's not going to be easy."

The assailant just stared at her with his dark brown eyes. Finally, he spoke. "I'm not interested in sex, and if you answer my questions honestly, you'll come to no harm."

The voice of the man in the ski mask was vaguely familiar, and then it hit her. "Chris? ... Chris O'Brian, is that you? What the hell are you doing? Let me up."

"Not until you tell me the truth. I know you or someone in Senator Goodman's office is directly or indirectly responsible for the murder of Jackie Goldberg," Chris said in a menacing yet eerily calm voice.

"Chris, you're crazy. Goldberg's death was an accident," McKay pleaded.

"Don't play dumb with me," Chris replied as he again pushed the knife against her neck and again cupped her mouth, both of his hands shaking in anger.

"I confided in you when we were in Brussels that Goldberg wasn't going to give up without a fight on EZ-15. No one but you and I knew that. But three days later, EMCO lobbyist Stanley Braxton gets a call from Senator Goodman's office telling him that Jackie intended to fight EPA's approval of EZ-15 and telling Braxton to take care of it. That night Jackie was murdered."

"That's crap," McKay mumbled, twisting her head free of Chris's grasp.

"That's not the answer I was looking for, Joanne. Either tell me the truth or I swear I'll cut your throat," Chris threatened as he put his other hand on around Joanne's throat.

"Okay. Okay, let's talk like rational human beings. Can you loosen your death grip? I can barely breathe," she gasped. "Chris, I'm on your side. Believe me."

Chris loosened his grip and let down his guard. Joanne had maneuvered her right leg so she could deliver a kick. With tremendous force, she kneed Chris in his groin, but instead of Chris screaming in pain, it was McKay who cried out—she felt like her knee had crashed into a stone wall.

As McKay writhed in pain, Chris said smugly, "I remembered that you bragged in Europe about your martial arts skills, so I wore a steel athletic cup just in case," Chris said triumphantly even though his protective device didn't completely prevent him from feeling some pain.

Then he slid further up her body so he could pin down her arms in case she planned to make another move. But in doing so, he freed her legs just enough. In one motion, McKay swung her left leg out to her side, raised it, and delivered a crushing blow to the right side of Chris's head. The force of the blow knocked him off her and caused Chris to drop the knife. With cat-like speed, McKay turned the tables, jumped on top of Chris, and now held the knife under his chin.

"For the record, if I was one of the bad guys, I could shove this knife into your heart. I could claim self-defense, and that would end the matter. After all, you're the fugitive from justice," she said forcibly. "Chris, I meant what I said. I'm on your side. Can we get up and talk about this?"

"Looks like I don't have a choice in the matter," Chris said cautiously, hoping that McKay might actually be telling the truth.

They both got up, McKay rubbing her knee, and Chris rubbing the right side of his head that was turning red and starting to bruise. Walking about ten feet to a park bench along the path, they sat down. Chris, noticing that McKay was shaking from the cold, took off his black sweatshirt and gave it to her.

"Chris, take off that ridiculous ski mask. I know what you look like," McKay said.

"Not anymore you don't."

McKay shook her head in frustration and dropped the subject.

Chris then suggested that she go first, and McKay reluctantly agreed.

"I did tell Senator Goodman when I returned from Brussels that Jackie Goldberg intended to fight approval of EZ-15. And, contrary to all of the press reports that he's anxious for EPA approval, my boss has his own concerns about the extraordinary pressure being put on EPA to rush it through."

"Was anyone there besides you and Senator Goodman when this information was passed along?"

"Only Damon Kowalski, Senator Goodman's chief of staff. But Damon is completely loyal to Goodman, and he would never—"

"Where were you, the senator, and Kowalski last Monday morning?" Chris interrupted.

McKay looked perplexed but answered, "The three of us were at a committee hearing all morning." But then on further thought, she added, "Damon did leave the hearing room briefly around ten thirty, which was a little odd because the most important witness was in the middle of her testimony."

Joanne turned and looked at Chris. "Let me guess—someone called Braxton around ten thirty to tell him about Goldberg."

Chris simply nodded. It was Chris's turn, but he chose his words carefully and only revealed enough information to convince McKay that she and Senator Goodman were right in having doubts about EZ-15 and that sinister forces were at work to ensure the EZ-15 approval.

After he had finished, she pleaded, "Chris, come on, I know there's a lot you aren't telling me. I want to help."

"Let's take this one step at a time. Tell me something I don't know, and we'll go from there."

"Okay. EPA is—" Joanne started to speak, but Chris interrupted her and finished the sentence.

"EPA is going to approve the EZ-15 application on Monday."

"How could you possibly know that? Senator Goodman only found out at five o'clock yesterday."

Chris offered no explanation but said, "Joanne, talk to your boss. I need a visible sign from Senator Goodman that he isn't buying into the EZ-15 crap. If you can get him to deliver, I'll be back in touch with a lot more information. In the meantime, don't trust Kowalski."

He then asked for and got Joanne's cell phone number. "You can't reach me. I'll call you."

It was nearly 9:00 p.m. Chris offered to give Joanne a ride back to her apartment, but she refused. "I need to do some thinking, and I think best when I'm running."

Chris patted Joanne on the back and said, "Sorry about my approach to initiating tonight's conversation. Keep my sweatshirt."

"I'll survive, but I'm not sorry about cracking you on the head with my leg," she replied.

As they parted, Chris called out to Joanne, "Watch your back."

CHAPTER 34

April 23
Prince George's County, Maryland—Evening

On the drive back to the farmhouse, Chris replayed everything that had happened that day. Rubbing his face where McKay had kicked him, Chris had to admit to himself that she was one tough female. He admired her courage, and more important, he now felt she was someone he could trust. He hoped his instincts were correct.

Looking at his watch as he approached the gate at the farmhouse driveway, Chris swore aloud when he saw it was well after 10:00 p.m. He knew Chet would be furious at him for leaving the farmhouse.

As Chris drove up the driveway to the farmhouse, he could see Sonja standing on the porch directly under the overhanging porch light. Her hands were on her hips. At first, she somehow looked taller, and he thought she might have on a pair of high heels. But as the car came to a stop, and Chris got out, he could see she had sandals on. Then it occurred to him that Sonja was standing perfectly straight with her shoulders back. He was so used to seeing her hunched over with her poor posture at EPA that standing there on the porch erect, she appeared much taller.

Sonja looked striking in the light of the front porch and appeared happy to see him. She came running to him, and he fully expected a warm welcome embrace. What Chris received was quite the opposite.

Sonja swung her fists furiously at him, pounding on his chest. "How could you do this? I was, I mean, we were worried sick ... I ... we thought something terrible had happened to you. I hate you for this." Sonja then turned, tears in her eyes, and stormed back into the farmhouse.

Hearing the commotion, several people gathered at the front door. But as Chris walked up to the porch stairs and entered the living room, everyone scattered, leaving Chris alone to face Chet.

"What the hell were you thinking, Chris?" Chet roared, his eyes glaring. "We're supposed to be a team. Each of us must be able to depend on and trust the other. We're dealing with some truly ruthless people, and all of us are in unspeakable danger. We can't afford for anyone, including you, to go rogue."

Chet continued his verbal lashing for another few minutes and refused to give Chris any chance to explain or defend his actions. When Chet was finally finished, Chris felt like he had been taken to the woodshed.

Finally, Chris was given the opportunity to explain where he had been all day and why he didn't tell anyone. Chet listened but made clear his feelings that Chris's decision to leave without telling anyone first was completely unjustified.

"I'm truly sorry, Chet. It won't happen again," Chris said quietly.

He turned to leave, but Chet called out, "Wait." Chet's mood changed, and he spoke quietly, pointing in the direction in which Sonja had gone. "After everything that has happened to that young woman over the past two weeks, she's barely hanging on by a thread. It's none of my business what's going on between you two, but it's pretty damn clear to me that she's depending on you. She was a complete basket case after you went AWOL this morning. She sat on the porch all day and evening waiting for you to return. Otto sat with her for most of the time and tried to provide comfort, but she simply was too distressed.

"Chris, I think you're a good guy, and I'll always be in debt to you for saving Leon and Tanya, but damn it, you're not the only one hurting here. It's time you got over yourself and started thinking and acting like the other people here matter too. You're great at strategy and giving orders, but showing a little compassion and appreciation wouldn't hurt." Having said his piece, Chet turned and headed to his bedroom.

Chris stood alone in the middle of the living room. He felt empty and lost. Trying to clear all the conflicting, troubling thoughts that were raging within him, he walked out of the farmhouse.

After the verbal dress down from Chet, Chris was hoping he would have the chance to be alone. But there sitting on the porch steps with their shirts off, which was a little odd since the temperatures had fallen below fifty degrees, sat Casey Randolph and Otto Simpson, with Billy McGuiness in the middle. From behind, the three buddies looked like two, huge, black granite rocks on either side of a thin slab of pale white limestone. They were obviously drinking something.

"Mind if I join you?" Chris asked.

"Hell no, have a seat," Casey said and then handed Chris a flask. "Have a drink. You look like you need it."

Chris hadn't had a swallow of alcohol since his dinner with Pamela Russell, but after all that had happened this day, it sounded mighty tempting. "I thought Chet frowned on having alcohol around," he said as he took a large gulp.

"What the hell is this?" Chris choked as he handed the flask back to Casey.

"Sweet apple cider, my friend," Casey answered. He laughed and added, "We're all alcoholics here. Thanks to Chet, I haven't had a drink in fifteen years."

Billy chimed in, "I'm an alcoholic, and I haven't had a drink for twenty years."

"Hell, I'm the biggest alcoholic of the bunch, and I haven't had a drink since 1982," Otto added.

"Then I guess I'm the newbie. I'm an alcoholic, and I haven't had a drink in about ten days," Chris said. While he was trying to be funny, it was the first time Chris had actually admitted to himself that he indeed had a drinking problem. With that realization, Chris resolved never to drink alcohol again.

Changing subjects, Otto turned to Chris and said, "Sounds like Chet read you the riot act in there."

"He verbally smacked me around pretty good. But I guess I deserved it."

"Chet's a great guy, and believe me, he meant well. His problem is he cares too much about the people around him, and sometimes he goes a little over the top," Billy replied.

"The simple fact is that the three of us and Freddie wouldn't be here today if it hadn't been for Chet," Casey added.

"Chet mentioned you guys were in Vietnam together."

"I'm pretty sure, knowing Chet, he didn't come close to telling you the whole, ugly truth about the final days in Vietnam. I think you need to know to fully appreciate the man that Chet Jones is and why the three of us and Freddie would do anything for him," Casey said, and without taking a breath, he began.

"Let's see, in 1975 … Chris, you were probably still in diapers, so you have no real recollection of the Vietnam War. All you know is what you've read, and my guess is you haven't read much."

"Guilty as charged," Chris said, somewhat embarrassed.

"The war in Vietnam was a complete cluster fuck. By the 1970s, the war was winding down, and most folks in America had completely lost interest in what was happening in Vietnam. By then, even the US soldiers in Vietnam knew the war could never be won and that the United States would soon pull out of Vietnam. Every soldier's mantra was: 'I don't want to be the last American GI killed in Vietnam.' Morale was horrible—drug addiction, emotional trauma, or combinations of both were commonplace. Not a great situation for a bunch of black MPs trying to maintain some semblance of order not only among our fellow GIs, but also among the Vietnamese citizens with whom we interacted."

Casey then went on to explain what happened to Chet's squad the days in April 1975 when Saigon collapsed. "You've probably seen those famous film clips of crowds of desperate Vietnamese people loyal to the United States climbing the walls of the US embassy in Saigon to escape the Communist forces. Our squad had been assigned to provide security in the general vicinity of the embassy. Total chaos ruled; gunshots came from every direction. Who was shooting—civilians, Vietcong, South Vietnamese army regulars, or all of the above, we didn't have a clue. The entire area had become a killing zone.

"We circled and created a defensive perimeter behind two partially destroyed vehicles. Then we saw a group of six school children, no older than seven or eight, wandering into the open street. Not far from them was the bloody body of a young woman who probably was their teacher. We raced into the street and carried the children back behind our barricade.

"We got the kids to crouch down as the intensity of gunfire and explosions grew. Then Chet yelled out that our only hope for survival was to try to escape. Each of us took off our helmets and flak jackets and put them on the children. We each grabbed and held a child with one arm and cradled our M-16s with our other arm," Casey explained, but then he choked up and couldn't continue.

Otto picked up the tale. "Within seconds, we came under fire, and the carnage began. The two boys from Mississippi were killed by mortar fire. They might have survived if they hadn't given their flak jackets and helmets to the kids. But, with Chet leading the way, we somehow fought our way through five blocks of intense enemy fire. In the process, Chet spotted and shot three snipers. Finally, we reached the American compound. The kids and the rest of us survived, but Billy here was shot twice in the hip, and Dyson Parker had his left leg blown off by a grenade."

Chris couldn't help but look at Billy, who was staring down at the ground, *My God, that explains why Billy looks so frail and walks with a limp.*

"At least Chet got the Bronze Star," Chris said somewhat meekly.

"What a joke that was. Do you know that lots of the army desk jockeys in Vietnam in the midseventies got bronze stars for so-called service in Vietnam for doing nothing more than spending a year in Vietnam behind a typewriter and staying out of trouble? Chet should have gotten the medal of honor," Otto said indignantly.

Billy then picked up the story. "Those of us who made it home had a horrible time readjusting to civilian life. Drugs, booze, and no jobs became part of our daily lifestyle. But one by one, Chet found us, helped dry us out, and found jobs for all of us. Over the years, each of us had moments of relapse, but Chet was always there to get us back on our feet."

When the men finished their remarkable tale, an awkward silence hung in the air. Chris struggled to say something, but his expression was more than enough to let his colleagues know that he had been deeply touched by their sacrifices and struggles.

As the three men walked into the farmhouse, Chris remained on the porch, alone. His amazement at the sacrifices and heroism that these men shared morphed into a self-realization that for his entire life, he had pretty much always put himself first and blamed others for any failures he had.

At that very moment, Chris became overwhelmed with a renewed sense of purpose and focus to protect his comrades and to crush the EMCO EZ-15 conspiracy—whatever it took. For the first time in his life, he truly accepted and embraced the fact that he couldn't survive alone; he needed other people, and they needed him.

*   *   *

Chris went up to his room, showered, and proceeded to toss and turn for at least two hours—replaying everything that had happened to him and trying to make sense of it all.

Finally, he fell into a deep sleep, only to awake suddenly with a start. Someone was in his room. His mind raced, but his body remained still. Had he made a mistake yesterday? Had someone followed him back to the farmhouse? He had been such a fool. He never should have gone to the soccer game or confronted McKay. Now he and everyone else in the farmhouse were about to pay the consequences of his stupidity.

Chris had one chance—the .45-caliber pistol he kept under his pillow. He often thought he was being silly to keep it there, but maybe this one time it would pay off. Slowly he slid his hand under his pillow, carefully grabbed the gun, and put his finger on the trigger. *Should I shoot first or confront the intruder?*

In one quick motion, he sprang out of the bed and pointed the gun at the unseen intruder, "Freeze, motherfucker!"

"And hello to you too, asshole," the intruder said in a strangely calm voice.

"Sonja?" Chris asked with a mix of confusion and relief. "You nearly scared me to death."

"Good. Then I guess we're even. I was totally freaked out yesterday. I didn't know if you're okay or dead."

"I'm sorry about yesterday. I didn't mean to cause you distress. I just needed to take care of a few things," he said quietly.

"Look, I've been more honest with you than anyone ever before in my entire life. I've told you things that were extremely painful for me to relive. Do you have any comprehension how difficult that was for me? And how do you pay me back," Sonja replied, with a touch of anger in her voice. "Christopher O'Brian, just who the hell are you?"

After a brief hesitation, Chris sat on his bed and replied thoughtfully, "Okay, you asked for it, and maybe it's for the best that you get the full story. You may think a whole lot less of me, but so be it."

Chris told Sonja everything. Not just about the soccer game, his son, and his wife, but his confrontation with Joanne and a lot more. He went back to the beginning about how he met his wife, their romance, marriage, and breakup. He painfully described his slow-spiraling decent into hell. How he planned but failed to end it all—and much, much more.

Sonja's response surprised Chris. She had come over and sat on the end of his bed as he began his tale. When he finished, she wept quietly, climbed into his bed, and whispered to him, "My God, Chris, I had no idea how incredibly fucked up you were. You were always such a snobby, confident prick at EPA." Then she gently kissed him on the cheek and said, "I can't make it without you, but maybe together—"

Chris interrupted her midsentence and kissed her gently on her lips. What followed was the most amazing lovemaking either of them had ever experienced. There was passion to be sure, but more than that was a wonderful sense of tenderness, vulnerability, and understanding. While they both experienced an amazing climax, it was the shared journey to that point that deeply and irreversibly touched them both. Exhausted and totally spent, they fell into a deep sleep closely together.

Several hours later, Sonja awoke first and had difficulty finding her clothes, so she slipped on her panties and grabbed Chris's oversized T-shirt. She tiptoed quietly down the stairs, hoping she could slip by unnoticed back into her room behind the kitchen.

As she walked through the kitchen, a familiar voice rang out. "Last night, I was worried that Chris wasn't concerned enough about your welfare. I gather that's not really an issue anymore," Chet, sitting at the kitchen table in the early-morning light, said quietly.

Sonja's face turned bright crimson in embarrassment, and she could barely speak. "Chet, I'm so sorry. I know you have strict rules of conduct, but—"

"Look, I know you all think I'm old-fashioned, and maybe I am, but the truth is that me and the misses, in our youth, did some things I doubt our parents would have approved of. I'm not in charge of morality here. All I can say is it's obvious to me that you two need each other, and the rest of us are depending on you both to help us survive this nightmare. Be good and be honest with each other—if you do, and with a little bit of luck, maybe we'll actually make it through all this."

Sonja went up to Chet and gave him a great big hug and a gentle kiss on his cheek. "Thanks. We won't let you and the Crew down." With that, she walked back to her room and had the best sleep she could remember in years.

CHAPTER 35

April 25
Silver Spring, Maryland

As he walked down the sidewalk, Cavanaugh recalled the miserable weekend he had endured. He had been called in the middle of the night by the police to come to the county jail and bail his worthless son out for drunk driving. For the rest of the weekend, he had endured the unending complaints of his wife. On top of that, his young mistress, who he supported financially, had stood him up. Now first thing Monday morning he had to meet with Petrovic, and Cavanaugh had nothing positive to report.

Cavanaugh arrived first at a coffee shop in Silver Spring, Maryland, just north of Washington. It was convenient for both, easy to get to, seldom crowded, and the coffee was decent. He was relieved that Petrovic hadn't yet arrived. Making Petrovic wait was never a good idea. Finally, Petrovic walked in, sat down, and without saying hello, barked, "Well?"

Cavanaugh reported that despite the stepped-up investigation, which was now official, the FBI had no solid leads in finding either O'Brian or Voinovich. Cavanaugh noted that the questioning of fellow EPA employees revealed that O'Brian and Voinovich weren't friends and didn't interact other than professionally.

"Each staff member we spoke to went out of their way to say how shocked they were that Chapman, O'Brian, or Voinovich would be involved in a conspiracy to doctor EPA data files.

"We also interviewed Ted Bennett, and he played the role of the innocent supervisor. But he went out of his way to accuse O'Brian and Voinovich of being involved in the conspiracy with Chapman. He claimed he was always suspicious of the three of them. Frankly, he overdid it, and I think Bennett is a loose cannon who thinks he's smarter than he is. We've got to make sure from now on he keeps his mouth shut," Cavanaugh said.

"I'll take care of Mr. Bennett if it becomes necessary. What else have you got on O'Brian?"

Cavanaugh went on to explain that he and Adams talked with O'Brian's wife, and she indicated that she hadn't spoken with or heard from him in over a year.

"While it was clear there was no love lost between her and her former husband, the woman didn't hide her annoyance at being disturbed at home and being subjected to endless questioning. After forty minutes, we came away with absolutely nothing. I think we can forget about her. We also searched O'Brian's apartment again, this time armed with a legitimate search warrant. We spoke to neighbors in the condo and opened and read his mail. But those efforts yielded nothing as well."

Petrovic stared at Cavanaugh, the displeasure at the lack of progress in the FBI investigation clearly evident on his stern face.

"We did track down his financial adviser. A guy named Daniel Witt, who told us that O'Brian had sold about $300,000 in stock and took the proceeds in cash on that Monday he returned from Europe. We've put a wiretap on Witt's phone."

"With that kind of money, O'Brian can dig himself a pretty big hole to hide in," Petrovic responded.

"From everything we've learned about O'Brian, he's not exactly the hero type. Maybe he's tried to get as far away from DC as possible and no longer poses a risk to us," the FBI agent offered up hopefully.

"Maybe, but we can't take any chances. Keep searching for the guy, and once you find him, you know what to do."

Cavanaugh simply nodded and then turned to the status of the search for Sonja Voinovich. "We searched her apartment but found nothing helpful. We also talked to her roommates and members of a band she performs with on occasion, but none of them knew the woman particularly well and had no idea where she might have gone.

"We checked about Voinovich's family. She was raised in Buffalo, but both of her parents are dead, and she apparently has no siblings or other relatives—she's just disappeared. Frankly, from what we know about the girl, my guess is she's not likely to cause us any problems," Cavanaugh said quietly.

Almost as an afterthought, Cavanaugh added, "Oh, there was one odd thing we came across in running a background check using Voinovich's fingerprints. But it's probably nothing—just some kind of error or something."

"What?" Petrovic said impatiently.

"The fingerprint background check revealed another name with the identical fingerprints—someone named Katrina Zimmer. This person, Zimmer, came to the United States from Germany as a child in the 1990s, and she was fingerprinted when she entered the country. Apparently, she died shortly afterward."

Petrovic replied without emotion, "Yes, that kind of stuff happens all too often—probably some kind of bureaucratic screw-up. Don't waste any more time on Zimmer. Put a wiretap on O'Brian's wife's home and office phones. Do the same for Voinovich's two roommates and the members of her band."

When the meeting between Cavanaugh and Petrovic came to an end and Cavanaugh had left, Petrovic lingered for a few moments, trying to absorb what he had just learned. Katrina Zimmer, daughter of Harold and Gertrude Zimmer, hadn't died that night during the horrific explosion Petrovic had orchestrated two decades before. Somehow she had survived and was now living under the name of Sonja Voinovich.

Petrovic lifted a steel sugar shaker, crushed it with his bare hand, and stormed out of the coffee shop. He understood well that Voinovich not only posed a threat to keeping EZ-15 on track to commercial introduction, but more important, she also could destroy him.

CHAPTER 36

April 25
Prince George's County, Maryland

While Petrovic and Cavanaugh held their clandestine meeting, Chris buried his head in a copy of the Sunday *Herald*. Checking the stock page, he saw that the EMCO stock price had risen, and Cloverleaf's value had dropped. Also he saw that Conrad Martin, Chris's old boss at EPA, had been named acting general counsel.

Leon, who was reading a follow-up article in the Monday online *Herald* on the Ronnie Chapman EZ-15 conspiracy story, noticed something also and called out, "Chris, Sonja, come here. There's a photo of a guy here who looks like one of the guys from your condo's security video feed that we got."

Chris and Sonja rushed across the room from opposite ends and positioned themselves behind the chair where Leon was sitting so they could look at what Leon had found. As the two crowded behind the chair, their bodies touched, and Chris, without thinking, put his arm around Sonja to make space so they both could see the article.

Rather than pull away, Sonja raised her arm up and gently put her hand on top of Chris's—a simple, innocent gesture had broken, at least somewhat, the awkwardness felt previously by both since their intimate encounter Saturday night.

The picture showed a group of people standing behind FBI Chief Calvin Wiseman. Sonja exclaimed, "That's definitely the same guy who chased and tried to grab me in the alley."

"And he's the jerk who broke into my condo—five days before you and I were officially named persons of interest in the FBI investigation.

That can only mean that this guy and his partner are FBI agents, and rogue agents to boot."

The photo identified the person in question as FBI agent Michael Cavanaugh, the lead investigator in the Ronnie Chapman conspiracy case. Chris, without speaking, walked over to the cork board and wrote on Cavanaugh's notecard "definitely FBI" and did the same on Adam's notecard.

When things settled down, Chris grabbed a cell phone from the box, went outside, and called Daniel Witt. "Hello, Robin, this is Christopher O'Brian. May I speak to Dan?"

"Mr. O'Brian, Mr. Witt isn't currently available. Would you like to call back or you may hold for a moment," she replied in a very business-like manner.

"I'll hold, thank you," Chris replied in an equally formal manner. Chris knew that in all the years he had dealt with Witt's assistant, she had never called him Mr. O'Brian simply because Chris had insisted from the first time they met that she call him by his first name.

Something's up, Chris thought.

Finally, Chris was connected with Witt. "Good morning, Mr. O'Brian. How may I be of assistance?"

Dan's tone confirmed Chris's suspicion, and he asked a question for which both he and Dan knew the answer. "I was calling to ascertain the cash balance in my FMA account."

"Allow me to check," Dan replied, and several moments later, he said, "Five thousand, the minimum amount needed to keep the account open. Was there anything else you needed?"

"No," Chris replied.

"Before we end this conversation, I must advise you that I was visited last Friday by a Mr. Michael Cavanaugh and a Mr. Richard Adams, both from the FBI. They've advised me that you have been named as a person of interest in an ongoing investigation into alleged tampering of government documentation. They've requested that in the event you contact me, that I inform you to contact them immediately at 202.555.1243. Also, as they have requested, I'm duty bound to notify them that you contacted me."

Chris hung up without uttering another word and decommissioned the cell phone. He knew the formality with which both Dan and Robin conversed constituted their attempt to let him know that Witt might be under surveillance and that his phone very well could be tapped.

Chris needed to get in touch with Witt, but thanks to Dan's warning, he knew he couldn't use conventional methods to communicate. He grabbed a blank piece of paper and wrote detailed instructions to Witt regarding the sale of certain stocks, the opening of a number of offshore accounts, the names to be listed on each account, and how the cash generated from the sale of the securities should be invested. He included in his instructions the dates that the transactions should occur.

Chris then addressed an envelope to Witt's home address with a phony return address. Chris hoped that the FBI would not be checking Witt's personal mail at home and that they would have lost interest in Witt by the time he executed the transactions. The only catch was whether Witt, upon receiving the instructions, would follow through on executing Chris's request.

By 10:00 a.m. all members of the Crew were engaged in various tasks. As they had done in previous days, the routine would be to gather and report in the late afternoon. They planned first to watch on C-SPAN the EPA announcement approving EMCO's application to sell EZ-15 in the United States and then provide their individual reports.

During lunch, Tanya approached Chris, holding a stack of typed pages in her hand. "I thought I would try to chronicle everything that's happened regarding EMCO and EZ-15," she said as she handed him the document and walked away without waiting for a reply.

After lunch, Chris went to his room to read her document. When he returned an hour later, he said to Tanya, "This is an amazing piece of work."

As 4:30 p.m. approached—the time for the press announcement on EZ-15—Chet turned on the TV. He found C-SPAN, which was covering the event live, and hit the record button.

"Everyone, gather around and watch for anything that might be useful to us," Chris declared.

After a brief voiceover announced C-SPAN was about to join a live press event at the White House, the feed picked up a group of people standing in the Rose Garden, with the White House in the background. After a few moments, a gentleman in his early sixties stepped to the microphone.

"Good afternoon, everyone. My name is Bingeman Foster, President Keller's chief of staff. Today is a truly historic day in the ongoing international effort to reduce the threat of global warming and climate change. I am truly honored to be appearing here as a stand-in for President Keller. As you all know, the president has a long-standing commitment to make the earth's environment safer for all of its inhabitants, and he would very much have liked to be here in person. However, as you also know, President Keller is in the Middle East, meeting with Arab and Israeli leaders and working to reduce the tensions that have flared up in recent months. You might say he's working to reduce a different kind of heat in that part of the world."

Everyone laughed and clapped at Foster's renowned wit.

"Today, I'm here to announce that the US Environmental Protection Agency, after a rigorous review, has approved EMCO Consolidated Company's application to market its greenhouse gas emission-reduction product, EZ-15. This product, which is a proprietary chemical emulsion, is designed to be added to gasoline at the end of the gasoline refining process. EZ-15 is currently being used on a test basis in Tokyo and Osaka and has demonstrated the ability to significantly reduce carbon dioxide emissions. With EPA's approval today, the Keller administration anticipates that EZ-15 will soon be added to all grades of gasoline sold in the United States and that, consequently, the levels of CO_2 emissions from motor vehicles will drop dramatically.

"We are standing here today as a result of the cooperative efforts of industry, EPA, Congress, and this administration. Today, the United States once again shows the rest of the world what can be accomplished when we all work together in a democracy."

Foster next introduced those standing on the podium: Newton Hill, EPA administrator; Ted Bennett, EPA assistant administrator for air quality; Chester Martin, now acting EPA general counsel; Congressman Alan Beasley, chairman of the House Environment Committee; Franklin Moss, Congressman Beasley's chief of staff; Barbara Simon, Protect the Environment Consortium; and Jorgen Johansson, CEO of EMCO.

Newton Hill, Congressman Beasley, Johansson, and Simon each made a short statement, patting themselves on their backs for the important role they had played. The press was given only a brief time to ask questions, and the event concluded about fifteen minutes after it began as Foster thanked everyone for attending.

Chet was about to turn off the TV when Sonja yelled, "Keep it running."

When the coverage ended and the feed was cut back to the promo for the next event to be aired on C-SPAN, Sonja said, "Okay. You can turn it off."

Chris turned to the group and said, "Well, what do you think?"

Sonja was quick to reply, "Well, I think the whole thing was a complete pile of crap: President Keller has completely ignored environmental issues during his entire term of office; regulated industries only cooperate with EPA when they get their way; and the so-called independent press decided to join in the mutual love fest over EZ-15 and failed to ask even one halfway probing question."

"Ms. Voinovich, I am sure no one here disagrees with your sentiments, but do you have anything constructive to add?" Chris asked sarcastically.

"As a matter of fact, Captain Crunch, I do," Sonja said with a wry smile, and everyone, including Chris, sat back to listen.

"As any EPA employee who works on industry applications to introduce a product into the United States will tell you, a company that has filed an application for product approval is entitled to only six hours' advance notice before the decision is announced publicly. To disclose this information sooner to the regulated industry is a violation of the EPA Code of Ethics. Jorgen Johansson, EMCO's chief executive office, no doubt operates out of the corporate offices in Brussels. But he just happens to be in Washington, DC, when the announcement is made. My guess is that someone, probably Stanley Braxton, gave him advance notice, as I'll explain in a minute.

"Next, no one from Senator Goodman's office was there. One would expect that someone from the office of the chairman of the Senate Environment Committee would be present at such an event. More important, Senator Goodman never misses an opportunity to grab a little media coverage. So, missing this event was uncharacteristic of the senator, to say the least. Chris, I would have to say that your Saturday night in the park with McKay paid off. I think Goodman's office sent you a pretty clear message.

"Finally, I think Keller's chief of staff may be one of the bad guys."

"Sonja, that's just plain ridiculous. Jackie Goldberg trusted Foster. They were close friends, and she listed him as one of the good guys," Chris protested.

"Chet, rewind the recording to the point where Foster thanks everyone for attending the event," Sonja replied.

When the segment was rerun, it showed Stanley Braxton going up to Johansson and shaking his hand and whispering something in his ear, at which point both men appeared to chuckle. Moments later, Foster walked over to Braxton and shook his hand. Braxton smiled broadly and patted Foster on the back. It was clear that Braxton and Foster knew each other.

"Sonja, what can I say? You may have a point," Chris said contritely. Changing the subject, he added, "Let's break for dinner and pick up our discussions after we've had a bite to eat."

As everyone got up to leave, Chris walked over to Sonja, put his arm on her shoulder, and whispered, "You're amazing. I'm glad you're on our side."

Without acknowledging his affectionate gesture, she said firmly, "We need to talk now and in private. Meet me on the porch in ten minutes, and we'll take a run. We can eat later."

CHAPTER 37

April 25
Prince George's County, Maryland—Evening

When Sonja arrived on the porch minutes later, Chris couldn't help staring. Her newly purchased blue spandex running pants and matching, tight-fitting nylon shirt showcased her athletic figure.

"Stop staring at me and let's go," Sonja said as she jogged off.

The pace was slower than Chris's normal routine to enable Sonja to keep up. For the next twenty minutes, they ran in silence. Chris figured Sonja would speak when she was ready, but as they approached the farmhouse on their return, he couldn't wait any longer and finally asked, "What did you want to tell me?"

Sonja stopped running and, after hesitating for a moment, said, "Chris, our early Sunday morning encounter was amazing, and being with you truly touched me in a way I've never experienced before. When I left your room, I never felt more alive. But, for reasons we both know, it can't happen again."

As they stepped up to the porch, Chris said quietly, "I understand what you're saying." But he understood absolutely nothing—he didn't understand why they couldn't continue to make love or how he truly felt about the young woman standing beside him.

*   *   *

Around seven o'clock, the Crew started getting situated for the evening meeting. Using another cell, Chris took the opportunity to check his messages and found a text message from Robert Levy.

When he opened it, he called out, "Sonja, come take a look. Not good news."

Sonja came over and sat next to Chris as he handed her the phone with the message. "So, Petrovic is a consultant with the Department of Homeland Security. How nice for him," she said without an ounce of fear and only resolve in her voice. Then she added, "Let's get the damn meeting started."

Chris kicked things off. "I received a text message from Levy at the *Herald*. Petrovic is tied to the DHS."

Everyone turned and stared at Sonja. She knew what they all were thinking and said, "I'm okay. It's going to make it easier for me to find and annihilate the bastard when I'm ready."

Next, Otto, Casey, and Ronnie put down boxes containing additional cell phones and computers. Chris had given Chet an additional $25,000 several days before to cover the growing expenses of the operation.

"Sonja, Leon, and Tanya, we need you to download everything important from the computers you have been using and then upload them onto these other computers. Then we'll destroy the hard drives of the old computers," Billy said. "If the DHS is in any way involved in trying to locate Chris and Sonja, we need to redouble our efforts to make sure we don't make any careless mistakes that could result in the US surveillance network tracking us down. Let's just say U-boat EZ-15 is going to have to submerge farther below sea level."

"Wait," Sonja interrupted. "Before you dismantle the computers, I'd like to try to access Ted Bennett's computer using the EPA access code Jackie Goldberg provided Chris. I'm sure Bennett or someone has tampered with the original EPA test data on EZ-15 that led Ronnie to his conclusions. If that's true, we'll have some very powerful evidence against the conspirators."

"Good idea, Sonja. But as soon as you're finished, let me know. We need to take that computer out of service immediately, so no one can track us down," Billy replied.

Without speaking, Sonja got up, went over to one of the computers, and began the process of trying to access Ted Bennett's computer.

Leon was next and reported that the shares of EMCO continued to rise on Friday, and again on Monday, not only on the US market, but the European and Asian markets as well.

"Looks like the Heritage Study Group boys and a few of their closest friends went on a buying spree after the Thursday meeting," Leon said.

"Wait till you see what happens to the EMCO stock tomorrow," Chris chimed in.

Tanya reported that the incidents of asthma attacks in Tokyo and Osaka continued to increase, and the death toll for the last month had risen to nearly seven thousand, mostly children and elderly people. Japanese officials had concluded that the rate of increase in asthma attacks could be explained by the hotter-than-normal ambient temperatures and a very high spring pollen count.

Tanya then added, "That theory is a complete load of crap according to the World Health Watch Center, but the Center couldn't offer an alternative explanation for the dramatic increase in asthma attacks or the related deaths. For a story this significant, it's amazing how little media attention it's getting. No one, and I mean no one, has made the connection between the increase in asthma attacks and limited use of EZ-15."

Chris went to the blackboard and in big letters wrote the number 30. "We have thirty days starting today to come up with the evidence EPA will need to withhold final approval of EZ-15. Up until the review period ends on May 24, new and credible evidence calling into question either the efficacy of EZ-15 or the potential adverse side effects may still be submitted to EPA. If EPA decides this new information is credible, the agency can delay final approval and stay the introduction of EZ-15 into commerce until the agency issues a revised decision."

Then Chris laid out the tasks at hand. "We need to do three things: we need to come up with the scientific evidence and a logical explanation for the link between the use of EZ-15 and those asthma attacks and related deaths; we need to continue to develop the documentation linking our growing list of bad guys to the variety of heinous crimes that have been and are being committed; and finally, we need to identify and work with some allies to make our case and publicize the story at the appropriate time.

"With regard to number one, at some point I'm heading out to find Karl Thurgensen, who's probably one of the greatest scientists in his field. He was last reported to be residing somewhere in southwest

Virginia. If anyone can find the link between EZ-15 and what's happening in Osaka, as well as Tokyo, he's the guy. If he can come up with a credible theory, the next step is to go to Los Angeles and have the California Air Resources Board test out his theory. Then—"

"Wait a minute. I thought we agreed earlier that you and I would go together to find Thurgensen," Sonja, who had returned to the group, interrupted angrily.

"We'll talk about that later. I—"

"There's nothing to discuss. I'm going, period," Sonja interrupted again and smacked Chris hard on his upper arm with her clenched fist. "You're such a pompous ass."

"Chris, Sonja, please. Can you two cool it for at least a minute? The rest of us would like to hear the plan," Chet said.

"As I was saying, if we can get the California Air Resources Board to run the tests needed to document Thurgensen's theory, we'll have credible evidence from a very respected source to help stop EZ-15 in its tracks.

"With regard to documenting the crimes of the conspirators, we already have a good start. Tanya, on her own initiative, has been documenting everything we've learned to date.

"Any comments, corrections, or criticisms, Ms. Voinovich?" Chris added.

Sonja stared at Chris and flipped him the bird.

"I'll take that as a 'no comment,' Ms. Voinovich, and I believe we can move onto the final item. We need some allies in the media and in the government to help us gather additional evidence and eventually publicize the truth about everything that's happened.

"On the media side, I suggest we work with Levy. He's familiar with the background on EMCO, EZ-15, and EPA. He trusts me, and he's a damn good journalist. Rob has already helped us identify several Heritage Study Group members and locate Petrovic. I think Rob's our best bet.

"On the government side, I think we may be able to work with Joanne McKay. I have a plan to check her out tomorrow, and it will be a four-person operation—Tanya, Leon, Sonja, and me. We need to leave tomorrow at 5:00 a.m., and I'll brief the three of you after we finish here. Also, Ms. Voinovich has raised a valid question as to whether we can trust Bingeman Foster, but for now I would like to leave him on the list of good guys."

Chris completed his review by asking, "Does anyone have anything to add?"

Chet spoke up. "Sonja gave me an idea earlier this evening, and I think it could work. She asked if I knew anyone who has the skills to shadow FBI agent Michael Cavanaugh. I have just the person in mind—Carson Bigalow—a retired plainclothes DC police detective. He's a good friend, very accomplished at his trade, and he owes me big time. If everyone agrees, I'll contact him tonight and see if he's willing to take the job. We're still going to need to pay him."

"Sounds good to me. Let's do it," Chris replied as he looked at Sonja, who was beaming in response to her idea being accepted.

"Good. Then let's call it a night," Chet declared.

"Not so fast," Sonja said. "I was able to access Ted Bennett's computer, and he had two copies of the EPA test data in his files. One set of data was identical to the data on the CD Ronnie Chapman gave me. The second set had obviously been tampered with and in all likelihood is the version Bennett gave to the FBI to support the claim that Ronnie tampered with the data. But the most telling information is the date on the tampered test data file. It's two days after Ronnie was murdered," Sonja concluded, putting her arms together in front of her chest and smirking at Chris.

"Well done, Ms. Voinovich," Chris said, smiling.

Chris, Leon, Tanya, and Sonja then gathered in a corner of the living room to go over Chris's proposed plan to approach Joanne McKay. Sonja had lots to say, and she and Chris bantered loudly back and forth.

Chet, Casey, and Billy sat on the other side of the living room and watched the continuing saga of Chris and Sonja unfold.

"It's like watching a couple of cougars engaged in a damn mating ritual," Billy said.

"More like a couple of teenagers," Casey countered.

"You two just don't get it, do you? You have two people who are socially dysfunctional and who have been alone for way too long. Suddenly they find themselves inexorably connected in a horrific situation fraught with danger and dependent on each other for their very survival. And on top of that, there's chemistry developing between them, and neither one has the emotional maturity to deal with it in a rational manner," Chet replied to his two friends. "All I know is that somehow they bring out the best in each other, and the simple truth is that our very survival depends on those two working effectively together. So I suggest you both say a little prayer. I don't know about you, but I'm out of here. See you in the morning."

CHAPTER 38

April 26
Washington, DC

Rebecca Bergman gently awoke as the sunlight crept through the window of her one-bedroom loft condo located in the trendy U Street corridor not far from where Chris and Sonja had met the night Jackie Goldberg was murdered. The thirty-five-year-old woman with curly, black, shoulder-length hair pulled the soft cotton sheets up to her shoulders and glanced affectionately at her good-looking companion, who was still sound asleep and totally naked under the same sheets.

The two lovers had met several years before through one of the growing number of Jewish Internet dating services. Ironically, they had lived within three blocks of each other. The couple often joked about how before their first computer date, their paths probably crossed many times at the nearby Whole Foods grocery store or at one of the numerous bars and restaurants frequented by young professionals.

Bergman and her mate didn't live together, but he often spent the night at her place. His abode, a studio apartment, was small and always a mess. They both were workaholics. She was the deputy director of a small nonprofit organization that focused on children's health issues in Israel.

The two young professionals' relationship worked perfectly. They enjoyed each other's company—they both loved live music and theater, biking and camping, good food and wine, and the sex was pretty fantastic as well. Most of all, neither of them wanted the commitment of a long-term relationship. However, while neither had ever used the word "love" in their conversation, the relationship was far more than mere friendship.

After a brief moment of just enjoying the warmth of the early-morning sun, Bergman quietly reached for her smartphone on the bedside table and scanned her e-mails, texts, and voice mails.

"Damn it, Rob. How many times have I asked you not to give my number to your sources," Rebecca complained as she playfully pinched Levy's nostrils.

The reporter struggled to awake from his deep sleep. "I promise, Becca, it won't happen again."

"You're hopeless, Rob," she replied, knowing full well that Levy had no intention of honoring her request as she handed him her phone.

Levy eagerly scrolled down and opened an e-mail from O'Brian sent late the night before.

As he read, Levy repeatedly exclaimed, "Damn" and "Amazing." Finally, he looked at Rebecca and said, "I've got to go. If Chris is correct, this is going to make one blockbuster story."

As he started to get up from the bed, Bergman playfully patted the spot in the bed next to her, hoping to coax him back for one more sexual interlude.

"Becca, I really can't stay, but I'll make it up to you tonight," he said as he leaned over, giving her an affectionate kiss on her moist, pouting lips.

Levy dressed quickly, kissed her one more time, and was out the door in five minutes. Fifteen minutes later, he entered the *Washington Herald* offices on Eighteenth Street, NW, took the elevator to the seventh floor, and headed to his cubical. As usual, his desk was hopelessly cluttered. With a broad sweep of his arm, he cleared all the loose papers off his desk, grabbed a new pad, and sat down in his slightly broken, gray swivel chair.

Levy had graduated from the prestigious Columbia School of Journalism near the top of his class. Immediately after graduation, he went to work for the *Herald*. Over the next twelve years, he had written a number of critically acclaimed articles and had won two local awards for outstanding journalism.

However, Levy's problem was that he cared too much about the various stories he worked on. He felt every tiny detail was important to understand the story behind the story, and he devoted way more time researching than any of his fellow colleagues at the *Herald*.

Print journalism had changed inexorably over the past decade, and to survive, newspapers needed stories that were sensational on their face, easy to understand, and no more than five hundred words. Unfortunately, that wasn't Levy's style of journalism, and he increasingly became a relic of the newspaper trade. But now Levy, thanks to O'Brian, had stumbled onto a story of epic proportions.

"If I can pull it all together, a Pulitzer Prize isn't out of my reach."

Levy tried to more fully digest the import of his friend's message. Chris reported that the Heritage Study Group appeared to be an investment club set up to provide investment opportunities in the stock market based on insider information. Chris had suggested that Rob check out the market activity on EMCO during the days since the last HSG meeting that occurred the previous Thursday. Chris also expressed his belief that there was a connection between at least one member of the study group, the murders of Jackie Goldberg, and the trumped-up charges against him. Chris didn't mention Sonja, where he was hiding, or the existence of the Crew. He did promise to provide Rob with updates but encouraged him to do some checking at his end.

But where and how to begin? Levy pondered. Chris's caution to be careful gave Levy pause. After considerable thought, the reporter arrived at a strategy. He grabbed his cell phone and made the call. "Frank, how's it going? How about lunch later this week?"

Franklin Moss, always open for a free lunch and a mutual exchange of gossip, replied, "How about David and Paul's at noon on Friday?"

"Sounds a little pricy for my budget; let's meet at the Hourglass."

"Okay. See you at noon," Moss replied, the disappointment of not being treated to a very expensive steak evident in his voice.

"Great," Levy said and hung up before Moss could change his mind.

* * *

Chris, Sonja, Leon, and Tanya had debated well into the previous evening how best to approach Joanne McKay and, equally important, how much they could trust her and how much information they should share. The result of the acrimonious discussion was a plan that they all reluctantly acknowledged was far better than any one of them could have devised on their own.

By 6:30 a.m., they had arrived at their destination and found a parking space near the Capitol building in a public parking lot that would be full by 7:30 a.m. They immediately set out for the Russell Long Senate building, where Senator Goodman and his staff's offices were located.

Tanya positioned herself at the staff entrance on the back side of the magnificent stone and masonry building that filled an entire city block while Leon took up his position on the front side near the grand columned public entrance. Chris and Sonja had positioned themselves kitty-corner at opposite ends of the building so that one or the other would spot Joanne McKay and determine which entrance the Senate staffer would use.

By 6:40 a.m., they all were in place. They tried not to look too conspicuous and carefully avoided standing anywhere near where the numerous security cameras were pointed. Chris had guessed that Joanne was an obsessed workaholic and would arrive early in the morning for work. He was correct. At 6:50 a.m., Sonja spotted McKay headed in the direction of the staff entrance.

Joanne pedaled her mountain bike up Capitol Hill, dismounted, and locked the bike to a tree. Then she removed her helmet and the pant clip from around her slacks and headed to the staff entrance.

As soon as Sonja spotted Joanne, she called Tanya to announce the staffer's impending arrival, what she was wearing, and from which direction she would be coming. Tanya spotted McKay immediately. When McKay approached, walking quickly and not paying particular attention, Tanya, who was wearing a blonde wig and sunglasses, stepped into McKay's path and allowed herself to be knocked down.

Looking in shock at the young woman she had crashed into, McKay turned and bent down on her knees, "Are you all right? I'm so sorry. I wasn't paying attention."

"Shut up and listen," Tanya said in a quiet but firm voice. She glanced quickly around to see if anyone was close by—they were alone—and continued, "If you want to learn more about the EZ-15 conspiracy, meet O'Brian at your and his favorite bench in Rock Creek Park precisely at 6:00 p.m."

McKay looked confused, but the message began to sink in, and she said, "I want to see Chris, but I work late and—"

"No buts. Be there precisely at 6:00 p.m. or you won't hear from Chris again," Tanya said as she got up, refusing any help from McKay, and started to walk away. Then Tanya turned back, looked at McKay, and said, "Don't try to have me followed. We get even a hint of something fishy on your part, and we're done with you."

A stunned Joanne picked up her backpack and helmet and began debating with herself what she should do as she headed to the staff entrance. Tanya, meanwhile, walked down the sidewalk and turned the corner to meet up with the other three at the designated meeting point on the back steps of the US Capitol building, two blocks away. When they were all gathered, Chris said, "Are we still in agreement that the meet with McKay this afternoon is a go?"

Although each of them had lingering doubts, they all felt that meeting with McKay was vital if they had any chance of eliciting Senator Goodman's support in stopping EZ-15.

"Let's head back to the farmhouse and go over every detail of our rendezvous with McKay. We'll head back to town by late this afternoon."

CHAPTER 39

April 26
Washington, DC—Early Evening

McKay spent the entire day debating with herself about whether she should meet with O'Brian and with whom, if anyone, she should confide. She had spoken with Goodman briefly after her first encounter with O'Brian in Rock Creek Park. Neither the senator nor Joanne wanted to believe the outrageous claims of the former EPA attorney who was now a fugitive wanted by the FBI. However, they both agreed to keep the lines of communication open if for no other reason than to eventually turn him over to the proper authorities if that turned out to be the appropriate course of action.

The senator hadn't had a problem sending a message to Chris by skipping the press announcement at the White House on the EPA EZ-15 decision. Goodman had his own doubts about the efficacy of EZ-15, and he certainly had no interest in having his presence add any luster to an event that would serve to politically benefit President Keller, for whom he had an intense dislike. Finally, Joanne decided she would head out to meet O'Brian per the instructions given to her, but first she needed to talk to a couple of people.

Chris, Sonja, Leon, and Tanya returned to the city around four thirty in the afternoon. Leon dropped Chris and Sonja off at their designated spots and then drove off to park the car near where he and Tanya would carry out their part of the plan.

Joanne was already running a little late when one of the young interns stuck his head into her office and said, "Kowalski's on the line and says he needs to talk to you. He said it was urgent."

By the time she had finished talking with Kowalski, it was nearly 4:45 p.m. Grabbing her backpack and bike helmet, she raced out of her office. When she finally arrived at her apartment building, the perspiration was pouring down her face. She wasn't sure if it was the result of the frantic bike ride home, a warmer than normal spring day in Washington, or her growing anxiety about meeting with O'Brian.

Running up the Rock Creek Park bike path, Joanne glanced at her watch. It was 5:40 p.m. *If I run faster than my normal pace, I should reach the park bench on time.*

Joanne heard someone running up behind her but didn't give it much thought since it was a popular time of day for a run. But as the runner came along side, he grabbed her on the shoulder and said, "Turn around; we're going to head in the opposite direction."

"Chris? What's going on?" she said as she slowed to a stop, looking totally confused. At first she barely recognized him. He was wearing a cap that completely covered his hair and had large, dark sunglasses on.

"Change of plans—just follow me and try to keep up," Chris declared, knowing full well that if Joanne and he ran at their fastest pace, he, not her, would be left far behind.

The two runners set off back down the bike path and turned up another bike trail that ran along the Potomac River past the Kennedy Center for the Performing Arts and toward the Fourteenth Street Bridge. Finally, they arrived at East Potomac Park on Hains Point—a huge, peninsula-shaped urban park that jutted out southward for two miles along the Potomac River.

While Chris and Joanne jogged south, Leon and Tanya were strolling along the Rock Creek bike path like a couple of lovers in a role that was pretty natural for them. They had been walking up and down the path in the vicinity of the park bench where Chris and Joanne had met the previous Saturday night and where the Senate staffer thought she would be meeting up with Chris. They had arrived about a half an hour before Chris met up with Joanne to see if they could spot anything or anybody that looked suspicious. If Joanne was planning to betray Chris and had brought in the authorities, Leon and Tanya were well positioned to spot anything suspicious.

Several times, Joanne tried to initiate a conversation, but Chris turned and motioned her to be silent. When they reached the southern tip of the peninsula, Chris motioned to Joanne to stop. The location provided a panoramic view down the Potomac River, but more important, it was the perfect place to spot anyone approaching the point.

Chris, moving toward Joanne, said, "Don't move an inch. I'm well aware of what you're capable of, but I need to check to see if you're carrying any listening or signal devices. Understand?"

Joanne nodded affirmatively and lowered her hands to her side. Chris reached out, untied the red ribbon that had pulled her hair into a ponytail, and ran his fingers through her hair. Next he ran his hands down the sides of her body and then gently touched her breasts, searching her sports bra for any electronic devices. Chris asked Joanne to take off her shoes, and he inspected them and checked her socks by rubbing her feet. Finally, he instructed her to spread her legs apart, and he reached down into her running shorts and felt between her legs. His intrusive body search had found nothing.

Anyone watching them would have thought they were two lovers enjoying a not-too-discreet moment of sexual foreplay. Nothing could be further from the truth. Joanne felt violated. For all she knew, the man groping her was a complete nutcase, or worse. She somehow mustered the willpower to control her temptation to forcibly stop the crude invasion of her body and deliver a karate chop to her assailant's throat that would crush Chris's windpipe and bring him to a slow, painful death by suffocation.

"I'm really sorry about all this, but if I could only convince you what's at stake. As much as you must hate me at this moment, you'd hopefully understand," Chris whispered.

Finally, Chris motioned Joanne to sit down on a nearby park bench, and he joined her.

"Okay. I don't have any listening devices. What do you want to tell me?" Joanne asked, unable to hide the depth of her anger.

"No conversations yet—just sit tight for another minute."

Moments later, Chris spotted Sonja jogging toward them from the same direction from which Joanne and he had come. Sonja had been stationed at a bench near the front entrance of the park to watch for joggers or anyone else who came after Chris and Joanne and who looked suspicious. As previously agreed, she had waited ten minutes and then started jogging down the path to the southern point of the park after them.

As she approached Chris and Joanne sitting on the bench with the sun low in the sky casting a glow on Joanne's beautiful face and blonde, flowing hair, Sonja felt an irrational sense of jealousy toward the athletically built woman. In response, Sonja substantially increased her pace to a flat-out sprint.

"Nice pace," Chris called out to Sonja as she passed by, which had been part of the plan, but nevertheless he was truly impressed with the speed at which she was running.

In response, and also as planned, Sonja turned to Chris and, without speaking, gave him a sexy smile and a thumbs up. Had Sonja spotted anything that had appeared suspicious, she would have given him a thumbs down that would signal Chris to end the meeting and get the hell out.

Chris started to speak, but his cell phone rang. Leon, at the other end, relayed that nothing suspicious had occurred at the place where Joanne had thought she would be meeting Chris.

Seeing that Joanne was becoming increasingly agitated, Chris decided to take the risk and tell her everything the Crew had discovered to date, without disclosing the identity of the other Crew members. He waited until Sonja returned running in the opposite direction, and he gave her a few minutes' head start. If she spotted something suspicious and started running back toward him, he'd kick Joanne in the knee to disable her, and Sonja and he would try to escape.

Finally, he turned to Joanne and said, "Let's head back. I'm going to tell you everything I know. You're going to find it hard to believe, and I know you probably don't trust me right now, but we can't stop these guys without your and Senator Goodman's help."

By the time Joanne and Chris reached the north end of the park, he had told her the whole story, providing far more information and in greater detail than he had the previous Saturday night in Rock Creek Park.

Joanne had lots of questions, only some of which Chris could answer. She told Chris that Senator Goodman didn't take much convincing to help send him a message at the EZ-15 press event. When she told the senator about Chris's suspicions concerning Kowalski, the Senator immediately sent his chief of staff to the senator's Detroit campaign reelection campaign office for a couple of weeks on a trumped-up mission of getting the campaign office better organized. Finally, Joanne told Chris that Kowalski had called her earlier that day fishing for any new developments related to EZ-15 in light of the EPA's announcement.

"He really sounded nervous and agitated."

Next, they talked about what Joanne could accomplish at her end, what steps Chris was planning to take, and how they would remain in contact.

"I'm truly sorry about what I had to subject you to," Chris said as they prepared to head in different directions.

"I really thought about disabling you out there, and you know I could have done it. I also have to admit I started to doubt your sanity. But while what you've told me today seems almost too preposterous to believe, with the little I know already, the whole thing sounds plausible. If you're wrong, my career is over. But I'm telling you now you can trust me."

"Thanks, Joanne," Chris said. "Be careful and don't involve anyone else besides the senator without checking with me first. I'll try to call you at least every other day to check in. If you absolutely need to call, use my cell phone number and leave a message. Do you still have the number?"

Joanne nodded affirmatively and with a note of concern said, "Be careful yourself."

Chris watched as Joanne jogged back up the trail in the direction of M Street. Moments later, Leon's car pulled up on a road that paralleled the bike path, and Chris joined his comrades.

"Well?" Sonja asked as they drove off.

"She's on board. I think she can really help make a difference," Chris said, trying to sound as confident as possible. But he thought to himself, *If I'm wrong about her, we're doomed.*

CHAPTER 40

April 26
Great Falls, Virginia—Evening

Retired Judge Thomas Worthington, sitting in the sumptuous study at his vast estate in Great Falls, Virginia, was enjoying a glass of fifty-year-old Douro Valley Portuguese Port. The day had been a particularly successful one, and he was savoring the moment in solitude.

The study was lined on two sides with bookshelves filled with a large collection of books, many of them quite rare and extremely valuable. Also displayed were plaques and other memorabilia chronicling Worthington's illustrious career and those of his ancestors. Noticeably absent were any recent photographs of Worthington or his immediate family.

Pushing himself out of his overstuffed leather chair, Worthington walked over to the magnificent granite fireplace and placed another log on the fire. Turning, he looked out the large floor-to-ceiling, wood-paneled window to the west across a vast lawn that sloped down to a rock outcrop. Standing on that promontory provided a fabulous view of the Great Falls of the Potomac River below and the skyline of the nation's capital about twenty miles to the southeast.

At one time, much of the surrounding countryside had been dotted with large estates like the Worthington property, but over the years, many had been sold and subdivided. The Worthington estate was one of the exceptions. The thousand-acre tract had remained intact since the mid-1600s when King Charles II deeded it as part of the Fairfax Grant to William Worthington, who was one of a consortium of allies who received land grants from the king for their loyalty during the English Civil War. William Worthington IV, the first of the clan to actually settle in the colonies, was fiercely loyal to King George III. But his son, Patrick, served with General Washington in the French and Indian War, and when the Revolutionary War began, Patrick, who had inherited the Worthington Estate from his father, served as a trusted aide to General Washington.

The current Worthington mansion was built in the early 1800s and had been a plantation and then a working farm until the late 1950s. Since the late 1700s, the estate had always been called the Worthington Plantation.

The Worthington men fought nobly for the Confederate army during the Civil War, and two of three brothers were killed at the battle of Gettysburg. After the war, Jacob Worthington, the sole survivor, retired from the military, but his oldest son, James, went on to West Point and began an unbroken 130-year period in which at least one Worthington was serving in the US military. Most of those men had been career military and had achieved the highest rank in their respective branch of the military.

Thomas Worthington attended the US Naval Academy, where he graduated near the top of his class. He served as a major in the Marine Corps in Vietnam in the late 1960s and early 1970s and was awarded two Silver Stars. His battalion received a distinguished unit award for the fighting near the Cambodian border. Worthington had a reputation for his aggressive, merciless approach to combat. His unit was implicated in an incident in which ten civilians were killed, but no formal investigation was every carried out, and no record of the incident was mentioned on Worthington's military record.

Worthington achieved the rank of general before his fiftieth birthday and led a command during Desert Storm in Iraq in the early 1990s. He was being groomed to become the top general in the Marine Corps, but he suddenly retired after Desert Storm as the result of a family tragedy.

Worthington's only child, Robert, had followed his ancestors into the military but had been a profound disappointment to his father. He graduated near the bottom of his class at the Naval Academy in 1985 and had a totally undistinguished career as a Marine. In 1991, after six years of service, he hadn't advanced beyond first lieutenant, while most of his classmates had reached much higher ranks.

During Operation Desert Storm, Robert Worthington commanded a platoon of new recruits who came under intense fire from Iraqi regulars, and half of his command was killed or severely wounded. The young Worthington should have ordered a tactical retreat but refused and was killed by friendly fire. Unsubstantiated rumors persisted that Robert Worthington was intentionally shot by one of his own platoon members when Worthington refused to retreat. However, a formal inquiry concluded Worthington's death was an accident.

Six months after his son's death, Thomas Worthington retired from the Marines. Everyone thought that Worthington was so grieved by his son's tragic death that he was unable to continue to serve in the military. In truth, Worthington retired because he was personally humiliated by his son's horrible military performance. In the elder Worthington's mind, his son had tarnished the distinguished, generations-long, proud history of the Worthington men in the military.

Worthington had obtained a Jurist Doctorate at the George Washington University in Washington, DC, by going to night school for five years while he was stationed at the Pentagon during the early 1980s. He had little trouble finding employment upon his retirement from the military with one of the law firms in Washington that represented defense contractors. With a sharp mind and a tenacious approach to representing his clients, Worthington quickly became a star litigator for the firm. For him, litigation was akin to a military battle, and he used the skills he had learned effectively in the Marines.

When a circuit judge seat opened up on the US Federal Court of Appeals for the District of Columbia in early 2001, Worthington, who had contributed to and worked on the incumbent president's campaign, made the short list of candidates and was eventually selected. Worthington was one of the more conservative members of the court, and in late 2001 shortly after the 9/11 terrorist attack, he was selected by the president to fill a vacancy for the chief judge position. Worthington didn't disappoint the president or his supporters. With his toughness and leadership skills, Worthington carried considerable influence as the court reviewed a number of cases that pitted personal freedoms against national security.

In 2005, Worthington decided to retire from the court. The reason was simple, though never stated to anyone. He needed money—lots of money. Worthington had a pension from the military, as well as from his service on the court of appeals, but those funds were nowhere near enough.

First, he was land poor. The property taxes on the Worthington estate were enormous. Worthington knew he was the last remaining guardian of the Worthington Plantation, and he wouldn't allow it to be broken up during his lifetime. Second, Worthington's wife of nearly fifty years, who had been a dutiful military spouse and a wonderful hostess for all of the obligatory social events a man of Worthington's stature was expected to host, had an insatiable compulsion to spend extraordinary amounts on exotic travel, clothes, and jewelry. The couple had never been close and had led largely separate lives except when duty called and they needed to be seen together. Decades before, when it became impossible for his wife to bear another child because she had a hysterectomy, any semblance of intimacy between them stopped. Worthington was alone in his mansion because his wife was on a two-month tour of the Mediterranean with two other rich, bored, elderly women.

Third, despite his dynamic public persona, Worthington was never the same after his son's ignoble death, and he drifted into a secret life of debauchery—gambling, heavy drinking, and spending more and more time with prostitutes.

For a while after he retired from the court, he traded online and did quite a bit of speculating. He was utterly terrible at it and lost heavily.

Then one night, several years before, while sitting in his beloved study, Worthington had an epiphany. He reasoned that the only people in the investment world who consistently made money were those who traded on inside information, whether they were friends of corporate officers or board members or learned of impending regulatory actions before those decisions affecting a corporation or industry's bottom line were made public. While there were all sorts of federal and state laws against making such investments, he figured that it still had to happen all the time.

While Worthington had no such direct access to inside government or industry information, he began to think about people he knew who might. He started to put together a list of possibilities.

The first person with whom he discussed his idea for making a killing in the stock market was a fellow veteran of the Marine Corps who served under Worthington in Vietnam and with whom the judge had become a lifelong friend. Though they had rarely discussed business when they got together, Worthington knew that, by virtue of his friend's position, he had critical inside information on a number of defense and national security companies. That friend was Parnak Petrovic.

The two ex-Marines met, and Petrovic, who indeed did have inside information on companies that were about to be awarded national security-related contracts, immediately embraced Worthington's proposal. After several follow-up meetings, Petrovic provided Worthington with advance information on one company that was about to receive a billion-dollar contract from the Department of Homeland Security when almost everyone else expected the company's competitor would win the contract.

Worthington, acting on the information provided by his friend, purchased a large amount of the company's stock. When the government announced the winning contractor, the company's stock value exploded upward, and Worthington made a financial killing. In return, Worthington gave Petrovic a plain white envelope containing $50,000, which represented only a modest portion of the profit Worthington made.

The transaction was so simple that the two men subsequently discussed identifying others in Washington who might be interested in participating. The idea they developed was that each participant would be required to provide inside information to the other participants on a regular basis to remain a member of the group. However, the person actually providing the information would agree not to purchase stocks based on the information he possessed. That person would benefit from other stock deals based on inside information provided by fellow members.

Worthington and Petrovic had agreed that in recruiting other participants, there would be three prerequisites: each member had to have access to inside information; each could be trusted implicitly;

and each had a little larceny in his heart and wouldn't be afraid to exceed the boundaries of ethics and legality. Thus, the concept of the Heritage Study Group was born, although its structure and name would come later. The first four members recruited for the group were Stanley Braxton, senior partner at Miller and Braxton; Alan Hastings, Federal Communications Commission board member; Roman Cherkoff, a Russian billionaire; and Lester Moody, Miles Hatfield Investing.

Since Stanley Braxton's firm represented a number of corporations in the national security/defense industry, Petrovic had known him both personally and professionally. Braxton had great contacts in the defense industry as well as the energy sector, and he was smart, discreet, and knew how to skirt the boundaries of propriety. Both Petrovic and Worthington thought Braxton was a perfect fit.

Worthington was a close friend of Alan Hastings. They both were members of the Congressional Country Club. Hastings's public reputation was impeccable. But Worthington knew from private conversations after both men had drunk way more than they should have after a golf outing that the FCC board member had, on at least two occasions, received gifts indirectly from companies regulated by the FCC. Worthington also knew from private conversations with Hastings that he too was having serious financial issues.

Petrovic had met Roman Cherkoff during Petrovic's days at the CIA. The Russian expatriate had numerous contacts with the CIA over the years, during which he routinely provided valuable information about Russian state-owned industries. Cherkoff was greedy as hell and since coming to the United States in the 1990s had amassed a fortune estimated in the billions. When it came to corporations outside the United States, there was no one who had more inside information than Cherkoff.

Worthington knew Lester Moody socially. The financial expert lived in Northern Virginia and frequented social events also attended by Worthington and his wife. On several occasions, Moody had mentioned to Worthington that he had a "hunch" about a particular stock that he was planning to buy, but he never explained the basis behind his hunch. However, the tips always proved correct, and Worthington made a nice profit. As he and Petrovic discussed possible members of their group, it dawned on Worthington that Moody had given him tips that were probably based on inside information.

Worthington and Petrovic invited each of the four men to join the group, and they all responded enthusiastically. Two weeks later, at the group's first meeting at the Worthington mansion, Braxton suggested that he recruit Franklin Moss, chief of staff for Congressman Beasley, chairman of the House Environment Committee, and Damon Kowalski, chief of staff for Senator Goodman, chairman of the Senate Environment Committee. Braxton reasoned that these two congressional committees were the source of virtually all legislation affecting energy and environmental issues, and they had enormous impacts on the regulated industries.

Braxton had worked directly with both Moss and Kowalski and reported that they had several characteristics that would make them good candidates for joining the group—most important was a willingness to pass along inside information for a price. Braxton also suggested Federal Reserve Board of Governors member David Rogers, because Rogers, in exchange for a personal favor Braxton had performed, shared information with Braxton regarding a coming Fed Board decision to increase the prime rate.

After becoming a member of the group, Lester Moody suggested Larry Wasserman, renowned attorney and champion of liberal causes. This seemed like an odd choice at first, but upon further explanation by Moody, Wasserman seemed a perfect fit for the group. Wasserman, who was a client of Moody's firm, was always looking for the inside tip on investments. The attorney's stock holdings hardly reflected his public image as a champion of environmental and social justice causes. A corporation's reputation, the way it treated its employees, or the nature of its product had little to do with Wasserman's investment decisions. As a member of the group, Wasserman could provide advanced intelligence on actions by various liberal groups against particular companies that could impact the targeted companies' stock prices.

As with the initial members recruited, the new members also were enthusiastic about being members of the club.

At his first Heritage Study Group meeting, Wasserman suggested recruiting the ultraconservative television evangelist, Jeremiah McCormick. Wasserman and McCormick often appeared on cable/

satellite television to debate opposite sides of an issue—be it banning prayers at high school football games or the rights of Muslims undergoing airport security. Even though the two men were on opposite sides of the political and religious spectrum, they became friends and found they had much in common. Both were interested in making as much money as possible, and neither was particularly concerned about how they did it. Just as Wasserman could provide useful insight into the activities of liberal political groups, McCormick could do the same with regard to conservative groups.

With the addition of Jeremiah McCormack and one other member high up in the Keller administration, the group of twelve was ready to go into action. Worthington provided the space for the weekly meetings at the Capital Club, and Braxton came up with the name Heritage Study Group. The name was perfect; it sounded prestigious and gave no clues to its purpose. There were lots of groups with fancy names fronting for a wide variety of activities, but Worthington had guessed that the Heritage Study Group was the only organization in town created explicitly to enrich its members by trading securities on insider information.

To ensure that no Heritage Study Group member decided to leave the group or developed a guilty conscience and disclosed the real purpose of the group, Worthington had his friend, Petrovic, conduct an extensive background check on each member. Any embarrassing information could be used to convince a wavering member not to leave or at least keep his mouth shut if he did quit the group. Petrovic had little trouble digging up lots of dirt on each of the group members.

Since the Study Group's inception, each member had provided inside information that had enriched their fellow members. Worthington's once rather bleak financial situation had improved considerably. But nothing could compare with the killing he made on the stock market this beautiful spring day when EMCO stock skyrocketed in the days following the EPA's announcement of the approval of EZ-15.

As Worthington sat at his desk, staring at his online stock portfolio, the smile on his face continued to grow. Beginning last Thursday after the Heritage Study Group meeting where Braxton had alerted members to the imminent EPA approval of EZ-15, he had invested $250,000 in cash, which represented nearly all of his liquid funds and leveraged another million dollars to buy EMCO shares that were then trading in the twelve-to-fourteen dollar range. At the close of market this Tuesday, EMCO was at forty-five dollars a share, and the stock was clearly headed much higher.

Worthington hadn't felt this content for years. He wanted to mark this extraordinary day but had no one with whom to share it. As he turned off his computer, a Colombian woman with shining black hair pulled back in a ponytail and dressed neatly in a gray dress with a white apron appeared at the door.

"Judge Worthington, everything is finished, and your dinner is in the oven. I'd like to leave now unless there is something else you require," his thirty-four-year-old cleaning woman, Rosanna, asked hopefully.

Rosanna Lopez had been employed by Worthington for three years, and while the pay was decent, she hated her situation. But she had no choice. She, her husband, and her seventeen-year-old daughter were all undocumented aliens who had fled Colombia fearing for their lives. Her husband, Jose, had been a skilled carpenter, but while working on a construction job, he had fallen twenty feet to the ground when an improperly designed and erected scaffold collapsed. Jose severely injured his back and was at least temporarily disabled and unable to work. He had no medical insurance. Her daughter, Anita, was an excellent student at the local high school and worked two part-time jobs. But Rosanna was the only real source of income. If they were caught and deported, death at the hands of the drug gangs would be their certain fate once they arrived back in Colombia.

Rosanna wasn't the only undocumented person working at the Worthington estate. Worthington was well aware that the various contractors he hired to maintain the grounds of the estate relied heavily on the use of undocumented workers. In fact, it seemed the entire region around the nation's capital thrived on the use of low-paid, uninsured, illegal immigrants. It didn't matter if someone was liberal or conservative or something in between—one way or another, they all benefitted from the system.

Much to Rosanna's dread, Worthington said, "Just one more thing."

Rosanna knew exactly what he wanted and without speaking walked slowly toward Worthington's desk. As she approached, Worthington turned the desk chair in her direction, unzipped his slacks, and motioned her to kneel at his feet. He then unbuttoned the top of her work dress.

It wasn't the first time, and it wouldn't be the last. When she finished, she rose without making eye contact, wiped her mouth with a tissue he had handed her, re-buttoned her blouse, and walked slowly toward the door to the hallway beyond.

As she reached the door, Worthington called out, "Rosanna, I haven't seen Anita in over two years; she must be sixteen or seventeen by now. Why don't you bring her with you next time to help out with the chores? I can find some special projects for her."

As Rosanna left the study, her head felt like it was going to explode in rage, and her heart felt broken in grief beyond repair. "You'll never see or put your filthy hands on my lovely Anita," she muttered as she wept silently. She quickly exited the mansion through the servants' exit.

Just as Worthington's ancestors had enjoyed abusing female slaves during the late 1700s and well into the 1800s, the judge was enjoying the fruits of his position as lord of the manor at the expense of someone who had no other options.

"A little sex with a fine-looking woman is the perfect way to cap off what has truly been a marvelous day," Worthington said as he poured another generous portion of port and toasted himself.

CHAPTER 41

April 27

Chris found himself standing in a dreary park that was deserted save a woman and her child. Both were dressed in heavy, drab coats. Even though he was wearing only a short-sleeve pullover shirt and shorts, he didn't feel cold. In fact, a few flowers blooming in the courtyard suggested it was springtime. The place looked exactly like a spot near the Brandenburg Gate that he remembered seeing during his short visit into East Berlin with his college buddies in the early 1990s. But from the few cars he could see parked on the nearby street, it appeared to be the present.

Then the woman, who was young and beautiful, with her auburn hair showing at the edges of the white, wool scarf she wore, started to walk in his direction. Chris tried to turn away but was transfixed. As she neared him, her face was taut with fear, her eyes pleading.

The young mother stared at him with her piercing, dark blue eyes and, placing her child's hand in his, whispered, "Take care of my child; keep her safe from harm. You're her only hope."

* * *

Chris woke with a start, his forehead and chest drenched in a chilling sweat. The young girl in his dream was no more than six years old and had curly, blonde hair and green eyes, but Chris had no doubt that the child was Sonja Voinovich or, more accurately, Katrina Zimmer.

Chris lay on his back, trying to make sense of it all. Finally, he resolved to himself, *Whatever triggered that vision and whatever the future might hold for me, I absolutely must keep Sonja safe from harm at any cost.*

Chris raised himself up by his elbow and stared affectionately at the beautiful young woman sleeping next to him. The night before, after they had completed the rendezvous with Joanne McKay and returned to the farmhouse, Chris, Sonja, Leon, and Tanya went down to the pond.

Tanya talked in more vivid detail than she did the first time the four of them sat at the pond. She described how she and Leon had fallen in love and the wonderful times they had spent together over the past two years.

As Chris and Sonja sat silently listening to Tanya and Leon's story of romance, they both separately felt a pang of envy and sadness that they never had experienced anything close to what Tanya and Leon had together. Chris's wife had turned against him, and his marriage had ended horribly. While Sonja had sex several times in college and with one of her fellow band members, she had never been close to any man.

Perhaps it was Tanya and Leon's tale of love, the events of the day, or Sonja's growing sense of dread that none of them would survive the nightmare they were living, but when Chris and Sonja went inside the farmhouse that night and turned to say goodnight, they both lingered awkwardly in silence.

Finally, Sonja leaned toward Chris and gently whispered in his ear, "I don't want to be alone tonight."

Without speaking, Chris put his arms around Sonja, kissed her, and led her upstairs to his bedroom. Once in bed together, Sonja and Chris's mutual vow of celibacy, made only three days before, was quickly broken.

Now awake from his dream and with the realization that even though it was only 4:00 a.m., he wouldn't be able to fall back asleep, Chris was content to lie next to Sonja and watch her sleeping restfully.

But then, as if she had sensed he was looking at her, Sonja opened her beautiful eyes and said, "Are you all right?"

"I'm fine, just enjoying the memory of last night," he said softly as he kissed her, deciding not to mention the dream from which he had just awakened.

"Last night was very special. I think I'm starting to fall in ..." Sonja replied but stopped in midsentence and changed her tone. "Thanks for being here for me. I couldn't survive all of this without you. Promise me you'll stay by me."

With his recent dream in mind, Chris chose his words carefully. "I promise I'll always do everything I can to keep you safe." Chris knew in his heart that keeping Sonja safe from harm most likely would mean keeping her as far away from him as possible as things became increasingly dangerous.

Sonja, aware at once that Chris hadn't really answered her question, began to regret daring to be so honest with him about her feelings. But then Chris embraced her and gave Sonja a long, deep kiss. At least for the moment, they were together, and for Sonja that was enough.

*   *   *

Petrovic sat impatiently as he waited once again for Cavanaugh, this time in a coffee shop near the Verizon Center sports arena. The upscale residential/business area was a perfect place to rendezvous. It was near the FBI building, so Cavanaugh could easily slip away from work to meet, and it was on Petrovic's way back from Capitol Hill, where he had just finished a meeting.

Petrovic didn't like the idea of meeting with Cavanaugh so often. Usually they met at most once every other week. But earlier that day, several disturbing developments had occurred that made meeting with Cavanaugh absolutely necessary.

First, Petrovic had received a call from Stanley Braxton. It seemed that Russell was starting to become a problem. As instructed, she had seduced the chairman of the Solid Waste Management Council in an effort to secure his vote to approve an application submitted by a Miller and Braxton client to construct a solid waste landfill site in a small town north of Des Moines. The project had been blocked as a result of growing opposition from residents living near the proposed site. After casting the deciding vote to approve the site, the chairman, a sixty-year-old, fat, balding, pompous ass, demanded a second sexual interlude with Russell. She complied, but then things turned ugly. In the course of their sexual encounter, he became increasingly aggressive and physically abused the woman, brutally striking her repeatedly in places that couldn't be seen when she was fully dressed.

For the heavily bruised and thoroughly humiliated woman, it was the final straw. Braxton had treated her unfairly by blaming her for what happened in Brussels with O'Brian and then exiled her to the middle of nowhere. Now she had been severely beaten and abused. Russell had called Braxton, explained in detail what had happened, and threatened to file a sexual assault charge against the council chairman, sue Miller and Braxton for sexual harassment, and finally, go public with the story behind her involvement with EMCO and EZ-15. Braxton wanted Petrovic to take care of the situation.

Second, Petrovic received a call from the White House. Concern was expressed that Senator Goodman seemed to be wavering on the issue of EZ-15 and potentially could cause problems during the thirty-day review period before the approval of EZ-15 became final.

Third, Crown Prince Abdul Syed had informed the White House that he was coming to Washington. The crown prince wanted face time with President Keller to discuss purchasing a fleet of attack helicopters and to obtain the support of the US government to promote the use of EZ-15 in other parts of the world once EMCO received final approval from the US EPA. Petrovic was being called on to provide security for the crown prince during his visit.

Finally, Petrovic was contacted by a former colleague at the CIA advising him that Robert Levy of the *Washington Herald* had called inquiring how Petrovic could be reached. Cavanaugh was ten minutes late when he finally arrived. Normally, Petrovic would have taken the opportunity to figuratively rip his head off for being late, but Petrovic had too much that needed to be discussed and little time to do it.

"Any new developments in the FBI search for O'Brian and Voinovich?"

"O'Brian contacted his broker, Dan Witt, but only asked for the balance in his FMA account. I think O'Brian must have guessed Witt's phone was being monitored and cut the conversation short. We tried to trace the call, but it was the number for one of those cheap pay-by-the-minute phones, and we couldn't track down the owner. Witt called me right away and accurately reported the conversation we had been listening to. I doubt O'Brian will try to contact him again, but we'll continue to monitor Witt's phone. Frankly, I think continuing to tail Witt is a waste of time and resources. If O'Brian tries to contact him, I'm confident Witt will call us."

"I agree. Any other developments?"

"No. O'Brian and Voinovich have simply disappeared."

Petrovic hid his growing frustration with the lack of progress and simply said, "Have the FBI put together additional composite drawings of O'Brian and Voinovich and circulate them to local law enforcement agencies and the media. Maybe have one of the composites showing Voinovich with curly blonde hair and green eyes."

"Can't hurt," Cavanaugh replied without giving Petrovic's specific suggestions for Sonja Voinovich's composite a second thought.

"We've got to do more to find those two. We need an international terrorist security hook to get the DHS and me more directly involved. With the Department of Homeland Security involved, it will be easier for you and me to communicate and meet directly, and I can access more of the DHS resources."

"Good idea. Any thoughts on how we can make this an international conspiracy?" the FBI agent asked.

"I've already started the wheels rolling. Documents are being planted at Sergio Sanchez's residence implicating Sanchez in a plot with O'Brian and Voinovich to kill Mueller and Goldberg. My colleagues in Europe already have pictures of O'Brian meeting with Sanchez in Bruges and Mueller in Berlin two days before the UBA laboratory blew up. O'Brian also was spotted at the scene of Goldberg's murder, and the rest should be easy to fabricate."

Petrovic then turned the discussion to the next items: the concern at the White House about Senator Goodman's possibly becoming a problem for EZ-15 final approval and Crown Prince Syed's visit to Washington.

"Concerning Goodman, Braxton knows Joanne McKay, one of Goodman's key staff members, pretty well, and maybe McKay can provide something useful," Petrovic said.

Then, leaning closer to Cavanaugh, he added, "With regard to Syed, all I need from your end is to arrange for some evening entertainment for him at his hotel during his visit. Make sure she's a natural blonde, beautiful, and young. If she can pass for sixteen or younger, so much the better. I'll provide the details later on about where he'll be staying."

Cavanaugh nodded affirmatively. He had provided female companions for visiting dignitaries in the past and had several young women in mind.

Then the discussion moved to the call Petrovic had received regarding an inquiry from Robert Levy of the *Herald*. "It's probably nothing, but can you discreetly check this reporter out?"

"Unfortunately, it actually may be a matter of concern for us," Cavanaugh warned. "Levy recently wrote an article for the *Herald* reporting that EPA was receiving undue pressure to quickly approve the EZ-15 application. O'Brian was identified by EPA officials as the source of the information. I'll have Adams tail Levy, and I'll also get a warrant to tap Levy's phone."

Petrovic frowned deeply at hearing Cavanaugh's information on Levy and quickly agreed that surveillance was the best action. Cavanaugh, thinking their business was concluded, started to get up and leave.

"Wait. There's one more thing, and you better handle this one personally," Petrovic said, motioning Cavanaugh to sit back down.

Petrovic then explained the Pamela Russell problem and the need for immediate action. He gave Cavanaugh all the pertinent information on how to locate Russell.

"I'll fly out tomorrow morning," Cavanaugh replied in a flat tone.

With the discussions completed, both men quickly got up and headed to the door. In their haste to leave, neither noticed the well-dressed, black, middle-aged man who sat at a table on the opposite side of the coffee shop and who discreetly clicked off several photo shots as the two men departed.

As soon as Petrovic and Cavanaugh disappeared, Carson Bigalow, who had tailed Cavanaugh from the FBI building to the coffee shop, texted the photos and a short note to a cell phone number Chet Jones had provided.

CHAPTER 42

April 28
Washington, DC—Morning

As agreed at the farmhouse the previous evening, Casey Randolph was a one-man operation conducting the surveillance outside the Capital Club where the Heritage Study Group was about to conduct their weekly gathering. Casey had positioned himself so he had a clear view of the side and front entrances.

Using a sheet of paper with Tanya and Leon's photographs of the HSG members who had entered the club the previous week, Casey mentally checked off each of the members as they entered the side door. By 11:00 a.m. all nine members previously identified had arrived, and he had spotted Judge Worthington arriving at the front entrance. He decided to stay a little longer just in case anyone else showed up.

Fifteen minutes later, Casey headed to the closest Metro stop.

No more than two minutes after Casey had left, a distinguished-looking gentleman, who wasn't a member of the Capital Club, arrived and was permitted to enter through the main entrance.

When the gentleman in question entered the study group meeting room, the various group members stopped their side conversations to acknowledge the arrival of their most distinguished and most powerful member. Given the stature of the other members of the group, the gesture was quite remarkable. The gentleman, in turn, acknowledged their courtesy and walked over to Worthington, who greeted him warmly.

In the waning minutes before the Heritage Study Group meeting started, Parnak Petrovic grabbed Stanley Braxton gently by his jacket sleeve and pulled him over to a corner of the room. "The White House tells me they are getting mixed signals from Goodman on the EZ-15 matter. Have you picked up any buzz about where Goodman stands?"

Braxton thought for a moment and then quietly said, "Nothing other than the fact that our friend Kowalski suddenly got shipped off to Detroit to organize Goodman's reelection campaign. I did talk with Kowalski, and he's not very happy, but he doesn't think it has anything to do with the senator's position on EZ-15."

"But Goodman wasn't at the White House press event on EZ-15. We can't take any chances on losing Goodman. We need to get some inside intelligence. If there's a problem, we need to move quickly. You know Joanne McKay in his office; can you feel her out on this without being too obvious?"

"Hell, I've worked with her a number of times on other issues, and I was actually able to help her out a couple times by getting support from several of my clients for some bleeding-heart legislation to provide alternative energy incentives sponsored by Goodman. She's damn capable and a real looker. Frankly, I wouldn't mind trying to get her in the sack, but I can't afford to lose her as a contact—she's that good."

"Give her a call and let me know what you find out," Petrovic replied. Leaning closer to Braxton, he whispered, "Two things: first, we need Goodman on our side—don't screw this up—and second, the Pam Russell matter is being taken care of."

Braxton looked up at Petrovic, who was staring directly at him. He couldn't tell if Petrovic had a smile on his face or was snarling at him.

"Don't worry. I'll take care of Senator Goodman. And thanks for the other thing."

As Petrovic and Braxton talked, on the other side of the room, Jeremiah McCormick was enjoying a hearty laugh at the expense of Larry Wasserman. Once again, Wasserman had been on the losing end of a bet and had to pay up.

The two friends always had a wager regarding which of their pet nonprofit groups would receive the largest amount of contributions in the twenty-four hours following their TV debate. For McCormick, it was the Holy Union Ministry church, and for Wasserman, it was the National Freedom Institute.

The previous Friday, McCormick and Wasserman had debated whether mosques should require special zoning approval to be located in the vicinity of a Christian church or cemetery. The two had argued ferociously, interrupting each other repeatedly, mocking each other, pounding their fists on the table, and speaking with great passion. When the donation contributions were tabulated, McCormick's church had raised over $200,000, while Wasserman's organization had raised a modest $90,000.

As Wasserman handed over ten hundred-dollar bills to McCormick, he said, "Hell, I should have won the bet on principal. Nobody in this country, besides Muslims themselves, gives a damn about religious freedom for Muslims."

Both men laughed as they shook hands.

McCormick's jovial mood was also a direct result of the news he had received the previous day. Thanks to some direct intervention by the White House, the Internal Revenue Service had abruptly ended a six-month investigation into whether McCormick's Holy Union Ministry church had violated the prohibition against engaging in political activity. Had the charges been successfully prosecuted, McCormick's church not only would risk losing its tax-free status, but the evangelist himself also would have been required to pay over a million dollars in back taxes.

As McCormick thought about the rather large bullet he had dodged, he caught the eye of, and mouthed the word "Thanks" to, the distinguished gentleman still speaking with Worthington.

Praise the Lord for having friends in high places, McCormick thought.

Around eleven thirty, Worthington called the meeting to order, and everyone immediately stopped talking and took their assigned seats.

"Let's start with an update from the man of the hour," Worthington said, motioning to Braxton.

"The news on EMCO gets better and better. The stock opened today at forty-seven dollars, a new high. We're already above the forty-five-dollar figure Lester predicted for when the decision goes final," Braxton reported. Then the lobbyist turned to Lester Moody, the financial expert of the group, and said, "Do you want to revise your estimates on EMCO's stock value growth potential?"

"Last week I was being conservative, which I think was prudent at the time. Our analysts at Miles Hatfield now estimate that EMCO stock will continue to climb over the next three weeks and reach a possible high of fifty-five dollars a share. Once EPA's approval is final, the stock is expected to jump another twenty dollars and could hit ninety dollars by the end of the year." Then Moody added, "Of course, these predictions are based on the assumption that no road blocks or problems arise with EPA's final approval of EZ-15 in twenty-six days."

Braxton replied confidently, "Everything points to EPA final approval of EZ-15 on time. There's simply no reason to expect otherwise."

What Braxton didn't say, but knew, was that there were still several land mines out there, most notably O'Brian, Voinovich, and Russell, that needed to be defused.

The rest of the study group meeting was uneventful. Petrovic updated the group on the Justice Department's ongoing investigation of fraud by Cloverleaf Security executives.

"DOJ will announce the indictments next Thursday. If you haven't sold your Cloverleaf Security stocks by now, do it immediately. The stock will drop to single digits within twenty-four hours of the announcement."

To a man, every member of the study group had already dumped his holdings in Cloverleaf after Petrovic announced the company's problems. Petrovic never got his information wrong, and when he counseled action, everyone acted quickly in response. The rest of the meeting was devoted to discussing several future regulatory actions to watch, but no further specific recommendations for action were forthcoming. The news on EMCO and EZ-15 alone was well worth the time spent at the meeting.

CHAPTER 43

April 28
Prince Georges County, Maryland

Sonja sat alone, staring at her computer. Everyone else was otherwise occupied and had failed to notice that now, as she had been most of the previous day, Sonja was completely lost in her own world. Beneath her quiet exterior, her thoughts raged. She debated with herself over and over again, asking the same painful questions and each time seeming to come up with a different answer.

Does he love me? Yes, I think so. No way; he's just trying to protect me. Absolutely not; he still loves his wife and kid. Do I love him? Yes, no, maybe. It's complicated. I don't even know what love is. Do we have a chance to succeed and survive? We can and will. It's hopeless. How can I possibly get through this nightmare?

Since her conversation with Chris when she awoke early the previous morning, they had barely said two words to each other. Once again the awkwardness between the two had returned.

A call in the late afternoon the previous day from Carson Bigalow helped distract Sonja for the moment. Bigalow reported the rendezvous between Petrovic and Cavanaugh at a coffee shop, thus providing helpful information: the two men knew each other and were most likely conspiring together. But the torrent of Sonja's conflicting emotions and endless internal debates quickly returned. Sonja looked at her watch, which read 1:30 p.m.

Now, after all those hours of inner turmoil, she sat up, leaned toward her computer screen, and said quietly, "Enough," as she began searching a long list of key words, names, and organizations to see if there were any new developments related to EMCO, EZ-15, or the FBI investigation.

After about an hour of dead-end searches, Sonja called out, "Chris, everybody, take a look at this."

Chris and the others quickly crowded in behind Sonja. There on the FBI's most wanted page were composite, digitized photos of Chris and Sonja next to their EPA ID photos. The composite showed Chris with short brown hair, a mustache, and a short, scraggly beard. The computer-generated photo of Sonja showed her with curly blonde hair and green eyes.

"Nice try, assholes," Casey said. "Those composites don't come close to looking like either of you right now."

Everyone agreed, but then Sonja spoke, her voice trembling slightly. "Petrovic has made the connection between Sonja Voinovich and Katrina Zimmer. He knows Katrina Zimmer is still alive, and now on top of everything else, he has another reason to hunt me down."

Everyone but Chris was thoroughly confused. Leon, trying to allay Sonja's concern, said, "You're a natural redhead and have blue eyes; you're not a blonde with green eyes."

"When Sonja was a young girl, and Petrovic knew her, she had blonde, curly hair and green eyes. Am I right?" Chris said, looking at Sonja.

"Yes, but ... how could you possibly know that?" Sonja replied with a mix of confusion and concern on her face.

"Lucky guess," Chris lied in response, having made the connection from his haunting dream the day before.

Everyone stood awkwardly, not knowing what to say next.

Sonja finally broke the silence and changed the subject. "Casey, you're right. Those pictures don't look anything like us now. They'll be more of a distraction than a help to the FBI. Also, we know that Petrovic knows who I really am, and maybe we can use that fact in some way to help us.

"This article says that the Department of Homeland Security suspects that Chris and I are part of an international conspiracy involving Sanchez and other unnamed conspirators in Europe to derail EZ-15. We're suspected of being involved in the deaths of Goldberg and Mueller. The article concludes by reporting that the DHS will join the FBI in its search for us."

Chris marveled at Sonja's composed demeanor and focus compared to the first time she learned that Petrovic was a member of the Heritage Study Group. As he bent over to read the computer screen showing the FBI's most wanted file on the two of them, he gently put his hand on the back of Sonja's neck and rubbed it. She tensed up at first and then, surrendering to his touch, relaxed and sighed. It was a nice moment for them both but wasn't destined to last long.

One of Chet's numerous cell phones rang, and he lumbered over to pick it up. "Okay, okay. That's kind of odd. I'll pass it along and thanks," Chet said, hanging up the phone and turning to the group.

"That was Bigalow. He tailed Cavanaugh to Reagan National Airport today. As Cavanaugh was standing at the self-check-in screen, Carson stole a peek and saw that Cavanaugh was flying to O'Hare and then on to Des Moines. When he checked in, Cavanaugh didn't show his FBI badge but used a personal driver's license instead. After a few minutes passed, and Cavanaugh was well on his way to the gate, Carson went to the woman at the check-in counter and asked if his business partner, Michael Cavanaugh, had checked in yet. The woman checked the flight in question and said no one named Cavanaugh was on that flight. Why would Cavanaugh be traveling incognito?"

Almost instantly, Sonja blurted out, "Chris, wasn't Russell sent by Braxton to Des Moines after he chewed her out about blowing things with you in Europe?"

"Cavanaugh may be heading out there to silence her," Chris said as checked for her cell phone number. When he found it, he grabbed one of the cheap phones and quickly dialed Russell's number.

"Come on, come on, Pam, pick up your damn phone," Chris pleaded, but no voice answered at the other end.

Finally, Russell's voicemail clicked on, and he shouted, "Pam. It's me. You know who it is. Believe me—your life is at risk. They're coming after you; get out of there. If someone you don't know comes to your door, don't answer it and call the police. Please, believe me; they've killed others and won't think twice about killing you."

Chris hung up, smashed the phone, and turned to Sonja, Chet, and the rest. "God, pray she gets my message in time."

*   *   *

239

Daniel Witt sat in his home office in his basement. His hands were sweating, and his throat was parched as he stared at the contents of the large, white envelope addressed to his wife that had been delivered by regular mail to his house earlier that day.

"I assume this is for you," she had said, sounding somewhat annoyed as she had handed Witt the envelope as he entered the house.

The return address was a phony, but Dan had recognized Chris's almost illegible handwriting on the envelope and knew instantly who it was from.

"I need to look at this now," Dan had replied as he headed downstairs to the basement.

"Don't be too long. Dinner's almost ready," Katie shouted down the stairwell.

Now, twenty minutes later, Witt still sat staring at the contents of the envelope. The contents consisted of a two-page, handwritten set of instructions. In meticulous detail, the document directed Dan to sell specific stocks owned by Chris but now in Dan's possession. Next the document instructed Dan to open a number of offshore accounts under different names into which the proceeds from the stock sale were to be deposited in equal amounts. Finally, Chris's note instructed Dan on how to invest the cash in the offshore accounts and the date the transaction should take place.

Chris ended the note, "I know what I'm asking you to do seems crazy, and the stuff with the FBI had to be unsettling for you. I can't explain why I'm doing this. You'll have to trust your old friend and godfather to those two wonderful kids of yours. I don't know how this will all end. If I die, make sure Sarah gets a copy of my will, which leaves my remaining securities in your possession to her."

Dan read Chris's note and instructions one more time, stood up, and started to walk in circles. "I've got to make a decision," he mumbled to himself.

"Chris is my friend. He was there for us when Katie had the miscarriage, and I've known Chris for years. He can be pretty exasperating at times, but the guy has always been honest. But if he's done anything illegal, I could be ruined. And what about Katie and the kids?"

Finally, Witt returned to his desk, flopped down in his chair, bowed his head, and put his two hands on his forehead.

"Dan, what are you doing down there? Dinner's getting cold," Katie called out.

Dan stood up, turned off his desk light, headed for the stairs, and called out, "I'm coming, honey."

By the time Dan appeared in the kitchen, he had made up his mind. He walked over to Katie, put his arms around her, and held her tight. Kissing her tenderly, he whispered, "I love you."

CHAPTER 44

April 29
Washington, DC

As Robert Levy approached the white-painted, two-story, brick Hourglass Pub, only three blocks from the US Capitol building, his face was flush with excitement. *One of the great joys of being a journalist is the moment when the object of your investigation knows he's toast and is going down,* Levy thought.

Upon entering the somewhat musty and dark eating establishment, he was immediately recognized by Regina Davis, the young black hostess dressed in a tight-fitting, low-cut, dark red dress.

"Going head-hunting today, or are you just having a social get-together," she asked coyly.

"A table in the back corner would be nice."

"Ah, the hunt is on," Davis replied as she led him to a spot where a discreet conversation could be had.

Levy had picked the restaurant for three reasons: it was close to Frank Moss's office; being a public place where everyone knew everybody, Moss wouldn't make a scene once confronted; and, Levy simply loved the place.

Once seated, Levy took the opportunity to look around the restaurant that had retained its cozy, earthy appeal but was less than half-filled with patrons. In years past, it would have been impossible for anyone but a congressional insider to get a table between 11:30 a.m. and 2:00 p.m., when Congress typically was in recess for the lunch hour. Stories were legend of Sam Rayburn, Lyndon Johnson, Tip O'Neill, and Howard Baker, when they were congressional leaders, hammering out tough but workable compromises with their counterparts from the opposition party at the Hourglass over lunch, cigars, and several scotches.

But things had changed. The art of building compromise in Congress had all but died in the last ten years. And so it appeared this grand old establishment had outlived its usefulness and was destined for the wrecking ball.

Levy, nursing his glass of Sauvignon Blanc, was deep in thought when Moss finally arrived at the table, looking very much like a man who was having a really bad day and in desperate need of a drink.

Once seated, Moss called out to the waitress, "Double Dewar's scotch straight up—STAT."

"Man, Congressman Beasley's on a tear about those idiot Democrats trying to repeal portions of the Patriot Act, and he's dumping everything on me. Looks like this will be the only time I'll be out of the office for the next week. My life couldn't get much worse."

"Sorry, my good man," Levy replied and then thought, *Actually, Frank, things are about to get a lot worse for you.*

They ordered lunch, and Moss knocked back a couple of drinks. After engaging in small talk for about fifteen minutes, Levy decided it was time to spring the trap. As he leaned toward Moss, Levy felt some regret in taking the congressional staffer down. He hung around with Moss mainly because Moss was so self-possessed with his own importance that he often spoke about what was going on behind closed doors just to show he was an insider. Consequently, Moss was a useful source for an investigative journalist. But Levy also knew Moss's wife and knew the congressional staffer was a decent husband and father.

"I wanted to ask you about the Heritage Study Group crowd you hang with," Levy asked casually.

Moss's body language said it all. His eyes opened wide, his jaw stiffened, and his entire body was instantly tense. He did his best to brush off Levy's question. "Oh, that's nothing. It's just a group of guys getting together for a drink."

"That's not what I hear."

"What do you mean?" Moss asked angrily.

"I have it on good authority that the study group is some type of investment group made up of the rich and famous here in Washington."

"Ridiculous. Absolutely ridiculous," Moss protested in a raised and almost trembling voice.

"Well, if you don't want to talk about it, maybe I could give a call to Judge Worthington, Stanley Braxton, Roman Cherkoff, Larry Wasserman, Jeremiah—"

"Where did you get those names?" Moss interrupted, his face now crimson and his eyes wild as sweat poured off his forehead.

"Thanks for the confirmation, Frank."

"You're crazy. You don't know what you're getting into. My advice as your friend is to drop this immediately," Moss pleaded desperately.

"Sorry, can't do. If you want to talk about this, you can always give me a call," Levy said calmly as he turned his well-hidden recording device off.

Moss raised his fist in a threatening manner but stopped. Getting up, he stormed out, nearly knocking the young hostess down.

"Got ya, Frankie boy," Levy whispered.

When Regina Davis came to Levy's table to give him the bill, she said, with a knowing expression, "Looks like your friend didn't exactly enjoy the lunch."

"Check out next Wednesday's edition of the *Herald*. It's going to be a ball buster of a story," Levy boasted and then paid the bill, leaving a generous tip. As he strode out of the restaurant, Levy sported an enormous grin.

* * *

Pam Russell, beaming, burst into her one-bedroom rental apartment. It was the first time in weeks she had smiled. Passing quickly through her starkly furnished living/dining room, she went straight to her bathroom. Russell looked in the mirror at the woman she had become and frowned.

"I'm out of here," she said to the image in the mirror. "Whether that asshole, O'Brian, was telling the truth or just trying to scare me into making a mistake doesn't matter, because I'm finished with all this crap."

Grabbing the small makeup removal cream from the shelf below the mirror, twisting the top loose, and scooping up a generous portion of the goopy gel, Pam slathered it all over her face. As she harshly rubbed the elixir deep into her skin, the slightly burning sensation made her feel a little better. Russell grabbed a towel and rubbed off a thick layer of skin cream, deep mascara, thick and tacky eyelash enhancer, and over-applied lipstick. She wet a washcloth with warm water and ran it through her hair, removing at least some of the sticky, perfumed, color-enhancing hairspray she had applied that morning and every morning for the past three years. She pulled her long, blonde hair back and stared at the mirror.

"That's better. Much better," Russell proclaimed as she felt her face, which had been restored to its soft, lovely luster, and touched her hair, which felt and smelled fresh and natural. She knew it would take a while to fully return to that young, innocent girl who had come to Washington from Green Bay, Wisconsin, so long ago to find fame and fortune. But she thought, *At least it's a start.*

Quickly tossing what she needed into a small carry-on bag, she declared, "The rest of this crap can stay. I'll buy what I need when I get home."

A look of satisfaction enveloped her face as she thought how surprised and thrilled her parents would be to see her. Russell took one quick look around the apartment, grabbed her smartphone, and raced toward the door.

"Good-bye, Des Moines, good-bye, Miller and Braxton, and good-bye to every other scumbag I've had to deal with since coming to Washington."

As she turned the knob to open the front door, her phone rang. Russell looked down at the screen but didn't recognize the number. As she opened the door, still looking down at the phone, she decided to answer it and didn't see what was coming. In an instant, Russell was staggering back into the living room, her arms and legs twisting and shaking sporadically like a rag doll. Her deep blue eyes were open wide in shock. She tried to speak but could only make a sickening guttural, gurgling sound. The knife, which had been thrust by the assailant who charged into her apartment, went into her neck and up into her skull. Her vocal cords had been severed.

Russell fell back and cracked her skull with a loud thud on the corner of the metal coffee table. She felt no pain. She was already dead.

As the assailant searched the apartment and took anything that might incriminate Miller and Braxton, he barely took note of his fallen prey. But then he stopped in his tracks when he heard a faint voice.

"Pam. Pam, are you all right? Pam, please, for god's sake answer me," a voice coming from the cell phone lying on the floor, pleaded.

Cavanaugh thought for a moment, picked up the phone, and said calmly, "Sorry, you've got the wrong number," and started to hang up.

"Cavanaugh, I know it's you, you sick bastard. You and your friends are going down."

Cavanaugh shouted into the phone, "Who is this?" But the person at the other end had already hung up.

Cavanaugh stood, shaking, his face flushed and his hands sweating. But after a moment, he gathered himself, finished his work, and exited the apartment unnoticed.

As he entered his car, Cavanaugh had a moment of instant clarity. *O'Brian. It had to be Christopher O'Brian. But how in the hell did he know it was me?*

CHAPTER 45

May 1
Washington, DC

For the thousands of passengers arriving and departing Dulles International Airport on Sunday morning, life had become a living nightmare. Despite the day's weather being magnificent, flights were being delayed for up to ninety minutes. As the overcrowded conditions worsened, people started shouting and pushing, and tempers were reaching the boiling point. The waiting areas in the already poorly designed and badly ventilated airport concourses began to feel and smell like an overcrowded gym locker room. But still no explanation for the delays was forthcoming.

The unspoken reason for the delay was the massive security blanket covering the skyways within two hundred miles of Washington, all traffic on the runways, and throughout the terminal. Such extreme security wasn't for one of the world's great leaders like the premier of China or the president of Russia. No, it was for someone far less known, but still of great political and strategic importance to the United States: Sheik Abdul Syed, crown prince of a Middle Eastern monarchy about half the geographic area and population of Bahrain and a country with little in the way of oil reserves. Nevertheless, because of its strategic location in the Middle East, it was critically important to the security of the United States.

* * *

That same Sunday morning, Parnak Petrovic and Michael Cavanaugh were led down what seemed like an endless corridor in the basement of a building that, from the outside, looked like some hideous, garish brothel. But it was, in fact, the Old Executive Building located right next to the White House. Numerous attempts to tear down the building by various presidential administrations over the years had failed, and the most famous eyesore in the nation's capital had remained standing. Indeed, many of the meetings "at the White House" were actually held in this building.

"You look terrible," Petrovic said to Cavanaugh, who, though well dressed in a pressed and clean suit, had enormous wrinkles under his bloodshot eyes and a deep frown chiseled on his chin.

"Christ, I had trouble catching a flight out of Des Moines, and I didn't get home until well after midnight, only to find your voicemail waiting for me. It's been a pretty rough week, you know," Cavanaugh whined.

"Hey, it comes with the territory. You can always quit if you can't take it anymore."

"Sorry, just dead tired today. I'll be fine," Cavanaugh said with a faint smile, knowing that quitting wasn't an option in his business.

"That's more like it," Petrovic said as he handed Cavanaugh a white envelope containing $5,000 in payment for Cavanaugh's services in Des Moines.

Cavanaugh did not tell Petrovic about the phone conversation with O'Brian. If Petrovic was aware that O'Brian had linked Cavanaugh to Russell, the FBI agent knew he would be dead meat.

Petrovic had commanded his colleague to attend the coming important security meeting at the White House for two reasons. First, Cavanaugh was the lead investigator for the FBI hunt for Christopher O'Brian, Sonja Voinovich, and possibly other conspirators. The other people who would be at the meeting were very interested in anything that had an impact on EPA's final approval of EZ-15. Second, Cavanaugh had personally arranged the evening's entertainment for the important visitor to the White House.

While Petrovic had a contract with the Department of Homeland Security and received his paycheck from DHS, he took his orders from someone outside of DHS. And while Cavanaugh was an FBI agent, he did what Petrovic told him, including killing Ronnie Chapman, Ann Hastings, and Pamela Russell.

When Petrovic and Cavanaugh finally arrived at the lavishly appointed meeting room, they waited a good thirty minutes before the other attendees sauntered casually in. The high-ranking White House official took command of the meeting, introducing all of the participants before inviting them to be seated.

Petrovic and Cavanaugh shook hands in turn with the senior White House official and then Hassid Kabar and EMCO's Jorgen Johansson.

"If I may," the good-looking, athletically built official began. "Please allow me to set the stage for this very important meeting by giving our guests from the DHS and the FBI a brief explanation of Crown Prince Syed's and the ruling family's critical importance to the United States' national security interests in the Middle East.

"The beautiful country, benevolently ruled by Crown Prince Syed's family for over eighty years, hosts a critical backup satellite relay station in the United States' worldwide satellite security network. Without the strong leadership of Crown Prince Syed, establishing this critical link in his country would never have taken place. Also, the prince has personally guided the rebuilding of the Royal Air Force that provides security for the relay station. Finally, the royal family has provided the United States with critical intelligence regarding terrorists operating in neighboring countries."

Petrovic, from his years at the CIA and DHS, was well aware of Prince Syed and the country his family ruled with absolute brutality. Syed's father had retained the title of king, but with advancing age and dementia, the king had been forced by the monarch's circle of advisers to unofficially abdicate his power to one of his sons, resulting in a fierce battle between Crown Prince Syed and his older brother, Aymid. Through guile, charm, and treachery, as well as a little help from the US security establishment, Crown Prince Syed had outmaneuvered his less-capable brother and seized control of the county.

Syed was educated in the United States, receiving a BS from Stanford and an MBA from the University of Chicago. During his twelve years in the United States, the crown prince had made close acquaintances with members of the CIA and DHS. Those ties proved invaluable later for both the Arab prince and US security interests.

"This administration and the United States have and will continue to do everything possible to support our important ally," the White House official continued. "With that, I'll turn things over to Dr. Kabar. Hassid, whenever you are ready to begin."

The short, slight, sixty-five-year-old Arab adviser to Syed began in somewhat halting English. "Thank you. Our beloved and benevolent king ruled his county for nearly fifty years after assuming the throne upon the death of his father. As our king aged, he relied increasingly on a group of advisers that horribly managed the royal family's wealth to the point that five years ago our kingdom was on the verge of bankruptcy. By the grace of Allah, Crown Prince Syed assumed management of the royal family's investments, and with some help from the United States, he has been able to restore our country's financial stability."

Pouring himself a drink of water, Kabar continued, "With the help of the United States, and using his keen business sense, Prince Syed was able to borrow well over one billion dollars at very low interest rates. With that money, he loaned $800 million to a global energy company at a substantially higher interest rate than the royal family was paying on its loan. The cash flow difference was enough for the royal family to continue to pay down our nation's outstanding debt to our other creditors." Dr. Kabar then looked at Petrovic and Cavanaugh and smiled. "You no doubt have guessed, given your involvement in the ongoing investigation to find the conspirators trying to sabotage the US EPA's final approval of EZ-15 and the presence of Mr. Johansson here today, that the energy corporation involved is EMCO Consolidated Company."

Petrovic and Cavanaugh both nodded.

"To continue, with the remaining $700 million, the royal family has been purchasing stock in EMCO. Before the development of EZ-15 and receiving a needed loan from the royal family, EMCO was in serious financial difficulty. However, today EMCO has a strong balance sheet, and with its new product, the company's stock price has soared. The value of the royal family's investment in EMCO is now $1.2 billion."

"Wow," Cavanaugh blurted out and then red-faced at his indiscretion, added, "Sorry."

Petrovic, on the other hand, sat silently, with an almost imperceptible smile on his face, as he quietly calculated how much money he personally had made, at least on paper, from his timely investments in EMCO. He had heard most of the rest of the background information from earlier conversations with the White House official now sitting directly across the table from him.

"Which brings us to the status of the joint FBI and DHS investigation into the conspiracy to discredit EZ-15," the White House official said, turning to Petrovic, and not Cavanaugh, even though the FBI technically had the lead in the investigation.

Petrovic replied confidently, "Our joint investigation is proceeding well. We have identified the main principals, we are closing in on them, and a series of arrests are imminent."

From Petrovic's overwhelmingly confident persona, no one at the table, save Cavanaugh, would have had any reason to suspect that so far the search for O'Brian, Voinovich, and anyone else possibly involved had gotten nowhere.

Cavanaugh added on his own, "The FBI agrees with the DHS assessment that we are very close to making arrests."

Petrovic, upset that Cavanaugh had spoken out of turn, frowned, but the others around the table seemed pleased with the FBI's confirmation that the investigation was nearing a successful conclusion.

To seize back control of the discussion, Petrovic asked, "While we are confident, is there anything else anyone around this table could tell us that would be helpful? Obviously, anything discussed here won't go beyond me or my colleague."

The White House official, Kabar, and Johansson took turns looking at one another and then each nodded, giving their respective consent.

"There is one matter," Johansson began. "A very small chance exists that there could be a small, unintended side effect from the use of EZ-15. We continue to investigate the matter, but we are confident that any potential adverse effects are minimal."

"So what's the issue?" Petrovic asked.

251

"We believe if the conspirators can identify the potential cause and nature of this possible side effect, they could force a delay in the final EPA approval of EZ-15, which we of course believe would be totally unjustified. Once EPA grants final approval for EZ-15 after the review period expires in twenty-three days, EZ-15's opponents' only option will be to challenge the EPA decision in court. They will have a heavy burden of proof to overturn the agency's decision. Even if they were successful, which is highly unlikely, the litigation will take years, and by then the royal family and the rest of us will have sold our stock, and EMCO will have made tens of billions from the sale of EZ-15."

Looking at not only Johansson, but the White House official and Kabar as well, Petrovic asked rhetorically, "So you believe there actually may be a problem with EZ-15? Are we talking about illnesses, deaths, or what?"

The question had been asked, and even though no one spoke, both Petrovic and Cavanaugh understood the answer.

Finally, the White House official said, sounding somewhat annoyed about the territory into which Petrovic's line of questions drifted, "Let me make this perfectly clear—the president has personally pledged his support to Crown Prince Syed and the royal family. The United States has a critical security interest in keeping the royal family financially strong and secure. Our government is committed to do whatever needs to be done to ensure that Prince Syed remains in power."

Then looking directly at Petrovic and Cavanaugh, the White House official said, "I assume everyone is on board and that DHS and FBI working together will bring the ongoing search for the conspirators to a quick and successful conclusion."

"Absolutely," Petrovic replied, realizing that his questions had dipped into troubled waters.

Either by coincidence or design, at that very moment, Crown Prince Syed, accompanied by his entourage, swept into the meeting room. The extremely handsome, forty-year-old prince unbuttoned the jacket of his Armani, black pinstripe suit as a gesture to reduce the formality of his arrival.

"I hope I'm not interrupting," the prince said in perfect English. Without waiting for a reply, he turned to Petrovic and Cavanaugh and continued. "My family and my country greatly appreciate everything the FBI and DHS are doing to capture the members of the international conspiracy trying to keep off the market a product needed to address the growing problem of global warming and climate change. Were these conspirators successful in their attack, the consequences would be catastrophic."

Right, catastrophic to your pocket book, Petrovic thought.

The prince ran his hand through his jet-black hair and proceeded to glide around the room, speaking with each person individually. He called each of them by their first name, even though he had never met Petrovic or Cavanaugh. With each person, the crown prince made a personal comment, showing he knew something about each person's family and their interests and always ending the conversation with a hearty handshake. Even Petrovic was a bit awestruck at how impressively the prince worked and controlled the room.

At the conclusion of his private chat with Cavanaugh, the crown prince whispered, "Everything set for this evening?"

"The same arrangement as last time—the packages will arrive at the presidential suite at the Excelsior Hotel precisely at midnight."

The two packages Cavanaugh had arranged for were two very young and very beautiful blondes. He had no clue whether either was even eighteen years old.

Having made the rounds, the prince exited as quickly as he had arrived, and the meeting came abruptly to an end.

Petrovic and Cavanaugh were escorted to the Old Executive Building's rear exit. As the two men turned to say good-bye, Petrovic whispered in Cavanaugh's ear, "So now at least we finally know why we've been asked to take such extreme measures in the interest of national security. We need to pull out all the stops and find O'Brian and Voinovich—now. I don't care what it takes. There are too many loose ends, and things could end badly for us, the president, and that slick piece of work, Syed—not that I give a damn about either of those two."

Cavanaugh nodded in agreement, and the two men walked off in opposite directions.

CHAPTER 46

May 2
Washington, DC

Ah, the games we play in Washington, Joanne McKay thought as she fidgeted in her chair, waiting for Braxton to join her for lunch. He had called Joanne the previous Friday to suggest getting together to "catch up on what's happening." The lobbyist picked the time, 2:00 p.m., a time convenient for him, not for her, the location that was two blocks from his office and eighteen blocks from her office on Capitol Hill, and the place, an expensive restaurant, which her budget could ill afford, so she couldn't offer to pay or even split the bill. To top it off, Braxton was twenty minutes late. All were signals designed to send MacKay a strong message that she owed him, and he was about to call in a debt.

Two can play at this game, Joanne mused.

Braxton had helped Senator Goodman, at her request, on several occasions by calling in some chips with several powerful trade associations that might not have otherwise been willing to help the senator on legislation he had proposed. In the process, her stature with Goodman had been greatly enhanced. Nevertheless, McKay disliked Braxton professionally and loathed him on a personal level. He was unethical and had subtly hit on her several times when she first went to work for Goodman.

Finally, Braxton arrived, and when Joanne stood up, he gave her a big hug, pulling her tightly into his body as her breasts pressed against his chest and his hand grabbed her back just a little lower than was appropriate.

What a pig, Joanne thought as she forced a smile and pulled away without appearing to be annoyed.

After they ordered, Braxton wasted no time. "I'd appreciate anything you can share regarding Goodman's current position on EZ-15."

"It hasn't changed. The Senator has clearly stated that he's seen nothing that would call into question EPA's final approval of the EMCO application. But as always, he'll keep an open mind until the thirty-day review period ends."

"Good," Braxton said, and his relaxed body language suggested he was satisfied with her reply.

But then his shoulders stiffened again as leaned toward her and in a somewhat menacing voice asked, "Have you ever spoken to that guy who got fired at EPA, Christopher O'Brian? You know he and another EPA employee have been linked to a terrorist group trying to disrupt the introduction of EZ-15 in the United States."

Joanne's mind raced, and she quickly chose her course of action. She already knew from O'Brian that someone had called Braxton about Goldberg having reservations regarding EZ-15. She was virtually certain her office mate, Kowalski, had been the one who called and told Braxton about her conversation with O'Brian in Brussels.

"O'Brian and I made presentations on EZ-15 at a symposium in Brussels last month, and we had dinner one night. He told me Jackie Goldberg had doubts about the efficacy of EZ-15, and I mentioned it to Goodman and Kowalski when I got back to the States. I gather from the newspapers that the guy dropped out of sight the night Goldberg was killed. He hasn't tried to contact me or, to my knowledge, anyone else in Senator Goodman's office, since."

Then in an effort to turn the tables, she added, "Why do you ask?"

Braxton uncharacteristically stumbled momentarily before replying, "As you know, EMCO is our client, and they have asked Miller and Braxton to provide any cooperation we can with the ongoing FBI/DHS search for O'Brian. I'm just making the rounds among folks in Washington to see if anyone has any information that would be helpful to the FBI."

"Well, I'll certainly let you know if I hear anything," she lied.

For the rest of the lunch, Braxton tried to pry information out of McKay, but she deftly parried every thrust he made. Finally, he gave up, and when the check finally arrived, Braxton took out his money clip, pulled out two hundred-dollar bills, and dropped them on the table. They both got up. Again he hugged her inappropriately, and they went their separate ways.

Well, I dodged that bullet, Joanne thought with a smile.

*   *   *

"That bitch is lying through those bright white teeth of hers," Braxton mumbled as he walked. "She's hiding something, and we don't have much time to find out what it is. I need to come up with something on her and confront her again."

As Braxton reached his office building, a broad smile came across his face. "Got it—Goldslide. I'll call McKay about meeting later this week and confront her. I've got just the thing to get her attention, and she'll have to cooperate."

Unnoticed by Braxton and McKay as they walked away from the restaurant was a well-dressed black man waiting at a Metro bus stop. Over the weekend, Chet had warned Bigalow to cease tailing Cavanaugh because the FBI agent knew he had been followed after Chris had blurted out Cavanaugh's name on Russell's phone when Cavanaugh was in her apartment. Chet asked Bigalow instead to start tailing Braxton. Bigalow snapped his final pictures with his cell phone, called the cell phone number he had been given, sent the photos, and left a voice message.

"Our friend Braxton just had what looked like an enjoyable lunch with that woman from Senator Chapman's office. When you sent me the folder of pictures, I thought you said she was one of the good guys."

*   *   *

As the sun's rays began to dip below the horizon, they cast a long, wavy shadow across the Potomac River, reaching the Jefferson Memorial on the opposite shore from where Levy sat in his Honda Accord, waiting impatiently for Moss. Levy had parked in the farthest, most remote parking area in the Lady Bird Johnson Park, a large track of land in the shadow of the Pentagon. By day, the gardens, with their numerous winding footpaths that passed by hundreds of species of flowering plants and trees, were a popular stop for tour buses and the hoard of tourists the buses carried, particularly in the spring. But at night, the type of visitors changed dramatically. As darkness set in, the area became a popular spot for men hoping to hook up with other males with a like-minded interest.

Maybe Moss is a closet homosexual. Why else would he pick this totally creepy spot to meet with me? Levy pondered.

When Moss called earlier in the day, Levy was leery about meeting with the congressional staffer. But Moss had promised to provide additional information about the Heritage Study Group in exchange for leaving Moss's name out of Levy's article.

If that worm doesn't show in five minutes, I'm out of here. And I'm going to put his name in the article's headline.

No sooner had the thought entered Levy's mind than a late-model BMW sedan pulled slowly into the parking area and stopped about fifty feet from Levy's car. Moss stepped out, looked around the area, and motioned Levy to follow him. Levy stepped cautiously from his vehicle into the now-misty, damp, and chilly evening air. Moss then turned and walked down a path and disappeared into the mist.

Every hair on Levy's body was standing up on its roots, and his mind screamed, *Get the hell out of here!*

But still Levy followed and wondered aloud, "What is he up to now?"

After walking down the barely visible foot path for about fifty feet, Levy could once again see Moss's figure standing in a small clearing.

Finally, Moss spoke, "I think this is a safe place to talk."

As Levy cautiously entered the clearing and moved ever closer to Moss, he could see that the staffer's whole body was shaking uncontrollably, and his eyes were darting in all directions.

"Frank, are you okay?"

At that instant, a soft, barely audible thumping sound came from the bushes, followed by a second. Moss instinctively spun around to look in the direction from which the sounds had originated.

Seeing absolutely nothing in the distant fog and bushes, Moss turned around back toward Levy, only to see the journalist stumbling

257

with an ever-growing, dark crimson patch dead center on his forehead and one on his chest.

Moss fell to his knees and retched. "What the hell have you done!" he cried out. "I thought the idea was to scare him, not kill him."

Petrovic stepped from the shadows, a Heckler and Koch UPD handgun with a silencer in his left hand. "Change of plans."

He stared at Moss and added with a note of frustration, "Come on, Frank, you had to know how this would end when you called me."

"No, no, I never thought it would come to this." Moss's voice was almost inaudible as he gasped for air.

"Stop whining, you little wimp, and listen to me. Go over and unbuckle his pants and pull his pants and underpants below his knees."

"What?"

"You dumb ass—just do it. We want to make this look like some homophobe stumbled on two dudes going at it and shot him dead."

When Moss finished the disgusting task, he looked back at Petrovic and asked, "What now?"

"You die," Petrovic said, devoid of any emotion as he aimed the pistol at his horrified victim and calmly shot Moss in the right temple.

Petrovic then put on plastic gloves and positioned the bodies so it looked like Levy and Moss were killed in the middle of a sexual encounter. Then he walked calmly back to his car, which was parked in yet another parking area, and drove slowly away.

As he made his way back to his modest carriage house in Georgetown, he called Cavanaugh.

Cavanaugh didn't answer, so Petrovic left a message. "Where the hell are you? Call me immediately." Then Petrovic hung up and reached for a cigarette.

CHAPTER 47

May 3

Prince George's County, Maryland—Morning

"Damn, damn ... *damn!*" Sonja shouted as she smashed her clenched fist on the dining room table and then winced as she shook her hand in pain.

Having heard similar outbursts of frustration from the young analyst over the past three days, no one sitting around the farmhouse living room bothered to look up. Spending painfully long hours at a time, Sonja had struggled unsuccessfully to find the key to unlock the mystery of what was causing the spikes in asthma attacks in cities where EZ-15 was being used. Her research had revealed that for long periods of time, the use of EZ-15 seemed to have no adverse impact, but in isolated instances, the rates of asthma attacks, as well as deaths, suddenly skyrocketed.

"I really thought I was onto something this time," Sonja said to no one in particular, the disappointment evident in her soft voice.

"Why don't you take a break?" Chris said sympathetically.

Sonja tilted her head toward him, and Chris felt her glare cut right through him.

Undaunted, he tried again. "Come on, let's go for a run. You could use a break."

Sonja tried but couldn't hide the smile that began to break through her stoic frown.

"I'll take that as a yes. Meet you on the porch in five minutes."

Sonja, without responding, got up, stretched her long arms, ran her fingers through her hair, and shook her head as if to clear from it all of the frustration she had experienced over the past seventy-two hours. Then she headed to her bedroom to change.

Moments later, she emerged, dressed in black, tight-fitting spandex running shorts and a matching form-fitted, black sports bra that showcased her increasingly muscular and attractive figure.

"Looks like all that running, sit-ups, and push-ups she's been doing the past two weeks are having an effect," Otto whispered to Chet as she passed by them.

"No, it's my home cooking that's made the difference. She's finally put some meat on her bones. God, she was so emaciated when Chris bought her to my house that night."

Chris, who had also undergone his own physical transformation, dropping over twenty pounds and tightening his abs, called out, "Let's go."

Breaking into a run, Chris asked, "What do you make of Joanne meeting with Braxton?"

"If she's in on the conspiracy, she had several opportunities to bring us down. I think we have to trust her. But we need to be careful. What do you think?"

"I don't know. She seemed sincere and honest."

"I hope it won't come down to us having to rely on her for anything important," Sonja replied.

"So do I."

When they finished fifty minutes later, both were breathing heavily.

Chris raised his head and looked at Sonja. "I'm really sorry you've hit a dead end with the EZ-15 and asthma connection."

"I'm convinced there's some connection between ambient air conditions and the degree to which EZ-15 affects asthma sufferers. It's got something to do with temperature, humidity, or other pollutants in the air."

"But incidents of asthma attacks already are affected by all of those factors," Chris replied.

"Yes, but in the case of EZ-15, it's way more than that," Sonja replied.

Raising her sweat-soaked head, Sonja put her hand on his shoulder as if for support. "I think I'm close. I'm not going to give up."

"I never thought you would," Chris said as he gently squeezed her hand.

As Chris and Sonja entered the farmhouse, still glowing from their run, Tanya called out casually to Chris, "Someone just called you on your cell phone."

Wiping the sweat off with a towel, Chris grabbed one of the cheap cell phones and dialed the number to retrieve the message. When he saw the number, he immediately recognized the number as that of Rob Levy's girlfriend, Rebecca.

Must be important. Rob's using his girlfriend's phone, Chris thought.

Chris grabbed another cell phone and keyed in the number. When someone picked up, he said, "Rob. Is that you?"

But it was Rebecca Bergman's, not Rob's voice, that cried out, "He's dead. Rob's dead, you bastard. Why did you have to drag him into that damn Heritage Study Group thing? I pleaded with him not to get involved, and now he's dead. You as good as killed him. The police just called me—Rob had listed me on his 'in case of emergency' card."

Chris tried to reply, but Bergman continued to shout hysterically, alternately screaming and crying.

Then the phone went dead, and Chris looked up at the group. His face once flush from his run had turned white, his eyes were vacant, and his mouth hung open. "Rob Levy's dead."

*　　*　　*

About the time Sonja and Chris were heading out for their run, Michael Cavanaugh was crawling out of bed. He had overslept, but after all that had taken place the last few weeks, he felt entitled to give his mind and body a chance to recharge.

As Cavanaugh checked his messages, he saw that Petrovic had called him sometime during the night. "Christ, what the hell does he want now?"

"Cavanaugh, where the hell are you?"

"So nice to hear your voice, Parnak."

"I don't have time for your crap. Levy's been taken care of, but we need to search his office and apartment before the DC police get around to doing it. We've got to find that article about the Heritage

261

Study Group—tear the place apart, if necessary. I found nothing on Levy's body or in his car. Oh, and Frank Moss won't be a problem anymore."

From his conversation on Sunday with Petrovic, Cavanaugh knew that Levy had confronted Moss about the reporter's plan to expose the Heritage Study Group. He also had learned that Moss, in a complete panic, had called Worthington, who, in turn, had contacted Petrovic. Finally, he assumed Petrovic would take care of things and probably kill Levy. But killing Moss surprised even Cavanaugh.

"How'd you pull it off? And have the authorities been informed?"

"Killed Levy and that little whiner, Moss, last night in the Lady Bird Johnson Memorial Gardens. Made it look like some homophobe offed two homos in the act of consensual sex. Then I provided an anonymous tip to the DC police earlier this morning."

"I'll get the FBI warrants immediately," a now fully awake Cavanaugh said. "Anything else?"

"Yes. When I had that tail put on Levy after I found out he was checking up on me, my guys discovered that he spent a lot of time with a woman named Rebecca Bergman. She lives at Tower Condominiums at Fourteenth and U Street. To be safe, pay her an unofficial visit. If she gives you any trouble, take her for a ride, and you know what to do."

*   *   *

Chris tried to call Rebecca once more, but she hung up without speaking.

"Chris, what do we do?" Sonja asked.

Chris hesitated for a moment but then stood up, the color returning to his face as he seized the moment.

"Everybody, gather around. We've got to move fast."

With everyone's eyes focused on Chris, he began, "Let me state the obvious. Rob was writing an article about the Heritage Study Group and had asked around about Petrovic. My guess is that somehow Petrovic got wind of it and sent his attack dogs after Rob. That bastard Petrovic is going to try to make sure that the copy or copies of Levy's article never reach the light of day. But if Petrovic knows that Rob was seeing Rebecca, she'll be on his list as well. So the first order of business is to get Rebecca out of her condo and hide her in a safe place. She won't speak to me. Sonja, let's have you try to talk to her."

"But she doesn't know me," Sonja protested.

"She almost certainly does. Rob knew you were on the run with me and that we were both involved in the EZ-15 business. He almost certainly told her everything he knew. You're also a woman; maybe that will help. We've got to try."

"Okay, but what do I say?"

"Tell Rebecca her life is in danger and she needs to get out of her condo. Let her pick the place to meet you as long as it's far away from where she lives."

Chris grabbed another phone, punched in Rebecca's number, and handed the phone to Sonja.

"Chris, damn it, leave me alone," Rebecca cried out.

"It's not Chris. My name is Sonja Voinovich. I think you know who I am. The man who almost certainly had Rob killed, Parnak Petrovic, brutally murdered my parents many years ago. This man is pure evil—he'll stop at nothing. Soon he'll come after you. You have to leave your condo now ... and don't bother to pack."

"Why should I believe you?" Rebecca responded cautiously.

"Meet me. You pick the spot. If I can't convince you, you've lost nothing but some of your time."

After what seemed like minutes, Rebecca finally replied softly, "Okay, but let's make it a very public place—the reading room of the Library of Congress."

After a moment, Sonja replied, "The Library of Congress won't work. Pick another place."

Rebecca hesitated and then finally replied, "Meet me at the moon walk exhibit at the Air and Space Museum. It's always crowded with people."

Chris, standing closely behind Sonja so he could hear, whispered, "Tell her you'll meet at 11:00 a.m."

Sonja relayed the message, and Rebecca agreed and added, "I'll be wearing a red wool sweater with a gold chain and black slacks."

"See you at eleven. But please leave your condo, now!"

"Great job, Sonja," Chris declared.

"What made you think of mentioning your parents?" Tanya asked.

"I've experienced the depth of paralyzing pain from losing your loved ones that she's feeling right now. I wanted her to feel the same hate I have for that wretch Petrovic. Believe me, primal hate is a great motivator."

"What was wrong with the Library of Congress?" Leon asked.

"I'll explain later."

CHAPTER 48

May 3
Washington, DC—Late Morning

Rebecca Bergman left her apartment, walked quickly to the nearest Metro station, and caught the train. Exiting at the Smithsonian Metro stop, she took the escalator that brought her up onto the National Mall and directly into the bright sunlight of a magnificent late-spring morning.

During happier times, she and Levy had spent hours on the Mall riding bikes, throwing a Frisbee, or just walking hand in hand along the tree-lined walking paths and beautiful gardens. But today, the spring splendor of the Mall was lost on her as she walked briskly toward her destination, her head down to hide the tears that still flowed and dried on her flushed cheeks. The young woman was so completely in a daze that she also failed to notice she had been followed from the time she left her apartment.

Moments later, Rebecca entered the vast Air and Space Museum from the Mall side and quickly walked to the moon walk exhibit on the first floor. It had been one of her and Rob's favorites. As she entered the dimly lit exhibit room, Rebecca's eyes scanned the room. Other than a group of school children, she was the only one there— or so she thought.

Out from the shadows, a lone figure approached her.

"Rebecca?"

Startled, Rebecca spun around and then pulled back at the sight of a woman dressed in black.

"It's okay, Rebecca. I'm Sonja, and we talked on the—"

"Like hell you are. I've seen Sonja Voinovich's picture in the newspapers, and you're not her," Bergman replied with an edge of panic in her voice.

"Rebecca, I had to change my appearance for obvious reasons. Look, we don't have much time. You may have been followed, and we need to leave."

Rebecca hesitated. But she knew she didn't have many options and decided to trust the woman facing her. "Okay," Rebecca said softly.

"Good. Let's get the hell out of here."

As the group of somewhat raucous third graders began to leave the moon walk exhibit, Sonja and Rebecca closely followed.

*   *   *

"I followed her, and she entered the Air and Space Museum about three minutes ago, but I've got the exit covered," Adams reported proudly by phone to Cavanaugh.

"You idiot, that woman just learned her boyfriend was murdered. Do you think she decided to go do a little sightseeing? She's either meeting someone in there or trying to give you the slip."

"Look, I can't go in the building. I'd have to check my gun and fill out a form," Adams protested. "Since I'm not exactly here on official business, I don't think that would be a good idea. Besides, I got the exit covered; she can't leave without me seeing her."

"There's another exit from the museum on the Independence Avenue side of the building, you dumb ass. Get in there now and apprehend her. We'll figure out what to do next later."

Without answering, Adams sprinted up the marble stairs and raced into the building, flashing his FBI badge in one hand and a government-issued handgun in the other.

"FBI! Everyone, down!" Adams shouted, the veins on his red and sweaty face and neck bulging, and his eyes darting in search of Bergman. "There's an armed terrorist in the building."

If Adams had thought that people, in response to his command, would quietly and calmly stop and crouch down on the marble floor, he was sadly mistaken. Instant chaos ensued as people screamed and scrambled in all directions. The wailing sounds echoed off the museum's high ceiling and reverberated back with even more volume in a wild symphony of panic.

The two museum guards at the entrance, trained mainly in reuniting lost children with their parents, promptly ran into each other and both tumbled to the floor as Adams raced into the center of the grand hall.

Then Adams spotted Rebecca on the far side of the school children who were now either shouting, crying, or in some cases laughing—but all running uncontrollably in every direction as their teachers tried in vain to rein them in.

Adams raced toward Rebecca, trying to cut through the unruly gaggle of school children.

"Sir, please. Please be careful—the children," a woman pleaded as she grabbed Adams's suit jacket with both hands.

"Out of my way," Adams shouted as he stared directly at the woman who appeared to be one of the teachers.

She refused to move out of his way or let go, and he shoved her hard. When she again refused to release her grip, Adams punched the young woman in the stomach, and she fell with a thud on the marble floor. The FBI agent then raced after Rebecca, who was heading out of the Independence Avenue exit of the museum. Adams's encounter with the woman had cost him valuable time, but he still had Rebecca in his view.

Rebecca scrambled out the exit door, down the steps, and then paused momentarily to search the street for the car Sonja had described would be her escape. At first she didn't see it and started to panic, but then …

"There it is!" Rebecca cried out in relief as she ran to the vehicle. As the vehicle's door slowly opened, a hand beckoned her to hurry.

Adams exploded through the museum exit doors, jumped over all of the stairs in a single bound, and landed with a thud on the cement sidewalk, quickly springing to his feet.

Adams raced at a full sprint after Rebecca.

In the next instance, Adams was flat on his back and dazed as his head snapped back and hit the cement sidewalk.

Standing over him was a huge, elderly, and shabbily dressed black man who said, "Are you all right? I'm sorry; didn't see you comin', and you ran right into me."

Refusing to take the hand extended and offered in a gesture of assistance, Adams yelled, "Get out of my way!"

But by the time Adams was on his feet, Rebecca had safely entered the car, which had sped away.

Adams stood for a moment and shook his head, "Damn, I didn't even see which car she got into."

As Adams walked away, the black man gently patted his shirt pocket and then entered the museum. He walked slowly in the direction of the crowd standing around the young woman who had been viciously knocked down by Adams.

"Did she make it?" the young woman asked as she struggled to get up with the help of several concerned bystanders.

"Elvis has safely left the building," the black man said with a smile. "Are you okay?"

"Other than what feels like a rather severely bruised tailbone, I'm fine."

Then to the amazement of everyone standing nearby, the young woman grabbed the hand of the shabbily dressed black man, and they headed off together.

"When he grabbed me, Adams looked directly into my eyes but didn't recognize me—amazing," Sonja said as she hugged Otto and kissed him on the cheek.

Otto gently squeezed the hand of the young woman.

"Let's blow this joint. Leon said he would pick us up at the corner of Independence and Third Street," Sonja whispered.

And with that, the odd-looking couple exited the building just before the DC police arrived and all hell broke loose.

CHAPTER 49

May 3
Prince George's County, Maryland—Afternoon

From the moment Sonja and the Crew left the farmhouse to meet up with Bergman, Chris was agitated, alternating between furiously planning the next phase of their strategy, slumping in one of the living room chairs, or pacing around the room.

"Chris, you're like a frantic mother hen worried about her little chicks. Can you give it a rest? You're driving me crazy. They'll be okay. Chet has never failed on a mission," McGinnis said with a mixture of sympathy and annoyance.

But before Chris could answer, they both heard the unmistakable sound of a car rumbling up the gravel road.

"They're back," Chris called out, and they both raced out the front door.

As the car pulled to a stop, Chris could see Rebecca slumped in the backseat between Tanya and Chet. As Chet helped the fragile, young woman out of the car, Chris hesitated, not knowing how Rebecca would react when she saw him.

Rebecca saw him and walked slowly toward him. He instinctively took a half step back in anticipation of the pummeling he expected to receive. But instead, Rebecca extended her arms, and they embraced.

"Chris, I am so sorry for what I said to you earlier. It's just that—"

"You don't have to explain," Chris interrupted as she wept uncontrollably in his arms.

After a long moment, Tanya said, "Rebecca, let's get you inside and settled in."

As Rebecca and Tanya walked away, Chris turned toward the dirt road, looking for the second vehicle.

"They made it out fine. They're just a couple of minutes behind us," Chet explained.

Moments later, the extraction team's other vehicle arrived. Chris audibly sighed, but when Sonja finally stepped from the second car, she was noticeably limping. He hurried to her, but she held up her hand, signaling she was okay.

"My butt's a little sore—those museum floors are hard," she said as she greeted Chris.

Chris gave Sonja a brief, gentle hug and whispered in her ear, "Looks like the Air and Space Museum worked out, but why did you reject the main reading room at the Library of Congress?"

Sonja looked coyly at Chris. "The reading room has only one entrance. I remembered from past visits that the Air and Space Museum has two exits."

Next, Chris greeted Otto and Leon as they exited the car and said, "Time to plan the next steps. Chet, let's you, me, and Sonja talk."

The trio entered the farmhouse and huddled, paper and pens in hand, taking notes in a corner of the living room. Billy and Otto watched the strategy session from across the room. Chris appeared to be laying out the makings of a plan for the next phase of the operation. Sometimes Sonja and Chet nodded in agreement. At other times, one or both seemed to be disagreeing. In the end, it was clear that a consensus strategy had been hammered out.

Finally, Chris called out, "Everyone, let's gather up."

When Chris saw Tanya enter the room, he asked, "How's Rebecca doing?"

"She seems to be okay, given the circumstances. She fell asleep almost as soon as her head hit the pillow."

As soon as everyone had gathered, Chris began, "If we continue on our current course, Petrovic and his associates are going to pick us off one by one. We need to go on the offensive."

"First, we need to shore up our defenses. Billy, we're going to need lots of additional surveillance and security equipment so we'll have an even earlier warning if they come after us. Also, we're going to need more weapons and lots of ammo. Second, I know a broadcast journalist at CNP, Nancy Carter, who owes me a favor. Tanya has done an amazing job of chronicling everything that's happened so far in this sordid affair. We're going to try to set up a meeting with Carter to see if she'll run a story at the appropriate time."

"Why don't we just use the Internet? It's a hell of a lot faster, and we can reach way more people," Leon said.

"Good question. We will. But if we're going to turn heads, we need a credible source of news to spread the story."

"Credible? Everyone here knows that the cable news is a joke," Leon pushed back.

"The EMCO EZ-15 conspiracy is perfect for cable news—corruption in high places, intrigue, murder, and conspiracies. If we can get this story on satellite and cable television, it will run continuously for two or three days or at least until the next sensational story comes along.

"Third, I'm going to try to reach Bingeman Foster, President Keller's chief of staff. He was a lifelong friend of Jackie Goldberg, and she trusted him implicitly."

"Damn, that's kind of risky, isn't it?" Otto exclaimed.

"It is, but it's a chance we need to take," Chet said quietly.

"Fourth, it's time to step up the search for Karl Thurgensen, the scientist who I hope can unlock the secret to EZ-15 and give us the technical proof that there's something very wrong with the product. As I mentioned awhile ago, we have a tip where he might be, but we haven't been able to locate him yet. It's getting near the time where we need to search for him.

"I plan to head out to Mason County, Virginia, next week to look for him," Chris continued.

"I thought we agreed I was going too," Sonja protested.

"We'll see," Chris responded weakly. "Any other questions?"

There were none.

"Good. Chet will work with Billy, Casey, Otto, and Freddie on getting the weapons and security equipment. Chet will also be in charge of the logistics for meetings with Foster and Carter. Tanya, Sonja, Leon, and I will work on the information to provide Foster and Carter. I think that's it. Thanks, everyone."

Everyone seemed enthusiastic about the plan, but as Chris turned and started to walk up the stairs to his room, his slumping shoulders

271

and bowed head telegraphed the enormous burden he was feeling for the safety of his comrades.

"You did good," Sonja said softly as she came over to him and touched him on his shoulder. Then she added with as much enthusiasm as she could muster, "The plan is going to work."

"It's got to work; there's too much at stake," Chris replied with more doubt than resolution in his voice.

"One thing, however. I'm going with you to find Thurgensen. You need someone who talks his language. I'm the scientist and analyst," Sonja said with conviction.

"Okay, you win," Chris lied.

* * *

Parnak Petrovic wasn't a happy man, and Cavanaugh knew that wasn't a good thing.

"But, Parnak, we got Levy's CDs from his apartment and his office. We searched his girlfriend's condo and found nothing. The odds are pretty good Levy never gave a copy to her," Cavanaugh said, feigning confidence and trying as hard as he could to put a positive spin on the disaster at the museum.

"Your boy, Adams, is a first-class screw-up. Take him off this case," Petrovic said angrily into his phone. In a more measured voice, he added, "What about the fallout from the FBI incident at the museum?"

"Got it covered. All we had to do was mention national security, suspected terrorists, and top secret. The park police and DC police backed off immediately."

"Did Adams think she had help in escaping? Did he see anything suspicious? Hell, did that moron see anything at all that might be of use to us?" Petrovic barked.

"No. He was confident she was alone. She just got lucky and avoided interception."

"Maybe you're right. Maybe we've got all the copies. But don't stop looking for Bergman."

Cavanaugh decided to take a chance. "Adams is a good agent. I trust him, and I guarantee there won't be any more problems with him. Besides, I need support, and I have no one at the Bureau I can trust on this matter."

After a long silence, Petrovic said, "Okay. Keep Adams on the mission, but no more screw-ups or I'll hold you personally responsible."

"We won't let you down," Cavanaugh replied as the sweat poured from his furrowed brow. He knew exactly what to expect from Petrovic if he or Adam made another mistake.

As Petrovic hung up, he thought, *Time for reinforcements.* He scrolled down his contact list and found the number for a former CIA agent and now chief operating officer for a mega defense and national security contractor.

When the voice at the other end said hello, Petrovic wasted no time with pleasantries.

"I need six of your best men for a Class Five operation, and I need them now."

The husky voice at the other end didn't need to ask who was calling and understood exactly what Petrovic meant by a Class Five operation. He needed well-trained, well-armed men for an assassination mission that would be conducted outside the normal CIA, Department of Defense, or DHS operations.

"Consider it done. Where and when?"

"I need them within the next forty-eight hours and will stage them in Alexandria. You know the place."

"This isn't going to be cheap."

"Cost isn't an issue, and the guys you send better be the best you've got," Petrovic cautioned and then hung up.

CHAPTER 50

May 4
Prince George's County, Maryland—Morning

Well before dawn, Chet, Freddie, Casey, Otto, and Billy headed out to obtain the necessary supplies and equipment for the next phase of the operation. By 11:30 a.m., they had returned with two cars laden with boxes and bags containing weapons, conventional and concussion grenades, flares, and other equipment.

Billy, Casey, and Freddie began the tedious task of setting up the enhanced security perimeter around the farmhouse and at the entrance gate. The three men installed motion sensors, trip wires, and surveillance cameras as well as clearing any brush that might impair line-of-sight visibility for spotting any intruders trying to close in on the farmhouse.

"Give me a hand with these boxes," Chet called out to Chris, Leon, and Otto. "We'll set up the firing range at the bottom of the hill over there."

"Anything we can do?" Sonja and Tanya asked.

"No, we're good for now. Why don't you change your clothes into something more appropriate for target practice and come back in about an hour."

The spot Chet had picked was perfect for a shooting range. The targets could be set up at the foot of a steep hill so that bullets from any shots fired would pass through, over, under, or around the target and would be stopped once they hit the hill behind the targets. The range pointed away from the road and the farmhouse.

About the time the men finished unpacking the boxes and checked and loaded the weapons, the two women walked down from the farmhouse. Sonja had changed into her spandex pants and sports bra, appearing ready to go. Tanya lagged behind and hadn't changed.

"What's up?" Chet asked.

"I don't believe in guns," Tanya said. "Sorry, Chet, but I simply can't do it."

"Okay, I won't try to force you," Chet replied, trying to hide his disappointment. "How's Rebecca doing?"

"She's a little better. I'll go back and keep an eye on her."

"I'm going to stay and shoot, if that's okay," Sonja said, looking at both Chet and Chris.

"That's fine. Ever shot a weapon before?" Chet asked.

"No, but I'm keen to learn."

Why am I not surprised? Chris thought.

The first weapons to be fired were the standard military-issue M-16 semiautomatic rifles.

"Let's limit the M-16s to me, Otto, and Chris. Billy, Freddie, and Casey can practice later today."

"Why not me?" Sonja asked with a hint of annoyance.

"Because Sonja each of us has been trained in M-16 weaponry, and learning how to shoot a pistol when you've never done it before is more than enough for you to tackle in the short time we have."

Chris was amazed when Sonja quietly acquiesced.

Chet and Otto, both who had fired the M-16 rifle extensively in Vietnam and regularly visited the firing range over the years, took little time before hitting the targets with great precision.

Chris was next. He cautiously stepped forward and took a rifle out of the box. It had been years since he had actually fired an M-16 in the army reserve. But suddenly he felt strangely comfortable holding the weapon. He snapped in a clip of twenty rounds and set the riffle on semiautomatic. Dropping to the ground, he spread his legs far apart, leaned forward, and rested the rifle in his hands, with his elbows bent and touching the ground.

Chris aimed and gently squeezed the trigger. He barely hit the upper left side of the target sheet.

"Nice shot," Sonja said sarcastically.

Ignoring her, Chris adjusted the sight and fired again—this time, he at least hit the outer ring of the target, but to the right and below the bull's eye.

Chris adjusted the sight again.

"Watch this," he said, confidently looking at Sonja.

Chris set himself and fired again. The shot hit the bull's eye at the outer edge. Once more Chris adjusted the sight and fired a shot that hit the bull's eye dead center. He then quickly switched the weapon to full automatic and fired the sixteen remaining rounds. All the shots found their mark.

"Damn fine shooting, Captain," Chet said.

Chris smiled and looked at the only person he really had hoped to impress.

Sonja looked back at him, smiled broadly, and said, "I want this guy covering my butt."

Next up was firing practice with handguns. Chet and Otto used DC police weaponry, and Chris chose his army-issue .45-caliber pistol. When it was his turn, Chris, remembering that fateful night in the park, carefully checked to make sure he had properly seated the clip. Again, the three men quickly found the range. Leon, who went next, had a considerable advantage over Sonja because he had gone to the firing range regularly with his dad. It took him a few minutes, but soon he was hitting the target reasonably well.

Sonja, who was last, exuded confidence as she stepped up. But as Chris handed her the loaded pistol, he could see her hands shaking and her palms moist with sweat.

Chris wiped Sonja's hands with the tail of his shirt, placed the weapon in her right hand, and folded her fingers around it.

"Take a deep breath and try to relax. You can do this."

He positioned her body toward the target, put his left hand on her bare hip just above her shorts, and, with his right hand, guided her arm into position. He tilted her head so she could properly line up the shot with her right eye.

"When you're ready, just gently squeeze the trigger."

His touch and soft words of encouragement had the desired effect. The tenseness she had felt was easing.

Sonja's first shot hit the target—barely. But she jumped up and down like a school kid, shouting with excitement.

She then fired two clips of bullets and showed slow improvement.

"Pretty impressive, " Chet said.

"I can do better."

"I've got an idea," Otto said as he pulled a piece of folded paper out of his pocket and continued. "What you need is a real target to shoot at."

Sonja and everyone else shook their heads, trying to guess what Otto had in mind. Walking down to the target, Otto pinned a photograph over the bull's eye. It was of Parnak Petrovic.

When Sonja saw the picture, she called out as she removed the now empty clip from her gun, "Someone, give me another clip."

Sonja reloaded the weapon, assumed the firing stance Chris had showed her, and squeezed the trigger once, then again, and again, and again until all rounds had been fired.

Leon ran down and retrieved the photograph. All the shots hit Petrovic's head. Two hit right between his eyes.

"I want this woman covering *my* butt," Chris said, smiling in admiration, and everyone patted Sonja on the back. Sonja whispered something in Otto's ear and then kissed him on the cheek.

Everyone took another turn shooting, and then Chet declared, "That's enough for today. Nice shooting, everyone."

As they all headed back to the farmhouse, Sonja came up to Chris and whispered in his ear, "Thanks. I couldn't have done it without you being there."

"I'm not sure how much I had to do with it. You simply continue to amaze me. I'm just glad you're on my side," Chris said tenderly and put his hand on Sonja's shoulder.

As the couple walked together up to the farmhouse, Chris asked, "By the way, I saw you kissing Otto on the cheek. You two seem to spend a lot of time talking together. Do I have some competition for your affections?"

Sonja stopped, and her look troubled Chris. "I was only making a joke," he said.

Sonja put her fingers on Chris's lips and then grabbed his hands and said quietly, "When Otto's wife left him years ago, she took their daughter as well. Otto has never seen his daughter since. She would be about my age. He keeps a picture of her in his shirt pocket and pats it every time he thinks of her. Remember that day when I was an emotional wreck and Otto gave me that big hug?"

"It was a nice moment."

"Ever since then, Otto and I just seem to have a very special friendship. He's like a father to me, and I know he loves me like a daughter. We can share things with each other that we don't seem to be able to share with others."

After an awkward moment of silence, Chris joked, "I hope you two don't spend a lot of time talking about me."

"No. You're way too boring a subject to occupy our time," Sonja answered and kissed Chris on the cheek.

*   *   *

After lunch as everyone moved into the living room, Sonja whispered to Chris, "If you don't need me right now, Tanya and I thought we might spend some time with Rebecca."

"Sounds good. How's she doing?"

"She's a remarkably strong woman, but she's still having a really tough time," Sonja replied as she and Tanya left.

After conferring with Chet for a moment, Chris removed from his wallet the now-somewhat-wrinkled business card that Nancy Carter had given him on the flight to Brussels.

*   *   *

Lost in thought, Nancy Carter was sitting in her office when her phone rang, and she was jolted back into reality. She grabbed the receiver, and the voice said, "You've got a call."

"Who is it?"

"Wouldn't give his name, but said he was a flight companion of yours on your trip to Brussels last month," Carter's receptionist replied.

"Must be a prank; get rid of him."

But then Carter remembered the flight in question and the man who came to her rescue when she was being harassed by an obnoxious passenger sitting next to her.

"Wait. Put him through."

"Ms. Carter, remember me?" Chris asked cautiously.

"I do and thanks again. But to be completely honest, I can't recall your name. Must be my advancing age."

"You told me, as we departed the plane, that if I ever needed a favor, you would help me out. I need a big favor, and by the way, my name is Christopher O'Brian."

The news announcer immediately made the connection. "Christopher O'Brian. You're a suspect in that ongoing FBI investigation regarding a deadly conspiracy to keep that carbon dioxide reduction product off the market. There's nothing I can do to help you. You should turn yourself into the authorities."

"Believe me, turning myself in isn't an option. I'd likely be dead within twenty-four hours. There's a conspiracy all right, but it's not me. EZ-15 is killing people, and there's a host of folks in government and industry who are trying to cover up the risks so that EPA's approval of EZ-15 becomes final in about twenty days. Lots of people stand to make lots of money once EZ-15 is on the market."

Carter sat up in her chair and grabbed a pen. "Why should I believe you? Do you have any proof to substantiate your rather preposterous allegations?"

"I do, but we're not going to talk any further about it over the phone. I have documents to prove my allegations, but we need to meet in person so I can show you."

"If you've got documents, e-mail them to me."

"I can't risk having these documents fall into the wrong hands. Will you meet with me?"

Her mind racing, Carter finally said, "Okay, I'll meet with you, but if you don't have solid proof, you're wasting your time."

"Good. Here's how we're going to do it."

Chris then explained the details of how the meeting would take place. When he finished, he asked, "Will you do it?"

"Yes," Carter replied with considerable reluctance in her voice.

"We see any signs that you've betrayed us, and you'll never hear from me again. This isn't about me. Innocent people are needlessly dying in Japan because of EZ-15," Chris warned and then hung up.

Damn it. What have I done? Carter thought as she mulled over the severe repercussions of agreeing to meet with a known fugitive who might be a killer.

*　　*　　*

Chris hung up and declared, "She'll meet with us."

Then, buoyed by what he considered to be a successful call with Carter, Chris declared, "Time to give Jackie Goldberg's old friend Bingeman Foster a call."

Chris walked over to the wall where Goldberg's note hung and wrote down the telephone number next to Foster's name. He started to dial the number.

"Wait!" McGinnis yelled as he lunged toward Chris, knocking the phone from his hand.

"What the hell?" Chris cried out.

"Sorry, pal, but you were about to call the White House, and they have the tracking technology to identify the location of any incoming call within thirty seconds. If you had stayed on the line longer, they would have pinpointed our location. Dismantling the phone in that case would have been worthless—they'd be here within the hour."

"Thanks, Billy. But what do we do?"

The technology wizard looked at Chris and then Chet. "Let's take a drive and make the call from somewhere else."

"Sounds good to me," Chet replied. In matter of minutes he, Chris, and Billy were on the road to another destination.

CHAPTER 51

May 4
Washington, DC—Afternoon

Bingeman Foster swiveled his high-back desk chair around and looked out his floor-to-ceiling window at the back lawn of the White House and the Washington Monument beyond. Although it was nearly 4:00 p.m., he still would need to spend at least three more hours at the office until President Keller left for the day. But he figured he had done all the heavy lifting earlier in the day, and what remained was going to be pretty mindless and routine.

The ring of his phone caught him by surprise; he wasn't expecting any calls.

"Mr. Foster, you've got a call on your private line," the voice of his receptionist came through the intercom speaker sitting on his desk.

"Who is it, Janet?"

"The caller didn't say, but ..."

"But what?" Foster replied with agitation.

"Well ... all he said was that he had a message from Jackie Goldberg ... a message ... from her grave."

Foster bolted up in his chair, thought for a moment, and said, "Put him through."

When the call was forwarded, the president's chief of staff quickly picked up the phone and barked, "Who the hell is this?"

"Mr. Foster, my name is Christopher O'Brian. I imagine you recognize the name."

"You bastard, you helped kill Jackie," Foster swore.

But before Foster could continue, Chris interrupted. "Jackie was my friend, and she asked me to help gather evidence to prove that EZ-15 has some serious problems. The night she was killed—murdered—she gave me some information she had collected that identified some of those involved in the conspiracy. She also told me you were her close friend and I could trust you."

"I find this all hard to believe. I don't—"

"I have the proof and will share it with you. But only if you agree to meet with me, alone."

"I can't possibly meet with you," Foster protested.

"Fine. Then I'll be saying good-bye."

"Wait, I'll meet. We can meet in my office."

Chris laughed at Foster's suggestion and added, "We'll meet at a location I choose. Be in your office on Saturday, early, and you'll receive further instructions."

Before Foster could reply, Chris hung up and looked at his watch. The call had been completed in less than two minutes.

*　　*　　*

Chris, Chet, and Billy drove back from a large shopping mall in suburban Baltimore about thirty miles away from the farmhouse. They had picked a shopping mall as the location to make the call so that if the Secret Service tracked the call and raided the site, the three members of the team would be able to blend in with the thousands of shoppers at the mall and never be detected.

When they arrived back at the farmhouse, Leon asked, "How did the call with Foster go?"

"Pretty well, I think. We set a meeting for Saturday, but we have lots of prep work to do between now and then," Chris replied.

After dinner, Rebecca came up to Chris and Sonja. "Thanks for everything. I want to help—I want to be a member of the Crew."

"Do you feel up to it?" Chris asked.

"I'm getting there. I thought this might be of help," she said, handing him a CD in a plain white envelope.

"Thanks. I'm sure it will be an enormous help," Chris replied, knowing, without asking, that the CD contained a copy of Rob Levy's article on the Heritage Study Group. Without speaking further, Rebecca turned and walked back to her bedroom.

Chris and Sonya spent the next hour carefully reading Levy's article. Rob had uncovered some additional background information on several Heritage Study Group members. When they finished, Chris rubbed Sonja on her upper arm affectionately, hoping that finally they could spend the evening together.

"Not tonight. Rebecca still needs Tanya and me," Sonja said as she leaned over and gently kissed Chris on his forehead, turned, and left to join Rebecca and Tanya.

Chris knew Sonja was right, but he couldn't hide his disappointment.

CHAPTER 52

May 5
Montgomery County, Maryland

The rain came down in torrents, and the numbing, cold wind nearly knocked over several of the older mourners huddled around the open grave. The shelter erected to protect those attending the funeral had been blown away by the blasting, near-vertical winds. The brief service completed, the casket was slowly lowered into what had become a muddy pit. Given the status of the deceased, the number of attendees was surprisingly small. Perhaps it was the awful weather, but more likely it was the rather bizarre circumstances surrounding his demise. People in Washington's power elite always needed to be mindful of the company they kept, and apparently this applied to which funerals they attended as well.

"I'm terribly sorry, Mrs. Moss," the bald-headed, well-dressed man said as he grabbed the trembling hands of the widow.

"Thank you for ... coming," was all she could say between sobs.

"Franklin did a great service to his country," the man added and then turned to speak to Congressman Alan Beasley. Beasley was standing next to the grieving widow, with one arm around her and the other holding an umbrella over her head, trying unsuccessfully to keep her from getting thoroughly soaked by the driving rain.

"Congressman, I'll be working with the FBI to track down Frank's killer," the man whispered quietly so that the widow couldn't hear.

"Thank you, Parnak. Please keep me posted."

Petrovic had testified many times before the House Environment Committee that Beasley chaired. His testimony often focused on domestic security issues related to preventing environmental terrorism, such as ensuring that public water supplies weren't contaminated by terrorists. Petrovic departed as soon as possible without seeming rude.

Even though the Heritage Study Group had canceled its weekly meeting for this Thursday morning, no other member of the group was present at the funeral except Stanley Braxton.

Moss had helped Braxton on many occasions by tacking obscure-sounding amendments onto major legislation for the sole benefit of Miller and Braxton clients. Moss and his wife dined socially on numerous occasions with Braxton and his wife. While both Braxton and his wife dreaded getting together with the incredibly boring couple, Braxton had told his wife on many occasions that those social interludes were critical to his firm's bottom line.

After Braxton finished paying his respects to Mrs. Moss, he spotted Joanne McKay, who had come representing Senator Goodman's office. Braxton made a beeline to the congressional aide.

"We need to meet again. My clients are becoming increasingly concerned with Senator Goodman's lack of support for EZ-15," Braxton whispered to the obviously surprised congressional staffer who hadn't seen him approach.

"I told you, as far as I know he's on board, and besides, Kowalski has the lead on that issue," she replied curtly.

"That's not what Kowalski tells me. Let's cut the crap. We need Senator Goodman's active support, and you are going to help him reach that conclusion."

Joanne tried to maintain her composure. "There is nothing I can do, and besides, even if you were right about Goodman, why would I help you?"

"Well, if you don't want to help, maybe I should have a little conversation with your boss about your involvement in that Goldslide debacle five years ago."

Joanne's face lost its color. After a moment, she regained some semblance of composure and said without emotion, "When do you want to meet?"

"Saturday at 7:45 a.m., and let's meet at Walker's Café in Georgetown. Come equipped with some information I can use."

There was no mystery with Braxton's choice of meeting place. It was at Walker's Café a number of years before where Joanne, for the only time in her career, breached the congressional code of ethics. Braxton had asked her for critical information on confidential committee materials about an investigation of a mining company named Goldslide. The lobbyist assured her that this kind of information was routinely shared with supporters of the senator and there would be no problems. In fact, Braxton said that with the information in hand, he could help the committee with its investigation.

Joanne, who was young, inexperienced, and naïve, gave the information to Braxton, and he shared it with several of his investor clients, who made a killing on Goldslide's stock. Subsequently, the leak somehow was discovered, and the Senate Ethics Committee ordered an investigation. Joanne was questioned and under suspicion for several months. It was the worst time of her life. But in the end, she was saved by the unrelenting support of Senator Goodman, who was convinced, and convinced others, that she was innocent. The source of the leak was never discovered, and Joanne's career was saved.

Joanne didn't speak further but nodded affirmatively to Braxton. She turned and slowly walked away into the mist of the pounding rain that had seemed to intensify.

* * *

At the very moment Franklin Moss was being lowered into his muddy grave, another funeral was just starting nearly seven hundred miles away in a small Jewish cemetery in a suburb of Chicago. The weather was frigid for this time of year, but at least the sun was shining as the family and hometown friends of Robert Levy gathered to say their final prayers for him.

Noticeably absent from the funeral was Rob's longtime girlfriend, Rebecca Bergman. Rob and Rebecca weren't engaged, but everyone who knew them figured it was just a matter of time before they married and started a family.

Rob's parents knew full well why Rebecca hadn't come. Earlier that morning, Rebecca, having had her cell phone confiscated by Chet, had used one of the cheap cell phones and called Rob's parents.

"The story about the cause of Rob's murder is totally fabricated. I can't tell you the details now, but Rob was a hero, and the truth will come out, I promise," Rebecca said as tears dripped down her face, and her trembling hands struggled to keep the phone near her mouth.

"I'm in danger too and must hide until ..." Rebecca hesitated, barely able to speak. "I loved Rob more than anything else in the world. I'm so sorry ..."

Chet, gently taking the phone from the young woman's hand, hit the disconnect button and put his arm around Rebecca, who sobbed uncontrollably.

As the funeral neared its end, the young Chicago-based FBI agent standing off in the distance, trying to look inconspicuous, continued to watch the funeral with a picture of Rebecca Bergman in his hand. As the last person began to leave, he crinkled up the picture, turned, and headed to his car parked at the far end of the cemetery.

CHAPTER 53

May 5
Washington, DC—Afternoon

Nancy Carter left her office at 1:00 p.m. and, as instructed, walked in a somewhat circuitous route to the designated meeting spot. Standing under a building marquee on P Street, NW that offered some measure of protection from the wind and rain, she looked at her watch, which now read 1:40 p.m.

What the hell am I doing here? she thought.

Carter knew that she had never been one to take risks, but she felt she owed O'Brian at least a hearing. Besides, if there was something to his claim, it might just be the ticket to saving her career.

In her youth, Carter had been a damn good researcher and journalist, but what got her in front of the cameras was a homey yet attractive face, a voice as smooth as silk, and more than adequate breasts. But CNP, like every other cable news network, had moved away from hard news and in-depth reporting to shock-value breaking stories and other fluff pieces designed to attract greater audiences. As a consequence, Carter had become what the industry called a "news reader."

Now approaching fifty, the wrinkles and thinning hair were harder and harder to disguise. Carter knew her career was nearing its end. She had less and less airtime, and the stories she got were mostly fillers.

"They're fifteen minutes late. I'm out of here."

But as she stepped out to leave, a cab abruptly turned into the curb on the street, spraying her with a wall of water from the oily pool that had collected curbside. The cab driver waved his hand, beckoning her to approach.

"What the hell are you doing? I didn't flag a cab, and you soaked my boots and raincoat," she shouted. That the boots were Dolce Vita and the raincoat a Burberry only added to her distress.

"Please get in, Ms. Carter, and don't make a scene," the cabbie instructed.

Surprised at first, she reluctantly opened the door of the rusting cab and slid onto the cracked and worn imitation-leather seat.

"Nice cab," she said sarcastically.

"It gets the job done," the cabbie replied. Then, without looking back, he handed her a black, silk blindfold like something one might wear to bed to block the rays of the morning sun and said politely, "Please put this on."

"Are you crazy? Absolutely not," she protested.

"As you'll find out, it's for your own protection."

She reluctantly put the blindfold on as the cab pulled away from the curb. After about a minute, a phone rang, and the cabbie answered, "Okay. Good. We're on our way."

Otto Simpson, who was staked out near where Carter had been waiting, watched for any vehicles that might try to follow the cab once it picked up Carter. When he was sure the cab wasn't being followed, Otto called Chet, who then headed off directly to the rendezvous point.

Other than asking three times, "Where are we going?" for which she received no reply, Carter sat quietly, becoming increasingly annoyed and frightened that she had made a very bad decision. After about twenty minutes, the cab, which Chet had borrowed from a friend, pulled up to the curb. Getting out of the car, Chet opened the door for Carter and said, "Please allow me to escort you into the building."

She reluctantly acquiesced and was led up a sidewalk and then up a short flight of stairs and through a door. Once inside, she was led into a room.

"You may take off the blindfold."

Cater removed the blindfold quickly, and it took her eyes a moment to adjust before she could see she was in a small room with the shades drawn. No pictures were on the wall, but nail holes were evident. The wood floor looked old and worn, and the only furniture was the chair she was sitting in and four other identical chairs facing her with what appeared to be two women and two men in them, all of whom wore caps to hide their hair and large-lens sunglasses to hide their identity. She guessed correctly that she was in a private residence, but she assumed incorrectly that it was an abandoned building.

The man sitting across from her on her extreme right spoke first. "Thank you for coming."

Carter immediately recognized the smooth, deep voice as that of the man she had met on the flight to Brussels.

"To be honest, I'm not convinced it was a good idea to come here. I think I'd like to leave."

"Please just sit and listen, and when we're finished, you may ask any questions you have."

The news reporter nodded, and Chris began. He covered in detail everything that had happened over the past horrific three-and-a-half weeks.

"Ronnie Chapman, Ann Hastings, Sergio Sanchez, Gerhard Mueller, Jackie Goldberg, Pam Russell, Franklin Moss, and Rob Levy all were connected in one way or another with EZ-15 and now they're dead."

Carter shifted nervously in her chair but said nothing.

Sonja spoke next. She talked about her conversations with Ronnie Chapman regarding his discovery of possible faulty test results on EZ-15, being chased by two FBI agents, the research she had done showing an increase in asthma attacks and deaths where EZ-15 was being used, her encounters in her youth with Parnak Petrovic, and much more.

Rebecca Bergman was the last to speak. "Rob was ready to submit his story on the Heritage Study Group to his editor, but he was murdered the night before. The story about Rob being killed by some homophobe in the middle of a sex act with another man is complete bullshit. I've been Rob's lover for nearly three years, and I can assure you he wasn't gay. Even if he had been gay, it wouldn't have mattered. But that his death looked like he was, clearly proves the killer staged the crime scene."

Chris then placed a computer on Carter's lap showing two icons: one was a link to Tanya's write-up of everything that had happened, and the other was Rob's article.

"Read these two documents, and then we'll try to answer any questions you may have."

Nancy Carter spent the next fifteen minutes reading the information. She said nothing, but several times she let out gasps and swore often in disbelief.

"Chris, you were right. This all is almost too outrageous to take seriously. But I'm inclined ... to believe you."

"Great!" Chris replied.

"Not so fast. There are several problems—perhaps fatal problems. First, you and Sonja are fugitives from justice and, in fact, have been accused by the FBI of being the perpetrators of many of the events you are now blaming others for. Second, while Rob Levy had a reputation for journalistic integrity, in his article he cites anonymous sources, which I assume are you and your female compatriot—again your credibility can be attacked. Third, while many of the events you have cited did occur, such as the deaths of various people and the explosion at the German EPA lab, there is no independent evidence that those events are, in fact, linked to a conspiracy to cover up any harmful side effects of using EZ-15. Finally, you have nothing that would explain the cause of any possible adverse impacts of EZ-15."

Lowering his head, Chris sat silently, but then he looked up and said hopefully, "What if we can, in fact, establish a scientifically-based explanation that proves the use of EZ-15 poses a serious health risk?"

"If you can find the link, I believe you have a story, and I'd be willing to run with it," Carter replied.

"We'll get the proof you need. The woman who wrote the report you read will deliver the evidence directly to you once we have it. I ask only that you give credit to her and Rob Levy when you broadcast the whole story."

Carter nodded affirmatively.

"One more thing—don't mention this meeting to anyone, no matter how much you think you can trust them," Chris warned.

"Chris, I'm a journalist, and I won't say anything to anyone that would place you or your colleagues in harm's way."

"Nancy, I'm not worried about us. You're the person who will be in grave danger if your involvement in this matter becomes known to the wrong people. Believe me, don't trust anyone."

With that, the meeting ended, and Chet led Carter out of the building, which actually was his house, and drove her back to within three blocks of the CNP office building.

Walking back to her office, Carter's mind was spinning. She felt an enormous rush of excitement and at the same time considerable fear with what she had suddenly gotten herself involved.

CHAPTER 54

May 6
Bethesda, Maryland

"Robin, I won't be in today," Witt explained to his administrative assistant. "The kids both have a touch of the flu, and Katie needs to run some errands, so I'll be working from home and playing nursemaid."

What Witt was planning to do, he needed to do in the privacy of his basement office. A week before, Witt had completed the first task requested by O'Brian. He had opened ten offshore accounts in different names and deposited $200,000 in each account from funds generated from selling over half of Chris's stock holdings. Today was the day designated by Chris to use all of those funds to buy "Puts" on EMCO stock in accordance with Chris's written instructions.

Stepping down the creaking wood stairs, Witt turned on his computer and quickly entered the necessary information, accessing each account and then completing the transaction. What Chris was asking Witt to do was a pure gamble. Chris was hoping that in less than a month, EMCO stock would fall in value, and Witt could sell the Puts at an enormous profit. In essence, Chris was betting the whole "pot of money" that EMCO stock, currently trading at over sixty dollars a share, would significantly drop on or before May 25. If it did, the return on the investment could be enormous. If the stock price didn't drop below the strike price on or before the date designated, each offshore account would be completely worthless.

Dan had followed the meteoric rise in EMCO's stock value over the past week since getting Chris's instructions. Everything he read

293

in the financial press predicted that the stock could eventually hit ninety dollars or more. As he turned his computer off and headed upstairs, Witt shook his head. "I just lost my client two million dollars."

CHAPTER 55

May 7
Prince George's County, Maryland—Early Morning

The debating and planning were over, and it was time to go. Billy and Tanya got into Billy's car, and Chet slid into the driver's seat of the GMC Sierra delivery van Casey had borrowed from a friend. The plates had been changed, just in case. Otto, Leon, Casey, and Freddie piled into the back of the van.

Chris was the last to enter the van, but as he turned to climb in, he saw Sonja standing on the porch, looking at the Crew. The young woman's shoulders slumped, her hands covered her mouth, and her eyes stared wide with concern. He walked slowly toward her and could see her shaking, her cheeks reddened.

As Chris grabbed her and pressed her body tightly into his, he said softly, "Everything is going to be okay."

She hugged him back. "I wish I could be there with you. I feel so helpless being left behind."

"You've got the most important job. If something bad goes down, you're the one who's going to have to guide us safely through it."

"I know, but please be careful," Sonja pleaded and then reluctantly released her hold on him.

As the two vehicles drove away, Sonja turned slowly toward the farmhouse. For the first time since just before she and Chris had rendezvoused, the night Jackie Goldberg was murdered, she felt alone and helpless.

* * *

When Foster arrived at the west wing of the White House Saturday shortly before 6:00 a.m., the security guards were hardly surprised. Foster was legendary for his penchant to begin the day early. Per his routine, he read all of the overnight international cables. If there were any looming crises, he wanted to be the first to know and to begin immediately scoping out a plan so when President Keller arrived, usually around eight thirty, he would be more than ready.

But today, happily, the six pages of cables presented nothing of particular consequence, so he could focus all of his attention on the meeting with O'Brian. His receptionist/administrative assistant had made coffee in anticipation of Foster's arrival. The young woman had flowing, light brown hair, and while the thought had crossed Foster's mind that she was probably fantastic in bed, he never approached her inappropriately.

Those days are gone forever, thanks to Clinton, Foster thought as he graciously accepted the cup of black coffee from the staffer and entered his office.

Foster didn't fit the mold for being a president's chief of staff. He was a career Washington bureaucrat—first, as a star antitrust lawyer in the Justice Department, before being named attorney general by President Keller's predecessor. Also, he was sixty, which seemed to many a little old to serve a young, dynamic president who was in his midforties. But Foster was a genius and a survivor. He knew Washington and the political community and how to work both crowds to his boss's advantage and his own. Foster also had the uncanny skill to deal effectively with any crisis that occurred.

As Foster sat at his desk, he let his mind drift to life after Washington. He had decided that his career in public service would end when Keller's reelection campaign was complete—win or lose. The chief of staff was in great physical shape and was looking forward to reaping the fruits of his labors and living a life of luxury, working in the private sector as a former Washington insider.

But any pleasant thoughts about the future were brought to a crashing close as the phone on his desk rang.

"Here we go," Foster thought as he slowly reached for the phone.

The first call from O'Brian on the previous Wednesday had been both surprising and disquieting. At Foster's urging several months before, President Keller had jumped on the EZ-15 bandwagon in an effort to bolster his diminishing support from the left wing of his party. The liberals in the party had complained that Keller had done little since being elected to address the issue of climate change—an issue Keller promised during the campaign would be a top priority if he was elected president. Keller faced a tough reelection campaign in the coming year, and he could ill afford losing the support of anyone who had supported him in his first successful presidential bid. If Keller were in any way tied to a product that had serious adverse health consequences, it could cost him the reelection.

"It's the call you were expecting, Mr. Foster," the young staffer from the outer office said when Foster finally answered.

"Put the call through."

"Good morning, Mr. O'Brian."

The voice that replied wasn't O'Brian's, but that of a young woman. "Do exactly what I tell you. Leave your office now and walk to the front steps of the Daughters of the American Revolution concert hall on Seventeenth Street. From your office, it should only take you fifteen minutes. If you're not there in fifteen minutes, there'll be no meeting. Give me your cell phone number."

"My cell phone number is 202-555-1001, but—" Foster replied, as the call ended abruptly. Foster looked at his watch. It read 7:20 a.m. He immediately jumped up and hurried out without saying a word to the young staffer.

*   *   *

"Done," Tanya declared as Billy continued to drive around the outer circle of the Washington Beltway. They needed to keep moving in case the White House tried to trace Tanya's call.

At 7:37 a.m., Foster arrived at the steps of the grand DAR building not far from the White House. Looking around, Foster saw no one who seemed remotely interested in his arrival. A block and half away, Leon sat at a small café with a clear view of Foster on the steps of the concert hall. Leon took a sip of his coffee and casually picked up his cell phone from the table.

"He's there. It doesn't look like he was followed. You've got the all clear."

Tanya waited five minutes and then called Foster. "Walk to the corner of Fifteenth and Constitution, and await further instructions."

"Listen, whoever you are, I'm not interested in playing your games."

"I can assure you, Mr. Foster, this isn't a game. The lives of hundreds of thousands of people are at stake."

Foster tried to reply, but again the call ended abruptly. He reluctantly continued his journey. Over the next forty-five minutes, he was sent to various locations within a five-block radius of the White House. At each stop, he was watched alternatively by Leon, Freddie, or Casey. Once Foster arrived at a given location and appeared not to have been followed, they would call Tanya with the all clear, and she would in turn call Foster with new instructions.

"Damn it. I've had enough," Foster barked into the phone.

Tanya remained calm and said firmly, "Go to the northeast side of Lafayette Park and sit on the park bench to the left of the blooming pink azaleas. Arrive there by 8:30 a.m. or you won't hear from me again."

Foster was furious, but he had come this far, and there was too much at stake to give up now. He walked back in the general direction of the White House and Lafayette Park. The park was directly across Pennsylvania Avenue from the White House, where Foster had begun his Saturday-morning odyssey over an hour before.

As Foster entered the park, he spotted the huge pink azalea bushes and made his way toward them, as instructed. For this early in the morning on a Saturday, the park was more crowded with tourists than normal because the flowers and bushes were in full bloom. When he finally spotted the park bench in question, it was occupied by an enormous black man clad in the most disgusting, dirty, torn, and odiferous attire. Foster looked around, shook his head in disgust, and turned to leave.

"Mr. Foster, I presume? Please have a seat," the man said calmly as he sat up and patted a spot beside him.

Foster reluctantly and cautiously moved toward the bench and sat down. "What the hell is going on here?"

"Be patient, Mr. Foster. Christopher O'Brian will be here momentarily," Otto Simpson said without looking at his newly arrived guest. Then Otto took an unwrapped, half-eaten Hershey milk chocolate bar and offered it to his guest.

"Get that disgusting thing away from me."

* * *

Shortly before Foster began his journey to meet up with Chris, Joanne McKay left her apartment building and made her way slowly to her breakfast meeting with Braxton seven blocks down M Street. The stark and determined expression on Joanne's face said it all. She was at once angry, fearful, and depressed. The next hour would determine whether her career and her life as a hotshot congressional aide would survive or come crashing down around her.

"This has got to work," Joanne said aloud, with a mix of hope and determination. She had spent a sleepless night carefully planning every element of what she would wear, say, and do when she met with Braxton.

Dressed in a tight, form-fitting, cream-colored knit sweater, a matching short, straight skirt, and open-toe, leather high heels, Joanne had strategically applied perfume, which she normally didn't wear. The congressional staffer hoped her attire, which showcased her figure and long legs, would both distract Braxton and send a message that she was available.

Arriving at the sidewalk café, Joanne spotted Braxton seated at a table. As the lobbyist stood up, she said pleasantly, "Good morning, Stan."

Braxton, his eyes popping wide open, and his jaw hanging slightly down at the sight and smell of the magnificent woman before him, gave Joanne one of his standard, inappropriate, and offensive hugs. But this time Joanne allowed his groping to continue for more than a moment as she pressed into his body and allowed her hand to gently brush his leg.

They finally sat down, ordered breakfast, and engaged in mindless banter. As they finished breakfast, Braxton lost the smile on his face and said, "So what do you have for me?"

Joanne was ready. "I wasn't completely honest with you when we spoke last week at lunch."

"Tell me something I don't already know," Braxton replied as he leaned menacingly closer to the young woman's face.

"Look, all I was trying to do was protect my boss. But I guess I don't really have much of a choice in this matter, do I?"

"No you don't. So get on with it."

"Goodman does have doubts about EPA's approval of EZ-15. It's nothing based on facts, but he respected Goldberg's instincts, and the fact that she believed there was a possible problem with EZ-15 matters to him. The circumstances of her death have further shaken his confidence in the product."

"What else have you got?" Braxton replied impatiently.

"Senator Goodman sent Kowalski to the Detroit office because he felt Kowalski was a little too cozy with you and EMCO on this issue. The senator wanted a person he felt would be objective, so he assigned me to the EZ-15 issue. He has my trust on this."

"Very good. Let me know what you need in terms of information and support. We can do a full-court press, if needed. I'll bring in all the big guns to meet with Goodman. Whatever it takes, including money," Braxton replied, smiling. But changing his tone, he warned, "You've got ten days to get Goodman on our side. Am I making myself clear?"

Joanne replied nervously, "I think a meeting would be a good idea. But there is one thing more."

"What?"

"You know that I told Goodman about my conversation with O'Brian in Brussels. For some reason, the senator thinks O'Brian may have some valuable information about EZ-15, and it's going to be hard to convince him otherwise," Joanne replied nervously. "It's not my fault Goodman feels that way. What should I do?"

"Don't worry about O'Brian. He's going to cease to be a problem later this morning."

Although Joanne felt like she had just been kicked in her stomach, she gathered what composure she could muster and asked without an ounce of emotion, "What do you mean?"

"That's not your concern. Watch the evening news, and you'll get your answer," Braxton said with a smile. "Just do your part."

"Okay," McKay responded as her mind raced.

With that, Braxton paid the bill and got up to leave. Grabbing Joanne one last time, he whispered in her ear, "After all this is over, let's you and I get together to celebrate EMCO's success."

Feeling both nauseous and panicked, Joanne nonetheless marshaled her emotions and said in silky, sexy voice, "That would nice."

As soon as Braxton caught a taxi and was on his way, Joanne instinctively reached for her cell phone, but she had left it back at her apartment. "Damn it," McKay cursed as she looked at her watch, which read 8:15 a.m.

With no taxi in sight, it would take her twenty-five minutes to walk back to her apartment. She had no choice. In an instant, she pulled off her high-heel sandals, took off her tight skirt, and ripped one side of her tight-fitting slip up to her waist to free her legs. Then McKay took off running down the sidewalk half-dressed and in her bare feet to the amazement of the few onlookers who happened to be out this early Saturday morning.

When McKay arrived at her apartment building a mere ten minutes later, she rapidly punched in the entrance code and raced to her apartment. It wasn't until she entered her apartment that she felt the agonizing sharp pain in her feet. Looking down, McKay saw the bloody footprints on her living room carpet and the mangled bottoms of her feet that had been severely lacerated by pieces of broken glass and all matter of debris on the sidewalk during her race home. Ignoring the excruciating pain, she grabbed her cell phone from the coffee table, hit the contacts button, scrolled down to Chris's number, and hit send.

"Come on, come on, Chris, damn it. Pick up," she shouted as the phone rang again and again, but no one answered.

Finally, she heard the recorded message and recognized Chris's voice. "Hi. Please leave me a message at the tone."

"Chris, it's me, Joanne. It's nearly 8:30 a.m. on Saturday. Wherever you are—get the hell out of there! Someone has set a trap for you."

Joanne reluctantly hung up the phone, slumped onto her couch, and sobbed uncontrollably. She had been too late. Her career was probably over, but far more important, Christopher O'Brian likely wouldn't survive the day.

"Everything Chris told me about EMCO, EZ-15, and Braxton was absolutely true," she sobbed, oblivious to the pain in her bleeding feet.

*   *   *

301

When Chris's cell phone rang, Sonja, who had been staring at the computer in her unending quest to find the connection between EZ-15 and the asthma attacks, literally jumped out of her chair. As a chill ran down her spine, she raced over to the ringing cell phone. Grasping the phone tightly in her hand, she started to answer it but caught herself. Then holding the phone and frantically pacing around, she waited, hoping that the person who called would leave a message. Her mind raced as she thought of one horrifying scenario after another that would explain why someone was calling at this particular moment.

Finally, she grabbed a cell phone from the box and entered the number to retrieve Chris's messages. When she was connected, Sonja saw a number she didn't recognize. She retrieved the message and listened in shock to Joanne's desperate message.

"Is this for real or is it a set up?" Sonja agonized before concluding that she really had no choice but to return the call. She grabbed another cell phone and dialed the number.

"Chris is that you? It's me, Joanne," the frantic voice at the other end said.

"No."

"Who is this? There's no time for games. Chris is in real danger. Is he there?"

"No."

"Sonja? Is this Sonja Voinovich? Sonja, you've got to get word to Chris immediately. He's in imminent danger. I don't have any of the details, but Stanley Braxton told me less than fifteen minutes ago that someone has set a trap, and Chris is the target. You've got to get word to him—"

Sonja hung up without saying another word and smashed the phone.

Was that really McKay? If so, is Chris really in danger? What should I do?

*   *   *

"Enough is enough." Bingeman Foster barked at his unwanted park bench companion as the president's chief of staff rose to leave.

"Just a moment, Mr. Foster," Otto said softly as he grabbed Foster's arm. "I see Mr. O'Brian approaching."

Foster's eyes looked around the park, but all he saw were two poorly dressed men ambling slowly in his direction.

Foster started to speak, but his train of thought was interrupted by a nearby cell phone ring. To Foster's surprise, his companion reached into his heavy coat, pulled out a cell phone, and answered it—but didn't speak.

Otto Simpson listened attentively to the voice at the other end for a brief moment. Then without any sign of emotion, he ended the call, placed the phone on the pavement, and crushed it with his massive foot. He sat motionless—his head bowed slightly almost as if he was praying.

Then without looking at Foster, Otto stood up, tapped his coat chest pocket over his heart, reached into his pants pocket, and pulled out a handgun. Foster, fearing for his life, sprang from the bench and dove into the nearby azalea bed.

"Please, please don't kill me," Foster howled like a little child.

But Otto wasn't interested in Foster. Otto knew he had to create a diversion to give Chris, Chet, and the others a chance to escape. And so, tapping his coat pocket one more time, he raised the pistol high in the air and fired four shots harmlessly skyward while screaming wildly, "Death to President Keller!"

A DC police officer walking through the park, without thinking, grabbed his service revolver and fired three shots at close range. The bullets ripped holes in Otto's coat as he spun completely around before falling dead on the sidewalk. Absolute chaos erupted as everyone in the park scattered in all directions. Chris instinctively moved toward Otto, but Chet grabbed his coat and pulled Chris down.

"Otto knew what he was doing. Somehow he sensed a trap and made the ultimate sacrifice to save us and the mission. We can't help him now, but I promise that when the time is right, we'll bring Otto home."

Without further discussion, Chet and Chris joined the other men, women, and children scurrying out of the park. As the two men slipped away, a team of secret service agents raced toward Foster. The agents had been tracking at a distance, Foster, who was equipped with a tiny tracking device. They had been instructed to wait until Foster activated his signaling device before they moved in. Foster had hit the signal as soon as Otto had pulled out his weapon.

CHAPTER 56

May 8
Prince George's County, Maryland

At the first light of Sunday morning, Chris carefully took Sonja's soft, limp arm that was resting across his bare chest and gently placed it on the blanket next to him. Late the night before, she had come to his bed and, without speaking, had lifted the covers and climbed in close to him. Neither spoke as he held her tightly. She began to sob deeply, her chest heaving, and her body shivering for many minutes. Finally, her breathing slowed, and she became quiet as she drifted off to sleep. Chris lay awake all night, replaying in his mind everything that had happened the day before and trying to figure out why things went so horribly wrong. He felt the disaster was his fault, and the guilt was crushing him.

But finally morning had arrived, and Chris grabbed his running clothes and moved, as quietly as he could, out of the bedroom and downstairs, where he dressed.

As Chris began to run down the gravel road, his thoughts drifted back once more to the horrific events of the previous day. Otto's incredible act of courage and sacrifice had its intended effect of creating utter chaos in the park, allowing Chet and Chris to make their way unnoticed back to the van parked four blocks away to join Freddie, Casey, and Leon. Chet immediately called Billy McGinnis and had yelled, "Abort—head back to base!"

When everyone arrived back at the farmhouse, Sonja raced to embrace Chris. "I was so scared."

But moments later, while still in Chris's arms, she had looked around in puzzlement. "Where's Otto?"

"Otto didn't make it," Chris said with great sadness in his voice.

Sonja lost all color in her face and fainted dead away in shock.

Now as Chris continued his Sunday morning run, he tried in vain to recall what had happened the rest of the previous day. He remembered carrying Sonja back into the farmhouse and to her bedroom. As best he could recall, members of the group wandered aimlessly around the farmhouse, took walks, or sat in silence.

By 8:00 p.m., everyone, including Chris, had gone to their bedrooms. No one had the stomach to eat anything. Three hours later, Sonja had come to his bedroom. A day that had started with such promise had ended in disaster, and the spirit of the group had been crushed.

Now as Chris neared the turnaround point for his run, he heard someone behind him, rapidly closing in. He immediately recognized the cadence and didn't need to look back to identify his pursuer.

"Thanks for being there for me last night," Sonja said softly.

He glanced over at the caring expression on the face of the person now beside him matching him stride for stride, and for the first time since the disaster in the park, he felt a spark of hope as his will to carry on the fight began to well up inside of him.

"How are you doing?" Chris asked.

"Not great, but I'll survive."

"Your quick thinking saved us yesterday."

"Don't thank me. Joanne McKay is the real hero. I can't imagine how she got wind of the trap, but I'm pretty sure she has probably put herself in danger."

"Right—we need to get a message to her quickly," Chris replied.

They ran in silence for a few moments, and then Sonja brushed her hand against Chris's arm and said forcefully, "We can't let those bastards win. We owe it to Otto, Ronnie, Jackie, and everyone else they've killed."

"I was just thinking the same thing," he said. "Let's get back and start figuring how we do it."

* * *

Twenty minutes later, everyone was seated in the living room. As Chris looked around, he could sense that the mood was still somber but somewhat improved from the day before.

But what came next was completely unexpected.

"If everyone would kindly stand and take the hand of the person on either side of you, I would like to begin with a prayer," Chet said softly, but in a tone that suggested he wasn't about to accept a no from anyone.

Chris grabbed Sonja's soft hand to his left and Casey's huge, callused hand to his right. Everyone bowed their heads, and Chet began.

"Dear Lord. Thank you for having allowed us to share the wonderful spirit of Otto Simpson in our daily lives. We know he is with you now, but we who remain miss him dearly. Give us the strength to move beyond the pain and sense of hopelessness we now feel. Give us the wisdom and courage to prevail as we move forward in our journey to save the lives of the young and innocent. And let us never forget that we are on the path of righteousness and that we will succeed if we open our hearts to you. In your name we pray. Amen."

The prayer was followed by a chorus of "Amens," and each person turned and hugged the persons next to them. Chris wasn't a religious person, nor were most of the other Crew members, but Chet's words and the group standing together gave Chris, and he suspected others, a comforting feeling of warmth and courage. Chris genuinely believed the moment they were sharing would help everyone move forward. As he glanced at Sonja, Chris sensed that she felt it too.

Turning to Chris, Chet said, "Captain, it's your show."

Chris looked around the room with heartfelt admiration at the most unlikely bunch of comrades he could have ever imagined. They had become a family, and after Chet's words, he realized that what mattered wasn't his survival, but bringing down the conspirators and making sure that everyone else in the room remained safe from harm. "First, I want to thank all of you for everything you've done since becoming a part of this. I don't need to tell you that we suffered a major setback yesterday, but it wasn't the fault of any of you. I'm the guilty party. I mistakenly thought we could trust Foster, and I was horribly wrong—"

Chet jumped up before Chris could go on. "Chris, trusting Foster was a chance we had to take. We all knew the risk. Let's move forward and stop looking back."

Regaining his composure, Chris carefully began discussing the next steps. He reviewed everything the Crew needed to accomplish going forward in order to block EPA's final approval of EZ-15.

After about ten minutes, he concluded, "Sonja and I will leave early tomorrow. We'll stock the vehicle with everything we'll need to help track down and convince Karl Thurgensen to work with us. Then we need to keep him safe, so we'll need guns, ammo, cell phones, computers, and other supplies. Anything else anyone wants to add?"

Freddie spoke next. "We need to shut down operations here and get the hell out by first thing Tuesday morning. It'll take the FBI at least a few days to identify Otto, do a background check on him, and identify his associates, including Chet, Casey, Billy, and me. They'll visit our residences, family, and friends. They'll discover that we have all strangely disappeared. Eventually, someone will figure out to come and check Casey's abandoned family farm. We need to immediately double check all of the surveillance equipment and, starting tomorrow, we'll need to have around-the-clock lookouts. Start packing what you absolutely need, and we'll destroy the rest."

Billy spoke last and reviewed how communications among members of the Crew would be maintained now that, starting the next day, Chris and Sonja would be in one place, and everyone else would be moving to a new place—a house on the north side of Baltimore.

"The area is notorious and so dangerous that even the police stay away. It's a perfect place to hide from federal and local authorities," Billy concluded.

"Unless there's something else, I think that covers everything," Chris said. "Except one thing." Chris reached behind his chair and handed Chet the bag filled with over $70,000 in hundred-dollar bills.

Chet looked inside, and his eyes popped open. "We don't need all this."

"I have all I need. It's for all of you. Spend what you need to complete your part of the mission and then divide it up among

307

yourselves," Chris replied to his friend as Chet graciously accepted the bag.

.   After the day's tasks had been completed, everyone gathered on the porch to say their goodnights and good-byes. No one was sure when, if ever, they would all be together again. A poignant sense of sadness was present in their final moments together. Chris and Chet stood face to face for more than an awkward moment.

Finally, Chris, somewhat choked up, said, "Thanks for everything. Be safe—we all know they'll be coming after you."

"Don't worry about us. We'll be out of here long before they come. You know how to reach me if you need anything from our end. You can do this, Chris. We can beat these bastards. But be careful and take care of Sonja. She's an amazing woman."

Chris thought, *I know exactly how I'm going to protect her.*

Chet and Chris then turned to join the others who had already entered the farmhouse. As the two men walked, Chet put his arm around Chris and patted his shoulder like a father saying good-bye to his son.

When Chris finally entered the farmhouse, Sonja was lingering by the door and quietly whispered, "Would you like a little company tonight?"

Chris turned and gave Sonja a deep kiss and held her tightly for several moments. Finally, he whispered, "We better not—we need to get some sleep. Tomorrow is going to be a long day, and we've got to get off early. I'll come to wake you in the morning."

While disappointed with Chris's answer, she knew he was right.

CHAPTER 57

May 9
Prince George's County, Maryland

Glancing at his watch which read 4:30 a.m., Chris opened the front door of the aging black SUV, got in, and turned the ignition. Nothing. He tried again and again, but the engine showed no signs of life. Sweating in frustration, he tried once more, and the engine first labored and finally started. He was on his way.

This thing is a real piece of crap, Chris thought as the vehicle bounced and shimmied down the dusty gravel road. His assessment was accurate—the outside of the vehicle was rusted and dented. But the vehicle, which Freddie had procured from U-Rent It Cheap, Inc. the day before, had one enormous advantage—it came with a no-questions-asked policy that included renting it without proof of identification or even a driver's license required. Of course, such a great deal came at a cost—$2,000 up front and cash only. For an extra $500, the SUV didn't even have to be returned.

Chris finally reached the paved road, and within twenty minutes he was on the interstate highway system heading south and then west. Lost in thought, he failed to notice that the passing landscape changed from office buildings and shopping centers to suburbs and finally to lush, green farmland with the mountains off in the distance.

By 6:15 a.m., Chris had reached I-81, the major north-south truck route between New York State to the north and Georgia to the south. In Virginia, the roadway for three hundred miles paralleled and passed through the heart of the beautiful Shenandoah Valley.

The early-morning traffic was light, and Chris made good time. But then it started, barely audible and intermittent at first, but increasingly more frequent and louder over time.

"What the hell," Chris said, totally exasperated as he spotted a sign indicating a rest area two miles ahead and quickly decided to check it out. While Chris knew absolutely nothing about motor vehicles, he hoped he could find someone at the rest stop who could help him.

The thumping noise continued until he slowed down to pull off the interstate. Parking near where several large trucks were parked, in case he needed to ask for help, Chris turned off the ignition, got out, and looked under the vehicle to see if anything had come loose. Seeing nothing, he shook his head in frustration and started to walk toward a nearby tractor trailer. But then the noise started again, louder and more rapidly than before.

The sound was clearly coming from the cargo area in the back of the SUV. He opened the rear hatch, and the noise grew even louder. Only now Chris thought he also heard a muffled voice coming from the same general location.

And then it hit him. "Damn."

Chris started to frantically pull boxes and bags out of the back of the vehicle, but at first he found nothing. Then he spotted a barely visible handle, which he pulled, revealing a well-hidden and surprisingly large additional storage area under the main back storage area.

"Thought you'd leave me behind, did you?" Sonja said, innocently looking up at Chris.

As he reached in and helped her out of the cramped space, Sonja said, "Chet figured you'd probably pull this stunt and leave me behind. We both felt you needed my help, so we got up before you, I hid in there—man was that uncomfortable—and here I am."

For one of the few times in his life, Chris was at a loss for words, and Sonja seized the moment. At first she approached him slowly as she tried getting the circulation back in her legs.

Then her expression changed as she frowned. "How could you leave me? You lied to me."

Chris didn't try to stop Sonja's verbal assault. He simply let her vent her anger, and when she finally finished, he put his arms around her and whispered, "If I told you the real reason I lied and left you, you'd never believe me. With all my heart I wish you hadn't done this. But now that you're here, I've got to admit I'm really happy to see you."

"You're so damn exasperating," Sonja exclaimed, but then she smiled as she wrapped her arms tightly around his back.

"Let's get back on the road," Chris said, but Sonja, after hiding nearly four hours in the back of the SUV, pointed desperately at the small stone building that housed the restrooms.

"Me too, but don't take all day. With any luck we should reach Mason County around noon," Chris called out to Sonja as she raced off.

* * *

As McKay pedaled her bike gingerly up Capitol Hill toward her office building, she debated with herself, as she had all weekend, what her next moves should be. She had spent a good deal of time on Saturday morning painfully removing, with tweezers, pieces of broken glass and other sharp debris that had deeply penetrated the balls, heals, and toes of her feet during her dash home after meeting with Braxton. The rest of the weekend, she soaked her feet and checked the *Herald*, cable news, and the Internet, but she had found no mention of Christopher O'Brian's capture. All she saw was a story about a black man who went berserk in Lafayette Park, threatening to kill President Keller, and who was shot dead by a DC police officer.

Sitting in her apartment early this Monday morning, McKay had finally allowed herself to think, *God, maybe my call to Chris paid off. Maybe Sonja was able to reach him in time.*

But as McKay dismounted and locked her bike, the reality finally struck her that she had to make contact with Braxton. Walking quickly toward the entrance, her mind in a complete fog, she immediately crashed into a pedestrian. McKay reached her hand out to help the young woman she had knocked off balance.

"Sorry ... what ... you again?"

"Chris, Sonja, and all of us thank you for what you did on Saturday," Tanya said as she slipped a small, folded piece of paper into the still-confused congressional staffer's hand. "Destroy this note

311

after you read it and please be careful. You can't believe how ruthless those people can be."

Joanne took the note and discreetly put it in her pocket. She started to speak, but Tanya had already turned and was walking quickly away to meet up with Leon.

When McKay reached her office, she quickly closed the door and eagerly grabbed the note from her pocket as she slipped on her glasses.

"That 'thing' in Lafayette Park that you no doubt read about was us. Bingeman Foster's in on the EZ-15 fix with Braxton. From here on out, be careful and don't do anything heroic. They'll be watching you, so play along with them. When the time is right, and believe me you'll know it, go viral."

Taking the note, McKay tore it into tiny pieces, put them in her month, and swallowed them with a big gulp of water from her water bottle.

She sat pensively for a moment and then decided her next move. Grabbing her cell phone, McKay called Braxton.

"I thought you said O'Brian was 'going down' on Saturday. I didn't see or hear anything in the news. If he's still out there making trouble, my job of trying to allay Goodman's concerns about EZ-15 becomes way more difficult."

"Don't worry about O'Brian. We're closing in on him fast," Braxton replied, his annoyance evident. And then he added, "Just do your part to keep your boss in line on the EZ-15 final approval."

"Okay, okay, I'll do what I can, but I need to get off the phone; Goodman's buzzing me. I've got to go with him to a committee meeting."

"One thing more, I'm going to an event at the Brazilian embassy on Friday, and I need a date. Are you available?"

McKay knew she had little choice in the matter. Braxton was holding all the cards because of what he had on her regarding the Goldslide matter, so she reluctantly said yes.

"Great! Wear something that shows off those amazing legs of yours. We can skip out early, catch a bite to eat, and spend the evening together."

Joanne fully understood what Braxton had in mind, but she didn't disclose the contempt she felt for him. "I've got just the thing to wear. I think you'll like it."

"I'll have a cab pick you up at 7:00 p.m. sharp, and I expect to hear some good news from you about Goodman supporting EZ-15," Braxton said and then hung up.

"Braxton, you filthy letch, you're goin' down, and you haven't a clue," McKay muttered, but deep in her heart she feared she might be the one who wouldn't survive.

*   *   *

By the time Tanya and Leon returned from Capitol Hill, the farmhouse was buzzing with a flurry of chaotic and seemingly random action. But Leon knew that everyone was carrying out elements of his dad's carefully designed plan for exiting the farmhouse.

By 4:30 p.m., everything was ready for the predawn departure to Baltimore and the new hideout. The computers, cell phones, documents, handheld weapons, the cash, and personal items they planned to take with them were carefully packed in seven oversized black nylon backpacks that would be loaded in the morning into the two vehicles parked in front of the farmhouse. About twenty yards in front of the farmhouse, everything else had been stacked in a huge pile of trash, smashed computers, and cell phones. When they departed the next day, the pile that had already been doused with gasoline would be lit. The resulting fire would destroy everything that could be of possible value to the EZ-15 conspirators if and when they arrived on the scene.

"Let's get dinner ready. We need to get to bed early so we're up and out of here by 4:00 a.m. tomorrow," Chet barked with a measure of satisfaction as he surveyed how well everything had been prepared.

CHAPTER 58

May 9
West Coast of Scotland—Evening

About the time Chet was declaring that everything at the farmhouse was ready, thousands of miles away, Sir Reginald Longshank sat on the open porch of his 250-year-old, modest, three-room, thatched-roofed stone cottage with Margaret, his wife of forty years. The couple sat together, his arm around her shoulder as she snuggled close on the cushioned wooden-swing couch with a faded blue wool blanket covering their laps. They looked out at a magnificent sunset over the North Atlantic along the cliffs of the west coast of Scotland. Though it was nearly 10:00 p.m. local time, the sun hadn't completely dipped below the horizon, given the northern latitude location.

"Care for another sherry, Maggie, my dear?" Longshank asked as he filled his glass and then hers.

"Here's to the queen," his wife proposed as the couple clinked their glasses and each took a healthy sip.

Following Chris's advice, Longshank had told his colleagues he was taking an extended leave from his post as executive director of IAECM to attend to a family medical emergency. Then he with his wife, Carin Holsten, and her infant child, Aaron, had disappeared to the summer cottage.

At first Longshank had fretted about how his wife would receive Carin and her child at their small cottage. But in the days that followed, Maggie and Carin grew closer and closer. So much so that at times Longshank felt like he was being ignored. For Maggie, Carin had become the daughter she never had, and Aaron, the grandson.

"The time here has been wonderful. I haven't been this happy in years, and I wish we could stay here forever," Maggie said softly as she kissed Longshank playfully on the cheek, her aging but still beautiful face staring deeply into her husband's eyes.

"You might just get your wish. I got an e-mail from Chris O'Brian last night, and it sounds like he hasn't made much progress. Says he's off to the wilderness to find Karl Thurgensen. If that fails, I don't believe there'll be any way to stop EMCO and EZ-15," Longshank replied, his bushy, gray eyebrows deeply furrowed.

"Don't worry, dear. I'm sure your Mr. O'Brian will succeed," she whispered as they both took another sip of sherry.

Lurking not more than a hundred yards from the side of the cottage, Hans Dietrich lay almost motionless in the tall, wispy grass. Adjusting the site of his German PSGI sniper rifle, he peered through the high-powered telescope at his four targets: Longshank and his wife on the front porch and, through a bedroom window, the young woman and her child.

Finding Longshank hadn't proven difficult. For while Longshank had taken great pains not to disclose to his business associates where he was going or how long he would be gone, his wife hadn't been so careful. She had told one of her closest friends and neighbors that they would be heading to their summer cottage in Scotland. Dietrich had canvassed the neighborhood, posing as a sewer inspector, and had skillfully plied the information from Longshank's neighbor. Once armed with that piece of information, Dietrich had little trouble tracking down the precise location of the cottage.

I'll take the woman and her child out first and then shoot Longshank and that old hag before they know what hit them, Dietrich calculated as his heart began to pound. Staring through the rifle's scope, the assassin watched Carin nursing her child as she stood gazing out the window, her ample white breasts fully exposed.

A twin kill—I can't believe it, Hans thought breathlessly as he positioned himself to fire the fatal shots. Dietrich had first read about twin kills in his favorite soldiers of fortune magazine. He learned that in parts of Africa, insurgents often lined up captured women holding their children and then fired one shot, killing both mother and child.

But this is even better—these victims have no clue they're about to die, he thought as the hint of smile emerged.

As Dietrich carefully took aim at his prey, he could feel an erection forming in his pants. He took a deep breath and gently placed his finger on the trigger. Two shots were fired in rapid succession, the glass pane of the cottage shattered, and blood exploded everywhere.

*   *   *

As Chet and everyone else slept soundly in the farmhouse after a long day of hard work, the thirty-man FBI SWAT team arrived in six black, windowless vans at the front gate entrance to the farmhouse. Petrovic, who had been invited by Cavanaugh to accompany the assault mission as the DHS liaison, sat in the passenger seat of the van Cavanaugh was driving.

"Finally, we were cut a break, and now we can squash those annoying roaches," Petrovic said with considerable relief in his voice.

Petrovic's reference to a "break" alluded to the fact that despite Otto Simpson's attempt to crush his cell phone before he was killed, he had failed to destroy the memory chip. The FBI agents in the lab were able to take the chip and trace the last call Otto had received to the farmhouse location.

"If we hadn't been able to trace the call, who knows when or if we could have found their hideout," Cavanaugh replied.

When the well-armed SWAT team, dressed in black, with riot helmets and Kevlar protective vests and leg guards, was assembled, the team commander spoke. "As soon as we open the gate, proceed down both sides of the gravel road. When I give the signal, spread out to the right and left, form a semicircle parameter, and then wait further instructions. We don't know how many are in the house, but we believe they're heavily armed. Our orders are to take the prisoners alive, but not at the expense of our team's safety. Shoot to kill, if necessary."

At that point, a behemoth FBI agent carrying a huge pair of heavy-duty wire cutters walked up to the gate and cut through the chain in one try. When the SWAT team came within sight of the dark farmhouse, they spread out as commanded. Then the team commander raised his arm high in the air and motioned for the team to move forward.

Moments later, all hell broke loose as one of the FBI agents broke an unseen trip wire that triggered a large siren. Suddenly, spotlights on the farmhouse flashed on, lighting the entire area and exposing the SWAT team members, who all immediately hit the ground for protection. Then two gunshots exploded in quick succession from the general direction of the farmhouse.

"Fire at will! Fire at will!" shouted the commander, and the SWAT team unleashed a barrage of gunfire.

In less than a minute, over two thousand rounds were fired at the farmhouse. That onslaught was quickly followed by the launching of several grenades through the now-shattered windows of the farmhouse. Suddenly, the bullet-ridden farmhouse exploded in flames. The soaring flames quickly spread and ignited the gasoline-soaked pile of trash and debris just outside the farmhouse. The resulting horrific explosion engulfed the house, causing the entire second floor to collapse, which, in turn, caused the walls of the first floor to collapse inward.

The heat was so intense that the SWAT team was forced to rapidly retreat back several hundred yards as the flames continued to rage. It would be hours before the team could safely approach the house, but those standing in the field knew that anyone inside the farmhouse couldn't have survived the horror of the flames and explosions.

Cavanaugh, now standing back and away from the perimeter line, looked at Petrovic, whose face was fully illuminated by the bright light of the raging fire. Petrovic was beaming with an enormous grin.

"At last, we got the bastards. But how could they have been so incredibly stupid to open fire on the SWAT Team? They must have had a death wish," Cavanaugh said.

"They didn't fire any shots," Petrovic replied as he held out his hand containing two cherry bombs. "Light one of these babies, and when it explodes, it sounds just like a gunshot. Had four of these just a moment ago; must have misplaced two of them."

* * *

"So much for getting to Mason County by 2:00 p.m.," Chris moaned as he looked at his watch, which read 11:10 p.m., and recalled the events of the day following his discovery of Sonja in the back of the SUV.

From the moment they had pulled out of the rest stop, the trip had turned into a disaster. First, after about an hour, the engine of the SUV began to sputter. By the time they contacted a towing service and had the engine repaired, they had lost six hours. Within twenty minutes after finally getting back on the interstate, the right rear tire went flat, and the whole process began again.

By the time they had reached the exit on the interstate that would take them in the general direction of Mason County, it was dark. Barely two miles off the interstate, the countryside was almost devoid of any signs of human life. It was like stepping off into the wilderness. There were no road signs, and after another ninety minutes of driving slowly in an increasingly dense fog, Chris was pretty sure they were lost.

"Damn," Chris cried out as he looked in his rearview mirror.

"What?" Sonja, half-asleep, muttered.

"There's a police car behind us with its lights flashing," Chris replied, the sweat breaking out on his forehead as he pulled off the road.

As Chris slowly rolled down his window, the moist, cold fog wafted into the SUV. He was shivering and wasn't sure if it was from fear or the chilling cold. Soon he could see the front door of the police vehicle open slowly and then the bobbing light of a flashlight as the police officer approached the SUV.

"Try to relax and look natural. We're just a couple of tourists," Chris cautioned Sonja.

"I'm fine; you're the one who looks like he got caught with his hand in the cookie jar."

Sonja's typically sarcastic response actually helped him relax a bit.

Chris fully expected that the policeman slowly approaching them would be a pot-bellied, fifty-something country hick, with a deep southern drawl. But the officer who arrived at Chris's window was fit and well dressed in his starched and pressed tan uniform with a big patch on the right chest pocket that read Deputy Sheriff Michael Stone. The officer couldn't have been a day over twenty-five years old.

With an engaging smile, he leaned on Chris's door and peered carefully into the vehicle, the beam of his flashlight darting around the SUV's interior.

Finally he said, politely and with only a hint of a southern accent, "Good evening. Do you know why I pulled you over?"

"Well, I'm guessing it wasn't because I was speeding," Chris replied with a nervous laugh.

As the smile disappeared from the young officer's face, Sonja cringed at Chris's effort to be amusing.

"You're left rear light is burned out. You're not from around here, are you?"

Chris, now well aware that his effort to be funny had backfired horribly, replied respectfully, "That's correct, Officer. My wife and I are from Montana and were heading to Mason County to find my wife's long-lost great uncle."

"Your vehicle has New Jersey plates," the officer said skeptically.

"It's a rental."

"May I see your license, rental contract, and registration, please?" The officer's voice suddenly sounded more officious, if not hostile.

"Dear, can you pull out the rental information and the registration from the glove compartment," Chris replied, trying to hide his growing anxiety as he pulled out his wallet and fumbled in trying to remove the license.

The officer then stared carefully at the registration form, Chris's license, and the rental agreement. "Never heard of U-Rent It Cheap before," the officer mumbled as he turned and walked back to his police cruiser.

"He's not going to be able to match my license in the Montana database," Chris said as his mind raced in search of a plan for what they should do next. Sonja grabbed Chris's hand in hers and squeezed it hard without uttering a word.

After ten minutes, the police officer returned with his service revolver drawn. "I can't access the database to check your license. They must go home early in Montana. Would you both step out of your car?"

Chris and Sonja stepped out as the police officer shined his flashlight into the rear storage area and surveyed the contents carefully.

When he was finished, the officer said, "Okay."

"Then it's okay for us to go?" Chris said hopefully.

"No," the officer replied. "Miss, would you please put both hands on the top of the car where I can see them. Sir, please open the back hatch," the officer ordered, the gun now pointing directly at Chris.

Damn. Why didn't I put those carry bags with the weapons, cell phones, and cash in the hidden compartment? Chris silently cursed himself and then said, "Just a bunch of clothes and stuff. My wife's freezing out here. Can't we just be on our way?"

"Please open the hatch, now," the officer said impatiently.

When Chris opened the hatch, the officer looked around and happened to grab the bag with the weapons and cell phones inside.

"Please open the duffle bag, sir."

Chris smiled but thought to himself, *We've successfully eluded the damn FBI and DHS for nearly a month. I'm not going to be stopped now by some young, local yokel cop.*

As Chris reached for the bag with his left hand, he slowly slipped his right hand into his right pocket and wrapped his fingers around a well-concealed, small .38-caliber pistol. He felt sick to his stomach. He had never intentionally killed anything, let alone a human, before, but he had come too far to be stopped now.

Sonja, aware that Chris was armed and seeing what was unfolding, looked on as if suspended in a nightmare. She wanted to scream, to stop this madness, but she was frozen in fear.

PART III

CHAPTER 59

May 9
West Coast of Scotland

The barely twenty-one year-old sharpshooter stood over the body of his fallen prey. What remained of Hans Dietrich floated in a pool of crimson blood and muddy water, making a surrealistic wavy pattern. The German assassin's head, which had taken the full measure of Her Majesty's Secret Service sharpshooter's rifle shot, had exploded on impact and looked every bit like a shredded head of red cabbage. Bending over at the waist and gagging at the sight, the lad spewed gooey vomit everywhere.

"Well done, young chap," a voice with a slight Irish brogue called out as a dark figure emerged from the underbrush.

Sergeant O'Malley, a grizzly veteran of thirty years in Her Majesty's Secret Service, gently but firmly placed his large hand on his young soldier's shoulder. "Killing is never easy, my boy, but, Private Fitzgerald, you've served your country and the queen very well this day."

Whereupon the young Scottish soldier heaved a second projectile of vomit—this time over his victim's body.

O'Malley, unable to control himself at the somewhat pathetic sight of his young charge, laughed but then, firmly grabbing the young soldier by his armpit, pulled him upright and patted him on the back. "You'll feel better soon. Let's check up on Sir Reginald and his family."

When the two soldiers reached and entered the cottage, they could see in the far bedroom Maggie and Carin huddled together with the infant pressed between them and Sir Reginald positioned at the bedroom door, gripping an old turkey shoot rifle.

As the soldiers entered, O'Malley spoke first. "It's over. Is everyone okay?"

Before Longshank replied, he sighed with relief, laid down his rifle, and rushed to Maggie, Carin, and Aaron. Then walking back to O'Malley, Longshank beamed and said, "We're all fine." Vigorously shaking O'Malley's hand, Longshank added with remarkable calm, "I must say, though, that bullet shattering the bedroom window pane was somewhat disconcerting."

"Sorry about that, sir," Private Fitzgerald said as he removed his black hood, revealing his matted and sweaty, curly red hair and his freckled and blushing handsome face. "The assassin was killed instantly when I shot him, but his rifle must have discharged as result of a reflex action of a dead man."

"No apology necessary," Sir Reginald replied as he shook the relieved young man's hand.

O'Malley assisted Longshank and his wife as they gathered up what they would need to take with them to a safer, more secure location. Private Fitzgerald, immediately smitten by the beauty of the young mother, dutifully helped Carin and her infant prepare to leave the cottage. Within moments, a helicopter appeared, rising up from the seaside cliffs, and landed in a clearing near the cottage. As they boarded the army helicopter, Maggie turned back and, staring at Longshank, said with the hint of annoyance, "You knew all along we were in danger and that the HMSS was out there protecting us. You never said a word to me."

"I thought it was better not to alarm you and Carin."

When they were both in the helicopter, Maggie gave Longshank a hug and whispered tenderly in his ear, "I love you, darling, and all is forgiven, but why us? Why would the pride of the Secret Service be sent to protect us?"

An enormous grin exploded on Longshank's face. "As I've said before, my dear, Knighthood has its privileges ... and it doesn't hurt that the Home Minister is a good friend of mine," Longshank said as he kissed his wife and they both took one last look at their cottage below.

Then the couple looked at Carin and Aaron, who were being well attended to by the young Scotsman. They both smiled at the budding relationship between the young man and woman, looked back at each other, and Longshank whispered to Maggie, "Looks like Carin has found herself a beau."

"And maybe a new dad for Aaron," his wife replied.

*   *   *

"Saigon Two! Saigon Two!" Chet screamed as an alarm, triggered when the FBI agents cut the lock and opened the gate, rang out in the farmhouse. Saigon Two, which was named in honor of the escape operation nearly forty years before, was the signal to evacuate the farmhouse.

Chet had concurred with Billy's assessment that it likely would take the FBI at least several days to track them down, and he had intended to use the next day to make one last inspection of the area to make sure nothing had been left that would help the FBI. But the former sergeant, who never left anything to chance, had also come up with a backup plan just in case the authorities arrived earlier than expected. He had gone over and over again with the Crew the meticulous plan for an emergency escape to avoid capture, or more likely, annihilation.

As soon as Chet shouted "Saigon Two," everyone was up instantly. Since they had been instructed by Chet to sleep with their clothes on, everyone was fully dressed and ready to go. Each person grabbed one of the fully loaded backpacks. In those backpacks was everything the crew needed to continue its tactical operations at the new hideout in Baltimore.

"Let's go. Let's move it," Chet barked as he herded everyone, still half-asleep and somewhat disoriented, through a passageway to stairs leading down to the farmhouse cellar. The cellar was little more than a musty crawl space that had once served as cold storage for perishables during the 1800s.

Chet at the back and Casey at the front of the single file of escapees were the only ones equipped with flashlights, and the going was treacherous over the unpaved, rutty dirt floor littered with debris. But each member of the Crew, as previously instructed, grabbed the shirt of the person in front, and they moved forward with surprising quickness. When they reached the far wall of the farmhouse basement, it appeared they had reached a dead end. But Casey grabbed a previously placed crowbar and quickly ripped the rotting wood planks off the wall. Soon a very small opening revealed what looked like a crawl space. The crawl space was actually a tunnel where escaped slaves hid in the 1860s during their treacherous journey along the Underground Railroad to the north where they hoped they would find a better life.

With considerable effort and a strong push from Freddie, Casey squeezed his enormous girth through the opening and into the slightly larger tunnel.

"If I can fit through that damn hole, the rest of you shouldn't have a problem. Hurry up." Casey's voice echoed from within the tunnel.

The damp, dusty tunnel extended for over a hundred yards and ended on the bank of a ten-foot-wide, semidry creek that ran the length of Casey's family property. As the members of the Crew emerged from the tunnel and into the creek bed, each felt a blast of heat. The sky, lit by the raging fire now consuming the farmhouse, was almost as bright as midday, only it was quickly becoming enveloped in black and gray smoke.

"Damn!" Leon exclaimed as tears welled up in Tanya's eyes, and Rebecca felt her heart racing.

Chet looked at the shock on the faces of his comrades and reacted quickly. "Don't look back. Stay down and keep movin'," he ordered as he quickly led the group along the rocky and slippery creek bed.

After following the serpentine bends of the creek for about two hundred yards, the cold, wet, and exhausted crew followed Chet as he scrambled out of the creek on to a dirt road that appeared to be in the middle of nowhere.

Chet raised his flashlight and flashed it quickly four times in a direction down the road away from where the fire was still raging. Almost instantly, two lights appeared like a pair of menacing eyes in the distance and raced toward them.

When the van pulled up and stopped, the double back doors soon swung wide open.

As Chet directed the members of the Crew to jump on board, he saw a familiar face. The man who greeted them was a former soldier whose life had been saved in Vietnam by Chet's squad.

He reached out his hand and shook Chet's hand heartily. As arranged by Chet earlier in the day, he had been waiting at a designated spot just in case the Crew needed to make an early, emergency evacuation from the farmhouse. "I've been waiting a long time to pay you back for what you did for me."

"I think this makes us even," Chet said as he hugged the man. "Let's get out of here, Corporal."

Chet, Leon, Tanya, Rebecca, Casey, Billy, and Freddie huddled close together under several layers of thick, musty, and scratchy wool blankets in the back of the bouncing, windowless black van with bold white lettering on the outside panels proclaiming "Prince George's County Emergency Response Team."

When the van began to slow down, Chet whispered to his dirty, sweaty, and exhausted companions, "Everyone stay perfectly still. We're coming to a checkpoint."

When the van finally halted, the driver, dressed in medical gear, lowered the window, leaned his head out, and called out to the FBI sentry blocking the van's path, "Officer, I'm Captain Richard Macon, Prince George's County Emergency Response Team. Heard over the wire about a fire and explosion." Then seeing the enormous ball of fire, he screeched, "What the hell happened over there?"

"None of your business," the stern-faced FBI agent dressed in riot gear barked.

"Careful, fella. Where you're standing is within the jurisdiction of the PG County Police and Rescue Authority. If anyone is injured over there, I'm here to help out."

"Don't need your damn help. It's a controlled burn, and we've got all the support we need. Turn around and leave," the FBI agent ordered.

"Okay, but can I just go through your checkpoint? If I have to turn around now and go back, it will take me twenty miles out of my way," the driver pleaded.

After hesitating for a moment, the FBI agent stepped aside and motioned the van forward. "And radio your home base and tell them to keep all their damn vehicles at least four miles from the scene while we complete the cleanup operation."

As the van passed through the checkpoint and headed off to Baltimore, everyone threw off the blankets and let out a spontaneous cheer.

*   *   *

"I gotta pee!"

"What?" Chris and the sheriff's deputy said in perfect unison as they turned and stared at Sonja.

"I gotta pee—now!" Sonja pleaded, dancing on her toes as if her bladder was about to burst. And then, without waiting for a reply from either of the two dumbstruck males, she turned and raced off into the darkness of the tall, grassy field adjacent to the country road.

The police officer's chain of thought was broken as Sonja disappeared into the misty darkness. But just as quickly, he regained his composure. "Sir, please step back and put your hands on the roof of the vehicle."

Before Chris could react, a primordial scream echoed from the darkness. "A snake—a rattlesnake. Help! Help me!"

Without hesitating, the deputy raced toward Sonja. "Don't move, ma'am. Stay perfectly still," the young man cautioned as he too disappeared into the darkness.

"Brilliant," Chris whispered to himself as in one continuous motion he reached into the cargo area, pushed all the boxes and bags to one side, lifted the trap door to the lower compartment, and shoved everything that contained weapons, cell phones, cash, and computers into the compartment, closed the hatch cover, and spread the remaining duffle bags with clothes, and bags with food around the cargo space to hide the cargo space trap door.

Meanwhile, the deputy cautiously approached Sonja, a flashlight in one hand and his gun drawn ready to shoot the rattlesnake in the other. Then he saw her, captured in the light of his flashlight standing in an open area, her slacks and panties still down at her ankles.

Sonja made a fleeting effort to cover up her exposed body with her hands as she called out, "I think you scared him off. I heard movement in the brush, and the rattling has stopped."

When he reached Sonja, she turned and threw her arms tightly around the flustered and embarrassed police officer. Try as he might,

327

however, the deputy couldn't help but stare at Sonja's fully exposed, rosy colored "Garden of Eden," as he would later describe it during the numerous times he recounted the story to his various drinking buddies.

Having achieved the desired effect, Sonja gently moved away and pulled up her panties and slacks.

"Thanks for saving my life," Sonja gushed as she hugged the sheriff's deputy again, pressing her breasts against his chest and kissing him playfully on the cheek as they made their way back to the SUV.

"Are you all right, dear?" Chris feigned deep concern.

"Yes, thanks to this wonderful man," Sonja swooned with the sexy smile on her face.

The poor, flustered deputy struggled to regain his composure and finally pointed his flashlight into the cargo area of the SUV. After a brief moment, he turned to Chris and said, "Wait here."

As the deputy walked back to the police vehicle, Chris whispered to Sonja, "Damn it. He saw something." Chris reinserted his hand into the pocket that hid his pistol.

But when the deputy returned, he was grinning and had a screwdriver and a small box. He went directly to the faulty rear light, quickly removed the cover, and, after several tries, replaced the taillight lamp bulb with a bulb he removed from the box. The rear light immediately lit up.

Pointing to his cigar box, the deputy said, "Always have a supply of these with me. You wouldn't believe how often I have to pull over folks with a tail or headlight out."

"I can't thank you enough, Officer," Chris said as the tension in his body began to ease.

"Me too," Sonja said as she hugged the deputy one more time around his neck and rubbed her long fingers up and down his back.

The deputy, his face flushed with embarrassment, said, "Ma'am, don't make it a habit of wandering in the woods in this part of Virginia—lots of rattlers and copperheads around here."

Then turning to Chris, the young man said, "Best way to get to Mason County from here is to turn around and head back up this road for about ten miles. When you come to Route 226, turn right and you'll hit the Mason County line in another fifteen miles."

"Thank you again, Officer," Chris said as he motioned Sonja to get into the SUV.

As the police cruiser pulled away, Chris turned the SUV around and headed off toward Mason County. He looked at Sonja, who was scowling at him.

"What?"

"I'm almost bitten by a killer rattlesnake, and who comes to my rescue? Not Christopher O'Brian. No, it was that nice police officer."

"Please, give me a break. I was onto your scheme from the get go."

"How did you know?"

"Hell, we stopped an hour ago so you could take a bathroom break on the side of the road. Given the fact that earlier today you went over four hours in the cargo compartment, I figured you had a pretty strong bladder and so ..."

A smile emerged on Sonja's face. "You've got to admit I gave a pretty good performance."

"No argument there," Chris replied as he squeezed Sonja's knee.

Within forty minutes, they passed a sign reading, "Welcome to Mason County—Come Stay with Us Awhile." They quickly found a small 1940s vintage motel with separate cottages that looked like they hadn't been painted in years. But the lights were on, and the flashing sign read "Vacancy," so the weary travelers agreed to stop.

CHAPTER 60

May 10
Mason County, Virginia—Morning

"Where the hell do you think you're going in that outfit? We're in the middle of hillbilly heaven, and it would be nice if we didn't stick out," Chris said as he entered the bedroom with a towel wrapped around his waist and his hair still dripping from his shower.

Dressed in a red plaid, cotton shirt with an unbuttoned, faded blue denim vest, a matching denim below-the-knee skirt, and high-top leather boots, Sonja shot back, "You're wrong about Mason County. This may not be DC, you Ivy League snob, and there may be some folks who live in abject poverty, some lingering pockets of racial prejudice, and folks who live far up the mountains without electricity or running water, but this place is really remarkable, if not eclectic."

Not waiting to give Chris a chance to respond, she added, "You're no doubt familiar with Courtney Sullivan, that woman who writes all those suspense novels. Well, she spends six months a year here. The county has wineries and breweries. They have an annual music festival that attracts thousands of people. Several pretty well-known bluegrass and country western performers have their roots in Mason County. In the 1970s, the county was a haven for several hippy communes. Today, there are artist colonies and meditation/spiritual centers."

"How do you know so much about this place?" Chris asked, somewhat defensively.

"Homework. I did a little research on the Internet about this place when we were back at the farmhouse," she responded. "Listen to what Sullivan wrote in an article in the *Washington Herald* about

Mason County. 'People in this County, white or black, rich or poor, are proud of who they are and where they live. They're quiet folks and hold dear their privacy. But once they get to know you, they're amazingly friendly and if you need a hand, they're always ready to help. I can't think of a better place to live.'"

Chris shook his head and then noticed Sonja had neatly laid out on the bed a blue plaid shirt and pre-faded jeans.

"You shopped for me?"

"I couldn't take the chance on what you'd bring to wear. Put these on, and you'll fit right in."

Chris stood silently for a moment and then walked to Sonja. He cupped his hand around Sonja's neck and kissed her softly. "As usual, you think of everything. You're right, and I'm wrong. Let's finish getting ready and get going. We need to find Thurgensen as soon as possible."

Moments later, Chris and Sonja were out the motel room door. As they looked out, the magnificence of the Blue Ridge Mountains in the early-morning sunlight burst into view.

"God, those mountains are more beautiful than I could have imagined. Wish we were here under different circumstances." Sonja sighed.

"Me too," Chris said quietly as they entered the cramped motel office to check out.

"Good morning," the balding motel clerk, dressed in a sleeveless, white T-shirt that barely covered his enormous stomach, greeted them. "Gonna do a little sightseeing today?" he continued, unable to take his eyes off of Sonja.

"Actually, we're here in Mason County hoping to locate my wife's great-uncle. Name's Karl Thurgensen. We think he moved down here about ten years ago. Happen to know him?"

After a brief but noticeable pause, the clerk replied, "Nope. Can't say that I do, and I know just about everyone in this neck of the woods." Then he added in a less-than-friendly tone, "You ain't from around here, are you?"

"My wife and I live in Montana, but I grew up in North Carolina, and my great-great-great-grandfather was a cadet at the Virginia Military Institute. He fought at the battle of New Market where the VMI cadets held the hill against the Union's forces."

331

The clerk pushed himself slowly out of his chair and with a broad smile held out his hand. "My great uncle, many generations removed, fought at New Market. Damn proud to meet a descendent of a New Market hero. Hey, you might try the county courthouse just up the road a piece. Maybe the county registrar can help you. Ask for Merilee Higgins. You can't miss the courthouse—big, white painted stone building on the right with the bronze statue of Johnny McCormick dressed in his rebel gear. Little Johnny rode with Robert Mosby—you know the Gray Ghost. Well, that is until a damn Yankee shot Johnny in the head," the clerk said, shaking his head sadly. "If there's anything I can ever do for you, just let me know."

"Thanks for the suggestion, and it's been a pleasure," Chris replied as he gave the man a firm handshake.

As they headed out the door, Sonja whispered, "Where do you come up with the stuff that you do?"

"Always knew studying those Civil War battles when I was in high school would pay off someday," Chris said. And then he added, with a note of sarcasm as they headed down the road in the SUV, "So Mason County is so 'very cosmopolitan'—150 years later, and these folks are still fighting the Civil War."

Sonja shook her head in frustration. "Chris, for all your studying, you're still so damn totally clueless. The memories of the Civil War down here have nothing to do with political beliefs. That war was fought on these folks' homeland. Farms and towns were destroyed by the invaders, and countless ancestors were killed, imprisoned, or left penniless as a result of the war. If you can't understand that, you'll never understand the people of Mason County. The pain, suffering, and loss of war—any war—should never be forgotten."

As they continued down the road, it occurred to Chris why Sonja had reacted so passionately. For her, the parallels to what happened to the folks in Mason County and the South during the Civil War and the horror Sonja's distant relatives suffered during the 1930s and 1940s in Germany and Eastern Europe weren't so different.

Arriving at the courthouse, the couple entered through the front doors of the wonderfully preserved pre–Civil War-era building and asked the first person they met for directions to the county registrar's office. They walked to the end of the narrow hall and turned left where they could see a sign hanging above an opening in the wall that said "County Registrar."

They looked into the cramped office on the other side of the service window, but it was empty. Chris rang the bell that sat on the window's counter. After a moment, a side door opened, and a pleasantly plump, sixty-something woman with rosy checks, sparkling blue eyes, and obviously dyed blonde hair pulled back in a bun entered.

"We're looking for the county registrar," Chris said politely.

"That's me—Merilee Higgins, and you are ...?"

"My name is Russell Smith, and this is my wife, Torrey. We're looking for Torrey's long-lost great-uncle, Karl Thurgensen. We believe he moved to Mason County about a decade ago. Does the name ring a bell with you?"

"Can't say that it does," the registrar replied politely. "I could check the county property tax records."

Without waiting for a response, Higgins turned and went to a floor-to-ceiling wood cabinet with multiple drawers. She busily thumbed through several drawers stuffed with what Chris assumed must be tax records and deed documents of some kind. After about five minutes, she returned to the window.

"Sorry, no record of your great-uncle. Of course, those records only cover property taxes. If your great-uncle is here, but he's renting property or squatting on some remote mountain property, we wouldn't have any tax records for him."

"Do you have any other ideas? We're desperate to find him," Sonja pleaded.

"Might try the State Department of Motor Vehicles office down the hall to your right. Doesn't open until 9:30 a.m. State offices open a half an hour later than the county offices and close an hour earlier. Can you believe that?" Marilee replied.

Looking at his watch, which read 9:15 a.m., Chris said as politely as he could muster, "Thank you."

After they waited fifteen minutes, the shutter to the service window at the DMV opened promptly at 9:30 a.m.

"Welcome to the DMV. May I be of assistance?"

Chris wanted to explode, but Sonja rubbed his arm, and he recovered. "Ms. Higgins, how nice to see you again. But I thought you worked for the county, not the state."

"We're a bit understaffed here, so I cover for the state folks when they can't be here, and they cover for me on occasion."

"That's nice," Chris replied politely. "Could you please check the DMV records for any record of Karl Thurgensen?"

"Absolutely," Merilee replied as she turned and went to a wooden cabinet similar to the one in the registrar's office and again searched through multiple drawers before returning to the counter.

"Sorry, if Mr. Thurgensen is in Mason County, he doesn't own a motor vehicle or have a Virginia driver's license."

Barely containing his growing frustration, Chris asked, "Do you have any ideas where we might get a lead on my wife's great-uncle?"

"You might try the post offices. We have eleven here in Mason County. If you're interested, you'll need a map. The Office of Tourism is up the stairs to your right. They have great maps and lots of fun information."

"Let me guess," Chris said with a smile.

"Yep. I'll meet you up there in five minutes. The door is open. Go on in and take a look around."

Fifteen minutes later, Chris and Sonja left the courthouse armed with a marked-up county map showing the location of the eleven post offices, a motel well up into the Blue Ridge mountains where Merilee had made reservations for them, and a restaurant/bar that Merilee proclaimed, "Serves the most amazing barbecued ribs in Mason County or anywhere else in the South for that matter."

As they got into the SUV, Chris said, "You know, I'm starting to like our Ms. Higgins. Can you believe she's also the mayor of Mason County?"

"I like her too. But I think both our friend at the motel and Ms. Higgins knew more than they're letting on."

"I'm with you, but let's play things out and see where we are tonight."

*   *   *

The next nine hours yielded no results. While the entire county had slightly less than fifteen thousand residents, it covered a geographic area of over eight hundred square miles. Visiting each of the eleven post offices, they found no record of Karl Thurgensen. The rest of the day, Chris and Sonja visited a number of small convenience stores and gas stations, seeking leads to Thurgensen's whereabouts. But again they came up empty.

"I know we haven't found anything suggesting Thurgensen is still here, but I've got a feeling we'll find something somewhere," Chris said as they pulled into the barbeque ribs place recommended by Higgins.

From the outside, Bar-be-Que Bob's, with its moldy shake roof shingles and warped and peeling, weathered wood siding, looked like a fire waiting to happen. Had it not been for the mayor's recommendation, Chris and Sonja never would have entertained the idea of stopping in. But once inside, the place had a rustic look, and at the same time, an intimate, friendly feeling to it.

A bar made out of a single slab of oak lined the length of one side of the dimly lit place. The kitchen, where the amazing, smoky aroma of barbecued pork wafted out, was at the back of the building. On the side opposite the bar was a small, raised stage with a variety of musical instruments and sound equipment. In the middle were about fifteen tables with red and white checkered paper tablecloths at which anywhere between four and eight patrons could sit. While it was barely 6:30 p.m., the place was nearly filled with a mix of patrons that seemed to match the cultural diversity of the county.

No one was at the door to greet them, and Chris quickly realized that Bob's was a seat-yourself place. The couple made their way toward an empty table, crunching peanut shells that covered the floor with each step they took.

They had barely sat down when a young woman came up and greeted them warmly. The menu she gave them was printed on a plain, creased, and greasy white piece of paper. The menu consisted of a list of barbecue dishes that seemed to differ only in the type of sides available and the number of ounces of pork to be served. They both ordered modest portions. The barbecue was fabulous.

Their table was front and center of the stage. A group of five young musicians—three males and two females, dressed in jeans— was warming up. Chris hoped the music wouldn't be gospel and was relieved when the band began to play a mix of rock, country, and blues.

As the music continued, Sonja began to fidget, and Chris became increasingly aware that she was itching to perform with the band. So when the performers stopped to take a break, he was hardly surprised when she declared, "I think I'll go over and talk to them. I really like their music. Okay?"

"Sonja, you played in a damn punk rock band," Chris replied, unable to hide his doubts about her musical abilities.

"It was a Euro-Pop band. Shows what you know about music," Sonja said. She then whispered, "Trust me. I know what I'm doing."

Sonja lost little time ingratiating herself with the band members. And when the band members returned to the stage, they had Sonja in tow.

"Let's give a warm Bob's Bar-be-Que welcome to Torrey Smith, straight from Big Sky Country—Montana," the lead vocalist said as the audience gave a warm applause to the new band member. Sonja looked completely at home as she settled onto the bench in front of the electric keyboard and tested the keys with her agile fingers. When the band finally started to play, everyone, including Chris, was surprised by the range of her talent and her ability to immediately mesh with the band.

Chris was so entranced with Sonja that he failed to notice the figure moving quietly but quickly toward him. When he felt a hand upon his shoulder, he jumped out of his seat.

"Sorry, didn't mean to startle you," the voice said quietly. "May I join you?"

"Mayor Higgins?" Chris exclaimed. Regaining some measure of composure, he said, "Please do. I'd love the company."

"Your lovely wife is rather talented."

"That she is," Chris replied as he thought to himself, *You have no idea how truly amazing she really is.*

Over the next two hours, Sonja sang, drank, and caroused with the members of the band—thoroughly enjoying every minute. Meanwhile, Chris and Higgins conversed loudly at times and at other times quietly.

At around nine o'clock, Sonja playfully grabbed the mike from the lead vocalist and said, "Thanks to these fantastic musical talents and a wonderful audience for letting me live out one of my fantasies.

You're all amazing. But I've got to take that bad boy home before Mayor Higgins steals him away from me."

The crowd cheered loudly as everyone in the band gave Sonja a hug. Sonja beamed as she walked over to Chris's table and said hello to the mayor. Then she gave Chris a long, hard kiss to the further cheers from all of the patrons.

"You have a wonderful talent, my dear, and I hope you didn't mind me stealing away your husband for the evening," Higgins said.

"Thanks for taking care of him. Hope he wasn't too boring a drinking companion," Sonja joked.

"Oh, quite the contrary," Merilee Higgins said as she got up and started walking toward another table. She turned back and added with wink, "Good luck in your search for your great-uncle."

As they left the barbeque arm in arm, Chris whispered, "Looks like you had a fun evening."

"Looks like you and the mayor were having an amicable chat."

"That and a whole lot more," Chris said. "Let's get out of here."

When they got in the SUV, Chris couldn't contain himself any longer. "She told me where we can find Thurgensen."

Sonja looked at Chris with a broad, sassy smile. "That would be up State Route 665 to Cup Run. Go about ten miles and then a right turn up a steep and barely passable excuse for a dirt road for about another half-mile—"

"How did you come by that information?" Chris interrupted her, feeling slightly wounded that he alone hadn't solved the mystery.

"Just being chummy with the band members and of course rubbing the inner thigh of the lead singer may have helped just a bit," she said.

"God, we males are a sorry species."

"No argument there," Sonja replied. "Thurgensen is a bit of a legend. Supposedly, he makes the best moonshine in the county. People know where to pick up the booze and leave the money, but no one ever sees him. He's a crafty, old geezer. They call him the Gray Fox. How did you get the honorable mayor to open up?"

Chris didn't respond immediately as he navigated the SUV up the narrow and increasingly winding road leading to their motel. Finally, he spoke. "I told her the truth."

"What? Are you crazy?" Sonja moaned.

"I told her about you, me, Chet, and the rest of the Crew. How we're fighting corrupt politicians, paid assassins, and a big multinational company who are conspiring to introduce a product that's already killing children and the elderly. As you might have guessed, fat-cat politicians and foreign corporations aren't so popular down around here. Merilee quickly grasped that we were the good guys and the only hope to stop the bad guys. She wanted to help."

Sonja leaned over and gave Chris a kiss on the cheek as she squeezed his leg. "I bet that old O'Brian charm helped as well. The mayor seemed quite taken with you."

Chris smiled and said, "It seems Thurgensen isn't only notorious for the moonshine he sells. The guy also is regarded as a local hero for helping people in the county—paper bags with cash left in the middle of the night on porches of folks in need and repairs to houses and barns when people are away. Children are a real soft spot for him. He leaves candy at Easter and handmade toys at Christmas for kids whose parents don't have the means to provide such trinkets. Like you said, no one has really gotten a good look at him in years."

As they pulled into the quaint motel atop the Blue Ridge Mountains, Sonja's heart was racing. "Tomorrow is going to be a very big day."

The couple checked in, and the room, while small, was everything Higgins had promised. A small deck off the bedroom had a double-wide reclining lounger. The view, with a nearly full moon shining, was breathtaking. To the left and right, the lush peaks of the Blue Ridge Mountains beckoned in the moonlight. Straight ahead, and nearly three thousand feet below, the Shenandoah Valley spread out before them with only a few lights visible in this very rural area. In the distance, the dark silhouette of the mountain ranges in West Virginia was visible over eighty miles away.

As they both undressed, Sonja grabbed a heavy cotton blanket and two fluffy pillows off the bed and proclaimed in a not too obviously sexy voice, "Let's sleep on the deck."

Without speaking, Chris, dressed only in his cotton undershorts, embraced Sonja, dressed only in a long T-shirt, and kissed her passionately as he led her outside. The temperature was cool, but the heavy blanket, to say nothing of the intense lovemaking that ensued, kept them both warm. Finally, totally exhausted from a long day, they drifted gently to sleep, wrapped tightly together.

CHAPTER 61

May 11

Chris, somewhat disoriented, walked cautiously down the narrow street that was lined with stone- and masonry-sided shops and sidewalk cafés with bright-colored awnings. He entered a large square with a huge, green, tarnished-copper fountain, with what appeared to be a military hero or statesman at the top.

He had to be somewhere in Europe, Chris thought, but couldn't remember whether it was some place he had visited with his former wife. Then he turned and saw a woman at a distance who at first he didn't recognize. She was smiling and waving at him to come to her. When Chris finally realized who she was, his heart raced. But as he tried to go to her, he couldn't move.

"Wake up, sleepyhead," Sonja said as she nuzzled close to Chris, who woke with a start from his dream. The morning sun had crawled above the eastern horizon. But it hadn't risen above the mountain ridge line, so the valley to the west below them was still wrapped in blissful darkness. He took a deep breath of the crisp, clean air as he opened his eyes and saw Sonja gazing affectionately at him.

The temperatures had dropped into the fifties, so Sonja snuggled tightly with Chris to share the warmth of their bodies. After a moment, she raised her head and whispered, "If we're able to survive this nightmare somehow, what would you want to do?"

Chris thought for a moment and then said, "I'd like to tell my son that I've always loved him and tell my wife how sorry I am for being such a horrible husband and that I never stopped caring for her. What about you?"

Chris's answer wasn't what Sonja had expected or hoped to hear, so she said the first thing that came into her mind. "I've always wanted to go to Argentina and dance the tango in the streets of Buenos Aries at midnight."

"That's really odd," Chris said as he seemed to ponder her reply.

Sonja bolted from the lounging chair and stormed off to the bathroom. While she really did want to dance the tango in Argentina someday, what she really wanted to tell Chris was that she loved him and wanted to be with him always. As tears welled up in her eyes, she resolved to put her feelings for Chris behind her and focus on completing their mission.

When they finally got into the SUV about twenty minutes later, neither had said a word to the other. Finally, Chris tried to break the tension. "I wasn't making fun of you."

Sonja simply glared at Chris.

Chris wasn't sure why Sonja had become so upset, but he did understand that silence was probably the best strategy, so they rode without saying a word over the winding roads in the Blue Ridge Mountains and past several severely dilapidated cabins. Eventually, they turned up Cup Run. Finally, they reached the double-track dirt road leading to Thurgensen's hideaway.

"Let's drive up a few hundred feet or so, park, and walk in from there. Okay?"

"Sounds like a plan," Sonja said, touching him on the shoulder. Try as she might, she simply couldn't stay mad at the man she loved, even if in the end they weren't destined to be together. Besides, she knew the only hope they had to survive and put an end to EZ-15 was to work closely together.

Sonja and Chris each grabbed a heavy, overstuffed backpack and made their way up the extremely steep, rocky road that ran parallel to a stunning creek with several cascading waterfalls. Periodically, the creek crossed under the road. It was nearly 10:00 a.m., and the sun was now high in the sky. However, the forest, a heavy canopy of oaks and ash trees, with a dense undergrowth of blooming wild rhododendrons and mountain laurel, nearly blocked out the sunlight save for a few places where beams of lights shined down and glistened on the evaporating moisture. It was almost like they were entering sacred ground—the forest silent except for the occasional eerie call of unseen hawks that soared high above the treetops in search of their next meal.

As Chris and Sonja drew near to where they thought they would find Thurgensen's cabin, Chris said, as he stopped to catch his breath, "Look at the stonework on this bridge; it's magnificent."

"And it was constructed fairly recently. Do you think Thurgensen built it himself?" Sonja replied, her hands on her hips as perspiration dripped off her face.

"I don't know. Who else could have done it? Merilee said that lots of people in the county know Thurgensen lives up here, but no one ever trespasses on his property."

"Out of respect?" Sonja asked.

"Out of respect for that shotgun and deer rifle he uses to ward off anyone stupid enough to enter his land," Chris answered. "Let's leave the backpacks here and move forward as quietly as we can."

Making their way across a tumbled-down barbed wire fence that had been stretched across the road, Chris and Sonja passed the first of several rusting metal signs nailed to trees on either side of the rocky pathway. Each sign delivered an ominous warning: "No Trespassing—Intruders Will Be Shot Dead."

"Wait," Chris whispered as he grabbed Sonja's upper arm. "I'm being stupid here. We're close enough that the crazy, old coot could pick us off. Let's hide behind those boulders, and we'll try to communicate from there."

Sonja and Chris crouched behind a nearby chest-high, moss-covered rock, and he shouted out, "Dr. Thurgensen. Dr. Thurgensen, my name is Christopher O'Brian, and Sir Reginald Longshank suggested I try to locate you."

After a long silence, a surprisingly friendly voice called out from about a hundred feet deeper into the woods, "Longshank sent you? Well, in that case, come on up."

Chris and Sonja stepped out from behind the rock and started to move in the direction of the voice. Two rifle shots rang out, and they heard the sound of bullets whizzing just over their heads.

"Christ!" Chris shouted as he pushed Sonja to the ground.

"Consider that a polite warning. You won't hear the next shots I fire because you'll already be dead when the sound waves reach you. Leave my property now!"

341

Chris started to stand up slowly with his hands raised high above his head. Sonja, with all her strength, tried in vain to pull him back to the ground.

"We've come too far to fail now. We have to take the chance," Chris whispered.

"Just hear me out," Chris called out calmly, disguising the fear that raced through his body. "When I'm finished, and if you don't believe me, shoot me, but let the woman live. She's been through enough hell already."

Then Sonja rose slowly and stood next to Chris. "You might as well shoot me too and put me out of my misery."

Chris looked at Sonja, somewhat shocked by her bold move. He grabbed and squeezed her hand tightly as the fear he had felt left him.

"How do you expect me to believe that Longshank sent you? He has no idea I'm living here," the unseen man replied. The sound of his voice revealed that he now was no more than thirty feet away but still hidden in the forest.

"Wrong. You sent Longshank a postcard years ago. It had a picture of mountains and words that read 'Come to Mason County, Virginia,'" Chris called out. He quickly continued, knowing he had only one chance to convince Thurgensen he was telling the truth. "Sir Reginald said to tell you that when it comes to good double malt scotch, he can still drink you under the table, but he wouldn't challenge you to a contest drinking that awful smoke-aged Kentucky bourbon you like so much."

Chris thought he detected a laugh in the distance, but otherwise he heard nothing. He quickly continued, "This is about a corporation called EMCO Consolidated Company. I know you're familiar with them. They're marketing a product called EZ-15 that supposedly can reduce carbon dioxide emissions from motor vehicles, but it's killing people, and we're trying to stop them."

Again silence, so Chris went on, the desperation growing in his voice, "Jackie Goldberg, Sergio Sanchez, Gerhard Mueller, and other innocent people all were murdered because they stood to disrupt the conspiracy to introduce this product, this agent of death."

Silence.

"Damn it. There's a lot more to this story, but we can't accomplish anything standing out here. For God's sake, please, we've got to stop them, but we need proof of EZ-15's horrible impact. You're the only person who can help—"

"Go away," Thurgensen interrupted. "I stopped caring about anything a long time ago. I'm an old man. Leave me alone."

Chris paused and then replied with a mixture of anger and sarcasm, "You're right. You're a pathetic has-been, and we were stupid to think you could possibly help us."

"Don't listen to him," Sonja said as she took a step closer to the unseen old man. "He's just one of those dumb government lawyers. What does he know? I'm an EPA technical analyst, and I've read your technical papers. You're a genius. I've also studied all of the technical documents and test data on EZ-15, and something doesn't add up."

Sonja took a deep breath and continued. "EZ-15 is being used in Tokyo and Osaka. Innocent children and elderly folks are dying by the thousands. If we don't stop EMCO, hundreds of thousands of children and others could die, and their blood will be on your hands."

Silence.

But then Thurgensen, whose considerable ego was bruised by Chris's well-chosen words, and his heart touched by Sonja's desperate plea, finally spoke, "Okay, come up here, but keep your hands high in the air where I can see them. I'll listen to what you have to say, but you're going to have to convince me. If you try anything or I don't believe everything you tell me, you're dead, and your rotting carcasses will be dinner for the turkey vultures that live out here."

Chris and Sonja raised their arms above their heads and turned to look at each other, both allowing themselves to believe that there was at least some small hope they might finally be able to stop EZ-15.

CHAPTER 62

May 11
Mason County, Virginia

Chris and Sonja made their way through the dense underbrush. If there was a path to Thurgensen's cabin, it was nowhere in sight. As they finally reached a clearing, they both froze, and Sonja couldn't stop herself from gasping. Not fifteen feet in front of them, on the front porch of a small wooden cabin, stood the menacing figure of Karl Thurgensen. His deep blue eyes were open wide and glaring from his well-weathered face—his rifle aimed directly at Chris's forehead.

Thurgensen was dressed in a pair of old, very faded and torn bib overalls—no shirt and no shoes. His long, unkempt, gray hair flowed far down his back, and his bushy gray beard spread across the full breadth of his chest and almost reached his waist. The old man was gaunt but surprisingly muscular for a seventy-five-year-old.

Without speaking, the mountain man motioned Chris and Sonja to come to him. As they walked forward, Chris spotted, to the left of the cabin, a wooden windmill. To the right was the stream with a fifteen-foot waterfall that flowed into a pond formed by a stone and mud dam across the stream twenty feet below. On the left side of the porch was a copper still, which from the steam that was rising, suggested it was hard at work turning out moonshine.

When they neared the porch steps, Thurgensen pointed with his long, boney index finger at Sonja and finally spoke. "Who are you?"

With her voice trembling, she replied, "My name is Sonja Voinovich, and I—"

"Stop right there, girly. Is Voinovich your married name?"

"No. I've never been married—"

"Leave now!"

"What?" Chris and Sonja both cried out.

"I told you I wanted the truth. Voinovich is a Slovak name. You have red hair and blue eyes. You're obviously not Slovak. My guess is you're Aryan," Thurgensen replied, unable to hide his satisfaction in catching his unwanted visitors in a lie.

At a total loss as to what to say, Sonja looked desperately at Chris, who whispered, "Tell him. Tell him everything."

"Wait," Sonja said, regaining her composure and staring directly into old man's eyes. "I did tell you the truth. My legal name is Voinovich, but my real name is Zimmer—Katrina Zimmer—and my parents were from Germany."

Without waiting for a reply from Thurgensen, Sonja told him everything—how her parents were spies in East Germany for the NATO countries and were granted asylum in the United States in a spy exchange. That they were subsequently murdered by a CIA agent, now DHS operative, named Parnak Petrovic, who was currently involved in the EZ-15 conspiracy. As she spoke, Thurgensen slowly lowered his rifle, and his cold, piercing stare disappeared as the taut muscles in his face softened.

When Sonja finished her story, Chris, without giving Thurgensen the chance to speak, picked up the saga, telling everything that had happened with EMCO, its coconspirators, and EZ-15.

When they finally finished, Sonja and Chris both looked at Thurgensen, who sat down on the porch steps as if he had lost the strength in his legs from the weight of the horrors vividly described to him. He sighed, shook his head, and mumbled, "Those miserable bastards."

After a long, awkward silence in which Thurgensen seemed to be wrestling with himself over what to do next, the old man finally spoke. "We've got a lot to do and not much time to do it."

The tone and inflection of Thurgensen's voice had completely changed. The once crazed-looking mountain man smiled almost warmly at the still-uncertain couple, beckoning them to come up on the porch. "You both look pretty hot and thirsty. Take a seat. I'll get you a drink. You've never tasted anything so delicious."

As Sonja and Chris sat in a beautifully handcrafted ash-branch, double-chair swing, Thurgensen went to the still, grabbed a nearby ceramic gallon jug, and returned. He pulled the cork from the jug and handed it to Sonja. "Take a swig, my dear," he said, the hint of álcohol on his breath.

At the restaurant the evening before, Sonja had heard the stories about the powerful kick of the "Gray Fox's" moonshine, but they had come this far, and she didn't want to offend Thurgensen, who eagerly waited for Sonja to take a drink.

Sonja reluctantly wrapped her long, slender fingers around the jug, lifted it somewhat tentatively to her lips, and took as small a sip as possible. Her eyes opened wide, and then, without hesitation, she proceeded to take two enormous gulps from the jug.

"That's amazing! I've never tasted anything as good as that."

Chris looked at Sonja with disbelief and then gathered his composure as Sonja handed him the jug. "And don't drink it all. Save some for me," she said with a laugh.

Like Sonja, Chris was reluctant, particularly since he hadn't had a drop of alcohol in nearly a month. But like Sonja, Chris's first sip was quickly followed by several healthy gulps.

"I never imagined water could taste that good," Chris said as he handed the now nearly empty jug back to Sonja.

"You city folk probably have never tasted untreated water before. This water comes straight from that waterfall over there. But what makes this H2O so fantastic is the mix of natural minerals. The spring headwaters of this stream are just above that waterfall—no risk of contamination from animals or humans."

As Sonja took the final sips, completely draining the jug, Thurgensen spoke. "Let's go back and get those backpacks you left behind and start getting organized."

"How did you know we had backpacks?" Chris queried.

"Your vehicle may have been designed to meet the government noise standards, but sounds roll up these mountains from miles away. When I heard you down there, I circled down and hid in the woods, tracking your progress. As you approached the cabin, I came ahead to give you a proper greeting."

Within fifteen minutes, the two men returned. Chris was sweating profusely, but Thurgensen, still barefoot, seemed totally unaffected by the trek up to the cabin carrying a forty-pound pack.

"It's pretty hot for this time of year if you're not used to it," Thurgensen said, as if he sensed Chris's ego had been bruised by a seventy-five-year-old who appeared to be in better shape. "Let's head inside and get started."

Entering through the front door, Chris and Sonja saw, in the surprisingly large room, a potbellied stove near the back, where several well-tarnished pots and pans were hanging on the wall. The furnishings—a table and four chairs, a large cabinet, a rocking chair near the fireplace—were all wooden and all handmade. No cushions, no decorations, no pictures save a faded color photo on the cabinet in a tarnished gold frame of a much younger Thurgensen, smiling, with his arms lovingly around a truly beautiful young woman—no doubt Mrs. Thurgensen.

The place was spotless, but papers were stacked helter-skelter everywhere, including on the rungs of a ladder that led to a loft over the back half of the cabin. A door at the back of the cabin was open and revealed a small room with a bed where Thurgensen apparently slept.

"You two can sleep upstairs. No bed, but the big mat I wove is surprisingly comfortable and is big enough for two. It's hot up there right now, but at night the temperatures drop precipitously, and there's always a nice breeze coming up the mountain and through the windows. The outhouse is around the back of the cabin about thirty yards to the south. It's a bit of a hike, but I don't want to contaminate the stream. Oh, and try to keep the noise down up there. I'm a very light sleeper."

Chris and Sonja both blushed at the not-too-subtle comment suggesting that they might be doing more than just sleeping in the loft.

"It's not what you think. Sonja and I aren't married or anything like that. We're just work colleagues who got caught up in this nightmare we've been living," Chris volunteered, somewhat defensively, as Sonja nodded in agreement.

"Look, I thought you two agreed to tell the truth. Anyone, including me, who watches the way you talk, look at, and touch each other isn't going to buy your story," Thurgensen said, grinning.

After yet another awkward moment of silence, Thurgensen said, "For God's sake, take your stuff up to the loft and let's get started solving the mystery of EZ-15."

When they returned ten minutes later, Thurgensen was transformed. He had changed into a white, short-sleeve shirt, wrinkled tan slacks, and a pair of well-worn, brown loafers covering his sockless feet. His hair was pulled tightly behind his head into a long ponytail, and he wore a pair of badly bent, steel-rimmed glasses. A rather ancient-looking computer was placed on the table in front of him.

As Sonja pulled her computer out of her backpack and sat across from Thurgensen, she exclaimed, "And I thought my computer was old."

"It's slow, for sure, but it gets the job done," Thurgensen said, turning his computer on and then waiting for what seemed like forever for its screen to light up.

The rest of the morning and well into the late afternoon, Chris, Sonja, and Thurgensen pored over every detail of what the two knew about EZ-15. Over time, the conversation was increasingly between Sonja, who had the technical background and knowledge, and Thurgensen, who seemed eager to absorb all he could about the test data that had been generated by various sources, as well as the information in Ronnie Chapman's notes.

The first surprise came late in the day when the battery on Sonja's computer began to run down. Thurgensen reached for an unseen adapter and plugged it into her computer. The cord ran back to the wall behind them and into, until then, an unseen electrical socket.

"Wind power. And I have a small battery where I can store power to use when the wind doesn't blow," Thurgensen said, without emotion.

Around five o'clock, Thurgensen stood up, stretched, and said, "I'm not a very good host. You two haven't had anything to eat, and I just simply lost track of the time. Sonja, please download all of your files onto my computer and then you two go take a break on the porch while I fix us some grub."

About twenty minutes later, Thurgensen called out, "Dinner is served."

The table had been transformed from a work station into a splendid dining space. Plates, cloth napkins, and utensils had been set. In the center of the table, a large, blue ceramic bowl filled with salad greens sat next to a large basket of homemade bread and a steeping hot, black kettle pot that contained rabbit stew.

When she finished eating, Sonja exclaimed, "That was wonderful, Dr. Thurgensen."

"Please, call me Karl," Thurgensen responded. As Chris and Sonja rose to wash the dishes, they heard a sound that nearly caused both of them to drop the dishes and bowls they were carrying.

"What the hell?" Chris exclaimed. "It sounds like my cell phone, but that's impossible. No way I could be getting a signal way out here."

"Not only cell phone service, but Internet service as well. I had to find some way to amuse myself up here the past ten years, so I erected a tower on an exposed rock outcrop high up on the mountain behind this cabin. I get an amazing connection, and you can't see the tower from any of the roads around here."

Chris raced up the ladder, rummaged through the pockets of his backpack, and pulled out his phone. He waited until it stopped ringing and allowed enough time for the caller to leave a message.

He came down the ladder with one of the many cheap cell phones they brought and dialed for his messages. As he listened to the message, a look of shock came over his face as he uttered the first of multiple expletives.

Sonja came over to Chris, the look of concern clearly visible on her face.

"It's Chet. They're all okay, but prepare yourself," Chris said to Sonja as he pushed the replay button and handed the phone to her.

Sonja gasped as she listened to Chet's message detailing the assault on the farmhouse, its destruction, and the Crew's miraculous escape. When she finished listening to the message, she slumped into Chris's arms. "Is this nightmare ever going to end?"

Chris quickly explained to Thurgensen what had happened to their colleagues. Thurgensen listened but said nothing. Chris raced back up to the loft, grabbed another cell phone, and called Chet back.

As Chris communicated with Chet, Sonja turned to the still-expressionless Thurgensen and warned, "These guys are ruthless as hell, and they'll stop at nothing. You don't have to risk your life by getting involved in this. We'd understand."

Thurgensen walked over to Sonja, put his hands on her shoulders, and said kindly, "You have no idea how much I want to stop them. Until you and that young man showed up today, I didn't have much of a reason to keep on living. Now I wouldn't miss the opportunity to help send every single one of those bastards straight to hell."

"Thanks," was all she could think to say. It was more than enough for Thurgensen.

About ten minutes later, Chris bounded down the ladder. "They are all fine. Hiding out in Baltimore and trying to lie as low as possible. I told Chet we've teamed up with Dr. Thurgensen, I mean Karl, and Chet will supply us a contact person in Los Angeles to meet us and provide us all the logistical support we need once we arrive."

"Los Angeles? I assume you're planning for us to pay a visit to the California Air Resources Board in the near future," Thurgensen said.

"Exactly, Karl. But we need to find some answers first."

"In that case, why don't you two finish up the dishes and call it a night. I need to digest everything you told me today, review the data, and start developing some hypotheses," Thurgensen said, turning on his computer and reshuffling his stack of notes taken earlier that day.

Sonja and Chris finished cleaning up and climbed quietly up the ladder to the loft. "Goodnight, Karl," they both said, but Thurgensen was lost in thought and probably wouldn't have heard them if they had shouted.

CHAPTER 63

May 12
Washington, DC—Morning

One by one, the Heritage Study Group members arrived at the Capital Club. Once again, they each were unaware that their presence was being duly noted, this time by Randall Walker, an ex-DC-cop and colleague of Carson Bigalow.

By 11:00 a.m., all the HSG members except Kowalski had arrived, including the most distinguished and frequently absent member, Bingeman Foster. At its beginning, the tone of the gathering was somber as members awkwardly waited for Judge Worthington to speak.

Finally, Worthington looked up. "This is our first meeting since Franklin Moss's tragic death. Franklin wasn't only a dear friend, but a true patriot and an outstanding public servant. We will all dearly miss him."

Turning to McCormick, the judge added, "Reverend, perhaps you could lead us in prayer."

McCormick, who never missed the opportunity to pray, bowed his head and droned on for several minutes before concluding, "And, dear Lord, please forgive our dear friend for his sinful and perverse ways. In your name we pray. Amen."

Petrovic almost choked with laughter at McCormick's not too subtle reference to Moss apparently being a homosexual, given the bizarre circumstances of his death. *What a joke. The good reverend is a flaming fag himself, and I've got the pictures to prove it,* Petrovic thought. And he did indeed have photos of McCormick's considerable indiscretions, as well as damaging evidence on every other HSG member sitting around the table.

Petrovic quickly regained his composure and solemnly said, "Amen." This was followed by a chorus of "Amens" from the others around the table.

Without even a moment's hesitation, Worthington barked, "Now, gentlemen, on to the matters before us today. Under old business, the chair notes that Parnak was right, as usual, with the intelligence he provided at our meeting several weeks ago. As he predicted, the Justice Department did launch an investigation into alleged bribery, fraud, and conspiracy by Cloverleaf Security executives, and two dozen indictments were issued earlier this week. I'm sure you all read in this morning's *Wall Street Journal* that Cloverleaf has filed for bankruptcy. I hope you all had the good sense to dump your Cloverleaf stock."

Everyone around the table nodded affirmatively, and a chorus of "Hear, hear," echoed throughout the room in recognition of Petrovic's scoop on Cloverleaf.

When the noise subsided, Worthington again spoke. "Stanley, would you be kind enough to give us an update on EMCO and EZ-15?"

All eyes turned to Braxton, who smiled broadly and said, "Nothing but great news. As of last night's market close, EMCO's share price hit a new high of sixty-two dollars. Only fourteen more days before the EPA approval of EZ-15 is final, and we see absolutely nothing on the horizon that could possibly derail that approval. Personally, I think EMCO is still a buy even at its current price."

Braxton's brash air of confidence belied the troubling truth that, despite the appearance of clear sailing for EZ-15 final approval, there were still too many loose ends.

"Well done, Stanley," Worthington said, and he turned to Foster. "Bing, I believe you have an item for the group."

"You've all no doubt seen or heard the rumors in the media that President Keller is about to announce a ten-billion-dollar high-speed rail network initiative. As a result, the stock value of several rail construction companies have recently soared by nearly 30 percent," the president's chief of staff began quietly. Then he changed his tone. "The rumors are complete bullshit! While President Keller is a big fan of infrastructure building, not even he's stupid enough to use his limited political capital trying to move Congress on such a costly initiative in this political climate. My advice to all of you is to sell BMDD, Ltd., and Weatherbee, Incorporated, short and enjoy watching these stocks drop when Keller holds a press event next week to debunk the rail infrastructure initiative rumors."

"Well done, Bing. If there is no further business, I suggest we adjourn," Worthington said, looking impatiently at his watch.

"Judge, I wonder if you, Parnak, and Stan could remain for just a few minutes," Foster asked deferentially. "I have a matter of national security I would like to discuss. I also took the liberty of inviting Michael Cavanaugh with the FBI, who's waiting in the lobby to join us. I hope this is okay with all of you."

Worthington did little to hide his displeasure with Foster's somewhat unusual request. The judge had a young, very attractive, and very expensive call girl waiting in a suite at the nearby Madison Hotel. He was already late, and he was paying her by the hour. But finally, Worthington nodded his approval, and the three gentlemen took seats near Worthington as the other Heritage Study Group members left the room.

Petrovic got up and opened the door to invite Cavanaugh to join them at the table.

"I would like to introduce FBI agent Michael Cavanaugh, who is leading the effort to track down the conspirators who are trying to disrupt EPA's final approval of EZ-15," Foster said.

"Do we have a problem here?" Worthington queried as the annoyance on his face turned to one of concern. "I thought things were moving forward nicely?"

"So far we've kept the conspirators on the defensive, but they continue to elude capture," Petrovic said, and then he explained how the trap set by Foster for O'Brian, the suspected leader of the group, failed when one of the group's lookouts created a diversion, and O'Brian was able to escape.

"We'd have caught them all if the idiot cop hadn't overreacted," Petrovic growled. "The dead guy got a cell phone call just before he went postal. Someone had to have warned him that it was a trap."

"Impossible. I talked with no one except the top secret service official and, of course, Stan here, who provided us with some very useful background information on O'Brian," Foster protested.

All eyes focused on Braxton.

"I told no one. Absolutely no one."

"Stan, relax; no one is accusing you. Gentlemen, let's move on," Worthington interrupted.

Petrovic next explained that the lookout tried to destroy the cell phone before he died, but FBI forensics, after several days of intense activity, was able to reconstruct and trace where the call had been placed—a nonworking farm in Prince George's County, Maryland. An FBI assault team stormed the farmhouse, but the conspirators had already left.

"Just great," Worthington said with a mix of sarcasm and frustration.

Cavanaugh quickly spoke up. "We did get one lead this morning during a subsequent search of the grounds around the farmhouse. Our agents found several pieces of partially burned paper in the rubble. We're checking them all out. One contained the words 'Karl Thurgensen' and 'Mason County, Virginia.' The FBI will try to identify this Thurgensen person, but Mason County is down in southwestern Virginia. As soon as we identify who Thurgensen is, my associate, Rich Adams, and I will head off for Mason County."

"I have some intelligence to offer as well," Braxton said. "I've met several times with Joanne McKay, Goodman's de facto chief of staff ever since Kowalski was sent to Detroit. My sources tell me Goodman is wavering on his support of EMCO's EZ-15 application, and I'm sure that blonde bitch is the reason. I'm taking her to a reception at the Brazilian embassy, and I'll squeeze her until she comes clean. I have some information I know she wouldn't like to see made public."

"Sounds good, Stan," Worthington said.

Unnoticed by the others, Petrovic leaned toward Cavanaugh and whispered, "After we leave, meet me at the southwest corner of the Park. We need to talk."

Shortly thereafter, the five men completed the meeting, left the Capital Club, and went their separate ways. Randall Walker, as he had done when the other HSG members left, duly noted each of the individuals, including Foster, who wasn't on the list of HSG members, but whom Walker recognized from the numerous pictures in the media as Keller's chief of staff.

Walker noticed, but didn't attempt to follow, Petrovic and Cavanaugh, who strolled together to the far end of the park and sat on a bench.

"That asshole Braxton leaked the information about the trap for O'Brian to someone; probably in an effort to impress some chick he was hitting on," Petrovic said, the veins on his temples bulging in anger.

"Do you think it's possible he told McKay? He's made no secret in the past that he has the hots for her. And if she really can't be trusted to turn Goodman to support EZ-15, she just might have been in communication with someone who sounded the alarm on the Lafayette Park trap," Cavanaugh pondered aloud.

"Damn, Michael!" Petrovic exclaimed. "You may just have hit upon it. We can't trust Braxton, and McKay is a big problem for us, whether she blew the lid on the O'Brian trap or not." After a moment's poise, Petrovic whispered in a barely audible voice, "Here's what we're going to do …"

CHAPTER 64

May 12
Mason County, Virginia

Hours before the Heritage Study Group gathered, Sonja made her way down the ladder, anxious to continue her quest to discover what caused EZ-15 to trigger asthma attacks.

"Good morning, Sonja. You're up early."

Startled, Sonja spun her head and saw Thurgensen sitting at the table, which was covered with small pieces of paper containing notes he had scribbled.

"You're up pretty early yourself," she answered but then realized Thurgensen was dressed exactly like he was the night before. The scientist had never gone to bed and looked exhausted.

"Any progress?" she asked hopefully.

"Lots of ideas, but no, nothing to report," Thurgensen replied, the disappointment evident in his tired voice.

"I'll make some coffee, fix breakfast, and then you, me, and sleepyhead up there in the loft will do a little brainstorming."

An hour later, Chris made his way down the ladder to join Sonja and Thurgensen, who were both staring at their computer screens. Grabbing a cell phone from his backpack, Chris checked for messages left on his phone.

Looking up, he said, "It's Longshank's number." Then he added in desperation, "We don't have international service on any of the phones I brought. We're screwed."

"No problem, my friend," Thurgensen said, without looking up from a document he was studying. "Grab the cell phone on the bureau in my bedroom. I hacked into the county's communication system, and we can use it to make calls anywhere."

Moments later, Chris returned and dialed the number. Finally, someone answered, and the British accent was easy to identify.

"Sir Reginald, are you all right?"

After a brief cordial exchange, Longshank detailed everything that had happened. "We're staying in a well-guarded safe house located just outside of London."

"Were they able to ID the would-be assassin?" Chris queried, and Longshank reported that the assassin had been identified by DNA as an independent security consultant named Hans Dietrich.

"Pam Russell told me in Brussels that Dietrich was on the EMCO payroll."

"Chris, the Secret Service shared a copy of the intelligence report on Dietrich, and there was absolutely no mention of EMCO. How are things going at your end?"

Chris paused as a chilling thought entered his mind. *What if British intelligence is working with the DHS or the FBI and is monitoring this call?*

"Everything here is fine. I'll contact you when the time is right. In the meantime, be careful and don't trust anyone," Chris said, abruptly ending the conversation.

"Longshank and everyone are safe, but they can't be of further help to us right now. I need to dismantle this phone. Is there any chance the authorities can trace this number?"

"Sure they can," Thurgensen deadpanned. "But they won't find us. That phone was given to me by a 250-pound, mean-ass biker named Killer in exchange for a jug of my special brew. Given that the phone is pink and has very large keypad buttons, my guess is that if the authorities successfully track its owner down, it will be a nice, old granny somewhere who will be receiving a rather shocking visit from an FBI SWAT team."

Sonja, Chris, and Karl looked at each other and laughed at the thought.

For the next eight hours, Thurgensen, with occasional input from Sonja and Chris, toiled at unlocking the mystery of EZ-15. Several times, the old man called out confidently that he had discovered something, only to grow quiet and distraught moments later.

Throughout the day, Sonja brought him a mug of cold, fresh water or something to eat. Each time, she touched his shoulder and whispered words of encouragement that seemed to give Thurgensen renewed resolve to keep on probing.

Sonja spent the rest of her time searching for the link between EZ-15 and the sudden increase in asthma attacks in Tokyo and Osaka. She was becoming increasingly convinced that local meteorological conditions did play a role, most notably high ambient temperatures. But like Thurgensen, her efforts failed to provide any answers.

Chris devoted his time to searching the Internet, hoping to find any news reports that someone, maybe in Osaka or Tokyo where EZ-15 was being used, had sounded the alert about the use of the product or was at least doing some research. But other than a few articles on the financial pages, he found absolutely nothing about EZ-15 or EMCO.

"It's as if no one but us gives a damn about what EZ-15 is doing to innocent people," Chris exclaimed as he slammed the cover of his computer down and stood up to stretch his aching back.

Chris knew what he had to do next and definitely wasn't looking forward to it. He needed to contact Steven Morris at the California Air Resources Board, the state version of EPA's Office of Air Quality. Chris and Morris had a long-standing dislike for each other. Some of the animosity resulted from the decades-old rivalry between California and EPA, but much of it was personal—very personal.

California, which did the pioneering research on the causes of ground-level smog, or "urban haze," that was suffocating Los Angeles and found the link to automobile exhaust pollution, established the California's Air Resources Board. That agency began developing and implementing emission standards for automobiles sold in California. When Congress enacted the Clean Air Amendments of 1970, establishing a comprehensive federal program to reduce both motor automobile and industrial air pollution nationwide, an exception was carved out for California to adopt its own pollution control standards for motor vehicles. The catch was that the US EPA had the authority to review and overrule the California standards based on a set of guidelines contained in the 1970 legislation. And thus was born an intense rivalry between the two agencies.

Over the next forty-plus years, the relationship between the US EPA and the California ARB resembled a not always happily married couple. Linked by legislation and a mutual desire to reduce pollution from automobiles, and later trucks, construction equipment, garden equipment, locomotive emissions, and marine vessels, the staffs of the two agencies at times worked well together. Both ARB and EPA had the right to claim credit for establishing automotive standards in the 1990s and early 2000s that, when fully implemented, would reduce exhaust emissions from cars, trucks, and other sources by up to 95 percent or more over the uncontrolled pollution levels of automobiles manufactured in the early 1960s.

But at other times, the relationship between the two agencies was strained, if not completely dysfunctional. Steve Morris, ARB's best technical analyst who had gained the confidence of the board chairman on policy issues as well, fiercely battled over the years with Chris on a host of issues. When Chris was eventually demoted, Morris had sent him an e-mail that simply read, "Good riddance, Asshole!"

Chris found Morris's telephone number on the ARB Web page, grabbed another cell phone, and dialed it. As the phone rang at the other end, he thought, *To stop EZ-15, we need Thurgensen to find the key to EZ-15, Morris's staff to run the tests to prove it, and the ARB Executive Board to endorse the findings at a public hearing—all this before the EPA EZ-15 approval becomes final in less than two weeks.*

Finally, a young female voice answered, "Good morning, ARB. Steve Morris's office."

"Hello, my name is O'Brian. Steve knows me. Tell him this is an emergency," Chris replied, the tension evident in his voice.

Even though Morris was the ARB's top technical staff member, he preferred a small office that was separated from his young administrative assistant by only a waist-high room divider. Consequently, all the young woman had to do was put her hand over the phone receiver, spin around in her chair, and tell Morris, "Someone named O'Brian—says it's important."

"Tell that pain in the ass I'm not available," Morris responded loudly.

"I'm sorry, Mr. Morris isn't available. May I take your num—"

Chris, recognizing Morris's voice in the background and hearing quite clearly everything Morris had said, shouted into the phone,

"Listen, Morris, you son of a bitch, EZ-15 is a killer. If you want the deaths of thousands of children in Los Angeles on your hands, then don't pick up your damn phone. I don't have any time to waste. I'm going to call Amos next."

"Amos Chandler would never a take a call from you," Morris shouted back.

The young assistant sat dumbfounded, holding the phone up in the air so the two men could yell back and forth at each other. Finally, Morris motioned her to put O'Brian's call through to him and whispered for her to leave the room.

"Make it quick, and this better be good."

Chris started with Mueller and Sanchez's discovery of asthma attacks and deaths in both Tokyo and Osaka. He recounted Sanchez's dire warning that EMCO was trying to hide something horrible about EZ-15. Chris next relayed his conversations with Goldberg and Mueller and how they both, along with Sanchez and many others, had died under suspicious circumstances.

Morris remained silent at the other end, allowing Chris to continue. Chris then discussed Ronnie Chapman's discovery of anomalies in the chemical balance of the EPA testing that showed carbon atoms had simply vanished. Finally, Chris reported Sanchez's theory about the carbon particles escaping during the emission testing and Mueller's plan to test the hypothesis by using a finer mesh test filter media.

"Has ARB run any tests on EZ-15?" Chris asked when he had finished his tale.

· "No," Morris replied somewhat defensively. "EZ-15 is a federal matter, and we simply don't have the money in our budget to run confirmatory tests on a federal initiative."

"But surely you guys have some concerns, some questions," Chris almost pleaded.

"Sure we do. But we need a lot more than you've given me so far for us to take on EPA, the president, the US Congress, and all of the EZ-15 private sector supporters."

"We do," Chris lied. "As we speak, an EPA analyst, who is an absolute genius, and Karl Thurgensen—you remember Dr. Thurgensen—are putting the finishing touches on an analysis that will provide the answers and blow the cover wide open on EZ-15."

"Tell me more."

"Not over the phone," Chris said, trying to buy more time for Thurgensen and Sonja to complete their research and find the answers needed. "Can we meet next Monday at your office? Have I given you enough to run one lousy test on EZ-15 using the finer mesh X10B19-0.0001 filter paper?"

"Wait. I need to put you on hold while I make a quick call," Morris replied.

In less than minute, Chris heard a click, and Morris said, "Ten a.m. Monday at Chandler's office. You know our address. And Amos has okayed running one emission test at our lab using X10B19.0.0001 filter paper. We'll start prepping the testing lab, and we should have the test results by Monday."

"We'll see you then," Chris said, unable to hide the sheer joy he felt. He was just about to say good-bye and hang up when Morris spoke.

"O'Brian, you know damn well that I know you've been accused of everything from murder to extortion to God knows what. I assume your genius technical analyst is Sonja Voinovich, who has been described from everything I have read as some kind of dysfunctional drug addict, social freak, and possibly a ruthless assassin."

"But—"

"Damn it, Chris. For once in your life, let me finish a sentence. You and I both know there's no love lost between us. But what you don't know is that I've on occasion, and somewhat reluctantly, respected your smart-ass opinions on legal matters. Frankly, I've missed sparring with you the last few years, and I absolutely hate dealing with that idiot boss of yours, Conrad Martin. Furthermore, you're too much of a wimp to go around killing people. But having said that, if I get even the hint that you are somehow involved with what the authorities are accusing you of, I'll turn you in myself."

"Fair enough ... and thanks," Chris replied and hung up.

"We're in—California, here we come," Chris said, looking at Thurgensen and Sonja.

"But we still haven't unlocked the mystery," the scientist said with a frown.

"But we will," Sonja replied.

Thurgensen continued to work well into the night without success. At one point, he reached for and started to fill a large mug with moonshine.

"No," Sonja said gently. "Let's wait until we have something to celebrate."

Around ten o'clock, Thurgensen, who had been up for nearly forty hours, fell asleep at the table. Sonja and Chris carefully guided him to his bed. Sonja leaned over and gently stroked his forehead.

CHAPTER 65

May 13
Mason County, Virginia

Friday at the cabin was the mirror image of the day before. The scientist, up before 6:00 a.m., had labored unsuccessfully for hours in his quest to unlock the mystery of EZ-15. Sonja, who had joined him thirty minutes later, pored over the modeling data she had generated on the spikes in asthma attacks but again made no progress. Chris spoke several times with Chet, arranging the logistical support they needed once they arrived in Los Angeles. Around six o'clock, Chris, sensing that Sonja's deteriorating mood was contributing to Thurgensen's already depressed state, approached her from behind and rubbed her shoulders.

At first she appeared annoyed at his gesture, but then she relaxed, put her hands on his hands, and whispered without looking up from her work, "Thanks."

Chris bent over and gently kissed the top of her head as he rubbed her neck.

"Damn!" Sonja yelled as she sprang from her chair.

Chris recoiled. "That's not exactly the response I was hoping for."

Sonja spun around and hugged him tightly as he stared at her, mystified by her bizarre behavior.

"I found it. The answer was staring right at me, and I couldn't see it. It's not simply the ambient temperature, the humidity index, or the level of pollution—it's all three. The asthma attacks occur when the temperature, humidity index, and the ground-level pollution levels each fall within a narrow range at the same time."

Without speaking, Thurgensen got up and walked over to Sonja, who was now pointing to show Chris the data. Thurgensen stepped to her side, leaned over the table, and ran his fingers over the data she had generated. Then without speaking, he returned to his seat and began writing.

Chris and Sonja looked at Thurgensen, both stunned by his apparent lack of interest in Sonja's breakthrough.

After five minutes of scribbling notes and mumbling to himself, Thurgensen got up and approached Sonja and Chris as an enormous smile spread across his face. He put his arms around both of them and proclaimed, "You found the key, my dear. The key that unlocks the mystery of EZ-15."

Motioning them both to sit down, Thurgensen explained, "EZ-15 contains a chemical catalyst that explodes a molecule of carbon dioxide, which, as you know, is one atom of carbon and two atoms of oxygen, into a carbon atom and a molecule of oxygen made up of the two oxygen atoms. Your friend at EPA, Ronnie Chapman and Gerhard Mueller, both discovered that some of the carbon atoms seemed to have disappeared in the emission tests. They both hypothesized that if a finer mesh filter media was used in the emission test, these carbon particles would be trapped. A good theory, but it won't provide the complete answer. These carbon atoms quickly explode and split into activated subatomic particles. These particles probably will be detected on the finer filter paper, but that's not going to be all the proof we need."

"But what's the link between these rogue subatomic carbon-based particles and the increased incidents in asthma attacks and death?" Chris asked.

"Thanks to Sonja, we now have the answer," Thurgensen replied. "If these activated subatomic particles enter the atmosphere when the temperature and humidity are just right, they become supercharged. When the pollution levels at ground level are elevated, there are toxic chemicals that are attracted to the super activated, subatomic particles. Because these particles are so small, when breathed in, the particles, with the toxic substances attached to them, pass through the lungs' respiratory filter system and lodge themselves deep within the lungs. Asthma sufferers are very sensitive to exposure of this toxic mix in their lungs. The result is an asthma attack, which, if severe enough, can cause death."

"You've done it, Dr. Thurgensen," Chris said as the three awkwardly embraced. "Finally, we have the ammunition to nail those bastards."

"Not so fast. We have a lot of work to do. It's going to take me the rest of the evening to write all of this up like a technical journal article, and, Sonja, I'm going to need your input on the details of the humidity, temperature, and ground-level pollution trigger zone you uncovered."

"I'll finish up on the logistics for getting us out to California and whip us up some chow," Chris volunteered as Sonja gathered her notes and sat down next to Thurgensen, where they would spend the next four hours hard at work.

When they finally finished hours later, Thurgensen, completely exhausted, got up and grabbed the brown jug on the counter and three glasses. "Time for a toast," he said as he filled the glasses with moonshine.

They clinked their glasses, and Thurgensen took a healthy swallow and wiped his lips. Sonja tentatively took a sip as her eyes popped open and she choked. "That's mighty strong stuff."

Thurgensen looked at Chris, who had politely put his glass on the table without taking a drink.

"Sorry, Dr. Thurgensen, I mean no disrespect, but I'm an alcoholic, and I've been sober for nearly a month," Chris said quietly. It was the first time he had actually admitted to anyone other than Casey, Otto, and Billy that he had a drinking problem.

Sonja came over and affectionately touched Chris on his shoulder, as if to say she understood.

"No apology necessary, young man. I admire your courage to quit. I wish I could have stopped drinking a long time ago," Thurgensen said, pouring himself another drink.

Sonja gently put her hand around Thurgensen's glass and pulled it away from him. "Tomorrow is another big day. We all need to get a good night's sleep."

Thurgensen looked at Sonja as if he was a scolded puppy, but then he said, "You're correct, my dear. Thanks for reminding me."

* * *

About the time Sonja and Thurgensen made their breakthroughs on the mystery of EZ-15, Joanne was tapping her foot impatiently in front of her apartment building, waiting for the taxi Braxton had promised he would arrange to take her to the Brazilian embassy. Once the taxi finally arrived, the trip to the embassy took less than fifteen minutes. The Brazilian embassy, like numerous other embassies, was located on Massachusetts Avenue, only minutes from the downtown business sector, the White House, and Capitol Hill.

As Joanne approached the main entrance to the grand reception hall, a man dressed in a black tux greeted her and opened the door. She glided into the room, dressed in her favorite black and flowing, below-the-knee-length silk dress. The low-cut, tight-fitting top showcased her lovely figure. She wore a string of pearls her mother had given her when she graduated from the University of Michigan, and her beautiful blonde hair was pulled fashionably back.

Joanne spotted Braxton and strutted across the large, lavishly decorated room toward him. "You look simply ravishing this evening," Braxton gushed.

"Thank you. You look rather dashing yourself in that tux," Joanne flirted as Braxton melted at her compliment.

The event was pretty standard for these types of affairs. The usual Who's Who of the Washington political, international, and business communities were in full attendance. Waiters circulated among the guests with sterling silver trays sprinkled with well-arranged, delicate canapés and ridiculously expensive champagne. The guests appeared to mingle aimlessly, but in reality, each person was on a mission to search out and make contact with the one or two people who were the reason for being at the event in the first place.

Braxton led Joanne around the room and displayed his female companion to those inside and outside of government like she was his trophy. The lobbyist's hands also got a little too familiar with various parts of Joanne's body. But all in all, for Joanne, the evening was tolerable.

She had fully expected Braxton to grill her on what she was doing to keep her boss on track to support EPA's final approval of EZ-15. But the conversation between them, while boring, was light. Braxton did seem intent on plying her with alcohol as he repeatedly grabbed a glass of champagne from a passing tray and handed it to her. Just as deftly, she placed each of the nearly full glasses on one of the many tables scattered throughout the room.

Finally, around ten o'clock, as the event was coming to the end, Braxton came up to her with two full glasses of champagne, handed one to her, and said, "Here's to Senator Goodman's continued support of EZ-15. Bottoms up."

Joanne had little choice, so she followed Braxton's lead and gulped down the full glass of champagne that had just the hint of an odd taste. *This champagne has been sitting out too long*, she thought.

As they left the embassy, Joanne turned toward Braxton and said, "Thanks for a nice evening. I can catch a cab home from here."

"It's early. Let's take a little walk down to the bridge over Rock Creek Park. The view of the city from there is always fantastic, and at night there's almost always a nice, refreshing breeze."

"I really need to go," Joanne replied politely.

"What's the hurry?" Braxton said as he firmly grabbed her arm above her elbow and pulled her in the direction he wanted to go. Then letting go, he said, "We need to talk."

Joanne's sense of dread was instantaneous, but she knew she should avoid making a scene. As they walked down the street in silence, her anxiety grew. Within minutes, there was no one else in sight.

Finally, as they reached the east end of the quarter-mile bridge, with its gothic-looking masonry towers at each end and dimly lit green-tarnish copper lampposts every twenty-five feet or so, Braxton asked, "What's your current read on your boss's support for EZ-15?"

"Senator Goodman is solidly on board," Joanne lied.

"That's not what my sources tell me. You and I both know you're trying to turn Goodman against EZ-15." The raw anger in Braxton's voice was increasing.

"That simply isn't so," Joanne protested.

As they continued to walk across the bridge, she failed to notice a black van with its lights off that had been tailing them at a distance since they left the embassy, or the two men walking toward them from the opposite end of the bridge.

As they reached the middle of the bridge, Braxton grabbed Joanne with both hands and spun her around so she was facing him. Staring at her like a madman, he uttered, "You bitch, I know you're lying about Goodman, and I know you're the one who tipped off a colleague of O'Brian that O'Brian was about to walk into a trap."

"You're crazy, Stan," she pleaded as she started to feel disoriented and nauseous.

At that moment, the two men who had been walking toward them raced up, and one of them grabbed Joanne and cupped his hand over her mouth, wrapping his other arm so tightly around her waist that she could barely breathe.

"She's guilty as hell on all counts," Braxton said, having carried out Petrovic's detailed instructions to bring the congressional staffer to the bridge for pickup. Then the lobbyist asked, "Are you going to do it here?"

"No, we'll take her with us. She might have some useful info about O'Brian. We know how to force it out of her before we dispose of her," the first man said, waving at a white sedan traveling from the same direction as the two men had come.

Joanne couldn't believe what was happening. She struggled desperately to scream, but only a muffled sound emerged from her mouth. Her mind was spinning, and she felt like she was losing consciousness.

"Well, I guess I'll be on my way," Braxton said.

"Not so fast," the man holding Joanne replied, nodding to his partner.

"What the hell!" Braxton screamed as the other man charged at him, wrapped his arms full circle around the lobbyist's legs just below his knees, and, in one continuous motion, lifted and flipped the wide-eyed, open-mouthed Braxton over the four-foot metal bridge railing and sent him on the way to certain death 150 feet below. The sound of Braxton's body slamming onto the two-lane Rock Creek Parkway was followed by the screeching brakes of a car that couldn't avoid skidding over the crushed and mutilated body.

As the two men glanced over the railing to admire their gruesome handiwork, Joanne struggled to maintain consciousness. Mustering all the strength she could, Joanne cocked her arm and delivered a short but powerful and sharp elbow blow to the lower ribs of the man who was holding her. Recoiling from the fearsome blow that cracked two of his ribs, he involuntarily loosened his grip on her. Joanne broke free and delivered a swift roundhouse kick that found its mark and dislocated the other assailant's left kneecap. With both men reeling in pain, she started to run back toward the east end of the bridge from which she and Braxton had come.

If I can make it to the end of the bridge, I can just throw myself down the steep embankment and disappear in the thick underbrush.

But the journey to the end of the bridge was proving arduous. The drugs Braxton had slipped into Joanne's last glass of champagne were now taking full effect. Finally, she neared the end of the bridge and looked back to see the two men she had incapacitated being helped into the sedan and then the sedan starting to move quickly toward her.

Joanne tried to pick up her pace, but she sensed she was slowing to a crawl as if she was in some horrible dream in which, no matter how hard she tried to run, she couldn't move.

Finally reaching the masonry statutes at the east end of the bridge, she stole one final glance back at the car chasing her. It was only about thirty feet away and closing on her rapidly. As she turned forward, Joanne crashed directly into a huge black figure and dropped to the ground. Barely conscious, she was vaguely aware that she was being picked up and put in the cargo area of a van.

"I don't want to die," Joanne tried to scream as she struggled to break free. She heard what sounded like two gunshots fired in rapid succession, and then she passed out.

CHAPTER 66

May 14
Mason County, Virginia

Sonja awoke before sunrise and felt fantastic, still enjoying the afterglow from the great breakthroughs achieved the day before and an evening of passionate, if not always quiet, lovemaking. As she opened her eyes, Sonja rolled over to give Chris a warm embrace. The bed was empty. She jerked her head around, looking for Chris, and saw him staring at her and sitting on a bench not three feet away. His expression was somber, but she couldn't tell if he was pensive, sad, or angry.

"You're up early," she said tentatively as she motioned to the bed, inviting him to come sit beside her.

"We've got to talk," Chris said sternly without moving from the bench. After a brief pause, he continued, "Sonja, you're not coming with Karl and me to California. It is simply too dangerous."

"What do you mean too dangerous?" Sonja protested. "We've solved the mystery, and all we need to do is get the California ARB on board. No one will possibly know we're in California. In a little over a week, this nightmare will be over."

"I wish I could agree with you, but what you believe to be the facts simply aren't true."

"Do you know something I don't?" Sonja said as every muscle in her body grew tense.

"Yes."

"What do you know? How did you get your information?" Sonja desperately pleaded.

"I had a dream."

"You what?" Sonja said, laughing. But when she looked at Chris, she could see he was serious. She wasn't sure if Chris was losing it or what he was thinking, but she got up from the bed, sat next to him, and squeezed his hand gently. "Tell me."

Chris hesitated briefly, but then began. "It's not just one dream; it's many dreams. How can I put it …? Well, let's just say I have the gift, or the curse, of sometimes seeing what will happen in the future. My grandmother years ago told me that she had had dreams that showed things that would happen in the future and that my mother did as well.

"My mother never talked about it with me and never knew my grandmother had told me. I don't know how much of the future she saw, but she sure had the uncanny ability to pick stocks to buy and knew when to sell and when to hold them. That all ended when she was killed in a horrific car accident in the early 1990s."

"But if your mother had the ability to see things in the future, why would she have even gotten into a car that she knew was going to be in an accident?" Sonja asked, struggling to make any sense of what Chris was saying.

"It's not that simple. Let me try to explain," Chris replied. "The dreams don't show everything that's going to happen. They're completely random and show only brief moments in time. I started having very strange dreams about twenty years ago, shortly after my mother died. Most of them I forgot almost instantly, and then I went years without having any. But during the last four months, they've started up again—this time much more frequently. Whenever I have a dream, it wakes me up. But many times I can't remember what the dream was about. Sometimes the dream comes back to me just at the right time."

"What do you mean just at the right time?" Sonja asked carefully, with growing fear that the man she deeply loved was dangerously close to slipping off the deep end.

Chris explained how when he was being chased by unknown assailants in Brussels and again the night that Jackie Goldberg was murdered, he found himself living an earlier dream that he hadn't until that moment remembered.

"In Brussels, when I was racing down a very narrow street, trying to outrun a car chasing me, suddenly it came to me that in a dream I had been running down the same street. In my dream, I finally spotted a recessed space in the side walls that could have provided me sanctuary from certain death, but I never reached it and was crushed to death. But that night in Brussels, I was able to run faster, and I jumped into the recess just as the car reached me and sped by."

Sonja's eyes were frozen on Chris in disbelief as he continued. "The night Goldberg was killed, while I was trying to escape from two men, a dream came back to me. In the dream, I ran down an alley that looked to be a dead end and jumped into a dumpster, where I was discovered by the pursuers and shot. The night Goldberg was murdered, I ran past the dumpster and found a way out of the alley."

Sonja, still staring at Chris, finally blurted out, "Chris, this is all insane. You can't expect me to believe any of this. You've got to get free of this crazy notion. You're delirious."

Chris seemed totally unaffected by Sonja's response. "Let me ask you a question or two." Without giving Sonja the opportunity to reply, he continued, "When you were around six years old, did your mother take you to a park near the Brandenburg Gate in East Berlin that had a large water fountain that was in disrepair?"

"Yes."

"Did your mother have auburn hair and did she have a gray cloth coat with a large animal fur collar?"

"Yes, but how could you know ..." Sonja's voice trailed off as the young woman struggled to comprehend all that she heard.

"Did you have a hooded red cape and a little dog—a gray terrier?"

Sonja said nothing, but the answer was clearly evident from the way she looked at him.

"I had that dream one night when we were back at the farmhouse, and in that dream, your mother motioned me to come to her. When I got close, she pointed at the young girl—you—and said, 'Protect my child.' And that's what I am going to do. You're not going to California. There's an Amtrak train that stops in Valley View in the northern part of Mason County. You can take the train all the way to Baltimore, and I'll arrange for Chet to pick you up. Karl and I will drop you off on our way to the airport tomorrow morning."

Sonja sat looking at Chris but said nothing, in part because she was still trying to digest everything he had just told her and in part because she had no intention of acquiescing to being left behind. How she would ensure that she was indeed on that plane the next day was something she would have to figure out later, but nothing would be gained by trying to dissuade Chris at this point.

Finally, she spoke. "You've also had a dream about California, and you know what's going to happen. Did we die in your dream?"

"No," Chris lied. "I think we've discussed all that we need to on this topic."

Without another word, Sonja and Chris got dressed and went downstairs to greet Thurgensen, who had already set the table for breakfast.

In silence, Chris, Sonja, and Thurgensen ate breakfast, cleaned up, and put the finishing touches on Sonja's document explaining the meteorological factors that created the environment for the EZ-15-induced spikes in asthma attacks and deaths, and Thurgensen's analysis of how the byproducts of post-combustion exhaust with EZ-15 created the chemical agents that caused the asthma attacks. Sonja then e-mailed copies of the documents to Tanya in Baltimore.

Next, the three collected and burned any loose papers and other material that would be of value to anyone who might show up at the cabin after they left. Sonja downloaded everything from Thurgensen's computer onto her laptop, and then she removed her hard drive. Next, she removed Thurgensen's hard drive, and Chris crushed it and all of the remaining cell phones, except three they would carry to California. Chris loaded the pieces of cell phones and the crushed hard drive in a large burlap bag, along with all of the firearms and ammunition, save one, a fully loaded pistol Chris would carry until they reached the airport. Finally, Chris carried the sack far into the woods, dug a deep hole, and buried it.

Chris, Sonja, and Thurgensen each packed a backpack with everything they would need for the journey. The bags were placed by the front door so they would be ready to carry down the trail and load in the SUV when they headed out early the next morning.

* * *

Before leaving the next day, Chris and Sonja needed to get Thurgensen ready for the trip to California. By the time the three reached the Mason County seat, it was nearly 4:00 p.m. First stop was a visit to Aunt Suzie's Hair Salon, which was two blocks from the courthouse. Sonja had remembered seeing it when they stopped to see Higgins earlier in the week.

"Good afternoon," Suzie Watts, a spry, sixty-five year old black woman greeted them with an enormous grin. "You must be the young couple from Montana who have been searching for Mr. Thurgensen. Looks like you found him all right. Let me guess. Mr. Thurgensen here is the one getting the haircut."

Thurgensen moved forward slowly and sat, with considerable anxiety, in the worn leather barber's chair, which was a relic from the 1950s. Suzie gently pulled the well used, white linen barber's cape over his shoulders. She then gently pulled his long hair out from under the cape, followed by his long, gray beard. Sensing his anxiety, she rubbed his shoulders, and he relaxed instantly.

"Just a trim," Thurgensen said as his eyes sparkled and a smile emerged on his hair-covered face.

"Oh, Mr. Thurgensen, you might need just a little more than that." Suzie chuckled.

"It's Dr. Thurgensen, and he's a renowned scientist. Suzie, you need to make him look like one," Sonja explained.

"Dr. Thurgensen. Isn't that grand. I'm getting a picture of what you need. You two take a seat over there. This is going to take awhile."

About an hour later, after shampooing, cutting, shaving, and blow drying his now wavy, silver gray hair and finely shaped, modest beard and mustache, Suzie pulled the cape off and had Thurgensen stand up so she could brush off the layers of loose, cut hair. Next, she spun Thurgensen around so he could see himself in the mirror. "There we are," the hair stylist declared triumphantly.

"Amazing," Sonja said as Thurgensen stuck out his chin, turning his head from side to side and admiring his new look.

"All you need now are some duds, and you'll be ready to wow them wherever you're headed," Suzie said.

"Speaking of clothes, any suggestions regarding a store where we can buy Dr. Thurgensen some new clothes?" Chris asked hopefully.

"If you're looking for new clothes, the closest place is Roanoke, but that's eighty miles away," Suzie said. Then seeing the disappointment on Chris and Sonja's faces, she added, "There's always the thrift shop just down the street on the left. My cousin, Sarah Beth, runs the place."

"Well, it sounds like our only option," Sonja replied.

"But before you go, someone else needs a touch-up as well. Those black hair roots of yours, young man, are starting to show. It'll only take a minute."

When they finally were ready to leave, Sonja said, "Just curious, Suzie. How did you know who we were when we first entered?"

"My son-in-law owns Bob's Bar-be-Que, and I heard all about you two and how you were searching for Mr., ah, Dr. Thurgensen. By the way, where's your next stop?"

"We're off to Montana," Chris replied.

"Oh sure you are," Suzie said sarcastically. "I know what you're up to. Hope you nail the bad guys."

"Does everybody in this county know everything?" Chris replied.

"Of course not, but Merilee told a few of us just in case someone comes around looking for you. We'll all give them the same misinformation."

"You folks are amazing. Thanks," Chris replied.

Upon arriving at the thrift store, Thurgensen was quickly outfitted with a full set of clothes and changed into one of the casual shirts, slacks, and loafers they purchased.

As they departed, Chris handed Sarah Beth four crisp hundred-dollar bills.

"This is too much," Sarah Beth protested.

"Please, we can't pay you enough for your help. I'm sure you can find some way to put the money to good use helping others in the community," Chris said as he pushed the money back into her hand and closed her fingers around it.

"Sarah Beth, we need to get a passport size photo for Dr. Thurgensen and get it laminated for his ID. Is there any place where we can get it done?" Sonja asked.

"Of course, the Department of Motor Vehicles office in the courthouse, but they're not open on Saturdays."

But before Chris and Sonja could react, the shopkeeper said, "You could always check with Merilee Higgins. Let's see. It's about six o'clock. She should still be at the farmers' market. It's just down the end of this street on the elementary school playground. That's where Merilee sells her cut flowers. They're beautiful this time of year."

The farmers' market consisted of a large tent with individual tables where vendors sold everything from crafts and small, handmade tools to flowers, homemade preserves, baked goods, and fresh meat. Chris spotted Merilee Higgins, dressed in a blue country dress with a white apron, at the far end of the tent. When they neared Higgins's table, Chris waved and yelled, "Beautiful flowers, Mayor."

Merilee put her hand over her opened mouth as if shocked to see the three of them. Then she motioned to them to come to her quickly.

"You've got to get out of here," she whispered in barely audible voice. "Chris, I called to warn you on that cell phone number you gave me, and when you didn't reply, I thought you three were long gone."

"Damn, I didn't have it turned on. What's wrong?" Chris asked.

"Two FBI agents were here earlier and were asking lots of questions about Dr. Thurgensen. They also said they were hunting down two murderers—a man and woman who were armed and dangerous. They didn't get anything out of me."

"Mayor, you lied to them. You can't put yourself in jeopardy," Chris whispered.

"I didn't lie. They just didn't ask the right questions. But they had already learned from someone down here with loose lips that Karl was known for his moonshine, and the FBI agents said they had a list of ex-felons who live in Mason County that they planned to visit today."

"Mason County doesn't exactly seem like a high crime area," Chris replied.

"Most of the guys on that list probably served time for making moonshine or growing marijuana. It's only a matter of time before someone tells them you and Sonja are here and where Dr. Thurgensen lives."

"We'll go back to the cabin, pick up our stuff, and scoot out of here. But first, we have a huge favor to ask." Chris whispered that they had a phony Montana driver's license with a fictitious name for Thurgensen, but they needed a photo and then to laminate the card.

"Let's go," she said.

Twenty minutes later, armed with a new driver's license for Thurgensen, they were standing outside the courthouse. They said their good-byes and headed back to the cabin.

CHAPTER 67

May 14
Mason County, Virginia—Evening

For FBI agents Cavanaugh and Adams, it had been a long and extraordinarily frustrating day. The day before, an FBI research specialist had informed Cavanaugh that Karl Thurgensen, a renowned automotive catalyst scientist, had dropped out of sight about ten years earlier. According to the information found at the farmhouse, Thurgensen apparently was now likely living in Mason County, Virginia. Cavanaugh had quickly made the connection that O'Brian or someone would try to enlist the chemist's assistance to discredit EZ-15. When Cavanaugh had called Petrovic late Friday night, Petrovic told Cavanaugh he should head to Mason County immediately.

After the long drive from DC, the FBI agents had interviewed numerous Mason County residents, who Cavanaugh assumed were either clueless country bumpkins or intentionally playing dumb in an effort to throw the agents off the trail. Now, they were down to their last possible lead—Lester Chase. The forty-three-year-old Chase was a former inmate at the Federal Corrections Complex in Petersburg, Virginia, imprisoned for illegally selling alcoholic beverages. They had tracked him down at his dilapidated shack at the end of a three-mile-long dusty and rutted dirt road.

At first, the inebriated Chase played dumb. Then Cavanaugh nodded to Adams, who circled around Chase and grabbed him from behind, locking the hapless farmer's arms tight against his body. Chase squirmed but couldn't break free.

Cavanaugh then pulled out his service revolver and shoved it up against Chase's throat. "You've got five seconds to start talking or I'll pull the damn trigger, and your brains, if you have any, will explode through the top of your head."

Chase struggled to speak, but the gun was pressed so hard against his Adam's apple that all he could do was choke out sounds as his eyes bulged in fear.

Having achieved the desired effect, Cavanaugh slowly pulled his weapon from Chase's throat and said, "Start talking."

Struggling to catch his breath, Chase blurted out everything he knew about Thurgensen, including where the "Gray Fox" lived. The now totally petrified ex-felon also divulged that two strangers, a man and woman, had been asking around the county about Thurgensen a few days before.

"If you're lying about anything you told us, we'll come back and shoot you dead," Cavanaugh barked as Adam pushed Chase to the ground, and the two FBI agents jumped back into their car.

"Within the hour, O'Brian, his female accomplice, and Thurgensen will be dead," Cavanaugh said, sounding almost gleeful.

"You mean captured or killed, right?" Adams said, seeking to clarify his boss's statement.

"I meant what I said. I want them dead, stone-cold dead."

*   *   *

By the time Chris, Sonja, and Thurgensen got back to the cabin and were ready to leave, it was nearly 9:00 p.m. and completely dark. What had been a beautiful day weather-wise had turned ugly, with heavy rain pounding down through an ever-increasing fog. The gentle stream that paralleled the dirt road down from Karl's cabin was rapidly becoming a torrent, overflowing across the road and making passage treacherous. Several times Chris thought the road was becoming impassible, but Thurgensen urged him on. Finally, they safely reached the end of the dirt road and started to turn left onto Cup Run Road.

"That's odd," Thurgensen said, looking down the mountain road.

"What?" Chris asked.

"Headlights of a vehicle that's coming toward us. No one, and I mean no one, ever comes up here at night."

"Cavanaugh," both Chris and Sonja cried out.

"Turn this thing around—we'll head up Cup Run to the Blue Ridge Parkway and take the back way into the Shenandoah Valley," Thurgensen commanded.

Without saying a word, Chris jammed on the brakes, and the SUV skidded to a stop. Quickly backing up the vehicle, Chris slammed the SUV into drive, and they took off in the opposite direction. As they climbed up the mountain road, the fog became denser. Looking behind them, Sonja saw the headlights of the vehicle rapidly closing in on them. "It's got to be Cavanaugh; that vehicle sped up as soon as we pulled out of the dirt road from Karl's cabin."

By the time they reached the parkway, a 469-mile, barely two-lane, paved road that meandered along the crest of the Blue Ridge Mountains from Virginia to northern Tennessee, the fog had reduced the visibility, even with the SUV's lights on, to about twenty feet.

Following Thurgensen's instructions, Chris turned right on the parkway and proceeded slowly—struggling to make his way along the wet, black road that had no painted lines or reflectors.

There's no way in hell I can outrun those bastards in this fog, Chris thought as his mind raced to come up with a plan of escape. Moments later, he saw it—a huge, towering, several hundred-year-old dead Chestnut tree with its gray branches overhanging the road and reaching out toward them like a ghostly apparition.

"Damn, I've seen all this before," Chris said as he tightly gripped the steering wheel. "Chris, you told me you've never been on the Blue Ridge Parkway before," Sonja said, somewhat mystified.

"Not in person," Chris muttered.

"In a dream? My god, are you reliving one of your dreams?" Sonja asked as she stared at him—her eyes wide open.

Chris simply replied, "Pull those seatbelts tight. You're in for the ride of your life."

And without speaking further, Chris pushed the accelerator down as they rapidly gained speed through the dense fog.

Looking back, Sonja could see that the vehicle pursuing them had reached the crest and had turned onto the parkway.

The SUV raced up the parkway at a perilous speed. But Chris, driving almost blind, followed his instincts and maneuvered the vehicle along the winding roadway.

"How does your dream end? Do we survive?" Sonja pleaded as she put her hand on his right leg and squeezed tightly.

"What was that? A dream?" a totally confused Thurgensen asked from the backseat.

Chris didn't answer. He just increased the SUV's speed. The vehicle swerved violently back and forth across the narrow road, often running up onto the narrow, grassy and gravel shoulders. Sonja and Thurgensen tossed back and forth, restrained only by the seatbelts that were cutting deeply into their skin.

"Chris, this madness isn't working. They're simply following our taillights. We'll never be able to outrun them," Sonja pleaded.

"I want them to increase their speed. Trust me," Chris said. Stealing a glance at Sonja, he whispered, "Do exactly what I say. In about a minute, you'll see a huge rock formation overhanging on your side of the parkway—you can't miss it, even in this fog. As we pass it, start counting slowly, one one-thousand, two one-thousand, and when we get to ten one-thousand, scream 'Now,' and hold on for dear life."

Moments later, Sonja spotted the rock formation, which looked like it was one new crack away from tumbling down on them. As instructed, she shouted, "There it is. One-one thousand, two-one thousand ..."

Chris immediately accelerated once more as the road temporarily straightened out.

When Sonja got to eight-one thousand, Chris, without reducing his speed, reached out and flipped the SUV's lights off. Thurgensen screamed like a kid on an amusement ride, but Sonja, who had closed her eyes in utter terror, just kept counting. When Sonja reached ten one-thousand, she screamed, "Now!"

Chris jerked the steering wheel hard to the right. The SUV spun out of control. Both Sonja and Thurgensen braced themselves for the anticipated crash into the rock formations that had paralleled the road for the last mile. To their surprise, but not Chris's, after spinning completely around twice, the vehicle came safely to a stop, half on the road and half on the shoulder and pointing in the direction from which they had come.

"Watch this," Chris said with an eerie sense of calm as he pointed out the front window.

The brakes of the pursuing vehicle squealed, but the car, which had reached a speed of over sixty miles per hour, skidded down the slippery, wet road toward the unseen ninety-degree turn in the roadway ahead. It skidded off the parkway onto the slick, grassy shoulder that had no guard rail and was launched off the top of a six-hundred-foot cliff into the foggy night air.

Seconds later, Chris, Sonja, and Karl heard the horrific explosion as the FBI agents' vehicle crashed onto the unseen rocks far below the parkway. Unbuckling her seatbelt, Sonja climbed into Chris's arms. Hugging him tightly, as she both laughed and cried, she said, "You did it. I'll never ever doubt anything you tell me. This ended just like your dream, right?"

"Not exactly."

"What do you mean?"

"Let me just say that I know how those two assholes must have felt when their car was launched into the air."

"What dream?" Thurgensen asked, still mystified but otherwise fine.

"Dr. Thurgensen, I'll explain all of this some other time, but right now we need to get the hell out of here and get ready to head to California."

"All three of us?" Sonja asked.

"For better or worse, all three of us," Chris said as he kissed Sonja gently. Then he turned the SUV back onto the parkway, and they headed off toward the Shenandoah Valley.

CHAPTER 68

May 15

As Joanne neared the end of her arduous journey back to consciousness, she still had no recollection of the events of the previous Friday evening or where she was. She slowly opened her eyes to complete darkness, thinking in horror, *I'm blind.*

But then she realized that someone had placed some kind of blindfold over her eyes that blocked out any light. She tried to lift her right arm and then her left to remove the device, but both arms were strapped down. It was then she realized she had tubes shoved up her nostrils and some type of apparatus jammed in her mouth, forcing her mouth open and pressing down on her tongue. She tried to shake her head, but it too was strapped down.

Struggling furiously to free herself, Joanne, her heart racing, suddenly heard something that sounded like an alarm begin to beep loudly. Next she heard what sounded like a door open and a voice calling out, "She's coming out of it. Hurry!"

Joanne heard someone approaching who said in a stern voice, "Don't struggle so, Miss McKay."

The person removed the tubes from Joanne's nose, the painful device in her mouth, and the plastic blinder from her eyes. Although the room was dimly lit, Joanne's pupils had trouble adjusting to any light, and for a moment everything was bright and blurry.

"You're not getting anything out of me. You might as well kill me now," Joanne cried out. She had tried to scream out her words for maximum effect, but they came out raspy and barely audible.

"Oh my," the voice of the person next to her said softly.

When Joanne finally was able to make out the person speaking, she was surprised to see a kindly-looking black woman with gray, curly hair smiling back at her.

"Dr. Michael, Tanya, come quick! Our friend has returned to the land of the living," the black woman called out.

Joanne then saw a fortyish-looking black man, wearing glasses and a white coat, with a stethoscope around his neck, and a young black woman with deep concern written over her face. Joanne instantly recognized the young woman and tried to speak. "You're the woman ... outside my building ... friend of O'Brian ..."

Tanya rushed to Joanne and grabbed her hand. "You're safe now. You're with friends."

Joanne squeezed Tanya's hand and struggled to speak, but exhausted by all the commotion, she drifted back into unconsciousness.

When Joanne finally awoke thirty minutes later, all of the restraints had been removed, with only an IV in her right arm to help keep her hydrated. She looked around the small room, which seemed more like a little girl's bedroom than a hospital room, and saw Tanya, three other black persons—the doctor, the nurse, a large black man, and one white woman, with her curly, black hair pulled tightly behind her head.

"You gave us quite a scare over the past thirty hours. Several times we thought we were going to lose you," the young doctor said, holding Joanne's hand. "What's the last thing you remember?"

Joanne thought for a moment and then spoke. "I was at a reception ... no, I was on a bridge ... with Stanley Braxton. I don't know. My mind is still spinning, and I have a crushing headache."

The other people in the room introduced themselves to Joanne and then provided her with details, starting with how Braxton must have drugged her at some point during the reception, and how she escaped from the two men who killed Braxton on the bridge. They told Joanne how she had stumbled into Chet, how he had put her in the van, and how, after shooting the tires of the car containing the men who were coming after Joanne, they escaped to the house of a friend of Chet's sister in Baltimore.

"But how did you happen to be at that spot at just that time?" Joanne asked, her voice beginning to gain strength.

Chet explained that they had been tailing Braxton, and when they saw Braxton and Joanne leaving the embassy, they decided to follow the couple. "We figured that since Braxton was in on the plan to catch Chris in Lafayette Park, and you alerted us, that he and his colleagues might have figured out that you were the one who tipped us off. So ..."

"We still don't know what that bastard poisoned you with. But one thing is sure, Miss McKay. If you weren't in such great physical shape, you probably wouldn't have survived," Dr. Michael explained. "As it was, you nearly did die. But you fought it like nothing I've ever seen in a patient. You thrashed around like a wild animal, refusing to completely give in to the drugs poisoning your body. That's why we had to strap you down—so you wouldn't physically injure yourself ... or any of us. It's also why we put that rubber device in your mouth—to keep you from swallowing or biting off your tongue."

"What day, what time is it?" Joanne asked.

"Sunday morning, about ten o'clock."

"I've got to go home. I've got to go to work tomorrow and tell my boss everything that's happened," Joanne cried out as she struggled unsuccessfully to pull herself up.

"Miss, you're not completely out of danger yet, so the first thing you have to do is rest and get your strength back. That's going to take two or three days," Dr. Michael lectured his uncooperative patient.

"And there's a lot you need to know about all of us and about this whole EZ-15 nightmare, but now isn't the time, Miss McKay," Chet added.

"Okay, okay, but please tell me one thing. Is Chris safe?"

"Chris left me a voice message on my cell this morning," Chet responded. "And while I'm happy to say he's still okay, I would be lying to you if I said he, or any of us, including you, is safe. Now, Tanya, Rebecca, and I are going to leave you to the care of Dr. Michael and Nurse Kathy, my lovely sister."

CHAPTER 69

The Sunday flight to Los Angeles was around five hours. During most of it, Chris, Sonja, and Thurgensen slept fitfully. They were exhausted from the last few days' adventures and a really terrible night's sleep. They had stayed the previous evening in a cheap motel near the Shenandoah Valley Regional Airport. There was only one room available, so the three of them crammed into a small, musty room with thin walls and noisy neighbors on either side of them. In the morning, they caught the first flight to Dulles International and connected with the flight to Los Angeles.

As they neared LA, Sonja tapped Chris on the shoulder, waking him, and handed him a copy of an airline magazine opened to a page with a beautiful cityscape picture.

When he stared at the page but said nothing, Sonja said impatiently, "Buenos Aires … Argentina … dancing the tango … in the streets. God, you don't remember, do you."

In frustration, she reached over and tried to grab the magazine back from Chris, but he held the magazine firmly in his fingers while he looked at the picture.

Finally, she ripped the magazine free from his clutches, crammed it into the pocket of the seat in front of her, crossed her arms in frustration, and mumbled, "Christopher O'Brian, you're totally hopeless."

When they finally landed in Los Angeles, Sonja helped Thurgensen out of his seat, and they moved down the aisle. Chris followed, but not before he grabbed a copy of the airline magazine from the seat pocket in front of him and stuffed it in his computer case.

As they entered the baggage claim area, Sonja, Chris, and Thurgensen were greeted by the most unlikely couple. The man, in his sixties, was dressed in wrinkled, white Bermuda shorts and a gaudy Hawaiian shirt. Smiling through his crooked, yellow teeth, he said, "Welcome, my friends," his bright red cheeks puffed out and his breath reeking of alcohol. Dyson Parker's dyed reddish-blond hair covered much of his pockmarked and overly tanned, round face. But his most noticeable feature was a prosthetic device below his left knee where his left lower leg had been before it was blown off in Saigon that fateful day decades before.

"Mr. Parker, I presume," Chris said as Dyson Parker consumed him in a hug.

"I'd like to introduce you to my lovely wife, Selma Hernandez," Parker replied as he turned and gently grabbed the arm of the Hispanic woman, easily twenty years his junior, standing beside him.

After brief introductions, they wasted no time exiting the huge, crowded, and chaotic airport terminal. Thirty minutes later, they pulled into a short driveway and stopped in front of the garage door of a small, quaint, and colorfully painted cottage. As they entered the house, Sonja could see a porch off the back of the house overlooking a small canal, lined on each bank with beautiful, blooming flowers.

"Your home is beautiful," Sonja gushed as Selma smiled broadly.

"Welcome to Venice Beach. My casa is your casa," Dyson replied.

Over the next hour Selma prepared dinner under the watchful eye of Thurgensen, who enjoyed practicing his rather rudimentary Spanish with the delightful Mrs. Parker. Chris, Sonja, and Dyson unloaded the car and went into a small den in the back of the cottage to check out the weaponry, computers, new IDs, and cell phones that Chet had instructed Dyson to obtain.

Sonja took out the hard drive from the computer they had destroyed in Virginia and reloaded all of the data onto two new computers so she and Thurgensen could each access the data they had stored. Chris and Dyson loaded the handguns, ammunition, and other armaments into a subfloor compartment in the back of a gray Subaru Forester that was parked in the Parkers' one-car garage.

Chris briefed Parker about what they anticipated would take place over the next week leading up to the ARB public hearing on EZ-15 in nine days.

With their work completed, Sonja, Chris, and Dyson joined Selma and Thurgensen, who were already fast friends, at the dinner table. The food was magnificent, and the conversation was intentionally kept light. Everyone around the table fully understood that the events of the next few days would determine their fate. After dinner, Chris and Sonja walked the two blocks necessary to reach the boardwalk on the beach and sat on a concrete bench, clasping each other's hands but saying little as they watched the sun set over the Pacific Ocean. When they returned, Selma, Dyson, and Karl were shooting shots of tequila and laughing loudly.

"He'll drink them both under the table," Chris joked as he and Sonja went up to the second-floor bedroom they would call home for the week.

CHAPTER 70

Early the next morning as Chris and Sonja came downstairs, they were surprised to see Karl and Selma already hard at work fixing breakfast. Neither one of them appeared the worse for wear. The same couldn't be said of Dyson Parker, who was snoring loudly on the couch in the same clothes he had worn the night before. Sleeping blissfully, Parker had the most ridiculous smile on his face.

After a quick breakfast, Chris, Sonja, and Karl were on their way to El Monte, California, and the meeting with Steve Morris and Amos Chandler. An hour later, they pulled into the parking lot of the ARB testing facility in an industrial park not far from downtown Los Angeles. Chris had been to the facility several times during his days at EPA, so he had no trouble finding his way.

Upon entering the two-story building, Chris, Sonja, and Thurgensen found themselves in a lobby with gray-painted walls lined with photos of the Los Angeles skyline with the Sierra Madre Mountains in the background. Each photo was obviously taken in the same spot and had the same date of the year posted on the bottom of the photo, but the pictures were taken in ten-year increments, starting in 1950. In the photos from the 1950s, 1960s, and 1970s, the skyline was barely visible, lost in the heavy smog that blanketed LA in those decades. In the photos taken in 1980 and 1990, the skyline was clearer, and the mountains in the background were starting to show through the greatly reduced levels of smog. In the 2000 photo, the visibility had improved further, and in the 2010 photo,

389

the skyline was pretty clear, and the view of the mountains had just a hint of haze.

"It's absolutely amazing. What incredible success the California and US automobile pollution-reduction programs have had on improving the air quality in Los Angeles and the rest of the United States. When the programs were first implemented, the naysayers predicted that the program would be a disastrous failure. But look what's happened. Cars sold today are 95 to 99 percent less polluting than cars in the 1950s and 1960s. The air pollution control technology and advances in engine designs necessary to meet the stringent standards created tens of thousands of jobs. It also opened up an enormous export market for US companies because the United States was the first country in the world to adopt the standards that required emission-reduction technology to be developed," Thurgensen said with more than a little pride in his voice.

The receptionist led them into a conference room. Sitting alone at the conference table, surrounded by five chairs and scribbling on a notepad, was a sandy-haired, forty-five-year-old man dressed in faded jeans. At first the man seemed unaware of their presence, but finally, without looking up, he spoke. "Amos will be with us shortly."

"And nice to see you again, Steve. Hope we're not interrupting anything important," Chris said, with a sarcastic tone in his voice.

Finally, Morris looked up. "Just finishing some editing of the test data we completed over the weekend." He then stood up and shook hands with Chris. It was patently obvious to Sonja and Thurgensen that there was no love lost between the two men.

Morris's demeanor immediately changed when he reached out his hand to Sonja. "Ms. Voinovich, nice to meet you. I've had the opportunity, over the past several years, to read some of your analyses for EPA. Very impressive."

Then Morris really turned on the charm as he shook Thurgensen's hand. "Dr. Thurgensen, it's wonderful to see you again after all these years."

Moments later, the door at the back of the room swung open, and a six-foot, muscular black man with short-cropped, gray hair entered the room, smiling broadly, and said, "Christopher O'Brian, nice to see you again. And you must be Sonja Voinovich. I'm very pleased to meet you," Amos Chandler said, shaking first Chris's hand and then

Sonja's. Then turning to Thurgensen, he frowned and exclaimed, "Karl Thurgensen, you scoundrel!"

Chris and Sonja were surprised at Chandler's apparent rudeness, but then the ARB chairman embraced Thurgensen, patting him on the back.

"Why haven't you been in touch with me? Shame on you. It's been such a long time. What have you been up to the last ten years, my good friend?"

Amos Chandler was an imposing figure, who was at once intimidating and, at the same time, disarmingly friendly and gracious. A firestorm of controversy had exploded when Chandler was first appointed over twenty years before by the then-Republican governor to serve as the chairman of the twelve-member California Air Resources Board governing body. Environmentalists and liberals railed against the appointment of Chandler as the state's top air-quality official. They likened Chandler, who had worked for the motor-vehicle industry throughout his career and had tenaciously represented the US auto manufacturers before the Air Resources Board for fifteen years, as the equivalent of "putting the fox in the chicken coop." The auto industry, conversely, was ecstatic over Chandler's appointment.

But the choice of Chandler turned out to be brilliant. First, he was extremely personable and always willing to listen to any point of view. Second, a lifetime of experience in the motor-vehicle industry had given him the wisdom to know when, in response to a particular regulatory initiative, the industry had legitimate concerns and when they did not. Armed with that knowledge, he helped guide the California air agency on its continuing path of leading the United States and the rest of the world in regulating and reducing pollution from cars, trucks, and construction equipment. Even Chris had to admit to himself that Chandler and his top staff member, Steve Morris, were a marvelous team. They often came up with tough but fair compromises that addressed legitimate industry concerns while achieving significant reductions in pollution levels.

As they settled in their chairs, Chris asked, "Where should we start?"

"From the beginning, the very beginning," Chandler replied as he put on his glasses and opened his notepad. "Steve gave me a quick overview, but I want to hear the full story."

Chris looked at Sonja and Thurgensen, who both nodded that he should take the lead. He began his saga with the death of Ronnie Chapman. He spoke of the deaths of Jackie Goldberg and the other victims, as well as the involvement of international hired killers, corrupt investors, possible rogue FBI and DHS agents, and even corrupt officials at the US EPA and in the White House. As Chris spoke, Chandler shook his head several times, trying to grasp the far-reaching magnitude and horrific impact of the EMCO EZ-15 conspiracy. Even Steve Morris, who at first sat back in his chair as if his mind was drifting off to other, more important matters, pulled his chair closer to the table. Placing his elbows on the table, Morris rested his head in his hands as he listened intently to everything Chris had to say.

When Chris finished, Chandler exclaimed, "How in the hell did you survive all of this?"

"Dumb luck, I guess."

"Luck had nothing to do with it," Sonja blurted out. "Chris has been brilliant at every turn. He's kept all of us alive and, more important, kept me, Karl, and the Crew focused on how to bring those bastards down." Then her face turned crimson, and she slumped in her chair, totally embarrassed by her outburst.

Chandler reached over and patted Sonja gently on her hand. "I agree. Mr. O'Brian is being way too modest, and I suspect you played a major role as well. But shall we continue? Steve, why don't you give our colleagues an update on the emission tests we ran over the weekend."

"As you recommended, we ran the standard emission tests on an engine using gasoline fuel with the EZ-15 additive, but we substituted the standard test filter media with the finer mesh X10B19.0.0001 filter. Chapman, Sanchez, and Mueller all were correct in their theory that ultrafine carbon-based particles were too small to be captured by the standard filter paper."

"Great," Chris said.

"Not so fast. While our tests did prove the presence of ultra-small carbon-based particles, from a health matter point of view, it's meaningless. In the real world, these small, solid carbon particles would fall to the ground within a matter of minutes after exiting the tailpipe. They would pose no health risk at all. So, unfortunately, we still don't have any proof of EZ-15's harmful effects," Morris said, the disappointment evident in his face.

"Your test results are exactly what we would have anticipated. But, Steve, let me ask you a couple of questions," Thurgensen said, sounding every bit like a professor about to pounce on his student. "I assume you used the standard US EPA Federal Test Procedures governing the ambient conditions for the emissions test in the test cell."

"Yes," Morris replied, unsure of where Thurgensen was headed.

"And I assume the ambient air in the test cell also was filtered to remove all ambient pollutants before the test?"

"Yes, the air was 99.99 percent clean. So ...?" Morris replied, struggling to understand where Thurgensen's line of questioning was leading.

"Finally, no doubt you ran tests on the carbon particles to determine if they had become activated during the engine combustion process."

"Of course, we ran the complete battery of tests. The particles were completely inert."

"How long after the emission test was completed did you test the carbon samples?" Thurgensen asked as he caught sight of Chris and Sonja nodding with approval, obviously enjoying the moment.

"Between two to three hours later, which is completely within the allowable timeframe called for in the EPA and ARB test protocols," Morris replied, growing increasingly defensive.

A poignant silence followed. Finally, Thurgensen, who had initially bowed his head as if he was lost in thought, looked up and said, "So, we'll need to run the test again. But this time we'll need to make some changes in the ambient air conditions in the test cell and in your protocol for testing the carbon particles."

"But ...," Morris stammered as Amos Chandler looked on, completely perplexed.

"Let me explain, Steve. Ms. Voinovich's analysis found that in the areas in Tokyo and Osaka, where vehicles fueled with the EZ-15 additive were in heavy use, such as in the vicinity of highways or central-city locations, the incidents of asthma attacks among sensitive populations spiked. But they only spiked when the temperature was above eighty degrees and the humidity was above 70 percent. These areas also had elevated levels of the typical ground-level pollutants, such as ozone, aldehydes, and other 'bad actors'."

"But couldn't those pollutants themselves cause the asthma attacks?" Amos asked.

"Not likely, because while the pollution levels were elevated, they were well below the levels deemed unhealthy by air-quality regulatory agencies throughout the world. However, if a carrier was present that could collect, in-mass, and transport these harmful pollutants deep into the lungs, then we would have a different situation," Thurgensen explained. "And that's exactly what we have with the byproducts of the combustion of fuel when EZ-15 is present."

Thurgensen, satisfied that he had Morris's and Chandler's rapt attention, continued, "My theory is that during the engine combustion process, the additive EZ-15 causes the carbon atoms in CO_2 molecules to explode, and the carbon atoms' electrons become electrically supercharged. Then, when those activated subatomic carbon electrons exit the vehicle's tailpipe, they attract, like a magnet, a host of toxic chemicals from the ambient air that become fixed to them. But, remember, this phenomenon only occurs if the ambient temperatures are above eighty degrees, the humidity is above 70 percent, and the ground-level ozone concentrations are 0.050 ppm or higher, which is below the current level of the 0.075 ppm ozone standard.

"These toxic-laced, subatomic particles are then breathed in by unsuspecting humans in the immediate vicinity of the vehicles' exhaust pipes, and because the particles are so incredibly small, they travel though the respiratory system's filter system and deep into the lungs, where they are released from the carbon electrons once it loses its active charge. I estimate that it takes about an hour for the carbon electrons to lose their activity once they leave the exhaust pipe.

"That's why you found the subatomic particles inert. The test was run well over an hour after they were collected. By then, the subatomic carbon-based particles had lost their charge. The critical point here is that if someone is suffering from asthma, their lungs are already highly sensitive and easily irritated by foreign, microscope toxins. Once these supercharged carbon-based particles, with their host of toxic chemicals attached, penetrate deep into the lungs, the effect on sensitive populations can be debilitating and often fatal, as appears to be the case in Tokyo and Osaka, where EZ-15 is being used."

"Karl, you've done it. Absolutely brilliant!" Chandler proclaimed.

"Ah, but unfortunately, at this point it's only a theory," Thurgensen responded cautiously.

"And a damn good theory at that," Morris, now fully engaged, chimed in enthusiastically. "It will take us the rest of the day to reconfigure the test equipment and the test cell, but we should be able to start running a new test first thing tomorrow morning."

"Great," Chandler exclaimed. "Chris and Ms. Voinovich, you're welcome to accompany Steve to the test cell. Karl, I'd love to have a chance to catch up on what you've been doing the past ten years."

Walking to the test facility, Steve turned around and extended his hand to Chris. "The three of you have done an amazing job."

"Steve, we still have a long way to go, but I'm really looking forward to being on the same side of an issue with you for once. It's a hell of a lot better than the alternative."

Ten hours later, everything was set to run the tests first thing the following morning, and Chris, Sonja, and Karl headed back to the Parkers' cottage in Venice Beach.

"For the first time since this nightmare began, I feel like things have finally turned in our favor," Sonja said hopefully.

"Maybe so," Chris replied.

CHAPTER 71

May 16
Washington, DC

Long before Chris, Sonja, and Thurgensen set off from Venice Beach to meet with Chandler and Morris, Petrovic was slouched in his leather chair in the living room of his modestly furnished, one-bedroom residence. He was lost in thought as his mind raced to plot his next steps in light of the unexpected and disturbing turn of events that occurred over the weekend.

The former CIA agent and now operative for the Department of Homeland Security rented his abode under an assumed name and had lived there for the past thirty years. His apartment actually was a three-hundred-year-old, renovated, white-brick carriage house that included an attached garage and was located just off an alley in Georgetown.

Petrovic had no mail delivered to his residence. He had any important mail sent directly to a PO box. For telephone calls, he only used his cell phone. He did have a small, hidden drop box on the alley side of the carriage house, where items that he didn't want sent through the mail could be left, such as the Chapman CD that Cavanaugh had dropped off the night the rogue FBI agent murdered Chapman's girlfriend.

Petrovic's apartment was his office. As a contracted operative for the DHS, he reported to, and took orders from, only one individual—Bingeman Foster. Foster, who had no official connections with DHS, was President Keller's choice to ensure that the vast organization, with its complex web of sub-agencies and private contractors, served the interests of the Keller administration.

In that capacity, Foster had assumed the lead role in ensuring that Crown Prince Syed and the royal family, who were critical in protecting US security interests in the Middle East, remained in power. When Keller learned that Syed had bet the royal family's fortunes on EMCO and EZ-15, Foster was the person charged to make sure there were no problems. Foster, in turn, immediately called Petrovic, who already was under contract to the DHS and was the person Foster most trusted to carry out the mission.

Everything seemed so promising the previous Saturday afternoon. Braxton had been disposed of, and while Joanne McKay had eluded capture, Petrovic was confident she would resurface soon, and he could have her killed. Also, Cavanaugh had reported that he and Adams had located Thurgensen's cabin in Mason County, Virginia, and that O'Brian and Voinovich were probably with the old scientist. The end was in sight, Petrovic had thought.

Sunday evening, in good spirits, Petrovic had taken his nightly stroll through the campus of Georgetown University, just two blocks away. Unfortunately, the joy of the evening's walk had been ruined when Petrovic returned and discovered that the FBI head, Calvin Wiseman, had left a disturbing message on Petrovic's cell phone that Cavanaugh and Adams had died sometime Saturday night when they apparently drove off, or were forced off, the Blue Ridge Parkway at high speed on a foggy, rainy night and were killed. The bodies hadn't been identified until late Sunday evening. Wiseman had called Petrovic as soon as he got the word from the Virginia State Police, and his message ended by asking Petrovic to call him first thing Monday morning.

Upon receiving the news, Petrovic had slumped into his leather chair. Initially, he was extremely upset, but not about the deaths of Cavanaugh and Adams. He had worked with Cavanaugh on and off over the years, and the FBI agent was fairly competent, but he hardly considered Cavanaugh a friend.

Petrovic didn't have or want any friends. He had been alone most of his life. His parents, who emigrated from Russia, died when he was very young. He subsequently moved from foster home to foster home because he was unruly and prone to violence. It wasn't until he joined the Marines and had his first taste of a "kill" in Vietnam that Petrovic came to peace with himself. There were very few people for whom he had any respect, his former Marine commander, Judge Worthington, being one of them. Petrovic and Worthington had weathered more than one storm together, including the time when Petrovic had needlessly killed innocent villagers in Vietnam, and Worthington covered up for him. They relied on and trusted each other completely.

What troubled Petrovic that night, alone in his barely lit apartment, was that, for one of the very few times in his life, he felt like he didn't have complete control of the situation. He had overseen and/or directly participated in dozens of high-risk missions, some authorized by the government, and some requested by others who were willing to pay the high price Petrovic demanded for his services. He had always been able to complete those missions successfully and had personally killed over twenty men and women without any hitches.

But now he was being outplayed and outsmarted by, of all people, a damn government attorney and a band of nobodies who seemed to have all but disappeared. Most aggravating was that Katrina Zimmer, who somehow escaped death when he blew up her parents' house decades before, was out there, somewhere, making life treacherous for him and others on the EMCO payroll.

Eventually, as the early-morning sunlight began to light the room, Petrovic regained his composure and slammed both of his hairy arms on the armrests of the chair.

"O'Brian and Zimmer have been incredibly lucky, but it will be only a matter of time before we track them down. First, I'll call Wiseman and learn what I can, and then I'll contact Foster. It's time to get the big guns involved in this!"

Pleased with the beginnings of a plan of action, Petrovic headed to his bathroom to take a shower and wash away the layers of self-doubt that had plagued him all night. First, though, he sat on the commode and reached into a large wicker basket filled with old and rather worn, foreign porno magazines, selecting one from Asia. The text he couldn't understand, but the photos, depicting young women tied up in an endless variety of contorted positions and being tortured, needed no written explanation.

Petrovic had never actually been with a woman, but he could find sexual pleasure in other ways. The graphic porno magazines were one way, but what really excited him was that moment just before a victim—man, woman, or child—realized, with eyes locked in fear, that he or she was about to die at the hands of Parnak Petrovic.

Refreshed from his shower and free of his doubts, Petrovic was totally energized. "Christopher O'Brian and Katrina Zimmer, wherever you are, I'm coming after you, and there's no escaping."

CHAPTER 72

May 17
El Monte, California

Chris, Sonja, and Thurgensen arrived at ARB on Tuesday morning, well before eight o'clock. Even though they would have no role in the actual emission testing, they all relished the opportunity to be spectators at the laboratory. If the test results confirmed Thurgensen's theory, California would have in its possession compelling evidence that the use of the EZ-15 did indeed pose a serious health risk, and the US EPA would have no choice but to withhold final approval for the product to be used in the United States.

By 9:30 a.m., the testing was under way and Chris took the opportunity to call Chet in Baltimore.

"Chris, how are you? Where are you?" Tanya asked, almost breathless at the other end.

"Tanya, I've got to make this quick. Sonja, Thurgensen, and I are safe in California. Tell Chet that Dyson and his wife have been incredibly helpful. We've made contact with Amos Chandler and Steve Morris. California is running the tests that we hope will prove Thurgensen's theory about the harmful effects of EZ-15. How are things in Baltimore?"

"We're doing pretty well under the circumstances," Tanya said. But then her tone turned more serious. "Chris, one thing—Joanne McKay is with us. They tried to kill her, but Chet, Leon, and Casey saved her."

"What?"

Tanya explained everything that had happened.

"Joanne's much better now, but she's becoming a growing pain in the butt, constantly insisting that we let her go back to DC and meet up with Goodman."

"Put her on the phone."

"Chris, I can't believe it's you."

"Thank god you're safe, Joanne."

"Chris, your friends have been wonderful, but I really need to get back to Senator Goodman."

"I know you want to go back, but you've got to stay put," Chris said. "We're making progress here in California. If you go back now, you'll be endangering not only yourself, but Senator Goodman and my friends in Baltimore as well. When the time is right, Goodman will need you, but for now, please do as we ask."

"I don't like it, but okay."

"Good. Can you put Tanya back on?"

"I'm here."

"Tanya, have you had a chance to integrate the information that Sonja and Karl developed on the connection between EZ-15 and the asthma attacks and his theory on why it occurs?"

"Yes, and with Rebecca's help and some information Joanne provided on Braxton, I've included some additional background information as well."

"Great. As soon as we have the test data, which should be by tomorrow, I think it would be a good time for the Crew to arrange another visit with Nancy Carter. Use the same MO as last time."

"Got it."

"I'll call tomorrow night. Say hi to Chet and everyone."

The rest of the day, Chris, Sonja, and Thurgensen paced, drank coffee, and slept in the rather uncomfortable chairs they were provided. When the actual emission testing was completed around four o'clock, Steve Morris said, with a huge grin, "We should have the data analyzed by 10:00 a.m. tomorrow. You three might as well head back to Venice Beach."

When the three arrived back at the cottage, Dyson Parker had a huge pitcher of margaritas and nachos waiting. Everyone but Chris enjoyed the tasty and rather potent concoction.

After dinner, Chris and Sonja decided to take a run on the beach. When they reached the beach, they ran north on the concrete

401

jogging and biking path to the Santa Monica Pier, with its famous Ferris wheel that seemed to make an appearance in just about every motion picture filmed in Los Angeles.

As they finished their run, the sun was beginning to set over the Pacific Ocean. It cast a pinkish hue over the beach as the shadows lengthened, until it dipped below the horizon, and the sky began to darken.

When they finally returned to the cottage around nine thirty, Dyson, Selma, and Karl had all gone to bed. Chris poured two tall glasses of ice water, and they went out on the back deck. Sitting in a love seat and looking out on the canal, Chris put his arm around Sonja. "I wish we could just spend the rest of our lives right here," he whispered as he kissed her on the cheek.

"Maybe we can … someday," Sonja replied hopefully.

*   *   *

While the ARB technicians were conducting the emission tests on EZ-15, Parnak Petrovic sat impatiently in the same conference room where he and Cavanaugh had met with Foster and the others a little over a week before.

Petrovic knew that, while Foster insisted that he be there no later than 10:00 a.m., the chief of staff, as usual, would be at least thirty minutes late. So, Petrovic decided to make good use of the time and gave Calvin Wiseman a call.

Petrovic had spoken with Wiseman late the previous day and urged him to send a major FBI task force to Mason County to try to uncover information on O'Brian, Voinovich, and Thurgensen and their possible whereabouts. He stressed to the FBI chief that all train stations, bus depots, and airports within a two-hundred-mile radius of where the three were last seen should be checked. While Wiseman had been somewhat insulted by Petrovic's detailed suggestions, in truth, he had planned a more modest investigation and had to admit to himself that Petrovic was correct to insist on a more aggressive search.

"Calvin, I'm sitting in the White House waiting to give the president's chief of staff an update on the progress in tracking down O'Brian and his accomplices. Anything to report?"

"Absolutely. We discovered that the three of them flew out of a small regional airport in the Shenandoah Valley up to Washington Dulles International Airport, and from there they flew to Los Angeles—"

"Los Angeles?" Petrovic interrupted, surprised by the destination O'Brian selected. *Maybe O'Brian and his colleagues have finally given up trying to derail EZ-15 and have decided get lost in LA*, he thought momentarily, but quickly dismissed the idea.

"But wait. There's more. We got pretty good pictures of the three of them taken by the airport security camera. O'Brian and Voinovich don't look anything like those composites you suggested the FBI put together."

Petrovic ignored Wiseman's dig about the composites he had requested and changed the subject. "Any progress in identifying and locating the other possible conspirators who escaped capture at that farmhouse last week after you guys blew the opportunity to nail them?"

Wiseman became agitated at Petrovic's not-too-subtle suggestion that the FBI had mishandled the mission but quickly regained his composure and said, "Some progress. We identified several close friends of that fellow, Otto Simpson, who was shot in Lafayette Park. Turns out that several of his friends we ID'd also served with Simpson in Vietnam in the 1970s, and two of them also worked with Simpson on the DC police force."

"And?" Petrovic asked impatiently.

"That's the weird part. All of these guys have disappeared. Most of them are loners with no families in the area, but one guy, Chester Jones, has a son. His son and the kid's girlfriend, who both worked at a temp agency, suddenly vanished the same time Jones disappeared. We're still following up on leads to find anyone who knows or is related to any of these guys."

"Send me copies of the airport photos and the names of the other possible conspirators you've identified. Keep me posted on any new developments. If I uncover anything, you'll be the first to know," Petrovic lied. He had no intention of giving the FBI anything he discovered.

Moments later, a grim-faced Bingeman Foster entered the room. "I don't like the way things are going. I'm getting nervous about this

EZ-15 thing. I had expected you to have matters under control by now. Where do we stand?"

Petrovic didn't appreciate being grilled by a clueless politician like Foster, but he nevertheless tried to spin things as positively as possible. He reported that Stanley Braxton, whose death had been reported as a likely suicide in the *Herald*'s Saturday addition, was almost certainly responsible for the leak that allowed O'Brian to elude the trap Foster had help set and was eliminated because he no longer could be trusted.

"Braxton was a loose cannon, and you should never have trusted him with the information about the trap set for O'Brian," Petrovic lectured, hoping to put Foster on the defensive.

Next, Petrovic recounted everything Wiseman had just told him, including that O'Brian, Voinovich, and Thurgensen had fled to Los Angeles. He expressed confidence that the three would soon be tracked down.

Bingeman's body language suggested that he was unmoved by Petrovic's efforts to sound encouraging. Then, almost as an afterthought, Foster said, "It's odd that you mentioned that O'Brian might be in Los Angeles. I got a call earlier today from Ted Bennett, who informed me that a member of his staff at the EPA Office of Air Quality was told by a California Air Resources Board staff member late yesterday that the California air agency was running emission tests on an engine using fuel with the additive EZ-15. The ARB staff member said the testing was routine, and Bennett didn't seem concerned."

Petrovic, who had slumped back in his chair, growing weary of his banter with Foster, suddenly sprang to his feet, his muscular arms held out, gesturing to Foster. "Damn! Don't you see? This guy Thurgensen, who's now with O'Brian in Los Angeles, was at one time one of the most revered chemists in the field of catalyst technology and motor-vehicle emission control. O'Brian and Voinovich tracked this guy down in the backcountry of Virginia, and now they're all in Los Angeles. All of a sudden, the California ARB is running emission tests on EZ-15. If they find something, the shit is going to hit the fan."

"My god, this is a disaster! What the hell can we do?" Foster almost screamed.

Petrovic seized the moment; this was what he lived for—to take charge. "The good news is we know where O'Brian, Thurgensen, and that EPA bitch are, what needs to be done, and how much time we have to stop them."

As Foster sat back in his chair, Petrovic strode around the conference table and stood uncomfortably close to him, staring down at the seated chief of staff.

"I can devise a plan to take care of everything, but I'm going to need to put together my own team of operatives. I'll take care of arranging for all of the logistics. But what I need to do can't be done under the auspices of the DHS. This is going to cost money—lots of money—and I'll need the cash in hand by noon tomorrow."

Foster stared blankly at Petrovic, paralyzed by indecision and self-doubt. "I don't know," he said meekly.

"Damn it, Foster! Get on your phone and call that damn adviser to the crown prince—Hassid Kabob, or Kabam, or whatever the hell he calls himself—and tell him I need two million dollars. He can send it to my offshore account," Petrovic shouted as tiny projectiles of spit sprayed from his open mouth onto Foster's bewildered face.

"Here's the damn number for my account," he barked as he scribbled and then shoved a small piece of paper toward Foster.

"But what if ... Kabar says no?"

"Then tell that camel jockey that the crown prince and his family are going to lose hundreds of millions of dollars."

"Okay, okay, I'll do what I can."

"You better do more than just try. If we don't stop that testing, and the California air agency finds something that will force EPA to withhold final approval of EZ-15, you, the president, and a lot of folks in Washington are going to be in deep shit."

Without waiting for Foster's reply, Petrovic turned, and as he walked to the exit, he muttered, "Don't get up. I know the way out."

Then, as he was about to exit through the conference room door, Petrovic turned back one more time, relishing the moment, and added, "I expect to hear from you by tomorrow morning at the latest. Don't screw this one up, Foster."

*   *   *

Foster sat motionless in his chair, his face a sickly, pale white. *Ruined?* Foster pondered. He cared little if Syed and his family lost hundreds of millions, even though the crown prince was an important ally to the United States. Nor did Foster really give a damn what happened to President Keller.

Keller had gotten his party's presidential nomination at the last moment when the party's overwhelming favorite, Senator Morris Beckman, removed himself from consideration on the second day of his party's convention. It turned out Beckman had committed some "indiscretions" with a very young staff intern twenty years earlier. When the scandal broke during the convention and created a media frenzy, Beckman had no choice but to step aside. The party picked Keller principally because the various factions of the party couldn't reach a consensus on the other potential candidates.

No, Foster was worried about himself. Looking forward to a lucrative career in the private sector that surely would follow his departure from the Keller administration, all Foster had to do was make sure he exited public service with a squeaky-clean record. The fallout from any problems with the EZ-15 approval and possible reports of conspiracies could ruin him.

Finally, after nearly ten minutes, Foster rose and walked slowly back to his office. He wasn't happy, but he knew what he had to do.

*   *   *

Daniel and Katie Witt stood alone in their kitchen, their arms around each other as they looked into each other's eyes. It was late, and their two children had long since gone to bed.

"Just do it," Katie said, hoping to sound positive.

"All of it?" Dan asked rhetorically.

"Dan, we've spent the last ten days and two hours tonight talking about this. We now both agree. If things don't work out, we still have each other and the kids."

Witt kissed his wife deeply on her lips, as if to seal the deal, and went down the stairs to his office. Everything was ready.

Eleven days before, Witt, following O'Brian's instructions, had purchased Puts on EMCO stock in each of the ten offshore accounts Witt had previously opened at O'Brian's request. If EMCO stock value fell below the trigger price by May 25, each of the accounts would be worth millions of dollars. So far, O'Brian's gamble that the EMCO stock would fall in value didn't seem to be working. Its current trading value had hit a high of seventy dollars a share, well above the trigger number.

Shaking his bowed head as if he still wasn't sure, Witt accessed an eleventh offshore account that contained the entirety of Katie and Dan's $80,000 savings. Witt keyed in the transaction and pushed the "Enter" button.

"What have we done?" he gasped as his hands shook violently.

CHAPTER 73

May 18
Georgetown, Washington, DC

Although Petrovic hadn't heard back from Foster, he was confident that Foster would be calling soon. Sitting at his desk, Petrovic turned on his laptop computer and keyed in the password to a secure page. He then accessed a folder that listed, with extensive biographical information, the names of forty-six operatives he had used over the past two decades on special missions. Some were experts in explosives, others skilled marksmen or masters of unspeakable techniques to extract information from uncooperative persons of interest. All were ruthless assassins who sadistically enjoyed their trade.

Some of the missions these men carried out were for government intelligence agencies that needed deniability if something went wrong. But in other instances, Petrovic had used his operatives to carry out contracts for private clients, including one for Crown Prince Syed involving an extremely messy incident.

During one of his visits to the United States, the crown prince had been overly aggressive with a very young prostitute, beating and abusing her ruthlessly. When efforts to pay her off failed, Petrovic dispatched one of his operatives to make sure the foolish girl disappeared.

"That stupid whore should have taken the money. When my guy finished with that kid, her sliced and diced body was never found."

Petrovic carefully scrutinized the list of operatives and their special skills in an effort to assemble the best team possible for the coming mission in California. He immediately eliminated from consideration the three operatives he recruited to kill Jackie Goldberg and the operatives he had contracted to kill Braxton and McKay. He always tried to avoid using the same operative more than once a year. And then, upon further thought, he decided to remove all the men used in the Braxton mission from his database—as well as the man who had recommended them. As he hit the "Delete" button, he thought, *Those incompetent fools completely blew the mission and let McKay get away.*

After an hour of poring over the list of remaining choices, Petrovic finally settled on ten men who, together, had the right mix of talents. They also could be summoned quickly to meet him in Los Angeles the following day. Without waiting for Foster's okay to fund the mission, Petrovic e-mailed all ten operatives. Within twenty minutes, all ten had responded affirmatively.

At slightly past 10:00 a.m., Petrovic's cell phone rang, and the voice at the other end said, "The money will be wired to your account, and you should be able to access it by two o'clock today. Kabar wasn't happy, but he understood the gravity of the situation."

"I don't give a damn how Syed's flunky feels. I'll contact you if I need anything more, and don't try to contact me. Call Wiseman and tell him to focus all FBI activities in a hundred-mile radius of Washington to track down the colleagues of that guy who got killed in Lafayette Park. If he asks about going after O'Brian and Voinovich, tell him I've got it covered, and I'll keep him posted," Petrovic barked.

"Bingie, you're going to owe me big time for this," Petrovic said, and then hung up. As a smile exploded on his face, Petrovic thought, *The hunt is on!*

*   *   *

Over the next several hours, Petrovic made a reservation for a 7:00 p.m. flight to LA, booked six rooms in the Crown Plaza Hotel near the Los Angeles Airport, and packed. He then sent a second e-mail to his ten recruits, detailing what supplies and armaments he needed them to obtain and where and when they all should meet.

On his way to the airport, Petrovic asked the cabdriver to deviate from the normal route to the airport so he could make one quick stop. As the cab turned into the entrance of Thomas Worthington's residence, Petrovic marveled at the size and lavishness of the estate.

An estate that he had helped Worthington keep by assisting him in accumulating the funds necessary to maintain it.

Upon entering the mansion, Rosanna Lopez led Petrovic to the judge's study. She was courteous but seemed agitated. Then Petrovic noticed her flushed checks and slightly mussed-up hair. He realized immediately that she must have just finished servicing, once again, the judge's needs.

Worthington, dressed casually in a yellow cashmere sweater and baggy, tan dress slacks, clasped Petrovic's hands in his trembling hands, greeting his old friend warmly. Petrovic noticed a small hole in the sweater and the rather crumpled look of the judge's slacks. Worthington appeared older, feebler, and more vulnerable than he had at the last Heritage Study Group meeting.

"Judge, how are you feeling?"

"Fine, just fine. But I wouldn't mind a little good news on the EMCO EZ-15 front. If EMCO doesn't hit eighty dollars a share by the end of the year, I won't be able to cover my debts."

Petrovic knew that Worthington had leveraged his financial future on the success of EMCO's stock value continuing to go up, and he tried to sound optimistic. "Judge, the stock hit seventy dollars yesterday, and EPA is on target to give final approval for EZ-15 next week. Once that happens, the stock will hit $100 by the end of the year. I'm doing everything I can to ensure that the EPA approval takes place. I've never failed you before. I absolutely won't fail this time."

"Thank you, my dear friend," Worthington said as his disposition improved noticeably. He patted Petrovic on the back and walked him to the front door.

Eight hours later, Petrovic's flight landed in Los Angeles. Entering the terminal with his computer case and small black bag, Petrovic had the appearance of any of the thousands of middle-aged, well-dressed businessmen who passed through the airport every day with high expectations of making a financial killing in Los Angeles. Petrovic had a different kind of killing in mind as he visualized, with utter delight, the exact moment he would kill O'Brian and Katrina Zimmer.

*   *   *

As Petrovic winged his way to Los Angeles, the ARB emission testing staff, Chris, Sonja, and Thurgensen were celebrating the results of the emission testing that seemed to confirm Thurgensen's theory about the adverse effects of EZ-15.

But the mood became less jubilant when Steve Morris cautioned, "Let's not get ahead of ourselves here. The test results are promising, but our agency's protocols require two tests, and the results must be within a small range to be statistically significant. We can't use today's test data alone at next week's Air Resources Board public hearing unless we have a second set of data to confirm the results of this test."

Looking at a room full of frowns, he added, "Hey, it's no big deal. We can prep the testing lab this evening and start the second set of testing tomorrow. We'll have test data results by first thing Friday morning. That will give us plenty time to get ready for the hearing next Tuesday."

A sea of happy faces returned, and Morris motioned to his staff. "Let's head down to the testing lab and get started." Then looking at Chris, Sonja, and Thurgensen, he added, "We can take it from here. You guys should head out. We'll see you bright and early tomorrow morning."

On the way back to the Parkers' cottage, Chris suggested they pick up a bottle of Don Julio Real tequila to celebrate the successful completion of the first emission test. Entering the cottage, Chris held up the bottle of tequila and said, "Major success today. The ARB testing proved Karl's theory, so we thought we'd celebrate the beginning of the end for EMCO and EZ-15."

But when they saw the stern expression on Selma Parker's face and Dyson's inebriated state, Chris and Sonja both realized that what they thought would be a nice way to thank the Parkers for their hospitality was ill timed. Having hit the booze earlier than most days, Dyson's eyes were dilated and bloodshot, and his speech was slurred.

But it was too late. "I'll get the glasses. Time to celebrate," Dyson said, grabbing the bottle.

Sonja, Thurgensen, and Selma took only a modest amount of tequila from the bottle, and Chris grabbed a glass of water. Dyson, however, filled a large goblet and took a healthy gulp.

At first the conversation around the table was pleasant, but as Dyson poured one after another glass of tequila for himself, he became increasingly agitated, a side of his personality his three guests had never seen before.

"You know, going after the EMCO conspirators is only scratching the surface. Hell, the president, Congress, the State of California, and the United Nations are all in it. It's way bigger than you could possibly imagine." Dyson spoke with surprising clarity for someone who was so hopelessly drunk.

"Are you talking about a conspiracy like the Trilateral Commission?" Sonja asked innocently. Selma shook her head and motioned to Sonja to stop speaking.

Dyson stared vacantly for a moment and then signaled for everyone to lean forward, as if he didn't want anyone else to hear. "Aliens. I'm talking about aliens from outer space. They're everywhere, and they control everything."

"What?" Chris responded without thinking.

As Selma Parker buried her shaking head in her hands, Dyson explained that he had been abducted by an alien spaceship in the 1980s. "They tried to take over my mind, but it didn't work, and I escaped. I know what they're up to, and they won't stop until they find me. But I'm ready for them."

Motioning to Thurgensen and Chris as he stumbled to his feet, Dyson commanded, "Follow me. I've got something to show you."

Reluctantly, Chris and Thurgensen followed Parker out of the room. Meanwhile, Selma removed her hands from her face. Tears were flowing from her eyes. With a soulful look, she spoke softly. "He's a good man, but he's a tortured soul. These outbursts don't happen very often, and he's never been anything but kind and loving to me."

Sonja reached across the table, grabbing both of Selma's shaking hands, and sat quietly as Selma continued. "When Dyson returned from Vietnam, he was physically and emotionally broken, and I don't just mean the leg he lost. After being discharged from Walter Reed Hospital, he struggled to adjust. Chet Jones, bless him, even came to California several times to try to help. But in the ensuing years, Dyson got into hallucinatory and other hard drugs and pretty much lived on the streets for over fifteen years. Finally, he was picked up for vagrancy, and mercifully, they sent him to a VA hospital."

Selma paused to brush away her tears and then continued. "That's where I met him. I was a nurse working in rehabilitation. Even though there was a significant difference in our ages, we hit it off. I had some bad stuff happen to me when I was young, and maybe that's why I could understand the emotional pain he was feeling. Within six months, Dyson was better—way better—and we've lived and loved each other for all these years. I know he still drinks too much, but really, he seldom goes off on the alien tangent anymore."

Dyson unlocked a huge padlock, opened a steel door at the back of the cottage, and entered a dark, ten-by-ten-foot room with no windows. When Parker turned up the lights, Chris and Thurgensen could see on each of the four walls an impressive array of firearms, grenades, and explosives.

"Wow!" Chris marveled at the sight of the arsenal, while Thurgensen stood silently in wonderment at what he saw.

"If the aliens come for us, we're not going down without a fight," Dyson boasted. Before Chris could speak, Dyson continued, "There's something else I want to show you—"

But Thurgensen interrupted him and said politely, "We should be getting back to the women. Perhaps you can show us another time?"

To Chris's relief, Dyson didn't argue, and they returned to the dining room table. Selma and Sonja brought out dinner, and the bottle of tequila had been removed. The two women also skillfully redirected the conversation, and there were no further references to aliens. About the time dinner was completed, Dyson folded his arms on the table, put his head down, and fell asleep.

CHAPTER 74

May 19
Washington, DC

Judge Worthington, looking much more energetic and imposing than the previous afternoon at his mansion, called the Heritage Study Group meeting to order. It wasn't just the freshly pressed, light gray suit the Judge was wearing. Petrovic's words of encouragement the previous day had their effect, and Worthington's disposition had improved greatly.

The meeting was sparsely attended. Foster was off putting out brushfires created when President Keller deviated from his prepared speech before the US Chamber of Commerce's annual dinner the night before and suggested that he might propose to Congress cutting some "tax loopholes" on US corporations' offshore manufacturing activities. Needless to say, the hosts were furious at getting blindsided by the sometimes flaky president.

Petrovic was in LA, and Kowalski was still in Detroit. With Moss's death and then Braxton's reported suicide, the group was reduced to Worthington and only six others. After saying a few words in remembrance of Braxton, Worthington opened the meeting up for discussion items.

Reverend McCormick jumped up and banged his fist on the table. "With Braxton gone, we've lost our most knowledgeable insider on EMCO. I've invested millions of my church's capital reserve in that damn EMCO stock, and I'm getting nervous. The stock value has skyrocketed. I want to know if we should sell now!" McCormick's expression of alarm drew similar comments from other members.

While Worthington had similar concerns, he had been bolstered by Petrovic's assurances the previous day that everything would work out. "Actually, while I cannot disclose the source, we're still privy to several inside sources of information, and one of my sources told me just yesterday that EZ-15 was absolutely on track for final EPA approval next week. I'm holding my stock."

Then Cherkoff, who rarely spoke, but who had made hundreds of millions in the stock market over the years and whose opinion was always respected, said, "I, for one, won't stand pat with my investment in EMCO ..."

In response to the billionaire's stern and direct statement, a chorus of moans emanated around the conference table, and Worthington felt his knees buckling beneath him.

"Please, if I may continue, I'm not holding my EMCO stock ... I'm going to double my holdings. Marshall Peterson, who I believe all of you know, and who is probably the most respected stock analyst in this country, is going to predict that EMCO stock will eventually hit $120 a share. He told me himself, in confidence, of course. But if you're going to buy, buy today. Once Peterson makes the announcement tonight during his evening *Market Watch* cable TV show, the stock will jump twenty points at tomorrow's market opening."

Once the chatter died down, Worthington seized control of the meeting. "While Bingeman is unable to be with us today, I would like to note that, as he predicted, President Keller on Tuesday announced that the high-speed rail system project would be delayed indefinitely. Those of you who took his advice to sell those two railway construction firms' stock short made a very tidy killing in the market this week."

Those HSG members who heeded Foster's advice rolled back in their chairs with big, silly grins plastered across their faces. Those who had decided to take a pass on the always-risky prospect of selling stocks short shook their heads in abject remorse.

Next, Wasserman reported on some inside information he had been given by his contacts in the environmental community about a soon-to-be-launched lawsuit against a pipeline company operating in the western United States.

"The Environmental Law Cooperative has uncovered evidence of unethical practices by several state officials in approving the permits for construction of the Purple Mountain Pipeline. Purple Mountain

Pipeline Corporation's stock has been rising steadily over the past year, and many of us have enjoyed the ride. But if you still own the stock, dump it now. ELC will seek, and no doubt receive, an injunction blocking further construction of the pipeline. The project is going to be delayed for years as a result, and the value of the company's stock is going to crash."

"Well done, Larry," Worthington, said.

When no one had any other investment ideas or information to bring up, Worthington quickly adjourned the meeting. He and the other members were all sitting impatiently, anxious to leave, call their brokers, and buy more EMCO stock.

* * *

As Tanya exited the Farragut North Metro stop, she lost herself in the midmorning rush of passengers riding up the escalator to the K Street, NW, exit. Dressed in a smart-looking skirt and matching jacket with low-heel, open toed shoes and an over-the-shoulder, leather carrying satchel, she looked every bit the young, aggressive female professional, with an air of confidence across her face.

But Tanya's outward appearance masked the growing anxiety she felt. *God, I hope I haven't made the wrong decision by going to see Carter.*

Following Chris's directions, Tanya had contacted Carter to arrange another pickup on Friday like the Crew had done previously with the CNP analyst. But then, Carter had called Tanya back very early this Thursday morning and said that if they wanted to meet with her, it would have to be that day before noon, and not on Friday. Carter also insisted that they meet in her office. Chet and everyone else were out on various errands, and Tanya had to make a decision on the spot. She agreed to meet.

When Tanya entered the CNP office building, she failed to notice the video monitor overhead. Taking the elevator to the eighth floor, she was greeted by a surly receptionist who led her down a long corridor. Entering Carter's office, Tanya was surprised at how small the space was for someone of Carter's elevated status as a well-known TV personality.

Almost as if she read Tanya's mind, Carter looked up and said, "Sorry for the cramped meeting space. Budget cuts, you know."

In truth, Carter had been moved three times in the past year, each time into a progressively smaller office and increasingly more remote location. A rather visible sign that Carter was on her way down and probably soon out as a CNP news analyst.

"I'm not comfortable meeting you here," Tanya said as she shifted back and forth in the seat to which Carter had directed her.

"It couldn't be helped. I'm pulling double duty here, and I simply couldn't get away to meet with you as originally planned," Carter replied, sounding more annoyed than apologetic. Then she added gruffly, "What have you got for me?"

Tanya thought about leaving immediately, but instead she reached into her satchel and, with her shaking fingers, slowly pulled out a CD.

Carter grabbed the CD and, without speaking, slid it into her computer. The CD contained everything Tanya had documented about the ongoing EZ-15 conspiracy, including the most recent, grizzly murder of Stanley Braxton and the attempted murder of Joanne McKay, as well as Thurgensen's theory regarding how and why EZ-15 caused significant increases in asthma attacks and deaths in Japan. For the next fifteen minutes, Carter didn't look up from her computer screen. Finally, lifting her head, Carter said, "This continues to be the most outrageous story I've ever heard. But if there's an ounce of truth in what you've reported here, we're dealing with a conspiracy of biblical proportions. However, as I said before, I can't run with the story without some additional corroboration from a credible source. If you can get me an independent corroboration on any of this, I'll consider running a story; if not ..."

Tanya slumped in her seat, struggling to fashion some kind of response. Pulling herself together, she sat up and, glaring at Carter, declared, "We'll get you that information, and it will be in your possession before the US EPA announces its final decision on EZ-15."

"I'll believe that when I see it," Carter said coldly. But then the CNP analyst looked at Tanya with a softer expression and added, "My door is always open to you."

Tanya left the CNP building lost in her thoughts. *Did I fail? Is there any chance Carter will actually run the story if we can corroborate any part of it, or was she only holding out hope to keep stringing me along?*

417

In her haste to return to Baltimore, Tanya failed to notice that she was being followed by a rather ordinary, middle-aged man dressed in a brown suit and wearing well-worn running shoes.

*   *   *

Petrovic, who had spent the morning in his hotel room refining the final details of the upcoming search-and-destroy mission, walked into the airport hotel's executive conference room precisely at 1:00 p.m. He warmly greeted the ten men already seated around the table.

To an outsider, the group of men—six Caucasians, two blacks, one Hispanic, and one Asian—aged thirty-five to fifty and casually dressed in golf shirts and slacks, looked exactly like the group of sales executives they were pretending to be. The only differences were they were more physically fit than the average group of sales executives, and they were all experienced and ruthless assassins.

"Let's get started," Petrovic said, and the pockets of conversation around the table ended abruptly.

As he walked around the table handing out packets of information, Petrovic spoke like a general instructing his troops. "These are the targets. The photos of the first three were taken four days ago by an airport security camera, and their appearances may have been altered subsequently. The rest of these people are government officials and should look pretty much like they appear in those newspaper photos in your packet. You all know the drill. Memorize these faces and the information about each printed on the back of the pictures. Write nothing down, including what I'm about to tell you. When we finish here today, I'll collect the packets, and we won't meet as an entire group again."

Over the next ninety minutes, Petrovic went over every detail of the mission. Teams of men were formed, assignments given, and in the unlikely case of an emergency, coded contact information was distributed that could be used to reach Petrovic.

Finally, Petrovic brought the meeting to a close. "Over the next few days, those team leaders who aren't out on reconnaissance will meet here precisely at 5:00 a.m. to go over any changes in plans."

Then Petrovic's tone turned more somber. "A few reminders before we disperse. Don't underestimate O'Brian or Voinovich. They have consistently outwitted and eluded the FBI. Next, my standard mission rules apply: if you screw up, I'll have you hunted down; if you're killed in action, your share will be given to the person you have previously designated; and finally, don't allow yourselves to be taken alive." Petrovic then passed out small plastic bags containing two cyanide tablets, which the men grabbed without hesitation.

"Any questions?" Petrovic asked. There were none, but the expressions on the faces of the men suggested that he had indeed left something out.

He knew what they wanted to hear, but he delayed for a moment to add to the suspense. "Oh, I almost forget. At the successful completion of the mission, you each will receive $100,000 deposited directly into your offshore accounts."

The usually quiet and stern-looking group of assassins couldn't hide their satisfaction as smiles broke out around the table.

After allowing his troops to enjoy the moment, Petrovic said firmly, "Okay, let's get this operation under way." In less than two minutes, the men were gone, and Petrovic stood alone with a look of complete satisfaction on his face.

* * *

First one, and then a series of ear-piercing and brightly flashing alarms went off throughout the ARB emission-testing facility. In response, the ARB staff sprang into action.

"This can't be good," Chris said to Sonja and Thurgensen.

Moments later, Morris approached, and his expression told them what they had feared had indeed happened.

"We had to abort the test. A damn gasket on one of the oxygen sensors failed—a lousy ten-dollar gasket—and now the lab is completely contaminated. We'll have to start all over. Five hours of testing down the toilet."

"How long will it take to repair the break, prep the test cell, and start testing again?" Thurgensen asked.

Morris slapped his hands on his head in frustration. Finally he spoke, "It's 3:00 p.m. We'll need a good two hours to exhaust the test cell and start working on repairs. Then we've got to decontaminate the entire test cell and recalibrate all the test equipment. If we work

419

all night, which I'm prepared to do, with luck, we can start new testing tomorrow afternoon."

Thurgensen asked, "Is there anything I can do to help?"

"Thanks, but no. We can handle this. We won't need you back until tomorrow afternoon around two o'clock. We should have the testing about ready to restart by then," Morris replied, sounding somewhat more positive than in his earlier outburst.

CHAPTER 75

Sitting on the back porch of the duplex in Baltimore, Tanya wiped the tears that freely flowed from her eyes as she finished describing her meeting with Nancy Carter. "I'm so sorry for what I did yesterday. It just seemed like the right thing to do when she called me."

Chet, whose expression was often difficult to read, moved slowly toward the young woman, who cowered as he approached. But as he reached Tanya, he simply put his arm around her back. "It's okay. You did what you thought was right. Sounds like you got Carter's attention and probably increased our chances of her running with the story."

Tanya hugged him, and the tenseness in her body subsided. A small smile returned to her face as she reached up on her toes, gave him a kiss on the cheek, and entered the kitchen to join Leon and the others.

What she's done has put us all at risk. There's only a remote chance that someone followed her, but we have no choice but to begin preparations for all of us to move once again, Chet thought, knowing that nothing could be gained by berating her after the fact.

Chet decided he would bring everyone together in the evening and plan the exodus for late the next night. "If, indeed, the house is under surveillance, we'll need to depart after dark, and we'll need to create some type of diversion, which is going to take a little time to plan and put in place. With luck, we could be out of the house by midnight tomorrow. I'll contact Bigalow and see if we can spend

421

the next few days at his house in Anacostia," Chet said quietly to himself.

*   *   *

As soon as Chris, Sonja, and Thurgensen entered the ARB testing building around two o'clock Friday afternoon, as planned, they could sense that something was very wrong. The doors of the test lab, which should have been closed, were wide open, and the test cell was filled with ARB staff checking various components of the testing equipment.

Their worst fears were confirmed when a sweaty, disheveled, and clearly agitated Steve Morris motioned them to come into the test cell. "Another damn equipment failure. This time the exhaust-emission collection container sprang a leak. We're done for the day."

"Can you start a retest tomorrow?" Sonja pleaded.

"No. Tomorrow's Saturday, and the only personnel allowed in this building on a Saturday are the cleaning crew and Freddie, our weekend security guard," Morris answered, with a frown. But then he added somewhat hopefully, "I'll put together a skeleton crew, and we'll come in early on Sunday and start testing at 7:00 a.m. I'll tell Freddie you'll be coming to join us on Sunday. Don't worry, I think we still have time to finish the testing so we'll have the data and accompanying analysis for Tuesday's hearing."

As they left the test facility, Chris looked at Sonja, and his expression said it all—one more testing delay or problem, and they would be out of time.

*   *   *

Petrovic flopped down on the love seat in his two-room suite on the Premier Executive floor of his hotel. He picked up, from the end table, an oversized, ice-filled crystal goblet that contained Chivas Regal from two mini-bottles. Sipping with pleasure one of his favorite elixirs, Petrovic beamed as he reviewed his notes reflecting all that he and his team had accomplished in less than thirty-six hours. But then the annoying ring of his cell phone rudely interrupted his pleasant thoughts.

He recognized Calvin Wiseman's number on the phone's readout as he glanced at his watch. It was 6:00 p.m., which meant that it was 9:00 p.m. back in Washington, DC.

"What the hell does he want now?" Petrovic grumbled. "What's up, Calvin?"

"Great news! We think we've located where O'Brian's coconspirators are hiding out."

"How did you manage that?" Petrovic asked in disbelief, having little regard for Wiseman.

"We got a break. You know that ongoing FBI investigation into possible rogue agents leaking inside Bureau information to CNP?"

"Yes," Petrovic answered as his mind struggled to make the connection.

"Well, awhile ago, the Bureau tapped into the CNP surveillance camera in the building's lobby. All persons entering and leaving the building are caught on camera. We pirated the ongoing video feed and linked it into the FBI's persons of interest database to see if we could match suspected rogue FBI agents with the people entering the building."

"Get to the point," Petrovic barked.

"Well our database also includes photos of fugitives, including known friends and family of Otto Simpson—you know, the guy who disrupted the capture of O'Brian."

"And?" Petrovic said, growing increasingly impatient.

"And who should come up as a match on the FBI database yesterday but a young woman named Tanya Williams. She's the girlfriend of Leon Jones, who is the son of Chet Jones. Jones was a lifelong friend of Simpson. When the database triggered an immediate match, we dispatched an agent, who followed Williams after she left CNP. The girl wound up in an aging duplex in North Baltimore. It's in a pretty rough area. Anyway, that's where we think the conspirators are hiding. We've got the place under surveillance, and we plan to make a move, possibly as early as Sunday."

"Good work," Petrovic said, feigning praise. "But why wait? Those guys are clearly professionals, and the FBI blew it last time. And for god's sake, don't invite them to surrender. They're cold-blooded killers. They almost blew up half of your SWAT team during that farmhouse raid."

"Look, Parnak, this is an FBI matter, and we, unlike you, are required to play it by the book."

"I can just see the headlines. 'Scores of Innocent Victims Slaughtered in Baltimore Residential Neighborhood when Botched FBI Raid Unleashes a Barrage of Gunfire,'" Petrovic responded sarcastically.

"Maybe you're right, but—"

"No damn buts. Keep me posted and don't blow this. The White House will be very unhappy if you mess up taking those guys down." And with that, Petrovic hung up and took another healthy gulp from the goblet.

"Finally, the end is near for O'Brian, Zimmer, and the rest of them," Petrovic mused as he leaned back in his chair and twirled the goblet in his fingers.

CHAPTER 76

May 21
Venice Beach, California

Chris lay in bed, his arms around Sonja, her naked body pressing against him. Her breathing was deep but relaxed. Even though the sweet scent of her hair aroused him, Chris didn't move for fear of waking her. The last eighteen hours they had spent together alone, and at least for that brief period, they had allowed themselves to become lost in each other's company—blocking out the horror that had engulfed them for so long.

Chandler had invited Thurgensen to join him for dinner at his home in Malibu on the Pacific Ocean shore and to spend the night. Thurgensen jumped at the chance so the two of them could relive the great moments of the battles to clean up motor-vehicle pollution over the past six decades. Then, when Chris and Sonja arrived back at Venice Beach, Parker announced that he and Maria were going to spend the evening with friends, leaving Chris and Sonja free to enjoy each other's company for a least one afternoon and evening.

Now, Saturday morning, Chris began to consider how best to use the day. While he was looking around the room for his notebook that contained all of his contact information to reach Chet and the others and his notes from the meetings with Morris and Chandler, the realization came crashing to him that he had left it in Steve Morris's office.

"Damn it!" Chris inadvertently blurted out, and Sonja awoke with a start.

· "What's wrong?" she asked as she nuzzled her nose on his ear and playfully kissed him.

"I'm an idiot, I—"

"No argument there, Captain Crunch," she interrupted and laughed.

"I left my notebook in Steve's office. I put it down for a second, got distracted, and left it there. I need to get it back."

"So we'll go get it. I'm sure the security guard will let us in. But what's the big rush?" Sonja said as she ran the sharp fingernails slowly down Chris's chest and below his waist.

As her fingers found their mark, Chris moaned and then turned, giving her a tender kiss.

"I guess we can pick it up later," he whispered.

Three hours later, Chris and Sonja drove into the ARB parking lot. It was empty except for two white vans with "El Monte Cleaning Services" painted on their sides. They walked to the front doors of the building and rang a buzzer. Moments later, a small, seventyish-looking man dressed neatly in a security uniform waddled down the hall toward the front entrance. When the security guard arrived, he squinted warily through his thick glasses and hit the intercom button. "May I help you?"

"You must be Freddie. My name is Russell Smith and this is my wife, Torrey. We're working with Steve Morris on some emission testing."

"No testing going on here today," the guard said with a touch of suspicion in his voice.

"I know that, but we were here yesterday with Steve and Chairman Chandler, and I left my notebook in Steve's office."

"Okay, but I can't let you both in," the guard replied. Looking at Sonja, who seemed far less threatening than the muscular, tall O'Brian, he added, "She can come in, but you'll have to wait outside."

Sonja entered and thanked Freddie as she headed down the main hall for about twenty feet and turned right down a side hallway in the direction of Morris's office. Freddie wasn't far behind.

The testing facility, usually bustling with activity, seemed eerily quiet, with most of the lights turned off and only a few of the office-cleaning personnel visible. As she neared Morris's office, Sonja noticed one of the cleaning workers with his back to her, standing idly by looking down toward the row of test cells. At the sound of her footsteps, the man turned in Sonja's direction.

"No!" Sonja screamed. Her face went ghostly white, and every hair on the back of her neck bristled. Instinctively, she spun around and started to run. But her shoes slid on the freshly waxed floor, and she couldn't gain traction. The harder she tried, the more she slipped—falling twice to her knees and frantically trying to regain any forward momentum she could. Her eyes almost bursting from their sockets, Sonja stared back in horror at the man dressed in a cleaning uniform who now was racing toward her and shouting.

As she reached the front door and pushed it open, she screamed to Chris, "It's Petrovic!"

Seconds later, Petrovic was closing in on Sonja after smashing his fist into the face of the befuddled security guard. Freddie crashed back into the wall and slumped unconscious to the floor.

At first, Chris froze at the sight of Petrovic, but then he noticed a bucket filled with soapy water just inside the entrance door. Before the door could close after Sonja had exited, he entered the building, grabbed the bucket, and dumped its contents across the floor. As Petrovic and now two other similarly dressed men raced toward Chris and Sonja, they reached the wet, soapy section of the floor. The three men went flying in different directions as their feet slipped out from under them. Each crashed with a thud into the walls of the hallway. By the time they were finally able to stand, Sonja and Chris had reached their SUV.

Chris turned the ignition, jammed the vehicle into gear, and squealed out of the ARB parking lot and into the street, narrowly missing an oncoming vehicle. Sonja was gasping for air and unable to speak. He grabbed her violently shaking knee and squeezed it gently. "Are you okay?"

"I wet myself."

"Don't worry about that. We've got bigger problems. Let's focus on losing these guys," Chris said as he squeezed her knee again and then gripped the steering wheel tightly with both hands, his knuckles turning white. "Grab the gun from the glove compartment."

As they raced down the road, Chris checked the rearview mirror and saw one of the vans closing in on them. Moments later, without signaling, he spun the steering wheel sharply to the right and raced down an access road onto the interstate, heading in the direction of downtown Los Angeles.

Traffic was light, even for midday Saturday, on the ten-lane elevated ribbon of highway that cut over numerous low-income neighborhoods, light industrial parks, and commercial centers. Chris slammed the accelerator down.

Sonja turned to look back to see if the white van was still following them. It was no more than a half-mile behind. As they approached the interchange with another interstate highway, congestion began to increase. Chris swerved back and forth, crisscrossing lanes and drawing a symphony of screeching brakes and blaring horns from the outraged drivers of the other vehicles he had cut off.

Looking in the rearview mirror, Chris saw that the number of vehicles between them and the van had grown considerably, but in terms of distance, Petrovic was closing in.

"Chris, look out!" Sonja yelled as Chris looked straight ahead and slammed on the brakes. Their vehicle screeched to a halt inches away from crashing into the car stopped in front of them.

"What the hell?" Chris cried out as he stared ahead at the five lanes of traffic that had come to a complete stop.

"Must be an accident or road construction," Chris said, looking at Sonja, and then he turned around and saw the cars behind him also stopping. In the distance, maybe a thousand yards back, was the unmistakable top of the white van that was chasing them.

After a minute, traffic started moving forward. But since the vehicles in all lanes were bumper to bumper and moving at the same speed, about fifteen miles per hour, there was no chance of breaking out of the pack.

"Well, at least they can't catch us in this traffic," Sonja said hopefully, having regained a measure of composure since first seeing Petrovic.

"We're screwed. All Petrovic has to do is call in backup from the Los Angeles Police Department or maybe the FBI, and we'll just slowly move toward interception," Chris said with resignation in his voice. "If we do run into an LAPD or FBI roadblock, get out of the car slowly, raise your hands high, drop to your knees, and let them take us into custody. Petrovic can't kill us in front the local authorities or the FBI."

For the next twenty minutes, the traffic moved in unison at an increasing speed that reached about twenty-five miles an hour, and the white van made no progress in closing the gap with Chris and Sonja.

"Why haven't we seen any helicopters overhead? If the LAPD or the FBI were going to intercept us, wouldn't they have arrived by now?" Sonja queried.

"That's it! They're not coming. Petrovic must be acting on his own, outside the authority of the FBI or any other federal or state agency. He couldn't take the risk of letting the LAPD or the FBI take us alive. We're only two of his targets here in LA; he needs to take down Thurgensen and possibly others as well. We've got to get off this freeway."

Moments later, Chris spotted his opportunity and quickly turned sharply to the right into a small space between two trucks. Next he swerved right again off the freeway on to an off-ramp, causing at least two vehicles to crash into each other.

Chris raced down the exit ramp and turned onto a two-lane, rather poorly maintained road with salvage yards on both sides. After going about three hundred yards, he turned right down a gravel road, hoping to lose Petrovic. To his dismay, the road quickly dead-ended. Chris, frantically spinning the SUV around, started racing back to the main road.

As he approached the intersection, the white van, its tires squealing, turned down the gravel road.

"We're trapped."

But then Chris spotted a narrow driveway just ahead to the right, but blocked by a dilapidated, rusting chain-link gate. He gunned the engine, and the SUV leaped forward, heading directly at the van. At the last second, he swerved to the right and easily crashed through the gate. As the SUV raced past the now-busted gate, Chris saw out of the corner of his eye a badly faded sign that read, in huge letters, "Long Beach Marine Salvage Company."

"So be it," Chris muttered to himself, knowing full well that he was about to live out the horrific dream he had had months earlier in his condo the night before his attempted suicide.

The marine salvage yard encompassed nearly a square mile maze of haphazard dirt paths that encircled the rusting iron hulls of easily two hundred marine vessels of all sizes. Some vessels were completely dry-docked, while others were half-sunken in the brackish and oily back waters of Long Beach Bay. The place looked like it had been abandoned years ago—no signs of life or even recent activity of any kind.

Spotting an abandoned maintenance building/garage, he drove the SUV inside. As he manually closed the barely functioning garage door, Chris ripped his wrist open on a rusty nail.

Chris and Sonja quickly unloaded weapons from the back of the SUV, stuck them into black bags, and set out to find a spot to hide from Petrovic. They raced in a zigzag pattern for almost twenty minutes, disappearing into the heart of the vast salvage yard. At last Chris found exactly what he was looking for—the dilapidated hull of a huge oil tanker, half of which was under water.

"We'll hide in there until first light tomorrow, and then we need to get back to the ARB testing lab."

After they entered the ship's hull, Chris and Sonja found and stacked some dead weeds and made a place to rest. Chris outlined the details of his plan and said, "Let's rest and try to get as much sleep as posible."

CHAPTER 77

May 21
Baltimore, Maryland

About the time Chris and Sonja entered the salvage yard, four large, black vans with "FBI SWAT" painted on the side panels cruised into a North Baltimore residential neighborhood. The four-square-block neighborhood was an island of sanity and tranquility surrounded by a huge, high-crime, and blighted area. The immediate neighborhood was populated almost exclusively by middle- and low-income black families. While many of the houses were in need of repair, the neighborhood was clean and vibrant. Adults, playing with their children or grandchildren, or working in the yard, stopped at the sight of such an imposing intrusion by the authorities into their quiet neighborhood.

Calvin Wiseman had decided to follow Petrovic's call for quick action to take out the band of coconspirators located in Baltimore. Unable to find a tactical leader to head the assault on such short notice, the FBI head decided to lead the assault himself. Wiseman, who had passable skills as a bureaucrat but lacked the judgment and leadership skills to run a field operation, made a number of critical errors in judgment. He chose a time when adults and children would likely be outside of their houses, he decided to use overwhelming force, and he failed to ensure that the SWAT team had at least one black agent present.

The SWAT team quickly surrounded the house—twelve agents in front and four more to guard the rear exit. As the growing, agitated crowd of residents began to collect across the street from the home where Chet and the Crew were hiding, Wiseman barked into a microphone, "This is the FBI. You're all under arrest. Come out one at a time with your hands up!"

Inside the house, everyone ran to the front windows and gasped at the sight of the FBI assault team. Tanya's eyes welled up in tears as she looked at Chet and mouthed the words, "I'm sorry."

Chet reached out his hand to Tanya and whispered back, "We'll be okay." And then he took command of the situation.

"Everyone, move away from the windows. We've done our best. Thanks to your efforts, Chris and Sonja are in California working with environmental authorities to stop EZ-15 in its tracks. But for us, it's over. We must surrender peaceably. Don't give them any reason to open fire. We'll walk out slowly, one at a time, with our hands up. I'll go first, then Leon, Casey, Billy, Freddie, and then Tanya, Rebecca, and Joanne. Kathy, stay in the house with the child and wait. Do exactly what they ask."

Freddie, who had gone to the back of the house to check the alley, reported that four agents were positioned in plain view. At that point, the Crew resigned themselves to their fate. All that was left was to give one another one last hug.

Chet opened the front door slowly and stepped out with his old police badge held high in his right hand—a gesture often used by police officers, active or retired, to ease the tension of the situation. "I'm Chester Jones, a former DC police sergeant and leader of this group. There are women and a child inside. We all surrender peaceably—"

But at the very moment Chet began to speak, a ray of the setting sun reflected off his badge, creating a flash of light. One of the SWAT team members, who was on his first operation and already spooked by Wiseman's admonishment that persons in question were suicidal killers, panicked and fired two shots in quick succession.

Chet, a look of utter disbelief across his face, stumbled back from the force of the two slugs that hit him in his upper torso. The large black man fell awkwardly to his knees and finally forward on his face. Blood quickly oozed out from under his motionless body.

"Nooo!" Leon screamed as he raced to his father, only to be gunned down himself. As rounds crashed through the front window, and glass projectiles flew into the living room, everyone inside dove to the floor. Everyone except Kathy Jones who, still holding her infant granddaughter, rushed out the front door to attend her fallen brother and her dear nephew.

"Hold your fire! Hold your fire!" Wiseman yelled frantically into his microphone as the gunfire stopped.

But the growing crowd of neighbors, witnessing the unprovoked violence and the sight of a grandmother and her granddaughter confronting the federal agents, exploded and charged en masse. The FBI forces scrambled in retreat into their vehicles as a firestorm of verbal assaults, as well as random rocks and bottles, were launched in their direction. At the sound of chaos, the four agents staked out in the alley scrambled to the front of the house to aid their colleagues but then quickly retreated as well into the vans for their own protection. Outraged neighbors, young and old in a rage, circled and then rocked the four vans back and forth.

Freddie, who had been watching the alley, saw the agents leave and raced back to the living room and shouted, "Tanya, Rebecca, and Ms. McKay, the alley is clear. You have to get out of here. The rest of us will surrender."

Tanya, dazed and disoriented at what she had just witnessed, was on her knees, swaying from side to side with her hands on her head and moaning hysterically. Rebecca and Joanne lifted her limp body and led her out the back door and into the alley.

A half a block down the alley, an elderly black woman appeared and motioned frantically for the three women to come to her. Rebecca and Joanne, carrying Tanya, scurried through the back gate and up the stairs. Looking frantically in both directions for the sight of any FBI agents, the elderly woman held open the door. "Hurry! You'll be safe here. You can hide in my basement."

It took nearly two hours for the FBI, with reinforcements from the Baltimore police, to restore some semblance of order. The disturbance did pause briefly when two emergency vehicles came to whisk Chet and Leon away. The onlookers hoped the ambulances were headed to the emergency room, but based on what they saw, they feared the morgue was the more likely destination. When the chaos finally subsided, Casey, Billy, and Freddie surrendered.

CHAPTER 78

May 22
Long Beach, California

The morning light crept through the endless cracks, holes, and crevasses of the rusting and broken oil tanker hull, casting rays of bright light almost like laser beams piercing, but not illuminating, the darkness inside. Chris, who hadn't slept, cradled Sonja in his arms, her matted hair brushing against his now-stubbled cheeks. The cut on his hand had stopped bleeding, but not before dark red ooze had covered his shirt and pants and Sonja's white, torn blouse. He knew that the time had come. He had been here before in his dream, but this time he was ready, and he tried desperately to convince himself that this time things would end differently.

"It's time," Chris whispered in Sonja's ear as she opened her sleepy eyes and looked up at him lovingly, forgetting for an instant where they were and what they were about to face. As she surveyed the surroundings, her expression morphed into one of awareness and determination.

"It won't be long now. Are you ready?"

"Ready," Sonja replied, and she shoved a fully loaded magazine into her handgun, turned Chris's face toward her, and kissed him hard on his lips.

*   *   *

As night turned into day, not far away, Petrovic was growing increasingly frustrated with his team's inability to track down their prey. He knew O'Brian and Voinovich were out there somewhere in the vast sea of rusted ships. Around midnight, his spirits had been lifted momentarily when first one and then the other team arrived from the operations they had undertaken in other parts of the city.

A simple nod from each team's leader signaled that each had successfully carried out their tasks. But now six hours later, there was still no sign of O'Brian and Voinovich.

Then a husky voice rang out. "Hey, over here, quick."

Petrovic and the other eight members converged on the area from which the voice had been heard.

"Fresh drops of blood and footprints. They continue in the direction of that tanker hull over there," the muscular, blue-eyed, blond squad team leader whispered as he pointed to a hull about twenty yards in front of them.

Using hand signals, Petrovic gave instructions to the two team leaders, who in turn gave more detailed signals of instruction to their men. The first squad of five men moved silently toward the target. Final signals were communicated, and a 250-pound squad member kicked the rusting hatch door open and ripped it from its weakened hinges, creating an opening into the inner sanctum of the dark hull through which a second team member raced in, firing his automatic weapon.

Chris and Sonja had moved behind a large, empty oil drum to the immediate right of the opening, out of the beams of sunlight that now cascaded through much of the inside of the hull. As they crouched down, bullets harmlessly whizzed by them and exploded through the walls of the opposite side of the hull, letting in even more beams of light.

As the assassin entered the space, Chris clicked his weapon to automatic and fired a burst of four shots. The intruder rocked from the blast and crashed against the side of the hull. His lifeless, bullet-ravaged body slowly slid down the side of the hull, leaving a bloody ooze on the wall behind. Three more men rushed through the narrow opening and immediately became disoriented by the streaming beams of sunlight. In their confusion, they fired their weapons haphazardly and harmlessly in all directions. Chris and Sonja took careful aim at the three heavily armed men who stood in the open, silhouetted by the beams of light, searching in vain for their prey.

"Now!" Chris shouted as he stood up from behind the large oil drum and fired the rest of his magazine rounds into the two men at the far side of the hull. Sonja took dead aim at the third assassin, who was no more than twenty feet away, and fired six rounds. Four rounds penetrated his upper body. Three more bodies now lay half-submerged in puddles of rust-colored, stinking water and oil on the floor of the tanker's hull.

"Are you okay?" Chris whispered to Sonja, who he could barely see in the dark and now dusty enclosure.

"Yes. Is it over?"

"Hardly. Reload and be ready to move."

In the next moment, Chris saw a small, round object fly through the hatch opening and clank as it hit and then bounced on a dry portion of the hull's floor.

"Get down!" Chris screamed as he vaulted over the oil barrel, dove in the direction of where the object had landed, desperately grabbed the object, and furiously hurled it back out of the opening.

Almost instantaneously, a huge explosion erupted just outside the opening that shook the hull's deteriorating walls and caused a rain of rusted metal flakes to fall over Chris and Sonja. They could hear the horrific sounds of blood-curdling screams and moans. And then there was silence.

"Let's get the hell out of here," Chris said. He grabbed Sonja's hand, and they raced down the slippery and often treacherous floor of the hull toward an opening at the far end of the ship's hull that they had scoped out the night before.

"Get them! Don't let them escape!" a voice eerily familiar to Sonja screamed as three men entered the hull in pursuit of her and Chris.

"Damn. That grenade took out some of them, but not Petrovic," Sonja cried out as Chris dragged her along.

Sonja pulled her hand free of Chris, turned, and aimed her pistol. She fired twice at Petrovic. The first bullet hit and passed through Petrovic's left calf, and the second ripped into his upper right thigh and lodged in his hip socket. He dropped to his knees and cried out in agonizing pain. Sonja took dead aim at Petrovic's head and pulled the trigger. The gun jammed.

Chris grabbed Sonja by the hand and yelled, "Come on; now's our chance to escape."

"But I didn't kill him."

"It's good enough for now. We need to get you out of here!" Chris shouted. An emerging source of light signaled the presence of a large hole in the hull through which they could escape, and he led her through it.

Once in the open air, Chris and Sonja raced hand in hand back to where they had hidden the SUV. As they approached the garage, they stole a glance back and saw no one pursuing them. Chris quickly opened the garage door.

"We made it. Let's get out of here," Sonja gasped in a barely audible voice, desperately trying to catch her breath.

Chris turned to her and, with a look of sadness, placed the keys to the SUV in her hands. "You've got to leave now and go back to the ARB testing facility. I'm staying here. As long as Petrovic is alive, this nightmare can't end."

"No! I'm not leaving you," Sonja said with a mix of defiance and fear on her face as she pulled her hands free from his and wrapped her arms tightly around him.

Chris forcibly broke Sonja's grip and placed his hands firmly on her forearms. He looked deep into her now-tearing eyes. "You've got to warn Morris before he begins the testing today. Petrovic wasn't at the ARB facility yesterday conducting reconnaissance. I'm sure his team was there rigging the test equipment with explosives. If Steve starts up the test equipment, the entire lab will blow up just like the explosion at the German test facility. If the ARB lab blows up, EMCO wins."

Chris felt the tightness in Sonja's body ease as she resigned herself to the truth of what he was saying. Hugging her tightly, he whispered the words that up until then he never could bring himself to speak, "I love you, Sonja. I love you so much. I know now that I started falling in love with you that night at Chet's house when you drifted off to sleep in my arms."

"You decide to tell me this now," Sonja whispered with a touch of sarcasm, as well as sadness, in her voice. Then she wrapped her arms tightly around Chris's shoulders and whispered, "I love you too, and you damn well better come back to me."

"That's what I plan to do," Chris said, forcing a smile. "Once I've taken care of Petrovic, I'll find a cell phone to borrow somewhere and leave you a message on my cell phone. The number to call to check my phone messages is in my notebook. It's still in Steve's office. Check for my message telling you where to pick me up."

Chris wiped away the mix of rusty dust and tears caked on Sonja's cheeks. The couple kissed and hugged each other tenderly.

When they finally and reluctantly pulled apart, Chris said, "One more thing. When you find the explosive device—and you will find one—keep checking because there likely will be another. Petrovic is too smart and diabolical not to have a backup device or plan."

Then, without speaking further, Chris went to the back of the SUV and grabbed the remaining canvas bag full of weapons and explosives. He came around the front of the vehicle and opened the driver-side door for Sonja to enter.

They kissed one last time before Sonja started the vehicle and pulled out of the garage. She stuck her head out of the window, the tears now streaming down her flushed checks. "Be safe."

"You too," Chris called out as she drove off to the salvage yard exit. Then with a look of determination, he headed back to the tanker.

As he rounded a corner, Chris could see two men racing toward him. Blinded by the rays of the sun now barely above the horizon, the men failed to spot Chris before he ducked behind a pile of rotting wood pallets. As the men approached, Chris sprayed the two killers with a freshly loaded clip from his weapon, jumped over the now lifeless bodies, and raced forward.

Reentering the ship's hull, Chris could hear a somewhat more subdued, but still wailing, Petrovic barking instructions to the two remaining team members attending to him. Chris slowly and quietly made his way through the hull toward Petrovic. But when he got within about twenty yards of Petrovic, Chris tripped on an unseen board sticking up from the floor and landed with a thud.

At the sound, Petrovic's two team members grabbed their weapons and fired in Chris's direction. Now hiding behind a pile of metal plates, Chris raised his gun above his head and fired back. A stalemate quickly ensued, and Chris knew that being outmanned three to one, he couldn't simply stay where was. He needed to take decisive action.

He reached into his canvas bag and pulled out a hand grenade, pulled the pin, and tossed it in Petrovic's direction. Chris could hear the desperate and futile screams of Petrovic and his men desperately trying to find the grenade before it exploded. The grenade went off, but rather than an explosion, it simply sparked and hissed.

Petrovic ordered his men to chase after Chris and yelled, "Nice try, O'Brian! Now it's your time to die!"

Petrovic glared at Chris and smiled smugly as the other two men took deadly aim at Chris, who had run out of ammunition.

But at that very instant, the small sparks from the defective grenade caused a pile of oil-soaked wood to catch fire. When the flame mixed with low levels of methane gas trapped in pockets throughout the ship's hull, the flame exploded into a wall of fire. With a look of utter disbelief on his face, Petrovic and his two men were quickly consumed in the flames.

Looking back in horror as he raced to escape, Chris could see the wall of flames now rapidly coming toward him. *If I can make it outside, I have a chance of surviving.*

Chris was no more than ten feet from the opening and his salvation when he felt a rush of hot air being pushed ahead of the intense flames. As he tried to accelerate his pace, Chris was blown forward—tumbling into the darkness. Moments later, the flames raced through the remaining portion of the hull, and it was over.

CHAPTER 79

May 22
Los Angeles, California

When Sonja reached the exit, she stopped and jumped out of the SUV to look back into the salvage yard. At that very moment, she heard a massive explosion and jerked her head around, capturing the sight of a tremendous plume of flames and smoke. Her legs went limp as she fell to her knees, her trembling hands held over her mouth that fell open in horror at the sight. While she told herself not to give up hope, she knew at that instant Chris wouldn't be calling her to say he was okay. After an agonizing moment, Sonja regained a measure of composure and got back into the SUV.

"It's up to me now to save Steve, Karl, and everyone else at the ARB Lab," Sonja cried aloud, still brushing the tears away that wouldn't stop flowing.

Sonja quickly made her way back to the ARB facility. As she swerved at nearly full speed into the parking lot, she could see Steve's Toyota Prius and the other staff members' vehicles parked in the lot. She looked down nervously at her watch, which read 6:56 a.m. Testing would start up at any time. Sonja didn't slam on the brakes of the SUV until she had driven up to, and nearly crashed through, the front door entrance.

Scrambling out of the vehicle, she raced to the entrance. The doors were locked, and no security guard was in sight. Her heart racing and with a look of desperation on her face, Sonja furiously pounded her fists in vain on the thick door windows.

Meanwhile, in the lab, Morris gave the final instructions to his lab technicians and then said, "Okay, start up the test engine."

But before the technicians could carry out the command, the sound of gunfire and broken glass filled the air. Everyone dove down and scurried to hide as the shooting continued.

When the gunfire finally stopped, Steve and the lone security guard cautiously raced down the hall in the direction from which the shots had been fired. The young security guard, his hands shaking nervously, pulled his revolver from its holster and took dead aim at the person screaming at the front door.

"Stop!" Steve screamed as he slammed his fist into the security guard's forearm. The weapon still discharged, but the bullet harmlessly lodged in the wall not a foot from Sonja's head.

"Don't shoot," Steve cautioned as he ran to open the door for Sonja, who by then had slumped to the ground.

As Steve opened the door to help Sonja to her feet, she warned, "Don't start the testing. There's a bomb."

Sonja, gasping for breath, explained that Petrovic and his men had been at the lab the previous day and had in all likelihood planted an explosive device that would be triggered as soon as the test equipment was turned on. Steve immediately called the LAPD bomb squad.

When the bomb squad arrived, they quickly found and successfully disarmed an explosive device. But over the next three hours, they searched in vain for possible other devices. Finally, the bomb squad gave the all-clear signal. Steve, taking no chances, had everyone except him leave the building as he started the test engine and the rest of the testing equipment. Everything went off without a hitch.

Soon the entire testing staff was at their appointed stations, and full testing was under way. Leaving the test area, Steve returned to his office and handed Sonja a mug of steaming coffee. As she sipped the coffee, she described all that had happened over the past twenty-four hours.

When she finished, she asked, "Is the security guard who was on duty yesterday okay?"

"Based on what you've told me, I'm afraid he isn't. When the evening shift guard showed up for work last night, everything seemed to be in order, but Freddie was gone. The security company apologized and said Freddie must have left, probably to have a drink. I'm afraid something far worse happened to him."

"Poor Freddie. Another innocent victim of this madness," Sonja said quietly. "But where are Chairman Chandler and Karl? I thought for sure they would want to be here for the final tests."

Steve explained that the last time he had talked to Chandler was early Saturday afternoon, when the chairman called to say he was driving to Venice Beach to drop Thurgensen off and that both he and Karl were planning on being present for the testing.

"I called the chairman this morning but got no answer on his cell phone. I'm sure everything is fine. I'll try again later."

Sonja started to speak, but then she saw Chris's notebook on an end table exactly where he had left it on Friday. She leapt forward, swept it up, checked for Chris's message retrieval number, and made the call on her cell phone. There was one message, and she quickly retrieved it.

Could it be Chris? she prayed, but then she recognized Tanya's voice, and Sonja immediately hit "Save" as her head slowly dropped.

"Are you okay?" Steve asked.

"I was hoping, by some miracle, it was a message from Chris, but it wasn't."

"You're obviously exhausted. There's nothing more for you to do around here. Hey, you've already saved the day. I can get someone to drive you back to Venice Beach."

"Thanks, but no. I'm fine. I just need to get back to the Parkers and check up on Karl. Maybe Chairman Chandler decided to stay with the Parkers overnight rather than drive back to Santa Monica."

Sonja was anything but fine. Steve walked her to the front exit and as he held the door open for her to leave, she turned and asked, almost plaintively, "Steve, do you really believe you have the time needed to complete the tests, do the data analysis, and be ready for the ARB hearing on Tuesday?"

"I don't know," Steve replied. But then he added, trying to sound positive, "But we're going to do everything we can to make it happen."

Steve's less-than-encouraging response only served to intensify Sonja's continuing spiral into the dark depths of despair.

Almost in a daze, Sonja drove slowly out of the ARB parking lot and headed for Venice Beach. Once on the freeway, her mind drifted aimlessly, and several times she weaved from lane to lane only to be shocked back into awareness by the blaring horns of the other drivers who had swerved to avoid being hit. Finally, she decided to get off the freeway, stop for a cup of coffee, and return Tanya's call. After taking several healthy gulps of coffee, Sonja called Tanya.

"Chris, is that you? Why haven't you called? Chet and Leon have been shot by the FBI. We think they're dead," the frantic voice of Tanya Jones screamed.

"Tanya, it's me, Sonja. What happened?"

But the only response she heard was Tanya's guttural wailing. Finally, Sonja could hear a voice in the background asking for the phone and sending Tanya away. Then someone else spoke. "It's me, Rebecca. Are you and Chris okay?"

Sonja explained everything that had happened. Then it was Rebecca's turn to break the bad news to Sonja about the FBI raid.

"We don't know if Chet and Leon are alive. The FBI hasn't released any information regarding the raid, but from all the blood, it doesn't look good. Tanya, Joanne, and I escaped; we're hiding out in Anacostia, in DC, at Chet's friend Carson Bigalow's place." Then sounding desperate, Rebecca added, "What should we do?"

Sonja, crushed by the news about Chet and Leon, didn't at first reply. After a moment, she regained a measure of composure and said, "Stay where you are. I'm heading to meet up with Dr. Thurgensen and the Parkers. When we come up with a plan, I'll call you back."

As Sonja ended the call and returned to the SUV, she shook her head in despair. She had no idea what to do next. Once on the freeway, she turned on the radio. *Maybe listening to some music might help me relax and focus on what we should do next.*

But any hope of that happening was obliterated when the regular programming on the contemporary rock station to which she was listening was interrupted by a special news bulletin.

"This is Mike Carlson reporting at the scene of a horrific explosion that occurred last night here in Venice Beach, where three homes where obliterated under suspicious circumstances. Authorities have just reported that fragments of explosive material have been found confirming that this tragic event, in which seven bodies have already been recovered, wasn't an accident. The police have no leads regarding the perpetrators, nor do they believe, at this point, that this explosion is in any way related to the massive explosion and apparent shootout at the Long Beach Marine Salvage Company in Orange County that took place early this morning. At that site, a number of bodies have been recovered, but no survivors have been found."

Sonja turned the radio off. She felt numb and didn't want to believe what she was hearing. Ten minutes later she arrived two blocks from the Parkers' home and stopped where the police had cordoned off the area. She could make out the precise spot where the Parker cottage had stood, but now there was only barren land, with what looked like a crater, and two nearly destroyed homes on either side of the Parkers' property. Sonja spotted several city morgue vehicles and a number of police and fire officials meandering around. It seemed clear to her that any search for survivors was over.

Pulling over to the curb, Sonja turned off the engine. Still staring at the devastating sight, she felt a cold chill consume her body as she shook uncontrollably. She quietly sobbed as droplets of spit drooled uncontrollably from her partially opened, quivering lips.

After what seemed like hours, but in reality was only a few moments, she made her decision. Chris, Chet, and Leon were dead. Now, Dyson and Selma Parker, Thurgensen, and probably Chandler were blown into oblivion. The ARB test result evidence needed to stop EPA's final approval of EZ-15, in all likelihood, wouldn't be ready in time. Even if it was, without Thurgensen's testimony, the test results alone wouldn't be enough.

"It's over. EMCO's going to receive final approval from EPA, and as a result, millions of innocent people around the world are going to die. There's nothing left for me or anyone else to do to stop the inevitable carnage."

But then Sonja, for the first time in her life, felt at complete peace. Having made her decision, she reached for the handgun that had fallen on the floor. She checked the weapon. One bullet remained, and that was all she would need. Sonja placed the pistol on her lap, closed her eyes, and allowed herself, before she ended her life, one last moment to think of the man she had dearly loved.

Sonja remembered the first time she and Chris had made love as the hint of a smile crept across her face. Moments later, all was black.

CHAPTER 80

May 23
Venice Beach, California

The LA police officer approached the parked vehicle cautiously. The driver's side window was coated with a thick layer of early-morning moisture mixed with dirt, making the glass panel opaque. Peering through the window, he could see a body slouched in the driver's seat with its head drooped downward. The officer tapped gently on the window, but he saw no movement in response. He tapped again, louder.

Sonja woke with a start from an eight-hour, deep sleep to the rapping sounds on the SUV's window. Disoriented, she tried to open her eyes. But they were stuck closed by the mixture of tears and dust that had dried overnight on her lashes, fusing them together. Finally, she rubbed her eyes clear, stretched her stiff neck, and raised herself up in the driver's seat. She struggled to remember where she was and how she got there.

Through the closed window, Sonja heard a muffled voice. "Open the door."

Sonja's eyes dotted around the vehicle, and then everything came crashing back painfully to her. She had drifted off to sleep thinking of Chris before she was able to carry out the act that would have put an end to her horrific life. Sonja's entire body trembled at the thought of what she had contemplated.

The police officer, seeing movement in the car, banged louder on the window and tried to open the door, but it was locked. Sonja, barely able to see the person on the other side of the window who was attempting to enter her vehicle, panicked and started searching in vain for the pistol that was lying on the floor in front of her where it had landed when it dropped from her grasp when she fell asleep. Resigned to her fate, she slowly opened the door, stepped out, and when she saw it was a policeman, raised her hands over her head.

"Ms. Parker, please, you don't have to put your hands up," the young officer said.

"I'm not Selma Parker."

"But this SUV is registered to a Ms. Selma Parker. Who are you?"

"I was a friend of hers and Dyson Parker. They let me borrow this SUV."

"So you know Dyson Parker?"

"Yes, I did."

"Are you a close enough friend that Mr. Parker would trust you?"

"I knew him well, but Dyson and the others are dead," Sonja replied, totally confused.

"Not exactly, Miss. But we could sure use your help if you would follow me."

The officer took Sonja's hand and led her to the huge hole in the ground where the Parker's cottage once stood. As they neared the crater, Sonja saw what looked like a large, square cement slab, cracked and pitted but otherwise still in one piece. Crossing the slab, she saw what looked like an exhaust pipe sticking straight up, and three uniformed police appeared to be speaking into it.

"Here's the problem, Miss. Dyson Parker is under that slab of cement with three or four other people. We don't know if they're hostages. We think this is some kind of bomb shelter. See that steel trap door over there? It's impenetrable and can only be opened from the inside of the shelter."

"I don't understand ... how can I be of any help?"

"Mr. Parker won't come out, and he won't let the others out either. He's convinced that we're aliens from outer space come to kidnap him," the officer explained.

"If you could just talk to him and try to convince him it's safe out here, we'd be deeply grateful. We've all been at this site for nearly thirty hours, and everyone is exhausted."

"I'll try," Sonja said as he directed her to the pipe that served as their only source of communication with Parker.

Speaking into the pipe, Sonja asked if Selma, Thurgensen, and Chandler were with him and if they were okay. She pleaded with Dyson to come out.

At first he resisted, believing she must be an alien as well. But eventually she provided him information only she would know. Finally, he acquiesced, and moments later, an unseen latch on the underside of the steel door clanked, and the steel door opened slowly.

Parker emerged cautiously and looked carefully around at the carnage that was once his neighborhood. He hesitated, but when he spotted Sonja smiling, he motioned to the others below that it was safe to come out. Selma, followed by Chandler, appeared. Their expressions of relief turned to shock as they surveyed the damage. When Thurgensen finally emerged, Sonja raced over and tightly hugged him.

"Remember the night Dyson showed Chris and me his weapons arsenal and said he wanted to show us something else really special?" Thurgensen whispered in Sonja ear.

"Yes, I remember you telling me about it."

"Well, that something else was the most amazing bomb shelter I've ever seen. He built it fifteen years ago as a place to hide from the alien invasion that he believed was imminent. We could have stayed down for a very long time. The place is incredible.

"On Saturday night, Dyson spotted two guys dressed in black slinking around in his back yard. He screamed 'Aliens, they're here,' and he marshaled all of us down into the shelter. Selma protested and was embarrassed as hell, and Amos was none too happy at the prospect. But frankly, I was fascinated by the place. Then we heard the horrific explosion above that shook but didn't damage the concrete shelter. For Dyson, that was the proof that the alien invasion was underway, but the rest of us were completely mystified by what was happening. Hours later, when the police finally tried to communicate with us, Dyson was convinced it was an alien trap, and he refused to come out. God knows how long we would have been down there if you hadn't come along."

The police immediately took Parker into protective custody. Selma accompanied him to the police station, where after four hours of questioning and a thorough psychological evaluation, the police released him and drove the couple back to Venice Beach to stay at least temporarily with friends of theirs.

Amos Chandler, who had parked his car several blocks from the Parkers when he came to drop Thurgensen at the Parkers the previous Saturday afternoon, drove home after agreeing to meet Thurgensen and Sonja at the ARB testing facility later that morning.

When Thurgensen and Sonja were finally alone, he asked, "Where's Chris?"

"He's gone," Sonja said in a barely audible voice and then had a full-body meltdown, collapsing in Thurgensen's arms. Sonja proceeded to give an account of all that had transpired the past two days. When she finished, Thurgensen fully grasped the depth of despair to which Sonja had fallen.

"Let's find a hotel where we can get a couple of rooms and get cleaned up," Thurgensen whispered into Sonja's ear.

They quickly found a hotel, rented two rooms, and agreed to meet in an hour. Sonja, who had been in the same, now filthy and torn clothes since Saturday morning, ripped them off and took a long, hot shower. The shower helped, and finding Thurgensen and the others alive raised her spirits a little. But as she sat in her white, hotel terry cloth robe, staring at the wall, she felt numb. At the sound of a knock on her door, Sonja startled and jumped up, relaxing once she heard Thurgensen's familiar voice.

"I bought you some clothes for today. We can shop later to get ready for tomorrow," Thurgensen said, somewhat embarrassed for having shopped for Sonja.

Sonja accepted the bag of clothes and pulled out a pair of jeans, a white sweater, and sandals.

"They're wonderful," Sonja said, trying to sound enthusiastic.

"A nice sales lady helped me pick them out. We guessed on the sizes."

Sonja managed a smile and gave Thurgensen a kiss on the cheek. "Give me ten minutes, and I'll meet you at the car."

The pants proved to be a little tight and the sweater a little too big, but clean clothes and Thurgensen's kind gesture gave Sonja a lift, however small. Fifteen minutes later, they were on their way to the ARB laboratory.

For the first ten minutes, Sonja and Thurgensen rode in awkward silence. Then the old scientist, looking at Sonja's expressionless face, spoke softly but firmly. "Sonja, you and I need to have a talk."

Sonja, without taking her eyes off the road or speaking, simply nodded her head.

Then Thurgensen continued haltingly, trying to find just the right words. "I know you loved Chris, and I know your life has been a living hell, not only for the past two months, but from your childhood. But now you need to decide whether you're simply going to give up or commit to fight this through to the end. Without you, we have no chance of beating EMCO. You're the leader now, and you need to guide all of us through the rest of this.

"When my dear wife died, I was devastated. And then when NJC fired me, I contemplated suicide. I ran away instead and spent ten years in the woods feeling sorry for myself. I wasted my God-given talents. But then you and Chris came along. It was your passion that woke me from my ten-year stupor of self-pity and gave me the courage to fight back. For the first time in years, I felt alive.

"Sonja, you need to decide. Are we going to fight EMCO and its allies or just let them win and watch millions of innocent children and adults die needlessly?"

At first Sonja continued to stare straight ahead as she drove up the freeway, but then she turned toward Thurgensen, tears in her eyes, and reached out to squeeze his hand. With a look of determination, she said, "Let's take the bastards down—all of them."

Sonja then pushed down the accelerator, turned the radio on, and hit a preprogrammed button for a classic rock station that Chris had loved.

* * *

As Sonja and Thurgensen walked down the hall to the testing lab, they immediately noticed that the testing cell was silent and dark.

"Something must have gone wrong," Thurgensen whispered to Sonja.

"Let's find Steve and Chairman Chandler."

When they reached Morris's office, they could see Morris and Chandler poring over a pile of spreadsheets.

"Is there a problem with the test?" Sonja asked.

When Chandler and Morris looked up with enormous smiles, Sonja got her answer.

"The test results are spot on. The correlation of the emission data between our first test last Wednesday and the one we just completed are well within the allowance for test variability. Dr. Thurgensen, your theory was absolutely correct, and now we have the hard evidence to prove it," Morris said.

"But how did you get everything completed so quickly? Yesterday, you were less than optimistic."

"I called in additional staff, and we worked through the night. Fortunately, everything ran smoothly," Morris replied. "The hearing is scheduled for tomorrow at 8:30 a.m. We still have a lot to do."

Sonja clapped her hands together in joy. "Dr. Thurgensen and I will start working on our testimony, but we'll need computers, and we'll need to download copies of the information we gave you previously. Our computers were destroyed in the explosion. Can we set up shop somewhere?"

Morris nodded and led them to the conference room. "I'll be back with everything you need in just a moment."

"Steve, will the hearing be covered by the press and will there be any TV coverage? We need to get the word out quickly to intensify the pressure on EPA not to issue final approval of EZ-15."

Morris laughed. "In Los Angeles, California Air Resources Board hearings don't exactly attract much attention in the TV or print media, what with one celebrity or another getting arrested for drunk driving and being sent to rehab. There is a video feed to the ARB website, and I'll try to stir up some interest with the *LA Times*."

After Morris left the room, Sonja looked fondly at Thurgensen and said, "Thanks for bringing me back to life."

Sonja then called to check for new messages. She was past having any hope that Chris would call, but she wanted to check in case Rebecca had called with any information about Chet and Leon. There were no messages.

Sonja hesitated for a moment, struggling to muster the willpower to call Rebecca, Tanya, and Joanne. Finally, she made the call.

"Rebecca, any news on Chet and Leon?"

"Nothing yet, but we're not giving up hope."

"Can you get Tanya and Joanne to come to the phone and then put your cell on speaker?"

When the three women had gathered, Sonja began. "First, great news ..."

"Chris survived," a voice interrupted at the other end.

"No, Chris is gone," Sonja replied in a barely audible voice.

But regaining her composure, she continued, "The ARB test results confirmed Dr. Thurgensen's theory, and we have the proof we need for the hearing tomorrow that EZ-15 is a killer."

The three women at the other end of the call tried to sound positive, but it was evident that they all were still reeling from the news of Chris's death.

"Chris would have wanted us to fight on. We've got to get the story—the whole damn story—out to the public. We need to create a media firestorm to fan the political flames so that EPA has no choice but to delay or deny final approval of EZ-15."

Then Sonja, seizing the moment, barked out instructions. "The days of beneath the grid are over for the Crew of U Boat EZ-15. It's just us girls now, and it's our time to go public. Here's what we're going to do. First, Tanya, e-mail the final version of your story tonight to Nancy Carter and give her complete license to use it as she sees fit. Also, tell her she can watch tomorrow's ARB public hearing on the ARB website. Second, Rebecca, once you and Tanya agree on the final draft of the newspaper article, e-mail it to your source at the *Herald* late tomorrow afternoon so they can put it in Wednesday's early addition. You can add to that story that Chris was murdered by Petrovic before Petrovic died in an explosion at an abandoned salvage yard near Los Angeles. You can also mention that Petrovic tried but failed to blow up the ARB test facilities on Sunday. Finally, Joanne, now is the time to go to your boss. We've got to have Goodman on our side. He's a vital key."

"I'll go to his office this evening. But I have something I need to confess to him first, and when I do, I'm not sure he'll follow my advice," Joanne said almost apologetically.

"Do the best you can. All you can do is try."

"The information is almost complete, and we'll take care of contacting Nancy Carter and getting the article to the *Herald*," Rebecca chimed in.

"Okay. We're good to go. Good luck, everyone," Sonja said, ending the call.

Thurgensen, his hands on his hips, said, "Now that's what I'm talking about, Sonja. Chris would have been proud of you."

"I had a good teacher ... I just wish he could be here ..."

"Me too, Sonja, but now's the time for the two of us to get to work."

CHAPTER 81

May 23
Washington, DC—Evening

Sitting in her office late at night, Carter lifted her head, rubbed her bloodshot eyes, and ran her fingers through her hair. She had read and reread the documentation prepared by the young black woman. The prose was exquisite, and the efforts at documentation of the events reported admirable. But the story still lacked any substantial confirmation from a credible source. After hours of internal debate, she turned off the computer, stood up, and stretched her back.

I can't run this story. It would be suicidal and most certainly would end my career. If I only had one piece of independent confirmation, I might take the risk. But I don't, she thought as she stared at the ceiling.

Moments later, the private line on her phone rang, and she fumbled to answer it. The person at the other end was silent at first, but then a voice spoke that was all too familiar. "Working this evening. Must be quite a story to keep you at your office this late."

"Foster, what the hell do you want at this time of night? Is President Keller about to announce his resignation in light of his growing incompetence?" Carter said sarcastically, unable to withhold the urge to poke a needle at the president's chief of staff, whom she once dated but now hated with a vengeance.

"Carter, I don't have time to listen to your crap. The White House has irrefutable evidence that you, on at least one occasion, met with a member of a criminal conspiracy. This group of conspirators has already killed several innocent people, all in an effort to derail EPA's final approval of a much-needed product to dramatically reduce global warming emissions. We have it on good authority that this conspiracy is being funded by a secret international cartel.

"I must advise you that you are under FBI suspicion for aiding and abetting this conspiracy. I can tell you that if you attempt to report any information the group may have provided to you, the FBI will arrest you immediately, and you will be charged with treason."

"Bing, I have no idea what you're talking about," Carter protested.

"Don't give me that line of bullshit. You know exactly what I'm talking about, and I swear the government will come down hard on you—real hard!" Foster threatened and abruptly hung up.

Foster, you just messed with the wrong woman. Then turning on her computer, she whispered, "I think I just got the independent confirmation I needed. Looks like this is going to be a long evening."

*   *   *

The time was approaching 11:00 p.m., but Senator Maxwell Goodman, who had the reputation for being the hardest-working member of Congress, gave no sign of ending his work as he sifted through piles of papers and reports on his desk. His concentration was broken when he heard a shuffling sound coming from the outer office. Slowly opening his top desk drawer, he grabbed a pistol he kept just in case some disgruntled crazy slipped through security.

Then a figure emerged slowly from the darkness and entered.

"Joanne, my God, where have you been? We've all been worried sick," he said as he got up, raced around his large oak desk, and awkwardly hugged her.

"I'm okay, but we need to talk."

Goodman led Joanne to the chair in front of his desk, motioning her to sit down. Pouring her a glass of ice water, he then pulled up another chair and sat next to her.

"You remember the Goldslide investigation and the committee report I worked on as a junior staffer years ago?" Joanne began, her hands gripped tightly on her lap.

"Of course. What about it?"

"I gave confidential information to Stanley Braxton before the committee made its results public. I know it was wrong, but Braxton convinced me that if he had inside information, he could be of help to us and the investigation. Instead, he used the information for his own benefit. Braxton held the fact that I leaked confidential material over me ever since, but I swear I never did anything unethical like that again," Joanne said, her voice shaking.

Goodman said nothing but looked directly at his young staffer.

"I'm prepared to resign right now, but I beg you to listen to what I have to tell you. It's going to sound crazy and beyond belief, but I swear everything I'm about to say is true," McKay pleaded as she lowered her head into her hands and wept uncontrollably.

Goodman reached out and touched Joanne gently on her shoulder. "Releasing that information was certainly inappropriate, but you didn't do it for personal gain. You thought it would help this office and serve a just cause. In our business, walking the line between trying to do what is needed to serve the greater good and always acting within the narrow lines of propriety is damn near impossible. When, or whether, to cross that line isn't always easy to decide. But I can assure you that anyone, and I mean anyone, who has been on Capitol Hill for very long has wrestled with that very question. Believe me, no one I know up here in Congress can claim to have never crossed over that line."

"But, I ...," Joanne said softly.

"If you try to resign, I'll refuse to accept it. Joanne, over the past five years, you've become not only my best staff member, but the committee's most valuable staff person as well. We have a lot of important work to do, and I need your help. It's time to put the Goldslide incident behind us."

Then Goodman said, "Now wipe those tears away and tell me what's so important."

Joanne told him everything that had happened, including the threats she received from Braxton, her alerting O'Brian that Foster had set a trap for him, Braxton's attempt to kill her, her rescue by O'Brian's comrades, and finally, the ARB hearing scheduled for the next day that would blow the lid off the EMCO EZ-15 conspiracy.

When Joanne finished, Goodman stood up and declared, "Joanne, you and I have a lot of work to do tonight. Are you up for it?"

"Absolutely. And this should help," McKay said as she handed him a CD with a copy of information Tanya Jones had given to Nancy Carter and the article for the *Herald*.

CHAPTER 82

May 24
Pasadena, California

The ARB public hearing, which was routinely held on the fourth Tuesday of every month, was scheduled to start at 8:30 a.m. in the historic Pasadena Civic Auditorium—a beautiful stone and masonry structure with a lofted, red-tiled roof. The cavernous, three-thousand-seat auditorium was less than a quarter filled with attendees, including about two hundred junior high school students. The hearing agenda was light, with only two items: approval of ARB funding for several University of Southern California research projects, and EMCO's EZ-15.

Standing at the entrance to the vast meeting room, Sonja saw to her left and near the front of the auditorium a group of well-dressed men and women huddled in conversation—the EMCO contingent, she surmised. To her right, Sonja spotted Barbara Simon from Protect the Environment Consortium, sitting alone.

As Sonja and Thurgensen moved quietly and took seats in the far back corner, she spotted a lone camera mounted on a less-than-stable tripod that would record the video feed of the hearing directly to the ARB website. She saw no one who appeared to be from the media.

Standing on the elevated stage at the podium and making final preparations for the start of the hearing, Morris nodded slightly to Sonja and Thurgensen as they took their seats. Neither Sonja nor Thurgensen had been listed as giving testimony at the hearing, and Steve intended to keep their presence a secret until just the right moment.

Diligently completing his preparation tasks, Morris was unaware that directly beneath his feet, below the stage floor, and connected to a bundle of dynamite, was a timing device ticking away. At precisely 8:45 a.m. the device would ignite the dynamite with enough explosive power to kill everyone inside.

Meanwhile, unaware of the impending doom, Sonja sat nervously in her seat at the thought of having to give a statement in public for the first time in her life. She wiped her sweaty palms on her black slacks. The courage and resolve she had felt moments earlier had disappeared as her time to testify grew near.

Thurgensen, who was relishing the moment, noticed Sonja's growing distress, grabbed her hand, and whispered, "Relax, my dear. This is our moment. I'm pretty sure that EMCO and their allies don't have a backup plan to resurrect EZ-15 after we testify. Today we're going to blow EZ-15 and EMCO away."

Sonja stared straight ahead for a moment and then turned to Thurgensen. "We've got to get out of here!"

"Sonja, now isn't the time to run away."

"I'm not talking about running away. The last thing Chris said to me was that Petrovic always had a backup plan. We didn't find a second explosive device at the lab, because I'm guessing some of his operatives put the device here. What better place. In one explosion, they kill the ARB staff, the ARB Executive Board, and us. Then there's nothing left to prevent EPA from giving EZ-15 final approval tomorrow."

Without giving the befuddled Thurgensen a chance to respond, Sonja jumped up from her seat and waved frantically at Morris, trying to gain his attention. When he finally saw her, Sonja motioned him to follow her out into the hall.

"What's up?" Morris asked.

Sonja, gasping for breath, explained her theory that a bomb had been planted.

"Sonja, they're not going to blow up the building knowing that their CEO is in the room."

"Steve, look. Johansson isn't with the EMCO group, and even if he was, they could easily find a new CEO. What they can't afford is having the EPA approval of EZ-15 delayed."

457

Finally, Morris nodded affirmatively and ran quickly back to the podium. "We request that everyone immediately evacuate the building," Morris said as calmly as possible. But when people in the audience were slow to react, he shouted, "We have a report that there may be a bomb in the building! Please—"

He needed to say no more as people scrambled to evacuate the building. The bomb squad arrived within seven minutes and began frantically searching the auditorium and the rest of the building.

The captain of the bomb squad nervously looked at his watch, which read 8:40 am. Then he spotted a utility trapdoor at the back corner of the stage and raced to it. Quickly ripping open the cover, the man lowered himself down the opening. Moments later, a voice rang out from underneath the stage, "Oh my God!"

After carefully and successfully disengaging the timer from the explosive device, with barely two minutes to spare, he emerged triumphantly through the trapdoor and said, "Got it!"

By the time the bomb squad finally signaled the all clear, it was nearly 11:00 a.m. The hearing participants, including Johansson, who had been conveniently absent earlier, filtered back into the room.

Amos Chandler formally commenced the hearing. The number of people in attendance had dwindled, and the school children had left with something far more interesting to tell their classmates and parents than simply attending a boring ARB hearing.

The first agenda item on the research grants was completed in ten minutes.

"Here we go," Thurgensen said as he squeezed Sonja's hand.

"The next item on our agenda is EMCO's global warming emission-reduction product, EZ-15. I see the first person signed up to testify is Barbara Simon from Protect the Environment Consortium," Chandler announced.

Barbara Simon presented pretty much the same information she gave at the conference in Brussels, but she included slides and information on the environmental benefits of EZ-15's use in California. Sonja noticed that several times Simon glanced in the direction of Johansson, almost like she was looking for his approval.

When Simon completed her testimony, Chandler spoke. "Thank you Ms. Simon. I have a question. Do you or the folks at Protect the

Environment Consortium have any concerns regarding any possible adverse environmental consequences of using EZ-15?"

Simon said with an air of complete confidence, "We have absolutely no concerns regarding any possible adverse impacts from the use of this product that is desperately needed to help reduce CO2 emissions in order to help address the growing threat of global warming and climate change."

In the back of the room, Sonja mumbled to herself, "That lying worm."

Simon started to leave, when Chandler asked a question to which he already knew the answer, "I'm sorry, Ms. Simon, one more question. Has Protect the Environment Consortium ever received monetary contributions from EMCO Consolidated Company?"

Simon froze, and her complexion turned pale. At first she stuttered, but finally she regained her composure and replied, "We receive contributions from many sources—concerned citizens, foundation grants, and limited contributions from the private sector. With regard to EMCO, I would have to consult with our financial officer and get back to you."

"Thank you, Ms. Simon. The ARB looks forward to receiving that information from your organization."

The next three witnesses were representatives from local commercial enterprises that planned to distribute the EZ-15 additive to refineries in California. They presented detailed statistics on the number of jobs that would be created in California, the stimulus effect to the economy from EZ-15, and the resulting tax revenues to the State of California. Neither Chandler nor the other board members had any questions for the witnesses.

Next Chandler called upon EMCO. Johansson confidently strolled up to the microphone. What followed was a dazzling, multimedia presentation that, no doubt, cost tens of thousands of dollars to prepare and was reminiscent of the presentation Russell gave in Brussels. Johansson showed slides and video clips of the ravishing effects of climate change, EMCO's research and development facilities, data and charts on the enormous investments EMCO had made, and the great benefits of using EZ-15 to reduce global warming emissions.

When the presentation was completed, Johansson said, "I would be happy to answer any questions the board might have."

"Thank you, Mr. Johansson, for a truly impressive presentation," Chandler said politely. "I have one question, which is similar to question I asked Ms. Simon. In EMCO's extensive research in developing the product and in assessing the effects of using EZ-15 on the environment, has EMCO or any of your consultants identified any evidence that would suggest that EZ-15 could possibly have any adverse impact on the public health and welfare?"

Johansson, looking every bit like he relished the question, puffed out his chest and replied, "EMCO has spent over twenty million dollars testing and analyzing the impact of EZ-15 on the environment, both in our testing laboratories and through independent testing facilities. We have found absolutely no evidence of any harmful side effects from using EZ-15. EMCO has shared this data with both the ARB and the US EPA, and as you know, EPA has given preliminary approval of EZ-15. We anticipate receiving final EPA approval tomorrow."

"Mr. Johansson, thank you again for your testimony," Chandler said.

Then the chairman added almost as an afterthought, "Mr. Morris, I believe that completes our list of persons who signed up in advance to testify at today's hearing. Have any additional persons or organizations signed up today to present testimony?"

"Yes, Mr. Chairman, two people," Steve Morris said, doing his best to suppress the smile that was trying to burst out across his face. Morris turned and handed a piece of paper to Chandler just as they had planned.

"Thank you, Steve." Then looking out into the audience, Chandler continued. "The first person listed is Sonja Voinovich. Ms. Voinovich, would you please step to the speaker's podium?"

As Sonja stood up and started the long walk down to the front of the auditorium, Johansson jumped to his feet. "I object! That woman is a fugitive from justice. She's a discredited and disgruntled former low-level US EPA employee."

"Mr. Johansson. This is a public hearing, not a legal action in a courtroom. With all due respect, you cannot object," Chandler said sternly.

"But ...," Johansson sputtered as the other EMCO representatives rose to protest as well.

"Mr. Johansson, I'm warning you for the last time. If you, or any member of your team, say one more word, I will call security to have you removed—forcibly removed, if necessary. Are we clear on this?"

Johansson nodded and slumped back in his chair.

Sonja continued walking nervously down to the podium. Her knees buckled, and she almost fell. She looked back in desperation at Thurgensen, who motioned her forward with his hands. She turned around but stopped.

Chandler asked, "Are you all right, Ms. Voinovich?"

Sonja didn't answer but begin walking forward again. As she glanced over at Johansson, who glared menacingly at her, she felt lightheaded and wanted desperately to flee. But she kept moving forward.

Upon reaching the podium, she dropped the unbound, written copy of her testimony, and pages flew in all directions. "Sorry," she said, almost in tears as she scrambled to pick up the pages.

Finally, Sonja began haltingly, "My name is Sonja Voinovich. I am a former analyst at the US Environmental Protection Agency ..." But as she looked down to read her prepared statement, Sonja realized the pages were out of order.

"This is ridiculous," Sonja heard someone in audience mutter, and she turned to look, only to see Johansson smiling smugly.

Sonja turned back, put her hands on the edges of the podium, bowed her head, and closed her eyes. Suddenly, she heard a voice deep within her speaking softly. *"Think of the children dying, the grieving families. You can do this."*

"Ms. Voinovich, are you able to continue?" Chandler asked, with concern.

"Yes." And as Sonja began, her posture straightened. She never looked at her written testimony again.

The young woman proceeded to weave a tale that kept everyone in the room riveted and the EMCO contingent squirming. She began by describing the analysis Ronnie Chapman had documented that proved a chemical imbalance in the emission testing on EZ-15, suggesting that pollutants were escaping detection by the testing equipment.

"Ms. Voinovich, I must interrupt you. The test data EPA submitted to this agency showed no chemical imbalance," Chandler said, knowing full well what would come next.

"The EPA data you received was doctored," Sonja calmly replied.

"That's outrageous!" one of the EMCO attorneys blurted out.

"Sir, I warned you—no outbreaks," Chandler said angrily. Pointing at the now sheepish-looking lawyer, he said, "Please leave this hearing room, immediately."

"Ms. Voinovich, what proof do you have to support your claim?" Chandler asked.

"I have one of the original EPA CDs that contained the data that was the basis of Ronnie Chapman's analysis and that proves my statement. I have given that CD to Mr. Morris."

Steve Morris nodded affirmatively and held up the CD.

"Ms. Voinovich, do you have a theory regarding the possible causes for and resulting impact from the escaping pollutants that caused the chemical imbalance?" Chandler asked.

"I believe the next witness will be able to answer that question better than I, but with your permission, I would like to focus on empirical evidence linking the use of EZ-15 with adverse environmental impacts."

"Please preceed, Ms. Voinovich."

"I have conducted a detailed analysis showing that in Osaka and Tokyo, where EZ-15 has been added to motor vehicle gasoline, a significant increase in the instances of asthma attacks and asthma-related deaths among children, the infirm, and the elderly have occurred when the ambient temperatures are eighty degrees F or higher, the humidity is in excess of 70 percent, and ground-level ozone reaches a concentration above 0.050 ppm level. I have given Mr. Morris a copy of my analysis."

Sonja completed her testimony by describing the suspicious deaths of Chapman, Goldberg, Sanchez, and Mueller, all of whom were linked in some way to trying to prove that EZ-15 posed a serious health risk.

When Sonja completed her testimony, Chandler asked the other board members if they had any questions. But they were so blown away by Sonja's testimony, they could hardly speak.

"Thank you, Ms. Voinovich. The next witness is Karl Thurgensen. Dr. Thurgensen, could you please come to the podium?"

As Sonja and Thurgensen passed in the aisle, Thurgensen whispered to Sonja, "You knocked them dead."

When Thurgensen arrived at the podium, Chandler asked, "Dr. Thurgensen, Ms. Voinovich has raised many serious charges about the effects of EZ-15, but she has offered no explanation to substantiate them. Are you here to enlighten us?"

"Indeed I am," Thurgensen said. He was in his element and loving every moment of it. He reviewed his impressive credentials as a scientist. Next he explained, in nontechnical terms people could understand, how the supercharged, subatomic carbon particles created during the combustion process when EZ-15 was added to the fuel escaped through the conventional test filters. Then he explained that these particles, having been activated by chemicals used in the EZ-15 formula, became a magnet, which under the right ambient conditions and air-quality levels, attracted a host of harmful chemicals that were then carried deep into the lungs.

Thurgensen concluded his testimony by adding, "For children, the infirm, and the elderly, who were asthma sufferers, these harmful chemicals triggered serious lung irritations that caused asthma attacks. In many cases, the asthma attacks were so severe they resulted in the death of the victim."

When Thurgensen finished, Chandler asked, again knowing full well the answer, "Do you have any test data to verify your theory?"

"That is a question your Mr. Morris can answer far better than I."

Amos Chandler thanked Thurgensen and then turned the proceedings over to Steve Morris.

Morris detailed the test protocols ARB used and the emission tests results collected.

"The two tests we ran had very close correlation and clearly confirm that Dr. Thurgensen's theory and the testimony of Ms. Voinovich were correct. The entire ARB staff unanimously agrees that the use of EZ-15 poses a serious health risk that potentially could result in the deaths of millions of people."

"Does the staff have a recommendation for the ARB Executive Board?" Chandler asked.

"We do, Mr. Chairman. The staff recommends that ARB submit a transcript of this hearing and all the related ARB test data immediately to the US EPA, that ARB adopt and submit to the US EPA a resolution calling for an indefinite postponement of EPA's final approval of EZ-15 pending further evaluations, and finally, that ARB adopt an order banning immediately the use of EZ-15 in California."

Johansson could contain himself no longer. "This is an outrage! You can't do this! I protest—"

"Dr. Johansson, silence! You are completely out of order, and I'm ordering security to escort you from this building immediately," Chandler barked.

Chandler then read aloud the previously prepared resolution and the order, which the board passed unanimously.

At the back of the room, Thurgensen and Sonja hugged each other as she jumped up and down like a little girl who had just won first prize. The EMCO contingent slinked silently away through a side door.

* * *

As the video feed of the hearing on the ARB website ended, Nancy Carter looked up at the clock, which read 5:15 p.m. Eastern time. She had forty-five minutes to work with her crew and make sure everything was ready for the six o'clock broadcast.

Three-quarters of an hour later, as the CNP cameras went live, Carter knew that this was *the* moment of her twenty-year career. Her heart racing, Carter began, "Good evening. Tonight's program will be devoted entirely to a shocking, breaking story. Today the California Air Resource Board revealed data that President Keller's solution to address climate change, a product called EZ-15, designed to significantly reduce carbon dioxide emissions from gasoline-powered vehicles and equipment, is, in fact, responsible for the deaths of thousands of people in Japan, where the product currently is in use. The ARB has called on the US EPA to withhold final approval of EZ-15, which EPA had intended to give tomorrow.

"But this shocking news is only the tip of the iceberg. Today, I will report on an alleged international conspiracy involving domestic and foreign corporations, overseas investors, and high-ranking members of the Keller administration, as well as rogue FBI and DHS agents working together to prevent damaging information on EZ-15 from reaching the public. The goal of these conspirators was to make billions in profit at the expense of the health and welfare of people here in the United States and around the world."

Over the next thirty minutes, Carter masterfully guided her TV viewing audience on a journey of intrigue, corruption, greed, murder, and mayhem. The telephone lines began to light up, and the Neilson tracking system reported a meteoric climb in viewership. As the thirty-minute show was drawing to a close, Carter still had lots more to cover, but she knew she needed to wrap things up. Then the show's producer, standing off camera, slipped a piece of paper on Carter's desk.

"Folks, I've just been informed that our program is being extended another thirty minutes. Stay tuned. There's much more to report on this story, and you won't want to miss a minute."

When the show finally ended at seven o'clock, the crew broke out in wild applause for Carter. The show's producer yelled, "We just hit an all-time high for viewership!"

Everyone started clapping again. Carter, who two weeks earlier was on the verge of being dumped by CNP, simply sat back in her chair and grinned.

CHAPTER 83

May 25
Washington, DC

At precisely one minute after midnight, the *Washington Herald* posted an article on the newspaper's website, "Keller Administration Linked to Conspiracy Promoting Lethal CO2 Emission Reduction Product." The article, which was designed to create a buzz to generate interest in the full story that would appear in the *Herald*'s early-morning addition, named names but was short on details. The Internet article had the desired effect, and when the *Herald* hit the streets at 5:00 a.m., people were already standing in line to get a copy. Among those anxiously waiting were reporters from other news sources, as well as congressional interns and low-level staff members in the Keller administration.

The "story" in the *Herald* actually consisted of three separate articles, all of which started on the front page. The first article covered the same elements of the EZ-15 conspiracy that Nancy Carter reported on her show, but included much more detail. The second article disclosed the alleged illegal activities and named the members of the Heritage Study Group, a topic that Carter hadn't covered. The bylines for the articles listed as the reporters Tanya Williams, Rebecca Bergman, and Robert Levy (in memoriam). The third article, written by a fellow *Herald* reporter and close friend of Levy, lauded Levy's considerable talents and contributions as a *Herald* reporter and reported that Levy allegedly was murdered by unknown assassins to prevent him from publishing his research on the Heritage Study Group.

The three articles, which were also posted on the *Herald*'s website, created a raging firestorm that spread throughout and rocked the nation's capital. EMCO, EZ-15, and the Keller administration quickly became the one and only story that was on the lips of every government official, lobbyist, and stockbroker. As news of the CNP reports and the *Washington Herald* stories spread to the European and Asian stock exchanges, which had already opened, the value of EMCO stock dropped precipitously.

*   *   *

At 9:00 a.m., Senator Maxwell Goodman stood in the stately, high-ceiling, wood-paneled Senate Environmental Committee hearing room and asked the hastily gathered press and media people to take their seats. As he began, Goodman was flanked by every member of his committee.

"Thank you for coming on such short notice," Goodman began, fully aware that no self-respecting reporter in Washington would miss this press event for anything.

"This morning I wish to make three announcements related to the ongoing EMCO EZ-15 situation. First, based on the unanimous vote of the committee members standing here today, the Senate Environment Committee will present EPA with a formal request to delay final approval of EZ-15, pending consideration of the new information and claims that have been reported on CNP and in the *Washington Herald*.

"Second, should EPA fail to delay approval of EZ-15, our committee has drafted and will present to the full Senate, legislation blocking, indefinitely, the introduction of EZ-15 in the United States. I have the assurances of both the Senate majority and minority leaders, as well as the Speaker of the House of Representatives, that our legislation will be introduced and voted on today in both houses of Congress with strong bipartisan support.

"Finally, our committee will commence a comprehensive investigation and hold extensive hearings on every aspect of the alleged illegal activity inside the government and in the private sector. To lead this investigation, I am appointing my new chief of staff, Joanne McKay. Ms. McKay has a long history of excellent service to me and this committee and is already intimately familiar with many aspects of the alleged conspiracy. I have every confidence that Ms. McKay will do a very thorough job in helping our committee get to the bottom of this horrible travesty and begin to restore the public's faith in its political leaders, which I am sure has been deeply shaken."

Then the senator introduced McKay to the press. The committee members and staff, who had been briefed by Goodman on her role in bringing the EMCO conspiracy to light, applauded loudly and cheered her appointment. Joanne's face turned crimson as she tried not to smile but failed. She beamed at the reaction from the committee members and her colleagues.

*   *   *

When the US stock exchange opened at 9:30 a.m., EMCO stock, which had hit an all-time high of ninety-five dollars the previous day, crashed immediately. When the trading price on the stock hit forty-five dollars, an automatic trigger halted trading for a mandatory four-hour period before trading could resume. The automatic trading halt trigger was designed by the Securities and Exchange Commission to prevent panic selling on a given stock that could cause a broader collapse in the market.

At 10:30 a.m., without any fanfare, the US EPA issued a written statement to the media that the agency would withhold final approval pending "an evaluation of the information submitted by the California Air Resources Board." This meek gesture by the Keller administration was simply too little, too late. Officials in Japan had already ordered an immediate halt to use of EZ-15's in Tokyo and Osaka. Everyone in Washington, unless they were hopeless optimists or completely clueless, knew that EZ-15 was dead, and EMCO with it.

When trading on EMCO stock resumed at 2:30 p.m., the share price dropped below four dollars. Shortly thereafter, the Securities and Exchange Commission announced that it would initiate an investigation into possible stock manipulation and fraud by EMCO officials and others.

*   *   *

Foster had locked himself away in his White House office as soon as the word of the EMCO EZ-15 disaster broke. President Keller's chief of staff racked his brain, trying to figure out how to escape from being destroyed along with every other person who had been involved in the EZ-15 quagmire. Finally, a plan began to emerge.

I'll demand a meeting with Keller immediately. I'll tell him my involvement in the EZ-15 matter was entirely based on supporting an important strategic ally of the United States in the Middle East—Crown Prince Syed and the royal family. I'll warn Keller that he should grant me immunity from prosecution based on considerations of national security. In exchange, I will resign immediately as chief of staff and make myself available to the appropriate authorities to provide any information in my possession regarding those who have been accused of misconduct.

Brilliant! Foster thought, clapping his hands together. He picked up the phone and hit the button for the president's private line. Twenty minutes later, Foster emerged from the Oval Office with an enormous grin on his face. Keller had enthusiastically embraced every aspect of Foster's plan.

Hell, I may come out of this looking like a hero. At worst, I'll have no trouble finding gigs on TV as a political analyst. Even better, I'll write a book, Foster thought as he waved good-bye to the president's personal secretary.

*   *   *

Shortly after four in the afternoon, Daniel Witt sat in his home office with an expression of complete satisfaction. Having sold the EMCO Puts well below the Put target price in his joint account, Dan and his wife had become instant millionaires. Behind Dan, Katie, her mouth and eyes wide open and her hands clutching her chest, let out a shriek of pure joy as she looked at the value of their investment account. Their children, who were playing in the kitchen, rushed to the basement stairs and screamed, "Mommy, what's wrong?"

"Nothing, children," Dan and Katie said almost in unison as they hugged each other tightly.

"Why don't you go upstairs to check on those two rascals? I'll be up in a minute, but I want to make sure the transaction is reflected in the other ten offshore accounts. We'll have a chance to celebrate later," Dan whispered as he playfully nibbled on his wife's ear.

*   *   *

As the grandfather clock in his study chimed five times, Judge Thomas Worthington sat at his desk, rocking back in his chair and staring at the ceiling. On his desk was a copy of his will, an opened mahogany box containing close to $15,000, and his Marine service revolver.

The judge had no illusions he could escape the firestorm that was about to consume him. By gambling that EMCO stock would continue to increase in value, he had leveraged all the family's wealth. With EMCO almost certain to go bankrupt, he would be left penniless save the $15,000 sitting on the desk. But far worse, his involvement with the Heritage Study Group would forever ruin his reputation and tarnish the proud heritage of the Worthington family.

He rocked his chair upright, grabbed the pistol from the desk, and took one last melancholy look around the room. "At least I can die honorably," Worthington said forcibly as he shoved the pistol in his mouth and pointed it at the roof of his mouth.

As he slowly squeezed the trigger, Worthington had second thoughts and attempted to remove the weapon. But the gun discharged, and the bullet instead of entering his brain, passed through the side of his throat—partially severing an artery.

At the sound of a gunshot, Rosanna, who was working well past her normal quitting time, dropped the cleaner and cloth she was using to wash the windows in the hallway. Racing into the study, she screamed in horror at the sight of Judge Worthington in his chair, wearing a grotesque expression on his blood-soaked face while massive amounts of blood sprayed from his neck.

Worthington pleaded to his housekeeper to call for help, but his words were incomprehensible as blood gushed from his open mouth. As she walked hesitantly toward Worthington, her sense of shock turned to fear and then to bitter hate. She stared without compassion at the man who had violated her so many times and who wanted to have sex with her dear, precious Anita.

When Rosanna reached the desk, Worthington's hands flayed as his head shook violently in desperation for help. The housekeeper spotted the box filled with $15,000 in cash. After hesitating, she reached over and clutched the money tightly in her fingers.

Then glaring at Worthington, Rosanna said, "You filthy pig, you'll never harm me again or ever touch my daughter. This money will help pay for Anita's education. You owe us that much for everything you've done to me."

Spitting on Worthington's desk and putting the cash in her apron pocket, she turned and walked out of the study, down the hall, and out the front door of the mansion, never to return. Ten minutes later, after unspeakable suffering, Thomas Worthington breathed his last breath.

*   *   *

Crown Prince Abdul Syed wandered aimlessly around his enormous, lavish, and beautifully appointed master bedroom suite on the top floor of the family palace. It had been a very bad day. His extensive investing in EMCO stock over the past year had, in one day, cost the royal family a fortune. But as the evening approached midnight, his spirits lifted. First, while Syed's investment had lost the family nearly two billion dollars, that amount was only a small amount of the family's incredible wealth. Second, he was and always would be the darling of the family. Third, even though he knew Hassid Kabar privately had counseled him not to invest so heavily in EMCO, he would blame Kabar for investing in the chemical company.

"After all, who would my family believe—the crown prince or a lowly employee?" Syed sighed smugly.

As the crown prince took another healthy swallow from the crystal goblet containing Frapin Cuvee 1888 cognac, he pushed a button on his intercom summoning Kabar. When Hassid Kabar entered, Syed quickly informed Kabar that he must take the blame for the EMCO disaster.

For a long moment, Kabar stood silently without emotion, but then he laughed.

Syed, outraged at the show of disrespect, started to shout, but his words became garbled. Gasping and choking, the crown prince clutched his throat with his hands and then frantically beckoned Kabar to come to his aid.

As the crown prince writhed in excruciating pain from the effect of the poison in the cognac, Kabar slowly walked over to him. His eyes now glaring and his face muscles taut with anger, Kabar said with scorn, "You have disgraced the royal family for the last time with your sinful debauchery, your Western ways, and your foolish mishandling of the family's wealth. Your miserable life in this world is about to end, and you must face the wrath of Allah in the next."

Kabar placed a suicide note on the bedside table, took out his cell phone, and called the crown prince's brother. "It is done."

CHAPTER 84

June 5
Washington, DC

Around four o'clock on a rainy Sunday afternoon, Sonja pulled into the driveway of a small Methodist church in the southeast section of the District of Columbia. She was already late, having stopped several times on the way, unsure whether she had the strength to endure the final gathering of the U-boat EZ-15 Crew to honor its fallen comrades.

As she reached the entrance, she paused and reflected on the madness of the past twelve days. The firestorm of media frenzy that had exploded since the EZ-15 conspiracy story had broken, and the numerous investigations now underway involving many of the nation's most prominent figures was unprecedented, even by Washington's always tumultuous standards. The EMCO EZ-15 scandal dominated the print, Internet, and broadcast media, featuring one shocking story after another. The FBI, DHS, and Department of Justice, as well as the House and Senate Environment Committees, all launched investigations and held hearings.

Each surviving member of the EZ-15 U-boat Crew endured endless, harsh questioning from one investigating authority after another, almost always outside of the public view. With one exception, they were treated with distrust and never thanked for their role in helping to prevent EZ-15 from potentially killing millions of people throughout the world. The exception was the Senate Environment Committee investigation led by Joanne McKay, which produced the most thorough information on the scandal, all of which would soon be released to the public.

While members of the Crew never were officially exonerated, no legal action was taken against them.

As horrific and exhausting as the past days had been for Sonja and her colleagues, it was nothing compared to what happened to the others involved in the scandal.

FBI chief Calvin Wiseman was forced to take early retirement because of his bungling of the raid in Baltimore and other "non-disclosed" reasons.

Members of the Heritage Study Group fared far worse. Kowalski was fired by Goodman the same day that Joanne McKay was named to replace him. Two days later, the US attorney for the District of Columbia issued an indictment on multiple charges against Kowalski.

Reverend McCormick had appeared on his weekly TV show the Sunday after the EZ-15 story broke. He tearfully pleaded for forgiveness, a Bible in one hand and a cross in the other, to his TV audience of millions and a live audience of two thousand parishioners in the huge sanctuary of his church. In response to the reverend's heart-wrenching appeal, McCormick received an overwhelmingly favorable response from his flock, and donations to his church were actually up for the week. Unfortunately for the good reverend, the US Department of Justice wasn't so forgiving, and he was indicted on thirteen charges of conspiracy, fraud, and stock manipulation. McCormick faced decades in prison.

Investment adviser Lester Moody had his broker license revoked, and he and the now former FCC board member Alan Hastings, former Federal Reserve Board member Thomas Rogers, and liberal talking head Larry Wasserman were also all facing multiple felony charges. Multimillionaire Roman Cherkoff, often rumored to have ties to the Russian mafia, was found brutally murdered in his lavish home in the outskirts of Moscow.

Finally, Ted Bennett, the now former assistant administrator for air quality at the US EPA was formally charged for his involvement in manipulating EPA test data and lying to federal officials and the DC police. The EPA bureaucrat faced life imprisonment for his crimes.

President Keller, who had accepted Bingeman Foster's resignation, was scrambling to push back the flood of ever-increasing bad press and falling popularity in the polls. First, he summarily fired EPA administrator Newton Hill—not because Hill was involved in any wrongdoing, but because Keller needed someone in his administration to take the blame. To replace Hill, Keller appointed the acting general counsel, Conrad Martin, to assume the position of acting EPA administrator.

Next, in an act of desperation, Keller, with great fanfare, announced his new Global Warming Initiative. The Keller administration would award a twenty-million-dollar grant to Medico Fuel. The Medico "Black Box" technology touted by its inventor as a fuel economy enhancer and therefore a "CO_2 emission-reduction technology" was almost universally regarded as a joke and was criticized openly by unnamed EPA officials, other scientists, and the environmental community. Even the Protect the Environment Consortium's Barbara Simon, who was trying desperately to salvage her own career, passionately criticized Keller's new initiative. By the end of the year, President Keller's approval rating would fall below 25 percent.

A week after EPA's decision, EMCO Consolidated Company filed for bankruptcy. But that wasn't the end to EMCO's problems. The European Commission also had established a special investigation committee, appointing Sir Reginald Longshank as the committee's chairman. Longshank was well qualified and had a personal grudge to avenge. His committee would be relentless in investigating EMCO officials and others involved.

Sonja finally mustered the courage to enter the church. The exhilaration she had felt immediately after the ARB hearing had quickly disappeared. In its place, the strain of the endless hearings and being called upon to relive again and again all the horrible events of the past two months had taken its toll. Sonja had spiraled deeper and deeper into a seemingly bottomless pit of depression.

The young woman took a deep breath and entered the church's basement. She saw sitting at the table members of the Crew and several other familiar faces. There were five empty seats: Sonja's, one for Otto, one for Chris, and the other two she assumed for Chet and Leon. One person at the table she didn't know. But when the young man turned toward her at the sound of her entering, she knew immediately who it was. Corbin O'Brian looked every bit like his dad.

The conversation at the table was very animated, which wasn't too surprising, since the Crew members had recently been informed by Daniel Witt that Chris had instructed Witt to open offshore accounts for each of them, and those accounts were now worth millions. When they saw Sonja, the conversation stopped, and everyone stood up.

First to greet her were Selma and Dyson Parker. Dyson, with his hair neatly cut, his face freshly shaved, and neatly dressed, was barely recognizable. As Selma hugged Sonja, she whispered, "Dyson's going to AA meetings and hasn't had a drink. It's only been a week, but I think he's going to make it this time. Of course, he still believes the house was blown up by aliens, but we're making progress."

Sonja saw Tanya and started walking to her when Casey hollered, "It's about time!" Everyone turned toward the entrance, and there was Chet, in a wheelchair, with one leg in an ankle-to-hip cast and his chest wrapped in bandages, being pushed by Leon, who had a cast on his left arm and a bandage around his forehead. Leon and Chet, both severely wounded in the Baltimore assault, were recovering well. Chet fully expected, probably a little too optimistically, to be back on his feet in a matter weeks. In the meantime, he decided to enjoy being waited on by Leon, Tanya, and his sister, Kathy.

When the EZ-15 story broke, all charges against Chet and Leon related to the Baltimore raid were quietly dropped, and they were released from custody. Why the FBI refused to disclose, immediately after the raid, whether Chet and Leon were alive or dead had never been explained.

Sonja turned back to Tanya and grabbed the young woman's hands, and then they wrapped their arms around each other. Sonja tried but couldn't speak as more tears welled up in her eyes.

"I'm so sorry about Chris," Tanya said softly.

But Sonja interrupted, "I'm okay, don't worry about me. What do you and Leon have planned now that this nightmare is over?"

"You're not going to believe it. Nancy Carter got me an interview with the director of admissions at the Columbia School of Journalism. Members of the admissions committee had read my story in the *Herald,* and I think I have a shot at getting accepted. Leon, who has always wanted to go to a top medical school, now has the money to do it."

Sonja made her way around the table as Karl Thurgensen stood up and hugged her awkwardly. "Sonja, I'm so sorry about everything that has happened to you, but you're personally responsible for saving untold thousands of lives. I hope that gives you some measure of comfort as you move forward with your life."

They hugged silently for a long moment as she quietly sobbed. Regaining her composure, she forced a smile and said, "Good luck in your new position as senior scientist at the National Academy of Sciences."

Finally, Sonja let go. "I'll be okay," she said, trying to convince herself.

Taking the vacant seat next to the young man, Sonja extended her hand to him. Corbin O'Brian responded politely but was clearly uncomfortable being with this strange group of characters.

"My name is Sonja Voinovich. I was a close friend of your father's. We asked you to come today because everyone in this room owes your father a great debt of gratitude. Don't believe anything you hear in the media about your dad. The simple truth is he was a hero who probably will never get the credit he deserves."

The young man seemed to relax somewhat as Sonja continued, "I once asked your dad the one thing he wished for, and he said that he wished that you would know that he loved you and that he never stopped caring for your mother."

Sonja looked into Corbin's eyes, but she couldn't decipher what he was feeling. So she continued. "Your dad saw you play soccer this spring against Virginia."

"What?" Corbin responded as he stared at Sonja.

"Your dad saw you set up the winning goal. He told me that when the two Virginia defensemen cut your legs out from under you, he almost ran out on the field to see if you were okay."

"Wow! I wish I had seen him. I always loved my dad, and I always will," Corbin said quietly.

"Your dad also saw your mom with another man at the game, and he said they both looked happy together."

"Yes, Mike Masters. He's a work colleague of mother, and they're planning to get married this fall. I think it's good. Mom and Dad just fell out of love with one another. It hurt me. But looking back, I know my dad's decision to move out was best for all of us. Still, I really miss seeing him."

Corbin smiled at Sonja and, rising from his seat, whispered, "I think I'll leave now. This is all a little too awkward for me. But I'm so glad I came to see how much my dad meant to all these people and to have the chance to talk to you. I'll tell my mom what my dad said about still caring for her."

Sonja gave Corbin a hug, and the young man was on his way.

When Sonja finished watching Corbin leave, she turned to Rebecca, who was sitting next to her. Rebecca struggled to speak but couldn't find the words to comfort Sonja.

Aware of the awkwardness Rebecca felt, Sonja simply said once again, "I'm okay." Before Rebecca could reply, Sonja continued. "What's next for you?"

"I'm going back to Chicago. I can't stand this city anymore. Too many painful memories here for me. With my share of the money we received, I'm going to start my own nonprofit that will operate a cultural exchange program for Israeli and Palestinian children. The future of the Middle East is going to be in their hands."

Sonja hugged Rebecca tightly, but before Sonja could speak, Chet tapped loudly on a glass and called the group to order. "Thank you all for coming. This is probably the last time we'll all be together, and I thought we should meet one more time to say our good-byes and remember all of those who are no longer with us." Then, looking at Sonja, Chet continued, "Each of us here has lost someone dear to us."

Everyone looked around the table to share their sorrow. They all were fully aware of the direction Chet was headed.

Chet then continued, sounding every bit like a preacher. "I know many of you aren't very religious. But I've got to say that the God in whom I believe looks down very favorably on those who try to do what's right, regardless of whether they believe in him. And I think God right now is looking down on all of you with a big smile on his ... or maybe her ... face because of all that you have done."

Everyone laughed, and then Chet asked for a moment of silence. All Sonja could think about was Chris and how much she missed him.

Everyone lingered for another forty-five minutes, but eventually they started to say their final, sad good-byes and leave.

Sonja had avoided speaking with Chet because she knew how painful their conversation would be. Finally, she slowly walked toward the big black man. Her lips quivered as she spoke in a barely audible voice. "Thanks for everything you've done and for being such a good friend." And then trying to rally her emotions, she added, "So what's a retired police officer going to do with his millions?"

"First, me, Billy, Freddie, and Casey are going back to visit Vietnam. Thanks to an official request from Senator Goodman, the State Department is going to help us locate those kids we saved in Saigon all those many years ago. They're all grown now and probably have kids of their own, but it will be great to see them."

"That's wonderful," Sonja began, but then the young, distraught woman fell apart and collapsed into Chet's arms, sobbing so violently that she felt a sharp pain in her rib cage.

Chet held Sonja for several minutes, patting her on the back and trying to comfort her. As she began to regain her composure, he whispered in her ear, "I have something to give you from Chris."

"What?" she cried out as she pulled away and looked at Chet with her bloodshot eyes.

"Chris mailed this to me awhile ago and, in his note, said to give it to you if he didn't make it back."

Totally bewildered and with her hands trembling, Sonja hesitantly took the envelope and opened it. Inside was a folded piece of paper with a handwritten note on the front. "If you're reading this note, the good news is that you're alive and hopefully EMCO and all the conspirators have been exposed and destroyed. The bad news is that we're not together, so look at the other side of this note."

Confused, Sonja looked at Chet, who was expressionless as she peered at the back side. There was a photocopy of a picture of a city setting. Written at the bottom, in Chris's easily recognized handwriting, were the words "Follow your dreams. Love forever, Chris."

At first she didn't recognize the scene, but then the memory came crashing through the layers of sorrow and into her consciousness. It was a copy of the photo in the airline magazine that she had shown to a seemingly disinterested Christopher O'Brian on the flight to Los Angeles. It was the picture of a small plaza in Buenos Aires, Argentina.

Again she looked at Chet, and again he simply stared at her. She picked up the envelope, which she had dropped on the floor, and looked at it. Her eyes opened wide as she turned once again toward Chet, who was now smiling broadly, his eyes twinkling. He answered the question he knew she was thinking with a simple nod and a playful wink.

She raced to him, hugging him so hard that he screeched in pain from his injuries.

"Thank you, thank you," Sonja cried out as she finally released her tight grip on Chet and literally ran out of the church building.

EPILOGUE

June 20
Buenos Aires, Argentina

Riding in the lavish airport limousine, the former Sonja Voinovich glanced out at the passing city scenery. Buenos Aires, with its broad boulevards, endless parks, and classic-style buildings reminded her more of Paris, which she had visited once on a high school trip, than other South American cities she had seen in movies. Nervously, she looked at her watch, which read 11:45 p.m. She didn't want to be late.

The past two weeks had been insanely busy. Sonja flew to Newark on the day after the final gathering of the Crew, where she visited the gravesites of her parents to say a tearful, final good-bye. Then she went to the city clerk to obtain a copy of her birth certificate. Next, she flew to Buffalo, where she visited the grave sites of Nikola and Jasna Voinovich. When she returned to Washington, DC, and with the help of Dan Witt, Sonja got her now considerable financial holdings in order. She applied for, and received, in a much expedited fashion thanks to the help of a certain staff person in Senator Goodman's office, a passport in the name of Katrina Zimmer.

Finally, she had one last, tearful good-bye with Chet and Karl at the airport and boarded the plane that would take her to Buenos Aires. Arriving at her destination, she quickly passed through security, stopping in a restroom to change and make a final check on how she looked.

When the limo finally stopped, Katrina took off her running shoes and put on a pair of high-heeled, black-leather dancing shoes. She told the driver to wait until she returned and then walked toward the plaza.

Katrina looked at the now hopelessly crinkled photocopy and compared it to the plaza at which she was now staring, just to make sure. She gazed around the plaza and saw a number of young, as well as older, couples gathering around the square, all of them in their dancing clothes, ready to "Tango in the Streets." But she didn't see the person she had traveled so far to find.

Then, at the far corner of the plaza, she saw him standing there. As her heart raced, and chills of joy spread through her body, she began to walk slowly and as sophisticatedly as she could toward him. The young, statuesque vision of complete beauty, with flowing, auburn hair, quickly caught the attention of those sitting at tables surrounding the plaza. She could feel the men staring, and she enjoyed the moment, but there was only one man she wanted to impress.

Katrina tried to retain her regal composure, but when she was about three-quarters across the plaza and could clearly see Chris brimming with excitement, she broke first into a trot and then raced toward him.

When she finally reached him, she jumped into his arms and wrapped her legs tightly around his waist. Chris kissed her with a passion stronger than he had ever felt before as the crowd around the plaza broke into spontaneous applause. Katrina would later learn that for nearly two weeks, Chris had been coming to the plaza, ready to dance if and when she finally arrived. He also told many of the other dancers his tale of adventure and love.

When he finally lowered her to the ground, Chris whispered, "Sonja, I love you. It seems like I've been waiting for an eternity."

She kissed him tenderly and said softly, "I'm Katrina Zimmer now."

"As it should be, Katrina," Chris replied.

Then looking into Chris's eyes, Katrina asked, "But how did you survive the explosion, and why didn't you contact us sooner?"

Chris explained that when the methane gas in the ship's hull exploded, it created a wall of flames that raced through the hull shell, pushing a pocket of air in front of it.

"I was trying to outrun the flame when I was blown forward by the wall of rushing hot air and fell. When I hit the ground, I fell through the rotted, rusty hull floor and landed in shallow water probably twenty feet below. The fire and subsequent explosions never reached where I had landed, and I survived the fall with just a few cuts and several large bruises. But I did hit my head and probably suffered a concussion. I couldn't make myself move, and I didn't get out of the salvage yard until three days later."

Katrina stared at him in amazement.

"By the time I got my senses back, the ARB hearings had already taken place, and I knew I was still technically a fugitive. Exposing myself at that point would have served no purpose. That's when I came up with this plan."

"But how did you know about this place, and how did you know I would come?"

"I had one of my dreams when we were in Mason County, and there you were, standing in front of that fountain just where I saw you for the first time tonight. Of course, when I had the dream, I had no idea where the plaza was. I thought it was in Europe. But then you showed me that picture in the airline magazine, and I knew where we hopefully would meet," Chris said. "You're here, so you must have figured out the clue I left you."

"Yes, I looked at the postmark; it was mailed from Los Angeles but was dated five days after everyone assumed you had died."

They started to kiss, but then the band began to play. As they stepped into the center of the plaza, to their surprise the crowd of people applauded but didn't join the couple to dance. This moment would be for Chris and Katrina only.

Five minutes later, when they completed their dance, the crowd cheered loudly. Chris and Katrina embraced once again, and it set off a second round of cheering, yelling, and clapping. The consensus among the experts watching the two amateur American dancers was that what their tango lacked in execution, it made up for in wonderful passion.

As they finished their tango, Chris asked, "Well, you just fulfilled your lifelong wish. What do you have planned for the rest of your life?"

"Tonight we dance and make love like never before. We'll figure out the rest tomorrow," Katrina whispered as they kissed, and the band began to play again.